Those Who Dwell In Darkness

Those Who Dwell In Darkness

Steve McHugh

Podium

For Harley

Cover design by Istvan Straban

ISBN: 978-1-0394-4697-7

Published in 2023 by Podium Publishing, ULC
www.podiumaudio.com

LIST OF CHARACTERS

The Assembly
Anya Makkya: Arbiter handler
Henry Shaw: ATO (Assault Team Officer) Commander
Megan Song: ATO (Assault Team Officer) Commander
Miles Watson: Arbiter
Church: Vampire enhanced Doberman. Best girl.

House Barbarous (The House of Blood)
Danica: First Lady of House Barbarous

House Umbra (The House of Shadows)
Vedran Vinko: First Captain of House Umbra

House Venator (The House of Justice)
Charlotte Henry: First Counsel of House Venator
Drest: First Lord of House Venator
Gideon: First Librarian of House Venator
Halime: First Captain of House Venator

No Affiliation
Carla Tanner: Illegal vampire
Oliver McCarthy: Criminal vampire
Danny Mortimer: Criminal vampire
Kyle O'Riley: Criminal

Magistrate
Blake Summers: Head of Seattle Branch of the Magistrate

Fortress Falls Inhabitants
Amber Lambert: Wife to Pamela Green. Fortress Falls Police Detective.
Doctor Beatrice Hammond: Fortress Falls Medical Examiner.
Lauren Gibson: Wife to Reese Gibson. Presumed kidnapped.
Yvonne Dent: Town Librarian
Paul Shilton: Fortress Falls Police Officer
Reese Gibson: Husband to Lauren Gibson. Fortress Falls Police Detective.
Rio Sheringham: Fortress Falls Police Officer
Pamela Green: Wife to Amber Lambert. Psychologist. Part-time Librarian.
Cody Sharpe: Criminal
Liam Fricker: Criminal

THOSE WHO DWELL IN DARKNESS

PART ONE

CHAPTER ONE

Oliver McCarthy had been, by his own admission, a truly terrible human being.

He'd been a thief, a liar, a killer, and probably a few other descriptors he couldn't quite recall. He once bragged to a priest that he'd broken most of the Ten Commandments, although he couldn't remember his mother and father enough to honour them. He was only little when they'd died.

He was twenty-nine when he became a vampire, and if he was honest, his awfulness had only increased.

At first, he thought it was going to be the best thing that would ever happen to him. Vampires were powerful; they were mysterious, dangerous, and above all, sexy. It had been the mid 1960s when he'd been turned. Oliver had been living in San Francisco at the time, taking part in free love and counterculture. He spent his days getting high and avoiding the law, usually at the same time. He figured that becoming a vampire would give him power to do what he wanted.

It hadn't turned out quite like that.

The man who had turned him, the name of whom Oliver couldn't remember despite having worked for him for nearly seventy years, had promised much and delivered very little.

That wasn't to say that his life had been awful—he'd seen the world; he'd made a lot of money—but he was, after all these years, beholden to the man who had made him. And would be for the rest of his unnaturally long life, unless the man were to die, and the likelihood of a powerful vampire just dying was infinitesimally small.

Oliver sat on the bare wooden floor of a third floor flat in Whitechapel. A part of London once known for the murders of one deranged psychopath, and a place that had been gentrified over the decades. Anyone who had been around during the latter part of the nineteenth century would probably find the place unrecognisable. Hell, Oliver had only purchased the building in the 1980s, and he found Whitechapel unrecognisable to back then.

He'd always known that he was going to need a place to go should he have to escape. The London Borough of Tower Hamlets—which Whitechapel was a part of—wasn't controlled by the vampires. He'd purchased the building under an assumed name, using cash, and rented out the bottom two floors to human tenants who had no idea who their landlord was. The third floor was officially an office space, although there was nothing in the flat that suggested it was used for anything but storage.

In reality, that was exactly what it was used for. Oliver had stored his valuables in the flat, retaining any information that he might need to save his life one day. Using one of two safes hidden under the floorboards to keep documents, fake passports, and cash, replacing the latter on a regular basis as currencies or notes changed. It had taken a lot of work to maintain, to keep hidden, but two weeks ago it had saved his life.

Oliver knew that his job was illegal. He was under no illusions that the man he worked for, the Boss, was not one of the good vampires. The Boss was involved in the creation of illegal vampires—those not sanctioned by the Assembly—in drugs, in spiked real blood packs, in extortion, gambling, and a host of other crimes that would probably get him a long stay in an Assembly prison.

It was the illegal vampires that were the big news, though. An operation decades in the making where people, paying obscene amounts of money, could bypass the long and often arduous official process of becoming a vampire. All of their documents looked official, because technically they were official—how, Oliver still didn't know.

It had gone well for years. Until two weeks ago, the most recent experience, when it had all turned to shit. When some old man wanting an extended life had gone wrong, and had become a monster.

Oliver lay down on the floor and closed his eyes. It was dark outside, and the windows were triple glazed, but with his hearing, Oliver could still make out the sounds of cars, of people out celebrating. He needed to find a place to hide. Away from London. Away from the UK. Too many vampires in the UK. Not Europe either; that was too close. Anywhere that spent all year being too hot or too cold was out, too; vampires didn't like the heat because it killed them, and they didn't like the cold because it made the need to feed too much to handle.

He knew if his Boss found him, he'd kill him. Slowly. Oliver couldn't go against his Boss; he was too well connected, too powerful, and while Oliver had killed plenty of people, he'd never hunted down and killed a powerful vampire. Besides—how could he hunt a ghost? Whatever psychic blocking had been done to his brain meant he couldn't remember his Boss's name, or what he looked like, and if he tried too hard it gave him a migraine. All he knew was that he couldn't win that fight.

Besides, they'd somehow found out that his loyalties didn't quite lie with his Boss. Fleeing was his only option.

"You don't need to check on them," Oliver said to himself, thinking about the two girls he'd managed to save from the catastrophe he'd just escaped. "Just run. Just run and don't look back."

Oliver tried to talk himself out of going back to the scene of the crime, so to speak. The two girls, Carla and Teresa, hadn't expected to become vampires almost the same day a monster tried to murder everyone. His Boss had wanted a clean slate, had ordered Oliver to kill them both, but . . . well, he couldn't. He'd brought them to his flat, but realised it was a terrible place to hide them, too risky, so he'd taken them to one of the halfway houses he'd arranged for new vampires in Soho. Somewhere his Boss knew nothing about, as Oliver was the only one who managed them. Though that wouldn't be the case if his Boss found him and ripped the information from his mind. Hence he needed to escape. For his safety—and the girls'. Oliver hoped they would never be found. Or at least not found by his Boss or those who worked for him.

"Fuck," Oliver snapped.

He could smell the blood on his jeans and hoodie, despite them being sealed in a ziplocked black bag. He'd risked showering when he'd first arrived, although he'd had to settle for a freezing cold shower, which had made him hungry. There was no blood in the apartment, synthetic or real. He never came back enough to make it necessary.

"Fuck," Oliver snapped again, feeling the pangs of hunger. He'd managed to feed once in the two weeks he'd been running, and even that was only one synthetic blood pack that he'd had to steal from a vampire emporium in Shoreditch, because he wasn't sure who was watching or tracking him. Avoiding the Assembly at all costs was his main goal now. That and anyone associated with his Boss. Basically, he couldn't trust anyone, he was all alone, and he was, frankly, utterly fucked.

Oliver got to his feet and stretched. He was six feet tall, and thin. He'd been disappointed to discover that while he was super strong, if he'd wanted a toned and muscular physique, he'd have to actually work out. It seemed like something he should have been informed of before he'd said yes to becoming a vampire.

He had pale skin, short blond hair, and two weeks' worth of beard growth. He wore midnight blue jeans, dark brown boots, and a plain black T-shirt.

"Right," Oliver said to himself. Despite having been born in France, he was raised first in Amsterdam, and then in California; his accent was more the latter, although occasionally the Dutch came through.

He ran a hand through his hair and went through the plan. "Blood, then fleeing," he said aloud as though that might make it a better plan. He had a fake passport in his pocket, along with ID and credit cards, all paid for some time in advance and hidden in the flat.

"Shit," Oliver said, realising there was something else he needed to do. He removed the burner phone from his pocket and dialled one of three numbers that were kept on the memory: *Danny*.

It rang three times, and Oliver began to feel anxious that Danny wouldn't answer. The feeling of relief when the phone was picked up was palpable.

"Oli," Danny said, his voice a whisper. "Where the fuck are you?"

"Doesn't matter," Oliver said. "I need you to get a pen and paper and write this down."

"Wait a sec," Danny said, sounding flustered. "Right, what is it?"

Oliver recited the address he'd left the two women. "Go there, find them, get them to safety."

"Shit, Oli, the Boss is looking for you," Danny said.

"I don't care, Danny, just fucking do this, okay?" Oliver snapped.

"Yeah, yeah, sure," Danny said. "Get the girls, keep them safe."

"I mean it, Danny; they don't deserve to be caught up in our shit," Oliver said. "I know you like Carla, so I know you'll do this. You tell anyone who asks that she's your insurance. That should make sure any other gang members leave her alone and don't ask too many questions. You wait until all this dies down, and you help them get out. The Boss has bigger issues than them to think about. Can you do that?"

Danny was silent for a moment. "Yeah, yeah, I can do that. Anything else?"

"No," Oliver said, feeling as if this was the last time he would speak to the young vampire. "Keep your head down, your mouth shut, and the Boss won't even bother with you. None of you were there when this happened. None of you are a liability. He needs you all to keep working normally. You don't know anything, got it?"

"Got it," Danny said. "Oli, take care."

"Be safe, Danny," Oliver said and hung up, feeling a weight lifted from his shoulders.

He looked over at the door and paused. He didn't know where he was going to flee. He removed a piece of paper from his pocket with *Fortress Falls* written on it in blue pen, and stared at it. That was his last option, but it was an option. Could he really do that to her? Could he really walk back into Yvonne's life and screw it over? He didn't want to. The last time she'd seen him, she'd told him to fuck off and never speak to her again. That was thirty years ago. He hadn't even known where Yvonne lived until he'd started digging a month ago.

Oliver screwed up the paper and tossed it aside, as his anger and need to feed threatened to overwhelm him. *Damn it.*

He flicked to the second number in his phone: *Barbarous.* He dialled it and waited for it to go to answerphone. "It's all gone to shit," Oliver said. "There's nothing that will come back to you. I'm going to see Yvonne; I *need* to see her before I disappear. Just do me one favour, and tell her I'm coming. I need to destroy this phone; I don't want anyone to track me. She'll be able to contact me if you need, but it's too dangerous to stay here. The *Boss*, he's fucked my memory, I can't remember his name, his face, anything about him. All I know is, he knows who I am, and he'll stop at nothing to find me. He can't risk me remembering something."

Oliver hung up again, feeling exhausted. He needed blood, not from a live person, he was too het up for that, but from an emporium. He took a deep breath and let it out slowly. Nothing good was going to come from anything that would happen next. He took a second deep breath, not letting it go until he'd stepped out into the hallway beyond.

He closed the door, posted the key back through the letterbox—he wasn't going to be needing it again—and carrying a black rucksack with everything he needed, mostly money, left his building once and for all.

It was a short jog through the early morning streets of the still fairly busy city to get to the emporium. All shops of the kind were named the same thing, at least in the UK; Oliver wasn't sure about everywhere else.

The windows of the shop were covered in dark fabric, and the door was made of metal, with a small grate at eye height. The sign above the door that said *Emporium* was in neon purple, giving everything an ethereal glow. Oliver knocked, took a step back, and waited as the grate opened.

"Need to feed," Oliver said, adding, "please."

The grate closed, accompanied by the sounds of bolts and locks being moved before the door was pulled open. "Weapons?" the deep male voice asked.

"No," Oliver said, turning to show his rucksack.

"Open it," the man said.

Oliver wanted to argue, but he was hungry, and needed food more than he needed to snap at someone. He unfastened his rucksack, showing the change of clothes inside, moving them aside to show his passport. The cash was inside a zip-up part inside the bag that was impossible to see unless you knew it was there.

The door opened wider. "Come in," the man said.

Oliver checked both ways on the empty road, finding nothing out of the ordinary, and stepped into the emporium.

The emporium smelled of lavender and pot, presumably the former to mask the latter. There was a till, behind which sat a middle-aged woman with dark hair and tattoos all over her arms. The large man who had opened the door took his seat next to a glass cabinet showing a variety of products that could be purchased; gummies, cakes, and sprays were all on show. Each one had a healing benefit to humans. Vampire blood cured cancers and helped humans heal from injuries; it had been a big part of why humans and vampires now lived side by side. Vampire blood had revolutionised the medical industry, although too much at once, and it could paralyse the human taking it. If they were lucky.

After someone figured out what happened if you mixed it with CBD, it revolutionised the drugs industry, too. It was heavily regulated and monitored, but it had brought humans and vampires closer together. And had oddly made vampires less feared by the human population.

Emporiums catered to the humans who wanted to use vampire blood as a way to get stoned out of their minds, or mellow out, just as much as for vampires who needed to feed.

"How much?" the woman asked.

"Two pint packs, please," Oliver said.

"What age?" she asked.

"Whatever is cheapest," Oliver said. Humans had to be at least eighteen to donate, and it was considered that the older the human, the better the blood.

"ID," the woman said.

Oliver fished it out of his pocket and showed her the card.

She practically snatched it out of his hand, turning it over and over. "Oliver Dent."

"That's me," Oliver said with a smile.

"You want anything else?" she asked, passing him back his ID and moving to a door behind her and opening it.

"No," Oliver said.

The woman shouted the order into whatever was behind the door, closed it, and retook her seat behind the till. "You ever tried the gummies?" she asked. "They mix the vampire blood with CBD and flavouring. It's a good mellow high, even for vampires. And all completely legal, of course."

"I need to feed," Oliver said by way of explanation.

"It's been getting cold," the woman said. "You need to be careful."

"Always comes earlier and earlier," Oliver said with a smile. He tried to maintain some kind of small talk, while trying not to show his anxiety.

There was a knock on the door behind the woman, and she got up to answer it. Someone passed her a small black wooden box, with the word *EMPORIUM* inscribed on the side in gold lettering. Oliver only saw the person's arm, but he felt the power that came off whoever it belonged to. No one in their right mind ever attacked an emporium. They were considered one of the safest places to work for good reason.

"That will be fifty quid, please," the woman said, placing the box on the counter.

Oliver smiled, removed two twenties and a ten from his pocket, and passed them over. Lots of vampires only used cash, as not everyone was able to move into new technology with ease.

The woman took the money, opening the till and placing it inside. "Please, enjoy your meal."

"Thank you," Oliver said, almost falling over himself in his hurry to get outside.

He walked down the street, carrying the box as though there were a bomb inside it, almost able to smell the blood it contained, despite that being impossible as it was sealed inside the box, and inside bags. All of his attention was on the box, so he didn't see the two people—a man and a woman—step out of the shadows and begin to follow him. If he had seen them, he'd have dropped the box and run.

Oliver walked for five minutes before finding a small park that was encircled in a four-foot metal fence. There was a sign on the gate that said *No entry after 9 PM* in red lettering. Oliver leapt over the fence as though it weren't even there, landing softly in the barely illuminated park, and walked through to find a wooden bench.

He placed the wooden box beside him and fought to calm his mind. He *needed* to feed. It was all he could think about. He pulled on the string on the box, and it unwrapped around the outside, letting him lift the lid to show the two blood pouches inside. Each one was exactly one pint. Enough to keep him going for two weeks before he would need to feed again, maybe three if he was sensible.

Oliver removed one of the pouches, twisted the top, and was almost overwhelmed when the scent of the blood reached his nose. He took a moment to savour it. It smelled good. Sweet.

He took a sip, letting it sit in his mouth before swallowing and feeling the warmth down his throat, letting it spread inside of him. Another sip, and another, and soon he was drinking it as if he'd just found water after a month in the desert. He drank the whole thing in seconds and let out a soft moan of contentment. It wasn't the same as drinking from a person, as feeling that connection, but it was definitely better than nothing.

Oliver sat on the bench and let the feeling of euphoria flow through him. He was in a happy place, a comfortable place, but he knew it wouldn't last.

He saw the man in the shadows outside of the park. He was watching him. Oliver didn't let on that he'd seen him and instead removed the remaining blood pack from the box, placing it in his rucksack, before springing to his feet and running as fast as he could. He reached the outer fence, leapt over it, and narrowly avoided a woman in a dark coat as she tried to grab him. The fresh blood in his stomach made him slightly light-headed, but it also made him stronger, and faster.

Oliver tried to dodge a second grab, but the man who had been outside of the park leapt over the fence, catching him in the chest with a kick that sent him back toward the woman, who punched him in the side with enough force to break his ribs. Oliver scrambled away, putting distance between him and his attackers.

Both wore dark trousers, black boots, and blood-red shirts under slate grey jackets. A white badge on their lapels, with a red circle and a black infinity symbol across it, denoted they were Inquisitors. And the number of dots above the symbol denoted their rank. Both had three dots out of a possible six. They had been at their jobs for some time.

They both had bald heads, and while the man was several inches taller than his female companion, they were both over six feet in height. The woman had dark skin, while the man's was pale; the streetlights illuminated the faint blue tattoos across their bald heads.

Oliver knew they were here to kill him. He ran.

He moved as quickly as possible, running across roads, dodging traffic which blared horns, drivers shouting a variety of obscenities in his direction. Oliver didn't dare look back as he moved down an alleyway, leaping over strewn detritus, until he'd reached the end, and was almost hit by a van as he ran across the road.

"Fucking idiot," the male driver said.

There was silence for a few seconds before the driver shouted, "You too, you fucking arsehole."

Oliver risked a glance and saw the two Inquisitors in pursuit. He turned a corner, ran down another alley, and at the end turned right and sprinted as fast as he could down a street full of restaurants and takeaways. He stopped outside of a kebab shop, stepped inside.

"Can I help you?" the man behind the counter asked.

"Exit," Oliver said.

"What?" the man asked, as though he hadn't heard.

"Fucking exit," Oliver snapped, showing his vampire side.

Fear filled the man, and he pointed through the kitchen behind him. Oliver didn't need telling twice—he vaulted over the counter, ran through the building, and burst out into a small garden beyond. He clambered up and over the twenty-foot high wooden fence, landing in a garden behind the kebab shop. He continued on through the gardens until he reached the end of the street, and landed on a footpath next to a road. He crossed it, risking a look behind him, but saw nothing as he stood in the dark mouth of an alleyway and watched the road he'd just crossed. The two Inquisitors arrived at the end of the street a few hundred meters up the road.

Oliver needed to leave the UK tonight. Fortress Falls it was. He just hoped Yvonne would forgive him.

CHAPTER TWO

The London Borough of Islington belonged to the vampires.

For the most part, vampire law and human law are pretty similar. Humans and vampires can move freely between vampire and human territory, but vampires committing crimes in human areas are dealt with by vampires. And humans committing crimes in vampire-controlled areas had better be able to run fast.

Miles Watson sat on a park bench in Barnard Park opposite Barnsbury Road. A chilling wind whipped through the whole park. Miles was happy to see that most people had wisely decided to stay somewhere warmer, or at least somewhere they could buy alcohol and feel warmer.

By half eleven, the last vestiges of people trickled by Miles on their way out of the park. One or two occasionally glanced his way, which Miles ignored as he continued to watch the road ahead.

The houses on Barnsbury Road were, according to the estate agent's website that Miles had checked, three-bedroom terraced buildings each with its own roof area. All went for approximately one and a half million pounds, which was almost certainly down to the security offered by living in a vampire-controlled territory, but it was London, so anything over the price of a shed was astronomical.

Miles wore a tailored charcoal suit, a white shirt, and a pair of thick black boots, along with a black and red striped scarf wrapped around his neck. He had an umber brown leather satchel bag beside him and wore a black Hamilton watch on his left wrist. He checked the time. *23:33*.

To the world, Miles looked like a man who had just finished an arduous day of working in a bank or office somewhere and needed some time to himself. He had long brown hair that fell around his shoulders, and a full dark beard that stretched to the top of his chest. He wore a bronze torc bracelet on his right wrist. The piece of jewellery gave the impression of strands of rope wrapped around one another, and was partially obscured by the sleeve of his long black winter coat.

Despite the layers, Miles was cold. The weather said it was going to be in the single digits Celsius temperature-wise, but the wind was going to make it feel several degrees colder, and they'd been right.

Miles pulled back the sleeve of his coat and checked the time again. *23:41.* He'd expected them to be done by now, but he also didn't want to have to spend his Friday night sat in the middle of a park during one of the coldest times of the year, so he guessed he was going to be disappointed on a number of levels.

A large black Transit van pulled up farther along the street, pulled over to the side of the road, switched its headlights off, and remained there. *Finally.*

He watched the van for a few seconds, bathed in the warm yellow glow of the streetlights above it. Miles looked back up the road as a Range Rover with tinted windows drove along it at a snail's pace, before eventually pulling over to the side of the road, where its engine was switched off. The four occupants inside the Range Rover were bathed in warm light for a few seconds before everything went dark.

The passenger door to the Range Rover opened, and a young woman stepped outside, closing it behind her. She wore typical tactical gear used by Assembly vampire assault teams; thick black boots, midnight blue trousers, a similarly coloured stab vest with ATO—Assault Team Officer—written in bright blue on it. The vest was worn under a zipped up black jacket, with just the letters showing over it. She had a gun holster against one hip, a dagger sheathed against her chest, and a long baton against her other hip.

The only ways to kill a vampire were decapitation and heat. Normal bullets could hurt, but they didn't kill. Incendiary bullets and shells were used by the Assembly in extreme circumstances, when taking the vampire in alive was either unlikely or far too dangerous. The rounds were regulated and monitored for vampire use only, and anyone not in the Assembly or a trusted organisation found using them was going to end up in a lot of trouble.

Throughout the centuries that humans had been aware of the existence of vampires, they had designed bladed and blunt weapons that could be used to kill or at least incapacitate vampires. Batons that discharged an electrical pulse or knives that become super-heated were more damaging to them than guns.

Humans and vampires might live side by side in society, benefiting both, but that didn't mean everyone on both sides liked it.

The woman's name was Megan Song, and she and Miles went back several decades. Although it would be fair to say that they had not always been on the same side. Megan was an ATO Commander, and fiercely loyal to the Assembly—the people who maintained the checks and balances of vampire and human coexistence, as well as being the political face of vampire kind—and Miles hadn't always thought that they were what was best for vampire kind. The fact that he now worked for the Assembly hadn't changed his mind. It had been a source of arguments between the pair. Many, many arguments.

"What the fuck are you doing here?" Megan demanded to know, speaking in a harsh whisper that she knew Miles would hear, even with the distance between them. She was five nine with long, braided black hair. She had piercing iceberg blue eyes, pale skin, and a Welsh accent.

"Good to see you, too," Miles told her as Megan reached him.

Miles had been born in a small village near the town of Stonehaven, Scotland over four centuries earlier, and despite working all over the world and having been brought up in London for the most part, he'd managed to keep a measure of his accent. The angrier or more excited he got, the more pronounced the accent.

"This is *my* operation, Miles," Megan said. "We're looking for a gang who have been spiking real blood packs with various drugs. They need taking off the street. You don't get to interfere here."

"Not here to interfere," Miles assured her, his hands up, palms facing Megan in a submissive gesture. "I'm here to find an illegal vampire. I'm pretty sure she's in that house right there."

Megan turned to look back at the three-storey building. The exterior of the bottom floor was painted eggshell blue, while the other two floors were standard pale brick used in all of the buildings around the area. There was a terrace on the roof, which a quick search online for a satellite image had shown was covered in plants and a sofa.

"There are illegal vampires in there?" Megan asked.

"One I know of," Miles told her with a smile. "We should share notes."

Megan stared at Miles for several seconds. "You wait until we've breached and cleared. You are not to involve yourself in the apprehension of gang members. Am I clear on that?"

Miles's smile broadened. "I am here only to let you do your job. It's the aftermath of your job I'm interested in."

"You could have let us know you were going to be here," Megan said with a sigh.

"Could have," Miles agreed. "Wouldn't have been as much fun, though."

"What do you really want, you irritating bastard?" Megan asked, with the tug of a smile on her lips.

"Her name is Carla," Miles said as Megan sat beside him.

"That it?" Megan asked.

"We both know that this ordinary looking house is a front for a vampire gang," Miles said. "That's why we're both here. The gang has been working the illegal vampire trade for years. Up until a few weeks ago when it all went to shit in a very public way."

Megan stared at Miles for several seconds. "Oh shit, you mean what happened in South Tottenham? You sure?"

"I do, and I am," Miles said.

"Are we likely to come across serious issues in there?" Megan asked him.

"You mean a desolate?" Miles asked. "No. Carla is just a scared kid from the sounds of things. No desolate. Just morons."

Megan stared at Miles for several seconds. "You sure?"

Miles looked over at her and nodded. "Two weeks ago, two humans were murdered and dumped in a block of flats, marked for demolition, in Lambeth."

"And this Carla is involved?" Megan asked.

"Carla and her friend Teresa were seen on CCTV in Lambeth the night of the murders," Miles said. "They were also seen outside of the nightclub Edge of Humanity with one Danny Mortimer. The second in command of the gang whose night you're about to ruin. It didn't take much to track Danny and Carla to this building."

"What about Teresa?" Megan asked.

"She's dead," Miles said. "She had a case of being decapitated. I don't know who by or why. I plan to find out."

"So, this Carla, she's one of the illegal vampires?" Megan said.

Miles nodded. "She's going to lead me to whoever turned her. I don't know what happened in Tottenham, but it ended up with a lot of dead vampires, and I'm hoping she has answers."

"You think she'll help you?" Megan asked.

"I think her options are help me or be executed in the middle of the park we're sat in," Miles said. "Not great options, I'll admit."

"You're just here to watch?" Megan asked, sounding less than convinced. Miles crossed his heart.

"That would mean a lot more if you weren't a vampire," Megan said with a smile as she got to her feet.

"I am here to watch you in the majesty of your work," Miles said, with a flourish. "Go, be an artist of violence and ruin."

"How long have you been thinking of that?" Megan asked.

"About three hours," Miles admitted. "Had some time to kill."

Megan looked up at the cloudy night sky and sighed. "What if Carla isn't in there?"

Miles's eyes narrowed. "Then Danny and I will be having an intimate conversation."

Megan nodded slowly and looked down at Miles, who met her gaze. "Okay," she said. "Stay here, don't do anything. Are you armed?"

Miles shook his head.

"Where's your shadow?" Megan asked.

"She's having a sleep under a tree, or a bush," Miles told her. "She's not going to be involved either."

Megan pointed a finger at Miles. "Don't make me regret this."

"Go hurt bad people," Miles said with a smile. "I'll be right here when you're done."

Megan walked back over to her people, who had exited the Range Rover, without looking back at Miles, who was busy watching half of the Transit van team run up to the end of the road and disappear from view as they made their way around to the rear of the building. At least, that's what Miles assumed. The other half of the team moved slow and low down the street toward the target house.

While Miles had never worked for any of the Assembly tactical teams, he'd worked with a few of them over the years. They were mostly competent, mostly diligent, and mostly uncorrupted by wealth, power, status, or any combination of the three. Mostly.

Miles was certain that with Megan in charge, no one would mess around and get away with it. She was known as a taskmaster and not someone to pick a fight with. They didn't always agree with one another, but Miles trusted her.

The six-person team with Megan remained crouched as they moved across the street, keeping low as they proceeded along the brick walls that separated the houses from the street. They joined up with the remains of the Transit team and together moved quickly as most of the team scaled the house, hanging from the underside of the window ledges, while four of the team remained on the ground by the front door.

Miles began to count in his head as the front door was kicked in by one vampire and something thrown inside. The vampires that had scaled the walls smashed through the windows, and every one of Megan's team was inside within a few seconds. It was well drilled and executed flawlessly.

There were shouts that Miles could hear even from the distance between him and the building, and he wondered if it was his vampire hearing that allowed it, or if humans could hear the noise, too. His question was quickly answered as several people along the road came out of their homes, only to be shooed away by the two vampire team members who had waited outside the building.

As soon as most humans were informed it was a vampire tactical group, they tended to do what they were told, and while people kept coming out, they never stayed out long. They did, however, open their windows and crane their necks to try and get a good look at whatever was going on. You see a lot of weird stuff in London, but vampire raids aren't an everyday occurrence.

One of the downstairs windows of the target house exploded outward as someone tried to escape, only to be clotheslined to the ground by a waiting Tactical Officer.

"Bad day to be them," Miles said to himself and wished he'd brought popcorn.

Someone jumped out of the window beneath which the Tactical Officer was restraining the vampire who had tried to make a break for it. There was a loud grunt, and suddenly someone was leaping over the wall and running across the road to the park.

They moved quickly, much faster than a human, and entered the park at full speed.

"Little help, Miles," Megan bellowed from the front door of the raided building.

Miles sighed. "Church," he said.

The vampire running toward where Miles sat was male and mid-thirties in appearance, although that meant little to a species who could live lifetimes. His long blond hair billowed behind him as he continued toward Miles's destination. He wore jeans and a white T-shirt with what looked like blood on it, and was barefoot. The runner's face changed from human to vampire in an instant, as his fangs elongated, his eyes turned red, and the skin around his skull sank back, giving him a haunted look. The runner saw Miles and leapt, his fingers now sporting three-inch razor-sharp talons.

Church intercepted.

The vampire bounced along the ground for a dozen feet, finally impacting a large oak tree and making an unpleasant crunch. Church stood between Miles and the injured vampire, her gaze only for the man she'd just knocked senseless.

Church might have had the same black and amber colouring of a Doberman pinscher, but she was almost one and a half times the size of any Doberman that had ever existed before. Most people who saw Church noticed her skull first, then her huge paws, and finally, when she opened her mouth, her teeth. She enjoyed showing people her teeth.

As a companion, Church was like a missing piece of Miles's life he'd never known he needed until he found her. She was his protector, too, but one side effect of her being around was that people were either immediately terrified or, as was the more common reaction, instantly disarmed by the large, affectionate dog. For ninety percent of her life, Church was just there, a constant source of companionship and love. Right up until she was needed for her job. And then she was a weapon without equal.

"What the fuck is that?" the vampire asked, pointing at Church as she stepped under a nearby streetlight, until she was next to Miles, who scratched her behind one ear as her tail wagged happily.

"This is Church," Miles said. "You're Danny, yes? I saw a photo of you."

"A dog?" the vampire named Danny snapped. He got unsteadily back to his feet and Church growled. It was the kind of growl that if you heard it at night alone in the woods, you'd begin to regret your life choices.

"Not so much," Miles told him as Church sat down, tail still wagging. "You see, Church's mother was a normal Doberman, and her owner was a geneticist. A vampire geneticist. His wife died, it's a long story, and he decided that he couldn't lose his dog too and to see if he could help her to keep alive longer. The mother gave birth to a litter of pups, but sadly only two survived. Church is one of them. She's not quite a vampire dog, but she's much stronger and faster than a normal dog. And vampire tricks don't work on her. Once she starts hunting someone, she doesn't stop until she's caught them. And catching them isn't much fun for the other person."

Church licked her maw, flashing her large canines as if to prove the point.

"Depending on how old and/or stupid you are, you might not know this," Miles continued. "But technically vampires can't be killed by sunlight itself; it's the UV rays that will kill us. Thankfully, most vampires aren't stupid enough to spend time outside during the day. Nearly all vampire deaths are done by decapitation or heat. Or one followed quickly by the other."

"Why are you telling me that?" Danny asked, his eyes firmly on Church.

"Church, yawn for the nice vampire," Miles said.

Church yawned.

It was dark, and despite his excellent night vision, it was still difficult to see emotions on faces, but Miles was pretty sure that Danny paled as he realised that Church's jaws would fit around his throat.

"I've seen her tear someone's head clean off," Miles said, just to make sure the point sailed home with everyone.

Danny turned and ran.

Miles sighed. "Church, fetch."

Church set off from a seated position into a flat-out sprint with almost no time in between. However fast a vampire was, they were no match for a dog born to vampire blood. Just as a human was no match for a dog.

Miles returned to his seat on the park bench and watched Megan frog-march several people out of the raided building. Their cuffs had a faint purple glow to them. UV cuffs—normal cuffs, except for the UV light embedded in them.

One press of a button on a remote and whoever wore them got a concentrated burst of UV light. It was about the same level as the ultraviolet index, and felt, to a vampire, as if they'd stepped outside during the day. At one, it was mildly discomforting. At two or three, the wearer would be in agony; at four, they'd be immobilised. At five, your arms would be incinerated, and any young vampires could well be killed. Anything over six, and even the most powerful vampires would find it unbearable. The cuffs went up to eleven, but no vampire on earth could survive over an eight for longer than ten seconds. Miles had only seen someone take that much a few times, and that had been for barely a second. The memory was deeply unpleasant. The smell of burning flesh had been even more so.

Megan left the cuffed vampires with her people and walked into the park. "Did you not bother to get Danny?" she asked, looking around.

Somewhere in the night of the park came the sounds of growling and yelping.

"You set Church on them?" Megan asked. "Damn, that's cold."

"He ran," Miles explained.

"We found Carla," Megan told him.

Miles nodded, although he couldn't tell if she was happy about it or not. "How is she?"

"Physically fine," Megan said. "Emotionally? She was turned into a vampire with no memory of who did it, where, or even why. She assumes she asked for it but can't remember. She remembers Danny killing Teresa."

"Why did Danny kill her?" Miles asked, accompanied by the sounds of someone pleading and another growl.

"She doesn't know," Megan said. "And I haven't been able to talk to Danny yet."

As if on cue, Church returned walking beside an entirely human-looking Danny, who had the appearance of someone who'd been pulled through several hedges. He was completely covered in mud, and his hair had a number of twigs and leaves in it.

Megan removed another set of cuffs and tossed them to the ground in front of Danny. "Put them on," she said. "Do not fuck around with me."

"Can I talk to him?" Miles asked.

Danny looked over at Megan with something akin to pleading on his face. "Not the dog," he said.

"Good girl," Miles said as Church returned to him, and he scratched her behind the ears. He noticed a slight cut on Church's leg and looked over at Danny. "Did you hurt my dog?"

"She was trying to kill me," Danny pleaded.

"Miles," Megan warned.

"Good girl," Miles said again to Church. He got up to his feet, walked over to Danny, and hit him in the chest with the palm of his hand.

Danny took a step back, blinked, and crumpled to the ground.

"What the hell did you do?" Megan asked.

"The bawbag hurt Church," Miles said, by way of explanation, his anger feeding his accent just a little.

"Doesn't mean you should disrupt his body like that," Megan said, remaining calm.

Miles crouched beside Danny. "You're going to answer a few questions," he said softly.

"What the fuck did he do to me?" Danny shouted. "I can't move."

"It's his bloodline power," Megan said. "He can use his energy as a psychical thing. Lashing out with it at a vampire, sometimes it just hurts, but when using enough of it at once, it sort of severs the vampire and human sides. Younger the vampire, the bigger the impact it has. Hurts like hell no matter who you are, apparently. How long does it last, Miles?"

Miles shrugged. "How long ago were you turned?" he asked Danny.

"Two years," Danny said.

"About twenty minutes then," Miles said. He didn't want to let anyone know that he couldn't use his bloodline gift again for a while, as it took time to charge. He usually only used it to sever the vampire and human sides of someone in dire emergencies, but Danny had hurt Church, and that shit just wouldn't be allowed to stand.

"I'll take Church to get something to eat," Megan said, scratching Church behind the ear. "She's earned it."

Church followed Megan, leaving Miles and Danny alone.

"Do you know who I am?" Miles asked him.

Danny shook his head.

"Do you know what I am?" Miles asked, raising his wrist so that Danny could see the bracelet.

"Oh fuck," Danny whispered. "You're an Arbiter, aren't you?"

Miles nodded.

Danny suddenly looked very ill. "Oh fuck," he whispered. "Oh fuck. Oh fuck. Please don't kill me. Please. I'll do whatever you want."

"I want answers, Danny," Miles said. "And we'll see about the other stuff."

Danny's eyes were wide with terror.

"So, shall we start?" Miles asked.

CHAPTER THREE

"Do you know the old saying about Arbiters?" Miles asked, taking a seat on the cold grass by Danny's head, causing the younger vampire to flinch slightly.

Danny nodded. "If they're knocking on your door, it's because you did something bad."

"That's the one," Miles said. "It's wrong. Do you know why?"

Danny shook his head.

"It's because if an Arbiter is knocking on your door, we're there to talk to you," Miles told him. "If you did something bad, we don't knock, Danny. We just take you. Or we kill you there and then. You shouldn't be scared of an Arbiter because they knock, you should be scared when you've done something bad, and we just appear in your house."

Arbiters were feared by pretty much anyone who had a working brain. They answered to no one but other Arbiters and the Assembly itself, and even then it was open to interpretation. They investigated crimes committed by humans on vampires, and between vampire Houses—both Minor and Great. It was the only way to make sure that the Houses didn't go to war every time there was some young idiot who wanted to make a name for themselves.

Danny looked terrified of what horror might befall him in the next few minutes.

"Why was Carla in your house?" Miles asked him.

"She was turned," Danny said without any prompting. "She and that stupid Teresa bitch killed some fucking stupid businessmen who thought they were up for a good time. Teresa used to work for me, called me, told me what happened. I went and helped. She . . . lost her mind, man. Just went bloodlust psycho, had to put the bitch down. She almost killed one of my guys. Took Carla because she was a witness."

"Why not kill her?" Miles asked.

"Didn't know who she belonged to," Danny said. "Can't just go offing a vampire."

Miles cuffed him around the back of the head.

"What the fuck, man?" Danny shouted.

"First of all, I'm right next to you, don't shout," Miles said. "Secondly, don't lie to me. I'm not in the mood. It would have been easier and cleaner for you if Carla had died too. Why keep her alive?"

"What do I get if I tell you?" Danny asked.

Miles stared at the prone vampire who'd just had his life ruined by a visit from the ATO, an Arbiter, and an especially large dog. He laughed. "Are you serious?"

"I gotta get something," Danny said. "What I know has to be worth something."

"How about me putting in a word on your behalf, so you spend a century in prison instead of dying horribly?" Miles asked. "Is it worth that?"

Danny thought for a second. "I like Carla," he said softly.

"You expect me to believe that you went against whoever has been running an illegal vampire operation for years, who is responsible for the deaths of a dozen vampires in the last few weeks, all for love?" Miles asked. "You want me to slap you around the head again?"

"Fuck no," Danny said, raising his hands in pre-emptive defence. "She's my insurance. Okay?"

Miles leaned closer to Danny, so his breath was on the younger vampire's neck. "Explain faster."

"Teresa worked for the gang," Danny said. "She also worked at the Edge of Humanity club. She'd help us find those humans with money and power who wanted to be vampires."

"Edge of Humanity?" Miles asked, wanting to clarify everything as they went.

Danny nodded. "Yeah. We did deals out of there, without the owners knowing. Because, well, because . . ."

"Claire and Ben would skin you alive," Miles finished for him.

"Yeah, that's about right," Danny said. "And that's if they were feeling nice."

"So, Teresa worked for you doing what?" Miles asked.

"She would do searches on clients, let it slip that we could do illegal vampires," Danny said. "There were always human assholes who wanted to be vampires but would never be accepted into a House. Rich assholes. We . . . facilitated it for them."

"And then what?" Miles asked. A lot of people were going to have to die because of Danny's activity. If they hadn't already.

"We take the humans to an apartment building in South Tottenham," Danny continued. "We hand them over to the people who work there, and we leave them to it. We get paid, that's all we're involved in. We never see the vampires again. They go back to their lives, or they get new ones if they wish. Either way they get all the documents to say they were legally changed into a vampire. It's all done properly, over ten days. The whole thing. The vampires are kept there for a month to allow them to feed and readjust; their memories are wiped of the meeting, the changing, every-thing. All very professional."

"How many vampires work down there?" Miles asked. "It's not just one vampire turning people."

"I think nine," Danny said. "Four who turn the humans, and the rest work in the building doing various jobs like lookout. Dogsbody shit. With someone to work as a buffer between us and them. Like I said, professional."

"Why do I get the impression there's a *but* coming?" Miles said, feeling his anger rise as the temperature dropped.

"A month ago, it all went to shit," Danny said.

Miles was well aware of what had happened; he'd seen some of the after-math personally, but he didn't want Danny to know what he already knew. "Keep going," he said.

"There was an . . . incident," Danny said. "I don't know what caused it, but vampires died. We were ordered to go down there and clean it up. It was fucked up, man. Just blood and gore fucking everywhere. We . . . we didn't get it all cleaned up in time. We were nearly done, but some Arbiter came and we had to scatter."

"Hi," Miles said with a wave.

"It was you?" Danny asked.

"Yeah, not all of the vampires died that night, Danny," Miles said. "A partially terrified new vampire managed to escape. Got to the Assembly building in Islington. Told us some of what happened. I've been tracking illegal vampires in London for a long time. Most of them yours, I imagine. They've gone out after becoming vampires and committed a host of crimes."

"What they do after becoming a vampire isn't my fault," Danny pleaded.

Miles wanted to hit him for that, much harder than before, but he let it go. "How many years have you been involved?"

"Five," Danny said. "First as a human runner, and then my Boss turned me."

"Your Boss," Miles said. "What happened when you came back and told him you hadn't finished cleaning up?"

"He . . . freaked out," Danny said. "Told us all to go on working, to wait for his call."

Miles stared at Danny. "So, why is Carla with you?"

"I told you, I like her," Danny said.

"That might be part of it, but I want the whole truth, Danny," Miles said, feeling little in the way of sympathy for the idiot vampire before him.

"I got a call," Danny said after a second of thinking about it. "Someone asked me to go find her and Teresa and get them to safety. I didn't go straight away. I was scared. By the time I got to them, Teresa had gone to the bloodlust. She'd killed people. I had to put her down."

"Who called you?" Miles asked.

"A friend," Danny said. "Name is Oli."

"He one of the vampires who worked there?" Miles asked.

Danny nodded and stared at the ground.

"You know where Oli is now?" Miles asked him.

"No," Danny said. "I swear. He'd never say anything to me. He knows that if the Boss found out he's alive, that he called me, I'd be dead. Teresa and Carla, they're meant to be dead, too."

"Meant to be dead?" Miles asked.

"The Boss wanted everything cleaned," Danny said. "Boss wanted everyone involved dead. Any humans there who had paid to become vampires, any vampires still alive. Complete salting the earth kind of shit."

"But you didn't kill Carla," Miles said.

"Couldn't," Danny said. "Like I said."

"You like her," Miles finished for him.

"She's nice," Danny said. "Teresa was always a . . . well, a bitch, but Carla. She's nice."

"So, you waited too long, and by the time you got to the two women, one had lost her mind?" Miles said, wanting clarification.

Danny nodded. "I tried to talk to her. Tried to calm her down. She wouldn't listen to reason, I hit her, she came at me. It was self-defence."

Miles felt dirty being close to Danny, and if he'd had his way he would have killed him there and then and done the whole world a favour. "Carla saw this?"

Danny nodded. "Carla freaked out, had to sedate her. Brought her here hoping to stash her someplace safe until I could help her get out, get away. I found out that the Boss was killing everyone involved in what happened at the place in Tottenham. Scared I was next, scared that if I let Carla go, she'd be grabbed and it would come back on me. Figured I'd keep Carla here until I could sort out how to use her to . . ."

"Save your own ass," Miles finished for him.

"Yeah," Danny said softly.

Miles got to his feet. "What was meant to happen to Teresa and Carla? Before everyone was killed?"

"The girls were meant to wake up in that block of flats in South Tottenham," Danny said. "There were rooms and shit that people were put in to acclimatise themselves. That didn't happen. Oli got them out when it all went nuts, drove them to fucking Soho, dumped them in some bedsit with two dozen blood bags in a fridge, and left. No details on the girls, no new IDs."

"Did you regularly take new vampires there?" Miles asked.

"No, mate," Danny said, sounding more confident. "There are bedsits and flats all over London. Only one man knew them all."

"Where's Oli?" Miles asked.

"No fucking clue," Danny said. "Dead, probably."

"Do you know why it all went to shit?" Miles asked him.

"Ah, yeah, sort of," Danny said. "Some old dude wanted a new lease of life. You know the type, rich, powerful, terrified they'll die and their kids will blow their money on shit. He came in, the operation went smoothly. And then it didn't. That's all I know."

Miles looked over at the house, where Church sat, but he couldn't see Megan. "I'll send Megan for you," he told Danny.

"So, I go to prison, yes?" Danny asked. "Not executed."

Miles stared at the prone figure of the idiotic gangster before him. "Do you even know what's going to happen to you?"

"Go to prison," Danny said, moving his hand. The paralysis was beginning to wear off. Miles guessed he had another ten minutes before Danny was able to do much more than wave.

"That is what I told you I'd arrange," Miles said. "But that's not the whole story. You see, you colossal waste of skin, it's a matter of whether or not they let you go into a stasis sleep for the length of your stay, or make you live through it like any human would. You helped an illegal vampire creation operation. That operation got people killed. Innocent people. *Humans.*"

"But they won't execute me, right?" Danny pleaded. "You promised."

"I did no such thing," Miles said. "I told you I'd put in a word, and I will. The more you do, the better it'll be for you. Right now, you're the one Megan has for it. Not got a lot of good options there, Danny, my boy. Maybe you should tell me who your Boss is."

"I can't rat on the Boss," Danny said.

"You *can*," Miles said.

"I *can't*," Danny repeated.

"What's your bloodline gift?" Miles asked.

"I don't know," Danny admitted, sounding more than a little ashamed.

"It's normal to be unable to access your bloodline gift," Miles assured him. "Not normal to be unaware of what it is. Could be from one of the Great Houses, could be a Minor House. Could be you come from a line of drifters, and if that's the case, who knows *what* your gift might be."

While the vast majority of vampires either worked for the Assembly or remained part of a vampire House, there were a minority who wanted nothing to do with any of them. They lived outside of the protection of the Assembly or a House and were known as drifters. Named because they tended to move from place to place to ensure that they didn't come under the watch of a House or the Assembly. A drifter crime boss was not unheard of.

"Okay, stay there. I'll go get Megan," Miles said.

Miles left a despondent Danny lying on the ground and made his way over to Church, who sat patiently at the park entrance. She nuzzled her head against Miles's hand, and he stroked her for a few seconds. "Keep an eye on that one," Miles said, motioning toward Danny. "Don't let him run off. Don't eat him either."

Church looked over at Danny and back at Miles. She licked her lips.

"Church," Miles said softly. "No eating the vampire."

Church licked Miles's face.

"Yeah, love you too, girl," Miles said, giving her a quick scratch behind the ear before walking across the road to where Megan and her team were still searching the house.

There were half a dozen people—a mixture of vampires and humans—on the concrete slab front garden, their arms cuffed behind their backs. Light from the open front door spilled out over the detainees, and despite the sounds of searching inside the house and the normal din of London at any time of the day or night, it was quiet.

Miles walked by one young male, who hissed.

Miles stopped walking and looked down at the angry-looking vampire, who hissed again. "Did you just hiss at me?" he snapped.

The vampire hissed for the third time.

"Have some self-respect, lad," Miles said. "You're not a fucking cat."

"How's Danny?" Megan asked from the doorway.

"Not thrilled about where he is," Miles said, stepping into the house. The hallway was short, with a staircase to the left of the front door. There was an open door at one end of the hallway that led to a kitchen diner, and next to it another door—a quick glance inside showed some kind of living room which stretched the entire length of the house. It smelled of cannabis, sweat, and blood. A solitary blood bag lay on a glass coffee table.

"They were feeding pretty regularly," Megan said. "The freezer is full of blood bags. We're tracing where they were sourced from. Shouldn't be hard. They used the blood to make margaritas."

Miles looked back at Megan. "Seriously?"

The Operations Chief nodded. "We've also found blood mixed in with vodka. Apparently, they were here to have a good time."

"Where's Carla?" Miles asked.

"Upstairs, top floor, back bedroom," Megan said. "I'll go get Danny then, shall I?"

"Church is watching him," Miles said as he stepped farther into the living room to get a better look. There were three ATOs inside, all looking through bookcases, tossing the contents onto the floor with little care of what they might be throwing around.

"You left Church to watch our criminal?" Megan asked. "Is she going to eat him?"

Miles moved his hand from side to side. "I told her not to, but depends on whether or not he runs."

"Someone go get that bloody idiot in the park," Megan bellowed to whoever was nearby. "Do not piss off the large dog."

"Good advice," Miles said to himself as he flipped over an orange cushion on a partially destroyed black leather sofa, and found the underside had several small bags of what he assumed were cocaine.

"This is why we're here," Megan said, tossing one of the blood pouches to Miles.

"This is spiked with something?" Miles asked, looking it over.

"No, these are all clean," Megan said. "We've found a second freezer in the basement, though, that is full of very much not clean blood pouches. You can smell the opioids the second you open one."

"They're making opioid and cocaine laced blood pouches?" Miles asked, tossing the blood pouch he held back to Megan. "Anyone buying one of these is going to have to be a moron."

"The industry of vampire blood and drugs is heavily regulated for a reason," Megan said. "And despite being able to go into any emporium and buy vampire blood mixed with a variety of substances, people just want to keep pushing that envelope. Doesn't matter how often we say that mixing vampire blood and opioids will kill a human, they just keep fucking doing it."

"Will confiscating all of this do much in the long run?" Miles asked.

"To us, no, not really, but to the human police, they'll be happy we got it," Megan said. "And there's always the possibility that some of the people buying the coke are also involved in moving the opioid blood. Might be able to press upon them the need to aid our investigation."

"These idiots can smoke and snort themselves into oblivion for all I care," Miles told her. "Human law enforcement cares about such things, not me."

"Nor me," Megan said. "But sometimes you need to show the human police that you're playing nice. You never know when you might need a favour, or access to some intel they have. And I do care that they have spiked blood. And so should you."

"Oh, I do," Miles said. "Spiked blood is not something we want getting into the hands of vampires, especially not new vampires who might not be able to control what happens after. Some vampires might like a shot of cocaine spiked blood, but I'm not sure I'd want to be around the vampire who took it. Surprised none of the idiots in here were taking their own product."

"Someone has them on a tight leash," Megan said. "And only three are vampires. The rest are human. I assume because humans aren't going to want to taste their own blood product."

Blood drinking by itself wasn't something that triggered anything more than a euphoria and the occasional need to have a lie-down. Doing drugs alongside it, even shots of alcohol, could have weird side-effects. You had to take a lot of the drug alongside the blood, but the result was never much fun to deal with. Whatever the effect it had on humans, vampires taking it with blood amplified the effect a dozen times over. Putting them directly inside the blood . . . well, that was going to be some potent level stuff.

"Some vampire in America killed his neighbour by drinking him dry," Miles said, remembering the less than pleasant investigation he'd been involved in. "He then ran out into the nearby park, where he tore the face off some elderly man walking his dog. Killed three human cops who were nearby before he was stopped. I ran the investigation. He'd drunk a dozen blood pouches spiked with fentanyl. If these idiots are selling blood spiked with drugs, I'd rather know about it now."

"What happened to the vampire?" Megan asked.

"Another Arbiter cut his head off," Miles said as he left the room. "Seemed to do the trick of stopping him."

Miles nodded to one of the ATOs as he took the stairs up to the next floor, where there were several more ATO agents in one of the three rooms. He didn't bother to hang around and took the stairs up another floor. There were three doors on the top floor; the farthest from the stairs was open, showing another set of stairs that led to the roof. The next along was a small, clean bathroom that smelled of jasmine, and the final door, which was next to the top of the stairs, was a large bedroom. There was a king-size four-poster bed in the middle of the room, with large windows on one side, and a dark wooden cupboard along the far wall, next to a huge television that looked almost comical in size. There were no paintings or photos anywhere in the room, nothing to identify who might actually use it. Just a place to sleep and store stuff.

Carla sat in the corner of the room, her knees up to her chest. She eyed Miles with distrust, which was fair, especially considering all she'd been through.

"I'm Miles Watson," he told her. "Did Megan mention me?"

"Said you're not a cop," Carla said with a South London accent.

Miles nodded and pointed to the floor under the still intact window. "You mind if I sit?"

"Free country," Carla said in a tone that suggested she wasn't really interested in a chat.

"I need to talk to you about some things," Miles said.

"Okay, but you're not a cop, right?" Carla asked.

"You're afraid of being arrested?" Miles asked. "And no, I'm not a cop, I'm an Arbiter."

Carla stared straight ahead for several seconds before nodding. "Teresa killed people. I didn't . . . I didn't kill anyone. I . . . I don't know what's happening to me. I meant, I know I'm a vampire, I just . . . it wasn't meant to be like this."

"It rarely is how you want it to be," Miles admitted. "So, why don't you start from the beginning and explain what happened to you?"

"Are you going to kill me?" Carla asked. "Danny said that Arbiters kill us."

"There are pieces of wet bread smarter than Danny." Miles said. "Despite what the stupid little shitehawk believes, we don't just kill people for no reason. We prefer to deal with problems without resorting to violence unless left with no choice. We want to see justice done. Something tells me that you're in way over your head and don't really know who to trust."

"And I can trust you, can I?" Carla asked.

Miles shrugged. "That's not for me to decide. I do know that I want to make sure that whatever is happening to you never happens to anyone else. I know that you were taken advantage of either by being turned into a vampire in the first place, or by not being cared for properly when you were turned. I know that you were turned illegally. I know that your friend is dead because she killed two humans and called the wrong person for help."

Carla shook her head. "No, it wasn't like that."

"Like what?" Miles asked, hopeful that he'd managed to break down any walls that Carla had put up.

"She changed," Carla said softly. "When we became vampires. She . . . wasn't Teresa anymore. She liked hurting people. Liked hurting humans. It was as if she was finally able to feel powerful. We robbed people; she said it was the only way we could survive after being dumped with no IDs. She

. . . scared them and didn't need to. She went further each time. Those two men she killed were dicks. They were rich, entitled, spoiled brats, but they didn't deserve to die. They didn't deserve to beg for their lives. She freaked out after, all full of remorse. She called Danny, threatened to go to the Assembly. He came, he . . . well, he freaked out, too. She . . ." Carla started to cry and buried her face in her knees.

Miles sat there silently for a moment.

"She attacked him," Carla said, barely looking up. "Danny, I mean. She attacked Danny. He cut off her head. He had a sword. A sword. Who carries around a fucking broadsword in London? He told me that if I behaved he'd help me, that I didn't have to end up like Teresa. I was in shock; I'd never seen anything like that."

"I'm sorry about your friend," Miles said. "About everything. No one deserves to go through that."

Carla nodded, but she didn't seem to be really paying attention.

"You want to tell me what happened from the start?" Miles asked.

Carla took a deep breath and let it out slowly. "Sure."

CHAPTER FOUR

I always wanted to become a vampire," Carla said. "Ever since I was a little girl. When I was about thirteen, we had one come to our school to talk to us about them. I was in awe of her. Vampires and humans coexisting, openly coexisting, but vampires were still mysterious and a little dangerous. The vampire who came to my school was so cool. I don't even remember her name, but she spoke to us about how vampires weren't allowed to turn humans without permission, about the mythology, about how their blood helps people. She told us about the old Christopher Lee films, *Dracula*, all of that. I had no idea you made it all up to protect yourselves."

"Yeah, it was a weird time," Miles said. "Fiction was put out to try and warn humans off, make us look scary. Turns out, we just made ourselves look cool instead. More humans wanted to become vampires, so we changed tactic, made vampires more human, gave them heroic stories. I don't know who was in charge of our PR back then, but it must have been a full-time job."

"There are still things being put out about dangerous vampires murdering people," Carla said.

"Because people like to be scared," Miles said with a shrug. "Also, scary vampires are cooler than ones that wear ruffled shirts and lament about the good old days."

"Are there vampires who do that?" Carla asked.

"Oh God, yes," Miles said. "Lamenting is practically a vampire hobby in some circles. Anyway, we digressed."

"Sorry," Carla said. "Anyway, I ended up working at the Edge of Humanity. The vampire club not far from here. I don't know if you've been before."

"Not by choice," Miles told her. Young vampires mixing with vampire wannabes, humans who think that partying with vampires is some kind of dangerous aphrodisiac, and the occasional genuine predator using it as a smorgasbord for their own desires, was not his idea of a good time.

"It was a good job," Carla said. "Nice people. Claire and Ben run a tight ship, but they were always fair to the humans who worked there. A few of us became familiars."

"To Claire and Ben?" Miles asked. It wasn't unheard of for a vampire of a certain age or power level to take a familiar. A human who shared a small portion of that vampire's power. It made them more durable, age slower—if at all—and capable of inhuman feats of strength and speed. Familiars were normally made when a vampire or human wasn't entirely sure about turning completely or didn't want to lose their human side. Familiars were trusted and spoke with the same level of command as the vampire themselves.

Carla nodded. "I never became a familiar, but these men started coming to the club. Teresa worked with me at the club, and she introduced me to Danny. We were only greeters, bar staff, whatever we needed to do, but these guys were VIPs, and Danny put in a good word for us. We got advanced to deal with the VIPs."

"Lots of vampires, I assume," Miles said.

"Yes," Carla said. "We got them blood from the emporiums, or food, alcohol, whatever they needed."

"Humans?" Miles asked.

"If they wanted them," Carla said. "Claire and Ben knew enough humans who were always willing to be fed on. They got off on it. There was never any shortage of them. Over time, we got talking, I said I always wanted to be a vampire, but it was illegal without going through the process of being part of a House, or going through the Assembly. They said they knew another way.

"We met them after the club, and they walked us through it. Told us how much it would cost, which we paid. We'd saved up a lot, and Teresa had an inheritance. I remember giving them the cash. I remember meeting the vampire who would turn us, but I don't remember his face, or his name. Or anything else. I remember going with Teresa to meet Danny at a coffee shop in Croydon. I remember being nervous. And then I woke up on the floor of an apartment with no memory of what had happened. That wasn't normal. I'd learned all about becoming a vampire, about how you might not remember the dying and being reborn, but you still remember the ten days of being slowly turned. Of time with the vampire who turned you. Of the bond formed between the two participants. I had none of it. No bond, no memories. Nothing."

"No bond?" Miles asked a little concerned.

Carla shook her head. "That's bad, right?"

"Yeah," Miles said. "You see, when you're made into a vampire, you make a bond with the vampire who turned you. That vampire basically cares for you for a month or two after the transformation. They're basically mother birds, bringing you food and keeping you safe until you can fly away on your own. No bond means it was mentally severed after the transformation, or someone ensured it was never there to begin with. Both are exceptionally dangerous for human transformations. It makes it more likely that the human will turn bad."

"What?" Carla asked, clearly scared she was becoming a monster.

"You ever heard of a *desolate*?" Miles asked her.

The act of becoming a vampire wasn't a quick one. It wasn't a one bite and done, so to speak. The vampire had to drain the blood of the human every day for ten days, each time letting the human drink more and more vampire blood. After ten days, the human was drained, and the vampire was reborn. Or not. Sometimes it didn't work. Sometimes you just got a dead body, and sometimes you got something much worse. A *desolate*. There wasn't a vampire working for the Assembly who hadn't been sent to kill their fair share of desolate. Usually after they managed to kill and infect a dozen more.

"They're monsters," Miles explained. "And they spread like a virus. If a vampire bites a human, nothing much happens long term. The human might forget the incident, or they might remember nothing but pleasure. Unless they went through the whole ten days of transformation, or the vampire purposefully wanted them to remember, the human would be none the worse for wear. If a desolate bites a human, that human becomes a *desolate*. Not a vampire, and definitely not human. Just a mass of rage, hate, and bloodlust, infecting everyone they bite. Having your link severed is one cause of a desolate's creation. It's one of the many reasons why vampire creation is regulated and done in safe conditions. It's not as romantic as the old stories of a human being seduced by a vampire, but it's definitely a lot safer for the rest of the population of the planet."

There had been occurrences where desolates ran out of control in cities and towns throughout history. The death toll was always high, and the cost to end the problem usually higher. It was also one of those things about vampires that they'd rather humans didn't know. Thankfully, the desolate were much easier to kill than vampires, and because they were nocturnal, they were easier to hunt during the day.

"Could I become one?" Carla asked, looking at her hands as if something might give it away.

"If you were a desolate, you'd already be one," Miles told her. "They're humanoid in appearance, but their arms and fingers are elongated, the fingers making almost spikes. Their jaws are wide, the sides of the mouth splitting open, and they have piranha-like teeth, not fangs. They only want to kill and feed. Not necessarily in that order. They'll hunt anything that moves. I once saw a group take down a grizzly bear, which was bad news for us when the bear revived a few minutes later. You're not a desolate. I haven't seen one for a few years, and when they do occur, it's sporadic at best. They're hunted down and dispatched as quickly as possible."

Miles considered explaining more about the desolate, but decided against it. Desolate kings and queens were a rare enough phenomenon to be almost mythological, and he didn't want to overwhelm Carla with information about every monster and horror that lived in the shadows of the world.

"No one told me any of this," Carla said. "I could have been made into a monster."

"Aye," Miles said, seeing no reason to sugarcoat it. "But you weren't, so we're going to call that a win. From what you've said, you don't remember Daniel's Boss or the vampire who turned you."

"It's just images," Carla said. "No names, no faces, just a nice suit. The Boss, that is. A smell of aftershave. I remember nothing about whoever transformed me. Not a single thing."

"Do you remember where the flat in South Tottenham is?" Miles asked, feeling concerned about the level of psychic control it would take to block out the bond with a newborn's maker. It was a lot more than the usual memory removal of the harder parts of that first month of becoming a vampire, of the rebirth, of dying. No one liked to remember those bits.

Carla shook her head. "I'm sorry, I'm not being much use."

"You've been a lot of help," Miles said. There was no need to tell her he'd already been to the flat in question. "Is there anything else you do remember?"

"I woke up in an empty flat," Carla said. "The floors were bare. Teresa was still unconscious; I think we'd been drugged. There was a man there; he said he was going to keep us safe."

"Do you know the man's name?" Miles asked.

"Oliver," Carla said. "I don't know his last name. He'd been nice to us when we were in Tottenham. I don't know what he did to get us out of there, but he saved us, I'm sure of it. We weren't at the empty flat long, maybe a few hours. When we were leaving, I recognised the street name. The next I woke up, Teresa and I were in Soho. We had blood packs, but Oliver was gone."

"What was the name of the street?" Miles asked. Oliver was definitely next on his list of people to find.

"Varden Street," Carla said. "It's near a church."

Miles removed his phone from his pocket, opened the *maps* app, and found the street in question, passing the phone over to Carla, who pointed to a spot on the phone that was further up the road, on the opposite side of the street to the church. "Thank you," Miles said.

"What happens to me now?" Carla asked him, fear etched through every word.

"It's going to be a hard year or so," Miles said, wanting to be honest with her. "You'll go with Megan, who will keep you safe. You'll be processed, and you'll have to tell them what you told me. At some point, you'll be taken to a vampire with telepathic abilities, who will try to get an idea of exactly what was done to your brain, and hopefully be able to fix some of the jigsaw they made of it. And then you'll be placed under a watch order for six months in . . . well, in a facility that allows the Assembly to watch over illegal vampires. They'll keep an eye on you, check on your well-being, teach you how to do vampire stuff. If you're not a threat, you'll be released into the care of one of the Houses, or maybe an Assembly faction depending on what you want to do with your life."

"And they'll watch me forever?" Carla asked.

"Not forever," Miles said. "But for a few years, aye. You broke vampire law. You might not have expected all of this shit to come along with it, but you still broke vampire law. Willingly. Humans died. I know, you didn't kill them. You did participate in the robbery of humans. As a vampire, you committed crimes against humans. I'll put in a good word for you, and the fact that you're clearly sorry . . ."

"I really am," Carla almost shouted. "I'm *so* sorry."

"I know," Miles said softly. "You were mentally severed and dumped, and that will all account for why I'll put in a good word for you. If I thought you were a continued threat, you'd be in cuffs, or worse."

"No trial?" Carla said.

"We're not human," Miles said with a sigh. "And when it comes to vampire law, the Arbiters are judge, jury, and more than once, executioners. I'd like to think most Arbiters will give people a chance to explain themselves, although not all, but humans outnumber vampires by who knows how many millions to one. They've already made weapons specifically designed to kill us, and we don't need to be giving them a reason to use them. And the more idiot humans who circumvent the law to get turned into vampires, the more likely it is that one of you becomes a desolate in the middle of a town. Do you have any idea how badly it would have gone in the middle of London if you had been a desolate?"

Carla wept as she shook her head.

"It's bad, Carla," Miles said, not wanting to frighten her, but wanting her to understand the seriousness of what she'd done. "It's happened before. Thousands of people died."

"I'm sorry," Carla said softly.

"Come on," Miles said. "We're going to get you out of here, and I'm going to go figure out how I'm meant to track down a vampire who severs their mental link with the people they're changing."

Miles offered Carla his hand, and she accepted it, using it to pull herself upright. She wore an oversized grey sweatshirt with the word *LONDON* written on it in letters that were coloured like the Union Jack flag. She had on black leggings and white trainers, although the latter had seen better days.

"I'm cold," Carla said.

"When did you last eat?" Miles asked. "Blood, not food."

"Two days ago," Carla said.

"You need blood," Miles told her as he guided her out of the room and down the stairs. "Do you know what happens when you get cold? When you get hot?"

Carla shook her head.

"Okay, let's go find somewhere to sit down and I'll explain it," Miles said. "Also, let's find you some blood that isn't laced with something."

The pair went back down to the entrance of the house, and into the living room, which still had ATOs searching.

"Can we get a blood pouch?" Miles called over to the ATOs, one of whom nodded and left the room, returning a few moments later with a fresh pouch. Miles tore the seal off and passed it to Carla, who practically downed it, licking around the seal when she was done in case she'd missed a drop.

"Feel better?" Miles asked.

Carla lay back on the sofa and let out a contented sigh. "God, yes."

"Good," Miles said with a smile. "Right, heat will kill us. Going outside in anything over about eighty-five degrees Fahrenheit—about thirty-ish Celsius—isn't good for you long term. Anything over a hundred Fahrenheit will kill you; how fast depends on how long you're out for, how powerful you are, and how old you are. It's not the sunlight, it's the combination of heat and UV; our bodies just can't cope with it. It's why most vampires either move to more temperate climates during the summer or hibernate during the day. Sunstroke in a human might kill them if not seen to properly; it *will* kill a vampire. No two ways about it.

"But it's not just UV and being outside that's a problem. Touching an oven pan for a human will cause a burn; for a vampire, it'll be down to the bone instantly. And I know this might sound stupid, but it hurts. Not like it hurts when you were human. It's the kind of pain you feel in your soul. It's all consuming. So anything that would burn a human will do us a considerable amount more damage."

"Right, heat bad," Carla said. "Can we drink hot drinks, and have baths?"

"Hot drinks aren't a problem," Miles said. "Don't go downing shots of boiling water or pouring it on yourself, and you'll be fine. As for baths, again, not really an issue. Our body temperatures are much lower than a human's, so what we'd consider a hot bath would be barely lukewarm for a human. We're talking a sustained, high level of heat. Fire bad, boiling water bad, any UV levels over about a two. Also bad."

"And the cold?" Carla asked.

"The colder it is, the more our hunger drives us," Miles said. "Anything below zero Fahrenheit will mean the hunger inside takes over. We become feral, more animalistic, and only interested in feeding. We're stronger and harder to kill, too. Basically, you need to make sure you stay between zero and a hundred Fahrenheit and you'll be fine."

"It's cold out tonight," Carla said.

"And you felt your hunger rising, didn't you?" Miles asked. "Because I know I did, and I'm several centuries older than you."

Carla nodded. "So, if it gets cold, I need to feed before . . . I hurt someone."

"Well, you need to get warm before then," Miles said. "But feeding will help. It'll keep that hunger at bay. If your body gets too cold, then no amount of feeding beforehand is going to stop what you do. And it'll be bad for anyone nearby. The Assembly has to execute more new vampires due to losing control during the cold than anything else. Keep going in freezing conditions without feeding or any respite, and your body will eventually shut down, and we go into a sort of hibernation mode. You do not want to wake up a hibernating vampire."

"Thank you for your help," Carla said.

"It's fine," Miles told her. "Just . . . look, I'm sorry this all happened to you. Just don't get into any more trouble where people like me have to turn up. You're a vampire now. You get to live a long time. Whatever you decide to do with that life, make it good."

"I will," Carla told him.

Miles left Carla alone and went to find Megan, who was outside the house, leaning up against the exterior brick wall drinking from a travel mug.

"Something hot?" Miles asked. The wind had turned colder and more ferocious in the few minutes that he'd been in the house. The pangs of his own hunger played at the edges of his mind. He pushed them aside and checked his phone, which told him it was minus three Celsius/twenty-six Fahrenheit, although with the wind it felt several degrees colder.

"Coffee," Megan said, "although I'm sure you can smell it. Staying warm any way we can, right?"

Miles smiled. "Anyone decided that throwing their Boss under the bus is better than jumping themselves?"

"Nope," Megan said in the tone of someone who was very close to losing their temper if they had to ask the same questions to one more person.

"You want me to try?" Miles asked.

Megan took a drink of coffee and let out a deep exhale, her breath visible in the frigid night air. "You going to kill them?" she asked eventually.

"Wasn't planning on it," Miles said.

"You going to maim them?" Megan continued.

"Not planning on that either," Miles admitted.

"No pieces cut off," Megan said. "No deaths. They all need to go to the Assembly and see how much they want to talk when placed in the care of an Inquisitor."

Miles allowed himself a grimace, but it came out more like a snarl.

"I'm fully aware of your disdain for them," Megan said. "But they get results."

"And you worry about *me* being too rough with them?" Miles said, trying to be diplomatic about it. "Look, I need to know who turned Carla and Teresa. If they keep this up, they're going to turn someone into a desolate."

"You don't need to tell me how bad that would be," Megan said, and had another swig of her coffee. "My job is to hunt down the spiked blood packs."

"Carla told me that Danny's Boss was involved in her being turned into a vampire," Miles said. "Gangs rarely do one criminal enterprise at a time. We find out who's behind the drugs or the illegal vampires, we get the whole thing closed down and we both win."

"Okay, just don't kill anyone," Megan repeated.

Miles stopped himself from smiling and turned to look at the eight men—a mixture of humans and vampires—who sat on the edge of the pavement on the opposite side of the street. They were still cuffed, their hands behind their backs, and Danny had been dragged over to join the group. Church walked out of the park, moving between two gang members who practically dove out of the way, and crossed the road without looking. She stopped in front of Miles, who stroked her head.

"That dog of yours scares them more than my officers," Megan said. "Maybe we should get some of them for the team."

"Which one of these idiots is the most likely to squeal when pressure is applied?" Miles asked.

Megan pointed to the skinny male third from the left. "Human. Kyle O'Riley. Twenty-six. No fixed address, no job, a string of criminal offences going back to when he was thirteen and smashed up someone's car. Mostly stealing stuff, a little aggravated assault. The human police wanted him for a stabbing a year ago. Two gangs went at it, four people got stabbed. One seriously. Police couldn't make it stick, though, as no one would talk. He's jumpy as fuck, and I don't think it's because he's taken something. I think he's terrified he's going to have to be tried under vampire law."

"Okay, we'll have one of your people bring Kyle up to the roof," Miles said.

"You are not going to throw him off the roof," Megan said. "That's a fifty-foot drop. He'd likely die."

"Megan, I'm not about to start murdering your suspects so that all of these lovely neighbours can film it, but he doesn't need to know that," Miles said with a sharp grin. "Just bring him up. I promise, he will come down here in the same state he went up in." *Mostly*, Miles thought to himself.

CHAPTER FIVE

One of the ATOs brought an exceptionally nervous-looking Kyle upstairs, chuckled, and left the roof.

"Kyle, sit," Miles said, leaving no doubt that it was a suggestion.

Kyle sat.

"Do you know who I am, Kyle?" Miles asked without looking at the young man.

"Arbiter," Kyle said. "Danny told us. Said you're . . . said not to trust you."

Miles slowly turned his face to look at Kyle, and was welcomed by the look of fear in the young man's eyes.

Miles's face had changed. He'd allowed the vampire side of his nature out, showing the bright red eyes that glowed as the meagre light touched them, the sunken features, the hardened bone ridges in his face. The fangs.

"Something wrong?" Miles asked with a smile, showing the fangs more clearly.

Kyle looked away and shook his head.

"For a human, you appear to be quite unnerved by being near a vampire," Miles said. He kept his tone conversational but pushed the thought onto Kyle that the tone was just the wrong side of pleasant, as if violence might happen at any moment. Violence that would happen to the only human in the vampire's presence.

All vampires past a certain age or power level could force their power onto a human to some degree. It didn't always work, and the weaker the mind the easier it was, but Miles didn't like it. Push too far, and you got to see into the mind of the human, but they also saw into yours. Or, if you pushed too hard too fast, you could crack their mind like an egg, and the psychic backlash was sudden and violent and could cause irreversible damage to all involved. Only one vampire House, Umbra, were experts at using psychic and telepathic powers, even on other vampires.

"Danny don't show his fangs off," Kyle said, trying to look away but being forced to stare into Miles's eyes. "You're in my head," Kyle said.

That was a surprise. Miles hadn't expected Kyle to know that. Which meant he was either stronger-willed than Miles had given him credit for, or another vampire had placed something in his head to counter what Miles was trying to do. A powerful vampire.

"Your Boss," Miles said, pulling back out of Kyle's head and turning his face to human once again. "He mesmerised you? Or is a glamour?"

"I don't know what you're talking about," Kyle said, fear leaking throughout his voice.

Miles slammed his hand down on the sofa between them, hard enough to make it creak. "Don't play games, Kyle."

"Everyone who works for the Boss undergoes the same procedure," Kyle said hurriedly.

"Danny said he *can't* rat the Boss," Miles said mostly to himself. "At first I thought it was just because he was a new vampire and his mind was weak. You knew I was in your mind, and while I'm no House Umbra, I'm not exactly a slouch in the power department. Danny physically can't name his Boss."

"I don't know what any of that means," Kyle said.

"Your Boss," Miles said, with a smile. "Has he wiped your memory of him? Do you know his name? His face? Where he lives? I'm not asking you to tell me, I'm asking if you know."

"And if I say yes, then what?" Kyle said. "You'll torture me?"

"No," Miles said. "I don't torture. I find it . . . unpleasant. Now, where Megan is going to take you, at the Assembly. Oh, the Inquisitors are going to torture you like nothing you've ever experienced. Quite a lot of them are . . . blessed probably isn't the right word, but a lot of them have the Umbra bloodline gift, or they're psychics in their own right. You know about gifts, yes?"

Kyle shook his head.

"Damn it, man, does no one even give you an orientation day with vampires?" Miles asked, exasperated. "Every vampire gets a bloodline gift and a second ability that's wholly based on them. The two are never the same, although they can be similar. Danny saw my bloodline gift earlier when I used my power to disrupt his vampire nature. Hurts like hell."

"And your other ability?" Kyle asked.

Miles reached out and a cushion floated across the roof toward his hand. "Telekinesis, Kyle. It's strong enough that I could use it to break your bones right now, without ever touching you."

Kyle's eyes widened in horror.

"But I won't," Miles said. "Because that would be cruel. Anyway, where was I? Oh aye, the Inquisitors. They're going to flay your mind like peeling an orange. And they're not too fussed about how messy it gets. And it always gets *messy*, Kyle. And for you it's going to be really messy because some vampire put a glamour in your head that means you can't say his name. There's a good chance that after they're done, you're not even going to know *your* name."

Silence hung between the pair as the wind gusted over the rooftops. Miles wasn't sure just how long to give it before speaking again, but he wanted the mental image of exactly what was going to happen to Kyle to sink in. The Inquisitors were little more than animals in Miles's mind, a great disease that infected the Assembly. He admitted that they were useful, and more than once had managed to avert horrific crimes or bring people to justice, but the horrors they inflicted to do so had weighed heavily on Miles's mind at the time. Not on the minds of the Inquisitors, however, as they all seemed quite happy to tear someone's psyche apart.

"His name is . . ." Kyle said and screamed in pain as he grabbed the sides of his face.

"Kyle," Miles said softly.

"His name . . ." Kyle shouted, and dropped to his knees, as blood poured out of his nose.

"Kyle, stop," Miles said, placing a hand on the young man's shoulder. "Please stop."

"What has he done to me?" Kyle asked, looking up at Miles.

"He's fucked your brain up," Miles said. "He's made sure that you can't betray him, and I'm going to guess that if you tried to write his name down or something, you'd be in the same situation. Some powerful bullshit mind-fuckery right there."

"I don't understand," Kyle said.

"I'm guessing you all just call him *The Boss*, yes?" Miles asked.

Kyle got back up onto the sofa, nodding. "We don't have many dealings with him."

"Okay, I have a slightly different question for you," Miles said, trying to think of a way to get answers without having Kyle name the Boss in question. "Did you go to the flat in South Tottenham? With Danny, when he had to clean it after the deaths there?"

Kyle suddenly looked quite ill, which Miles took as a yes.

"Where's the block of flats?" Miles asked.

Kyle's face was a picture of pain as he sought to recall it. "Don't know," he said eventually.

"Okay," Miles said. "Most telepaths, people who can mess in your brain, they only limit things, people, places. Not events. It's too complicated. So, you remember going to this block of flats, you know it's in South Tottenham. How many bodies were in there?"

"Eight, I think," Kyle said with something bordering on relief. "There were not whole. They'd been torn to pieces by . . . I don't know what. Something strong because they were vampires."

"Did you see the bodies?" Miles asked.

"Yes," Kyle said. "I saw three of the vampires who worked there. I don't know names. It hasn't been blocked from me, I was never allowed to know them. I only went when I had to drive Danny up there for something or other."

"Did Danny go often?" Miles asked, feeling confident about the direction the conversation was taking.

"Every few days," Kyle said. "He would go, pick up money, drop off whatever they needed. I was never allowed inside. Not until we had to . . . not until the cleaning."

"What can you tell me about the bodies?" Miles asked.

Kyle took a deep breath and let it out slowly. "They were a mess. One had no head, but weird arms. They were . . . long. It was like he'd turned into a vampire's monster form, but there were no wings."

A dark foreboding fell over Miles. "You've seen a vampire's beast form?"

Kyle nodded. "Once. It was . . . scary. Genuinely scary. Not like you are now, you know, a vampire just sitting, looking normal. There's no *normal* for shit like that."

Only vampires of a certain power level could turn into what some called their true form, or beast form. Or occasionally, their monster. Miles considered it less of a true form and more of a visualisation of the power they possessed. They were larger in their beast form, with big bat-like wings, and there was no mistaking them for anything else. Those calling it a true form were usually the same people who liked to romanticise everything about vampires, or considered it some kind of religious thing. Both were idiots in Miles's mind.

"I'm guessing that what you saw wasn't a monster formed vampire," Miles said. "It was something else altogether. Do you know Oliver?"

Kyle nodded. "Yeah, he's missing. No one knows where he's gone. Do you know if he's okay? He was nice."

"I'll look into it," Miles said. "Let's go back down, and I'll hand you over to Megan."

"Will I still have to see the Inquisitors?" Kyle asked.

"I hope not," Miles said honestly, although he knew in his heart that he would.

The pair walked back down to the house entrance, where one of the ATOs took Kyle back over to the rest of the gang, who were being loaded into the Transit van. Danny and another were the last, still sitting on the side of the road.

"Leave him a minute," Miles called out, pointing to Danny.

The ATO gave a thumbs-up and motioned for the one other seated on the ground to get to their feet.

"Was Kyle helpful?" Megan asked.

Miles told her everything he'd learned. The look of horror on Megan's face told him everything he needed to know about where she stood on the practice of tearing apart people's minds to hide something.

"All of these guys have had the same thing done to them," Miles said. "Even Carla, although it didn't appear to be as invasive. Whoever this Boss is, he's blocked all use of his name from their minds. They can't even say what he looks like."

"That's some high-level shit," Megan said.

"Do all you can to keep them out of the hands of the Inquisitors," Miles said. "Please. These guys are assholes, thugs, and undoubtedly criminals, but they're no threat to vampires. No threat to any of the Houses or the Assembly. All they're going to do is turn a bunch of idiots into vegetables."

"I can have a word," Megan said. "But . . . I can't stop them. As you know, even the Arbiters can't stop the Inquisitors from doing their job; they're a law unto themselves. Oh, they'll send a nice psychic to talk to

Carla. She's had her link severed at transformation, she's been helpful, and while creating an illegal vampire is bad, actually being one is little more than someone wagging their finger at you while tutting. Besides, she's a new vampire. In the long term, she might be of benefit to the Assembly or a House, but these idiots are fair game to them. They helped actively threaten vampire law. Human or vampire, doesn't matter much to the Inquisitors if you've willingly broken vampire law."

"I know," Miles said with a sigh. "I just thought I'd mention it. I'm going to talk to Danny again."

"You going to hurt him?" Megan asked.

"Maybe," Miles admitted, crossing the road. "Get up, Danny."

Danny got up. He looked the figure of a broken man. He had no favours to call, no one to ride to his rescue, no pleas of ignorance or being forced into something. He was well and truly fucked, and he knew it.

"That headless body you cleaned up," Miles said. "You see its arms? Its hands?"

Danny looked around as if to see who was nearby. "Yeah," he whispered. "Like a vampire's monster form. Their true form."

"No," Miles said, pointing a finger at Danny in anger. "We both know it wasn't anything like that. You lied to me, Danny. You know what killed those vampires."

Danny looked away. "Don't know what you're talking about, man."

Miles grabbed Danny by the throat and lifted him clean off the floor, forcing the younger man to look down at him. "Do not cross me on this," Miles said, his voice deeper and angry, his eyes turning red.

"It was a desolate," Danny practically spurted out.

"Miles," Megan said softly, almost a whisper, but Miles still heard it as clear as if she stood beside him.

Miles dropped Danny to the ground and took a deep breath, calming himself. He looked behind him as the sounds of Megan's boots sounded on the road. Megan nodded down the road to the humans looking out of their windows. Some had phones.

"They made a goddamned desolate," Miles seethed. "That's what happened, yes?"

Danny said nothing.

Miles crouched down in front of the young vampire and took his jaw in one hand, forcing him to look up at him. "This is your only chance to avoid the Inquisitors. Make yourself useful to Megan and her team, and you get to stop having your mind turned inside out. You understand?"

Danny nodded. "I don't know how, but it attacked the vampires, it killed nearly everyone."

"How many vampires survived?" Miles asked.

"Five," Danny said. "The vampire who ran off and went to the Assembly, Oli, and three others. Oli and the other one who found you, they knew what was coming. The Boss turned up, had everyone executed, they were long gone by then. One of them ran for it when the Boss arrived, got away."

"So, of the five, three survived," Miles clarified, more for himself than anyone else. "We have one. Oli is the other, and the third is?"

"No idea his name," Danny said.

"Who killed the desolate?" Miles demanded to know.

"One of the vampires," Danny said. "The one who was there when the Boss arrived and ran. He was older than most of the others."

"You know their names?" Megan asked in horror.

"Only a few," Danny said. "The Boss didn't like us knowing one another. I only know Oli because he was in charge of the security for the new vampires."

"You know the name of the go-between?" Miles asked.

"Tony Company," Danny said, rubbing his neck. "He was barely alive when I arrived. He'd had an arm ripped off," Danny said. "The Boss . . . he killed him. Tore his head clean off in rage. I don't remember anything else. Just rage. I thought I was next."

"Any other names?" Miles asked.

"I don't remember," Danny said. "It's all . . . foggy."

"Your boss scrubbed your memory of them," Miles said. "But there was so much that happened, he couldn't scrub it all. Probably not enough time if he was going to get the surviving vampire away."

"So, you then got a bunch of humans from your gang to help clean that shit up?" Megan asked.

"Boss said clean it," Danny said. "Didn't say how. I don't think he cared. Hell of a first week for Kyle, though. Thought he was going to throw up."

"First week?" Miles asked.

Danny nodded. "Boss brought him in, told me to put him to work. Poor bloke didn't expect to be cleaning up vampire pieces a few days later.

By the time we arrived at the bloodbath, Oli had already run off with Teresa and Clara. Boss was not happy about that."

"What's Oli's surname?" Miles asked.

"I don't know," Danny said. "We're not big on surnames here."

"And you haven't spoken to your Boss in how long?" Megan asked.

"About two weeks," Danny said. "Like I told this guy."

"Danny, if you've lied to me about any of this," Miles said.

"No lies," Danny told him. "Can't really afford to upset the people who might stop me from a long chat with the Inquisitors."

"The old dude you sent there," Miles said. "The rich one. He was the last one to be turned, yes?"

Danny nodded.

"Was he the desolate?" Megan asked.

Danny shrugged. "I guess, but I can't say for sure."

"You know who he is?" Miles asked.

Danny shook his head. "He was important. I know that. I know it was going to be a lot of money passing hands. I was never told his name. Never allowed to be alone with him. He had a proper posh English accent, though. He was white, old, and rich. He was clean-shaven, he was balding, he had a bit of a gut on him." Danny patted his belly for reference and let out a chuckle.

"You met him at Edge of Humanity?" Miles asked, allowing himself to hope that Danny's big mouth could be a break in finding his Boss.

"I have no idea," Danny said. "I wasn't there when the original meeting happened. It was . . . at a club. Not a club, club, but like, one of those old-time gentlemen's clubs. You know, with wood panels on the wall and paintings of some old geezers."

"You don't know more?" Megan asked.

"That's it," Danny said, sounding smug about having made himself useful.

"Thank you for your help, please enjoy prison," Megan said, and Danny was dragged away by one of the ATO's and almost thrown into the rear of the Transit van.

"Fuck," Miles shouted, feeling the need to vent his anger. "These stupid little pricks could have spread a goddamned plague of certain death."

"But they didn't," Megan said. "And now they won't."

"Okay, so we've got an unidentified Boss who is probably in hiding because his idiot employees created a desolate," Miles said. "And one Oli who at the very least saw what was happening and managed to save the lives of two women. On the plus side, at least these idiots won't be making more anytime soon."

"And we got a lot of bad blood packs off the streets," Megan said. "That's got to be worth something."

"It is," Miles said, thankful that his friend was there. They might not always agree, but he knew she was always able to look on the brighter side of life, even if no one else could.

Carla was taken out of the house by an ATO as a black Mercedes-Benz C-Class pulled up. She looked tired and scared, but at least she was safe.

Miles crossed the road and waited for the ATO to tell her what was going to happen. Carla nodded as she heard a rehash of what she'd been told not long ago. When the ATO was done, she walked away, leaving Carla alone for a moment.

"Thank you," Carla said. "For not clamping me in irons and shipping me off somewhere."

"I haven't done much iron clamping for a while now," Miles said with a smile. He removed a card from his pocket and passed it to her. "This is my number. Show it to whoever you see at the Assembly, and they'll contact me if they need anything. Also, if they know you've spoken to an Arbiter, they'll know to behave and not try to freak you out. Remember, this is going to be a process for a while. You've got something to prove to the Assembly now."

"I will," Carla said. "I promise."

"I'll keep an eye on her," Megan said. "We'll make sure that no matter where you end up, House or Assembly, you'll be comfortable there."

"Thank you," Carla said again. She climbed into the back of the Mercedes and was driven away.

"You think she'll be okay?" Megan asked Miles.

"I hope so," Miles said. "I don't think it'll be an easy year."

"Was it easy for you the first year?" Megan asked.

Miles shook his head. "And I was vetted. I was transformed by a House member. That first year is hard. Really hard. And for Carla it'll be even more difficult."

"You ever look at the place in Soho they were dumped?" Megan asked.

"Yeah," Miles said. "Name who owned it is fake, nothing to link anyone. No CCTV. Only one used flat, which was the one with Carla and

Teresa. Working fridge, with three months' worth of real blood packs. Most of which had been used. There was a phone number of a nearby hospital they had reserved for drifters. This Oliver bloke had dumped them there with as much care and attention as possible."

"This old guy who wanted to be turned," Megan said. "Maybe we should be looking into missing persons. Might be able to figure out who it is."

"London is full of posh, old, rich, white geezers," Miles said.

"At least it's narrowing it down," Megan said helpfully.

Miles looked up at the night sky and sighed. "I've got a lead, I'm off to Whitechapel."

"As much as I'd love to help," Megan said, "the team needs me. We've got some processing of prisoners to do."

"Thanks for everything tonight," Miles said, offering her his hand, which she shook.

When the ATO had left and it was just Miles and Church alone, the latter sat down by the former's leg.

"So, we have a lead," Miles said, looking down at the huge dog. "Oliver someone or other. Varden Street, Whitechapel."

Church barked softly.

"Too right," Miles replied. "Let's go hunt."

CHAPTER SIX

Miles's home was a five-acre estate in the Scottish Highlands. His five-bedroom home was north of the town of Dingwall, in a small village known as Evanton, about half an hour drive north of Inverness. He'd purchased it many decades earlier and enjoyed the solitude and peace it gave him.

Unfortunately, as an Arbiter, the days that he got to actually spend at home were fewer and fewer every year. He missed being able to go for walks among the many trails and spend time with Church where she could run freely.

He especially missed it when he found himself walking the dark streets of London early in the morning as it started to rain.

When he was on a job, it was hotels at the Assembly's expense. At first it had been quite nice to go to fancy, expensive hotels with someone else paying for it, but after a while it made him long for home again. He would deal with this job and take some time off. The Assembly had plenty of Arbiters who could fill in for a few months.

Miles had a large suite at the Royal London, a vampire-owned hotel in Finsbury Square, Islington. The bar was open twenty-four hours a day, and the staff during the night shifts were a mixture of vampire and human. Some people became vampires and expected themselves to be thrust into a life of intrigue and wealth, but that just wasn't the case. Many vampires who lived under Assembly rule lived normal lives for much of the year. Living in a vampire controlled district or city usually meant you got free room and board, but you still had to make your own way.

The only exception to this were those who were taken into a Great House from the beginning. They were given good jobs, usually accompanied by the lifestyle that many envied. The downside of this lavish life of wealth and privilege was twofold. Firstly, you wore a target on your back that some of the other Great Houses, lesser Houses, and drifters would like to aim at. And secondly, you had no room to move within the vampire House structure unless those in charge of that House agreed to it. You did what you were taken on to do, and you didn't complain. That was how it had been sold to Miles, which hadn't been much of a pitch at all, but then he'd not really had much of a choice at the time.

Each of the Great Houses had a speciality. House Umbra dealt in paranoia and manipulation, House Barbarous in warriors and combat, House Venator in stealth and intelligence gathering, House Phalanx in illusions and coming together for the common good, and lastly, House Nix in demonic entities and darkness. No House was technically more powerful than any of the others, but accepting your place in one meant accepting the House and rules therein.

Miles had left the Great House he'd been taken into and joined the Arbiters. He'd seen one too many House members get away with murder, one too many feel as if their position in vampire society made them untouchable. It had angered and disgusted him for many years until he'd finally grown the courage to walk away.

He'd considered going back to the hotel, having a nice drink, maybe a little food, and relaxing in bed, after a shower that would hopefully wash away a lot of the less pleasant parts of the evening. He knew he wasn't that lucky. He couldn't leave a clue alone when there were still several hours of darkness to operate in.

So, instead of resting and relaxing, Miles had taken a cab to Whitechapel, stopping around the corner from his destination. He'd thanked the driver, given him a good tip, and walked in the drizzle around the corner, with Church padding dutifully beside him.

The building that Carla had pointed to was a three-storey pale brick building with a metal grate on the front door, large bay windows at the front of each floor, and a dark tiled roof. It was on the end of a terrace, with an alleyway between the building Miles was there for and the next one in the row.

"Stay here," Miles said to Church. "Let me know if there's trouble."

Church made a slightly whining noise and looked up at the sky.

"I know it's raining," Miles said. "You have fur on."

Church whined again.

"Fine," Miles said and walked up the steps to the front door. There was a mailbox next to it, with slots for three flats, each one labelled. Flats one and two had a name beside them, written on a piece of card behind a plastic seal, but flat three had nothing.

Miles had done some searching on the building on the ride over and discovered that flat three was owned by a company, which appeared to do absolutely nothing except exist for several decades. It had no register online, no income, no expenditure. It was just a thing that existed. Clearly this Oliver didn't expect anyone to look into it closely.

Miles rang the doorbell for flats one and two.

"Yes?" came a tired and cranky sounding voice. "Do you know what fucking time it is?"

"Apologies for waking you," Miles said. "My name is Miles Watson, and I need access to the third floor."

"Fuck off," the voice said.

"I'm an Arbiter," Miles said quickly. "You either let me in, or I kick the door down. Pick one." He showed his torc to the camera doorbell.

"Fine," the voice said after a few seconds, and there was a click as the door unlocked.

The hallway beyond was short, with only a set of stairs and some landscape paintings on the walls. Miles took the stairs quickly but quietly, and was greeted on the second floor by a burly looking man holding a baseball bat. He did not look happy.

"Arbiter," Miles said. "Thank you for letting me in."

"You know I have to get up for work in in a few hours," the man said, lowering the bat.

"Apologies," Miles said with a broad smile.

"Is there anything dangerous in flat three?" the man asked. "It's been empty for years."

"I doubt it," Miles assured him. "I hope to be here and gone quickly. Did you know the resident?"

"What resident?" the man asked, looking down at Church, his eyes widening. "That's a big fucking dog."

"Yes, she is," Miles said. "So, the resident in flat three. Someone named Oliver?"

"Oliver?" the man asked, his eyes flicking back to Church. "You mean

McCarthy? He's not a resident; he works for the landlord or some shit. Never met him until a few weeks ago. Caught him walking up there when I was coming back from a late shift. Asked him who he was, said he worked for the landlord. He said his name was McCarthy, didn't give a first name."

"He say what he was doing?" Miles asked.

"Something to do with the flooring up there," the man said after taking a few seconds to think. "Heard a bit of banging, but it soon went away."

"Thank you," Miles said. "And again, I apologise for waking you at this hour."

The man nodded, took another look at Church, shook his head in disbelief, and went back inside, locking the door behind him.

Miles continued on upstairs, trying the door for the third flat and finding it locked. He made a mental apology to the man in flat two, and kicked the flat three door in.

It splintered as though it were made of balsa wood, the heavy wooden door slamming into the wall adjacent to it, leaving a deep gouge from the door handle as it ripped into the white painted wall.

Miles stepped inside the flat, waited for Church to join him, and closed the remains of the door as best he could.

"I don't think anyone lived here," Miles said, switching on the lights to find bare wooden floors and no furniture, not even a chair.

He made a quick search of the entire flat and found nothing of note in any of the rooms, except one bedroom. No bed, no nothing, not even a light shade.

Miles returned to the main living area, spotting a slightly ajar floorboard. He knelt beside it and prised it open, finding a safe, the door of which was still open, beneath it. The safe was empty. "Damn it," Miles snapped, getting back to his feet.

Church made a chuffing noise behind him, and he turned as she dropped something at his feet. He bent down and picked up the crumpled paper. "*Fortress Falls,*" Miles said. "I don't know what any of that means. What's Fortress Falls?" He removed his phone and typed the name into the search engine, which brought up details of a town in northwest Oregon, Washington state.

"Okay, so either Oliver is an idiot and left this here, or he was preoccupied," Miles said. "Either way, I guess I'm going to need to make a phone call."

Church barked.

"Yeah, I know," Miles said with a deep sigh. "Nothing here, but let's see if I can call in a few favours." He checked his watch; it would be dawn soon, and the call could wait until he'd had some sleep. It was a Pandora's box he would rather open after some rest.

He called an Uber and took it back to the Royal London hotel, getting out in the car park a few minutes' walk away. It was a habit he'd never quite gotten out of. Get out and walk so you can check no one is following you, or waiting for you. On this occasion, it turned out to be the right decision when he spotted two people watching him from a small green park close to the hotel. They were standing under some trees, either trying to keep out of the rain or trying to keep hidden.

Miles crossed the road and continued on down toward the park, stopping by the metal fence. "You're both pretty shit at hiding," he said. "My advice is to come out now, and not make me come in there after you."

"Is your dog safe?" a deep voice asked.

Miles looked down at Church, who had at least tried to look as sweet and innocent as possible. "Depends if you're dangerous or not," he said.

"Arbiter Watson," a female voice said as she stepped out from under the darkness of the trees. A larger man stepped out behind the woman.

"Inquisitors," Miles said, taking note of the bald heads, the tattoos on their scalps. Both had the same white badge on their lapel with a red circle and a black infinity symbol that went across it, each with three dots on the symbol. "Either of you want to explain why you're waiting for me?"

Technically Arbiters weren't the bosses of Inquisitors, as they operated in different branches of the Assembly, but Arbiters could, and had, made the lives of Inquisitors difficult if they felt they were overstepping their legally designated jurisdiction.

"We were told to find you," the male Inquisitor said.

"Aren't I lucky," Miles said, trying not to think of anything about the two vampires in front of him. He settled for replaying parts of *Enter the Dragon* in his mind. It was illegal for an Inquisitor to use any telepathic abilities on a fellow vampire without due cause. What they considered due cause, and what anyone else might, differed on a sometimes daily basis. "You must both be a great boon to your Inquisitor family."

They both bowed their heads. "We went into the hotel but were told you were not there," the female Inquisitor said. "We decided it best to wait out here and not disrupt the hotel guests."

Vampires didn't like the Inquisition. No one wants to sit near the people many consider to be a secret police.

"How'd you know I was here?" Miles asked.

"We were told you were staying at this hotel," the man said. "It's the best vampire hotel in this part of the city."

Not exactly high-level deducting, but Miles figured they were probably telling the truth, although it was hard to tell with Inquisitors. The world of the Inquisitor was not one Miles ever wanted to spend any real time in.

"You want to tell me out here in the rain, or go inside?" Miles asked.

"I think it would be wiser to give the information without prying ears," the man said, which Miles figured was a fair point.

"We were asked to let you know that someone has confessed to the crimes of illegal vampires that you are currently investigating," the female inquisitor said.

"Someone confessed?" Miles asked, not even trying to hide his surprise. "Who?"

"We were not given that information," the female Inquisitor said.

"Who told you to tell me?" Miles asked, feeling confused. "Why didn't *they* tell me?"

"I do not know the latter," the female Inquisitor said with a slight nod of unnecessary apology. "The former was Umbra First Captain Vedran Vinko."

"Anything else?" Miles asked, when he couldn't think of anything else to say.

"Vedran offers you an invitation to come to the Great Houses gathering in Glen Affric," the male Inquisitor said with a slight smile. "He says you can talk to the confessor there and hopefully it will aid your investigation."

Miles wasn't sure when the Inquisitors started doing grunt work for House Umbra, or if it was just Vedran they were running errands for, but something felt off. The Assembly and Houses were meant to work in harmony, so there was nothing wrong with one of the Houses asking Assembly members to inform someone they personally couldn't get ahold of, but Miles wondered if there was more to it.

House First Captains were in charge of the security for that vampire House. In times past, they'd been in charge of warfare, but it had been a long time since any of the Great Houses had gone into open warfare with one another. Over time, the position had been modified to still work during times of peace.

When Miles said nothing for several seconds, the Inquisitor said, "You have a pleasant day now, Arbiter Watson."

"You too," Miles said.

He made his way back to the hotel, his mind racing with possibilities of what was going on. Miles and Church went to the bar, he ordered a pint of German beer, and he took it to an empty booth at the rear of the establishment.

The bar had five booths down each side, with a collection of various sized tables in between. There was a stage at the far end, with a midnight blue curtain surrounding it. There was a sign in front of it detailing the upcoming acts over the next few weeks. Music, comedy, and at least one magic show were the offerings. Although Miles had heard of none of them, he would like to at least come down and see them when he could.

Next to the stage was an emergency exit door. There were no windows in the bar, as it was in between the foyer and a large hall used for company gatherings. A second bar at the rear of the hotel was much more popular with a younger crowd, and the hall and bar could be opened up to create a large nightclub-like space. Miles tended to avoid the place when it was in full flow. The level of vapidity from the people he'd spoken to who frequented it made his head hurt.

The bar had a black marble floor, with deep burgundy seats and golden accents on everything. The hotel kept the theme into the foyer and reception area, although the lighting made everything appear quite bright during the day. At night, the lights were lowered, giving Miles the impression it had been designed by someone who had watched an old vampire film and thought to themselves, "Yep, that's the one." He doubted that a vampire had even been consulted during the decorating stage, although at least nothing was made of velour and the doorman wasn't wearing purple crushed velvet.

The bar was fairly quiet, although as it was midweek, early in the morning, and considering the majority of humans would need to get up for work in a few hours, it was hardly surprising. The eight people inside the bar were spread out into three groups. Four men in suits were huddled in a booth together, whispering over a bottle of bourbon. There were a man and woman on the opposite side of the bar, and a second couple of two women a few booths down. All were human. Vampires knew their own.

There was music playing throughout the bar, a low background of classical pianos. It was unobtrusive, and Church went to sleep under the booth table.

As Church snored softly, Miles removed a notepad and two fountain pens from his satchel, placing them before him. One pen, a black Visconti Homo Sapiens Bronze Age, was filled with black ink, while the other, a bright blue Sailor Professional, was filled with a forest green ink.

The tan leatherbound notebook had fountain pen paper inside which, for Miles, was a must-have so his writing didn't look like an abstract painting. The notebook leather was heavily marked and had been battered for several years. After every case, he removed the paper and replaced it with a new stack, placing the old note-filled paper in a safe at his home. Just in case he ever needed it.

Miles wrote down everything he'd seen and heard during the night's investigation. Vampire memories were a double-edged sword. They remembered pretty much everything in minute detail, and that was both the good and bad thing about it. Miles could recall something from two years ago or a hundred years ago with the same clarity. It just needed for him to close his eyes and pick the memory in question. He considered it possibly his most useful trick when undergoing an investigation.

When he was done, he sat back and drank his beer while staring at the words on the page. He circled *Oliver McCarthy, Illegal Vampires, The Boss, Fortress Falls*. He put an arrow between *Illegal Vampires, The Boss,* and *Oliver*. A second arrow connected *Oliver* to *Fortress Falls*. Oliver was his best bet to find out who this Boss character was.

He wrote *Vedran Vinko* under the other names and put a question mark next to it. He'd met Vedran many times over the centuries and found him to be hard work. He was jovial and outwardly pleasant, but everything was a competition to him, and it quickly became tiring. "Why can't things ever be easy?" he asked Church, who snorted without looking up.

Miles removed his phone from his pocket and texted the First Lord of House Venator, Drest: *I need to talk to you. Urgent.*

Miles put his phone away. Dawn was coming soon, and while the sunlight wouldn't kill him—not during the winter when the UV was so low— he needed sleep. He rubbed his eyes, put away his things, and retired to his room, where Church took up residence on the floor behind the door, her usual spot when they were in a hotel. Miles had as hot of a shower as he could stand, got dried and dressed, and practically fell into his bed, as a single thought swirled around his mind: what the hell was the First Captain of House Umbra doing being involved in his investigation?

CHAPTER SEVEN

Miles woke in the early afternoon, feeling refreshed and ready for whatever the day ahead was about to throw at him, which, considering the previous day's lot, was probably going to be annoying. Church had stayed on the floor beside the hotel room door, putting herself between the door and Miles, as she always did.

He removed a synthetic blood pouch from the hotel room fridge and drank it down. Real blood was rarely kept in hotel rooms, even ones run by vampires. A vampire more than a few months old could survive on synthetic blood without any problems, and over time those making it had spliced in flavours to get it close to real blood. It was harder to spike synthetic blood with illicit substances, as it was designed for the smell or colour to change almost immediately.

But it wasn't quite the same thing as real blood. And that wasn't quite the same as taking the blood from an actual living being, from having the emotional and physical connection with someone. It was good enough, though, and in Miles's mind, a lot easier and less messy than taking from a living person. Safer, too.

Miles got dressed in jeans, a black T-shirt with a forest green hoodie over it, and black trainers with green stripes. He packed away everything he'd brought with him, and with Church taking the lead, he left the hotel room, making sure to check out at the reception.

"Mister Watson," the young female receptionist said. "A car is waiting for you."

"A car?" Miles asked. He hadn't been expecting a car. "Where's it going? Who sent it?"

"We were told to tell you to read your messages," the woman said, with a small smile.

Miles placed his leather satchel bag on the ground next to his black suitcase, removed his phone from his pocket, and switched it on. He vaguely remembered switching it off before going to sleep. It had been a long night, and if Vedran Vinko or any of the Umbra lackeys needed to get hold of him, because someone had confessed, he'd rather it wasn't by interrupting his well-earned rest.

There was one phone message.

The voice in the message was instantly recognisable, the deep Scottish accent warm and friendly. "*Miles, it's Drest. It was good to hear from you. Feel free to come to the estate at Glen Affric as soon as possible. A jet is waiting for you at Heathrow. As soon as you can would be good, though.*"

"Where's the car?" Miles asked the receptionist as he replaced his phone in his pocket. Drest had said *soon* twice in the same message. That was his less than subtle way of saying it was urgent.

"Out front in the parking area," the receptionist said, helpfully. "It's a silver Audi Q7. I hope you had a good stay."

The daylight sky outside was overcast, but Miles checked his watch again just to make sure the UV level was low. It said *one*, so Miles was in no concern about being threatened by ultraviolet rays. If he was going to be out in the sunlight for long, he'd have put sunscreen on, just for a little extra protection, but five minutes in an overcast London wasn't about to cause him to spontaneously combust. He spotted the Audi almost immediately, even among the other prestige cars in the car park, and headed toward it. He felt a slight tingling feeling being out during the daylight, a warning not to dally. The driver, a man Miles had never seen before, waved him over with some enthusiasm.

"Sir," the driver said, offering his hand. He wore a smart looking charcoal suit and black chauffeur hat.

"Miles is fine," he said, shaking the driver's hand.

"Tim," the driver said with an earnest smile as he helped load Miles's belongings into the boot of the car. When done, he opened the rear car door and let Church jump in to get comfortable.

Miles climbed in after Church, who had curled up on the floor behind the passenger seat.

"You need to stop anywhere?" Tim asked.

"No, I'm good; let's just get to the plane and get going," Miles said.

After a short distance, Tim said, "You okay with me putting the radio on?"

"Be my guest," Miles said, looking out of the heavily tinted rear windows.

The rest of the hour and a half drive through central London was done to the sounds of people discussing the previous night's football match between Arsenal and Liverpool. Miles tuned out pretty quickly, not because he disliked football—he'd been to several matches over the year and had enjoyed his time—but because he just didn't care who won.

They were soon at their destination.

Once the car was parked in the private parking area, Miles let Church out to the nearby small greenery, which was basically a few bushes and the odd tree, the former of which she took full advantage of.

"Thanks, Tim," Miles said as he stood by the driver's side window and waited for Church. "You work for the Venator House?"

Tim moved his lapel to show the badge, a white bow over a black sun. "Have done for a decade now," he said.

"How's everything going at Glen Affric?" Miles asked him, hoping for some information before he reached his destination. Vampire politics was a tricky thing to navigate at the best of times.

"It's Venator's turn to host the Assembly," Tim said. "That's all I know, sorry."

Miles already knew which vampire House was hosting the Assembly for the year, which, considering it had just gotten started, meant lots of vampires moving around the globe to get to Scotland to stay for the next twelve months. Or to prepare for next year when the host would change to . . . well, no one officially knew until a few weeks beforehand.

While the Assembly had several buildings dotted around the globe, they didn't meet in one building every time. The Assembly was gathered at the headquarters of each of the five Great Vampire Houses, moving from one to the other every year. It meant that every Great House estate was home to members of the other four Houses and several dozen Assembly members every year, as well as a smattering of Minor House members.

The majority of Assembly buildings were home to Inquisitors, Arbiters, ATOs, and various other clerks and members of the administration that helped run the vampire world.

"Thanks anyway," Miles said as Church returned and snorted. No clear-up for Miles this time. Having a hyper-intelligent canine had its perks.

It didn't take long to get through the check-in system, and to be taken across the airport to the private runway where the Gulfstream G700 was waiting. The jet seated twenty people normally, although as Miles climbed the short set of stairs and entered the fuselage, he saw that the plane only seated eight. The rear of the aircraft was turned into a bedroom—the door of which was open showing the large bed inside—and a bathroom beside it, with a small kitchen toward the cockpit. It was basically a flying hotel.

Miles thanked the two female crew members who greeted him and took one of the two seats that sat opposite a comfortable looking couch, with Church jumping up on the couch itself to look out of the window, her tail wagging furiously. She loved flying, although for the life of him, Miles couldn't figure out why.

Miles stowed away his suitcase and satchel bag behind the seats, figuring he wasn't going to need anything in either of them, considering the large TV on a nearby table.

One of the two female crew members went through into the cockpit, while the other came over to Miles as a third—whom Miles hadn't seen—sorted out closing and locking the door.

The female crew member who came over to Miles had long blonde hair tied back in a ponytail and wore a navy blue shirt and jacket with a white blouse and black shoes. She had multiple earrings in both ears and wore a silver necklace with the symbol of House Venator medallion on it. She was definitely human, although that didn't preclude her from being a familiar to one of the older Venator vampires.

"Master Drest sends his warmest regards," the woman told Miles. She had light blue eyes, and her perfume was subtle and floral in nature. Over-powering scents did not sit well with a vampire's senses, so those who worked for the Houses tended to be more thoughtful in their deodorant choices. "My name is Lily, and I'll be attending you on this flight. It's expected to last only an hour and forty minutes, and we should be disembarking soon. Is there anything I can get you?"

Miles smiled. "Some water for me and Church would be excellent."

Lily looked over at Church, who had decided to lie down on the sofa. She gave the flight attendant her best "woe is me, I'm so in need of atten-tion" look, which worked a treat as Lily went over to make a fuss of the dog.

The jet began to taxi and Lily took a seat as the Gulfstream soon took off. Once airborne, Lily brought over a glass of water for Miles and a bowl for Church, who lapped up the cool refreshment as though she'd never been given water before.

"What a cute dog," Lily said. "Are you sure you don't want anything else? It's free."

"It's free now," Miles said. "Just wait until I meet Drest and he's got an itemised bill to tell me exactly how much I cost him."

"He makes you pay it back?" Lily asked.

Miles shook his head. "No, he just wants you to know exactly how much he's let you off with. This time. Because he's such a nice guy."

"Lord Drest has always been very kind to me," Lily said, slightly irritated by the insinuation that Drest was anything other than the perfect boss.

"No, he's a good man," Miles said. "He just likes me to know how much I cost him. It means when he asks for a favour he feels less guilty about it."

"Aren't you an Arbiter?" Lily asked. "I wasn't aware you worked for the Houses."

"I don't," Miles said. "Doesn't stop people asking, though."

"A car will be waiting for you at Inverness," Lily said. "We don't usually have Arbiters on our flights, so this is all a bit exciting for everyone."

"I should fly with you all more often then," Miles said with a warm smile.

"Yes," Lily said, not breaking eye contact with Miles. "You really should."

Miles watched Lily walk away, which he was pretty sure was the point. He looked over to Church, who had something approximating a smile on her face.

"Don't you start," Miles said.

Church snorted and went back to looking out of the window.

The rest of the flight went quickly, with the jet beginning its descent to Inverness after a short announcement from the pilot.

Lily came back over to Miles. "You should know it's been snowing in Inverness, and minus six Celsius as of right now. The jet will land fine as the runways have been cleared, but it's going to be cold. Have you got a warm jacket?"

Miles tapped the suitcase behind him. "Thick winter jacket all ready to go," he told her. "Not my first time in Inverness."

"You're Scottish, yes?" Lily asked.

Miles nodded. "Born near a small village south of Aberdeen, not far from Stonehaven," he told her. "English father, Scottish mother. My dad's family—who were all English—were not best pleased about it."

"You grew up in Scotland?" Lily asked, taking her seat close by as the seatbelt sign flashed.

"No," Miles said, buckling up his own seatbelt. "My parents died when I was very young. I was shipped out to London to be with my dad's parents. They were . . . not great. I kept the accent to spite them to begin with. Wealthy landowners weren't thrilled at having a Scottish grandchild to begin with, but they were duty-bound—apparently—to give me an education, if not their love and understanding."

"I'm sorry," Lily said.

"You can't pick your family," Miles said. "It's why picking your friends is so important. You from England?"

Lily nodded. "Liverpool," she said.

"The vampire capital of England," Miles said with a chuckle. Liverpool had been a vampire city for well over a century and was easily the largest one in England. "You don't have the accent."

"Grew up in Winchester," Lily said. "Lost the accent as a kid. It comes back a bit when I go home, though. It always comes back a lot when I go to the football." Lily laughed and tucked the strands of hair that fell across her face behind her ear.

Lily and Miles continued to chat as the jet touched down in Inverness with a slight bump and jolt, and when the jet had stopped moving, Miles unbuckled, got up from his seat, and fetched his belongings.

Church yawned and lazily removed herself from the sofa, looking to all the world like a dog who wished to remain on the sofa and not venture outside into the Scottish weather that awaited them.

The second flight attendant opened and secured the door, as the steps lowered down to the ground automatically.

He nodded thanks, before disembarking and walking across the tarmac as the cold wind whipped all around him.

Church bounded off ahead, jumping into the snow that had been piled up on the edge of the runway beside the door to the terminal, which Miles entered, glad for the immediate warmth it offered him. Church stalked in after him, shaking the snow from her head.

There was no check-in for an Assembly Arbiter, although Miles still had to show the bracelet on his wrist to a large guard, and give his name and reason for being there. The guard checked his electronic pad and nodded after finding Miles's name, beckoning him through the metal detector, which beeped and was immediately ignored by everyone.

Miles left the terminal and found the Audi Q7—an identical one from what had taken him to Heathrow Airport—waiting nearby. The driver, a dark-haired human woman of about fifty, came over and shook Miles's hand.

"You taking me to Glen Affric?" Miles asked after he'd put away his bags and climbed into the rear seats of the car next to Church.

"Only to Cannich," the woman said.

"You live around here?" Miles asked as they set off on the hour and a bit journey.

"In Cannich, sir," the woman said.

"Miles is fine," he told her.

"I'm Diane," she said. "Pleasure to meet you."

"So, any particular reason why we're going to Cannich and not on to the Glen Affric estate?" Miles asked.

It was dark outside, and he felt a pang of regret that he wouldn't get to see the majesty of the scenery he was going to be driving through. Night vision is great for when you're on foot, not so useful looking out of a heavily tinted car window.

"All I know is that I've been asked to drive you to Cannich, where future transport will meet you," Diane said.

The mystery deepened, but Miles had long since gotten used to the idiosyncrasies of the vampire world. While the Assembly and the various vampire Houses—Great or otherwise—officially were all working off the same page, unofficially a large number of them all distrusted each other to various degrees. Some even hated others. Grudges could be held onto for centuries.

The conversation ended there, and Miles settled back as Church rested her head on his lap, looking up at him as if asking him what the hell they were doing. Miles sighed; he wished he knew.

CHAPTER EIGHT

The village of Cannich sat in the Highlands of Scotland and had a population of around five hundred people. Everyone who lived there worked for the Glen Affric estate in some way or another, with all of them considering the Great Vampire House of Venator as their employer and protector.

In the 1990s, a large hotel had been built roughly ten minutes' drive outside the village, near the tiny village of Tomich. When full, it almost quadrupled the population of the village. For most of the time, it sat empty, a skeleton crew making sure everything was clean and fresh, but apart from a few tourists it remained way under occupancy. Right up until the Assembly came to visit.

The Assembly with their security and personnel completely took over the hotel. Several of the other vampire Houses stayed on the estate itself, accommodated on several hundred acres of land and more than a dozen buildings. Empty for most of the years when not utilised by the Assembly.

All of the five Great Houses had similarly large places to house everyone when they came to stay. A few even had their own islands, and one House had a hundred-storey skyscraper in Manhattan, but of all of them the Glen Affric Estate was the only one where Miles felt somewhat at home. Or at least moderately at peace.

He'd called the estate home for several centuries and knew every nook and cranny of the vast wilderness it contained. The nearby lochs, Càrn Eige and other mountain peaks, the forests, even the vast emptiness of so much of the land around it. Miles was pretty sure that leaving the House and going to work for the Assembly had been more difficult simply because of what he had to give up in terms of his living arrangements, although he'd found a beautiful home since.

The car stopped, which took Miles out of the daze of memory he'd found himself in.

"We're here," Diane said.

"Thank you," Miles said. He opened the door and stepped outside, looking around at the expansive nothingness illuminated by two nearby streetlamps, although considering the size of the area they were trying to light up, it was probably not worth their electricity consumption.

After retrieving his luggage, Miles found that Diane had gotten out of the car, too.

"What now?" Miles asked, pointing to the lights in the distance. "I assume that's Cannich."

"It is," Diane said. "I was told to bring you here."

Miles looked around, his night vision illuminating what would otherwise be pitch darkness. It was a car park, although not a particularly large one. It was usually used for coaches that would bring day-trippers in during the summer months. Some people came to the area to see its natural beauty, and some came because they hoped to see the vampires. Either way, it was empty now.

The car park had a low stone wall surrounding it, with high hedges just beyond that protecting it from the fierce wind that whipped across the place even during the warm months. A number of trees at the far end, just beyond the hedges, creaked and groaned. They were maybe three hundred meters from Cannich proper. A brisk walk would see them there in a few minutes, although Miles was damned if he wasn't going to find out exactly why the cloak-and-dagger nonsense was necessary, and yell at someone about it.

A black electric BMW X5 pulled into the car park and stopped beside Diane. The driver's side window lowered, and Miles tried to listen in to the conversation, but it was short and to the point, and he managed to catch none of it beyond the greeting.

"I'll be going then," Diane told Miles.

"Thank you for your time," Miles said with a nod of his head. "Take care."

"Aye," Diane said. "You too, lad."

Miles was quite possibly several centuries older than Diane, but he imagined that she called everyone *lad* if she didn't have to call them *sir*.

Diane got back into the car and headed away, the red lights of the car vanishing into the darkness as she drove down toward Cannich.

The rear passenger door of the car opened and a woman stepped out. Even bathed in the less than flattering streetlights, she was, in Miles's opinion, radiant. Long dark hair that fell over her pale bare shoulders in loose curls. She held a red shawl with black swirls across it in her hands. It matched her strapless evening gown in colour and elegance. There was a slit in the dress from ankle to upper thigh, and she wore strappy high heels that were probably not ideal footwear for the loose pebble of the car park. Her name was Charlotte Henry, and she was the First Counsel of the House of Venator.

"Are you getting in, or are you just going to stare?" Charlotte asked, her accent French, her tone playful.

"Are you going somewhere fun?" Miles asked as Church went over to Charlotte so the latter could make fuss of her, which she did immediately.

Charlotte made a mock laughing noise. "You, my old friend, are a hoot."

Miles walked up to Charlotte and the two embraced warmly. "It's good to see you again," Miles told her as they pulled apart.

"It's been far too long," Charlotte said. "Now get in the blasted car, it's freezing."

Miles let Church get in first, and he climbed in after as Church decided to clamber over the seats to sit in the front passenger seat. The driver opened his mouth to complain, took one look at the large dog inches from his face, and patted her on the head instead.

Charlotte climbed into the rear of the BMW, closed the door with a flourish, and turned up the heating in the rear of the car to max. "I am not dressed for such things."

"Why are you dressed like that?" Miles asked. "Also, why did Drest ask for me? Why are you meeting me out here with the cloak-and-dagger routine? And where is your Blood Guard?" The questions weren't all connected to form a coherent train of thought, just a random assortment of thoughts that were bouncing around his mind.

"That is a lot of questions in a short time," Charlotte said. "Drive."

The car set off silently into the darkness, something Miles still wasn't entirely used to, despite so many electric cars now being the norm.

"No guard because I don't need one," Charlotte said.

All vampire First ranks had a three-person Blood Guard. They were a dangerous trio, who had come up through the House to be placed in positions of protection. They were, for the most part, vampires who knew their principle well, who had served with the House for many decades. If you wanted to harm a First, you had to get through their Blood Guard, and very few people managed it.

When Miles had left House Venator, it had meant leaving his Blood Guard behind, too. In some ways, that had been more difficult than actually leaving. They'd been good vampires, and he'd trusted them with his life, but they were House Venator before all others.

"I am dressed like this because there is a formal event on," Charlotte continued. "I am obviously thrilled about having to spend time with people from the other Houses, and being leched over by, let's be honest, men who wouldn't have a chance if they were the last people on earth. I've already had to stab one particularly handsy man with a fork. He went crying to his House betters, who slapped him for pissing me off."

"I think anyone who ever met you can definitely attest to not wanting to piss you off," Miles said.

Charlotte smiled, showing a little fang in the process. "Thank you. Anyway, it is at the estate and it is boring, but as First Counsel, I'm required to be there. Lucky me."

"Okay, so the second question?" Miles asked.

"What was that one?" Charlotte asked him.

"Why the cloak-and-dagger?" Miles repeated.

"Ah, we'll get to that," Charlotte assured him. "Why did you get a message from Drest? Because we need to talk. Tomorrow. It's going to be a late night, and people are drinking a lot, and honestly, I'm going to stand back and watch the inevitable fireworks when two of the Houses who hate each other start to get into it."

"I'm not getting a lot of information here," Miles said.

"House Umbra has someone who came here and confessed to the crime of illegal vampire creation," Charlotte said. "Vedran contacted you about it."

"Yes," Miles said. "Two Inquisitors handed me Vedran's message. I texted Drest last night and asked him to contact me. He told me to come here. I assume all three things are connected. Although, honestly, I'm not sure if that's a good thing."

"Sounds like you've been busy," Charlotte said.

"Unfortunately, yes," Miles agreed. "What can you tell me about the confessor?"

"Officially, nothing," Charlotte said with a sparkle in her eyes. "It's House Umbra business, and I have zero information on them."

Miles remained quiet and waited for Charlotte to tell him anyway. House Umbra wasn't known as the House of Shadows for no reason, but Charlotte had the uncanny ability to know the *exact* person to talk to, in order to get any information she needed.

"The confessor drove from London to here, to confess *personally* to the First Captain of House Umbra," Charlotte said. "Unofficially."

"Are you and Vedran still fighting?" Miles asked.

"Do *you* trust him?" Charlotte countered, with a little more snap in her voice.

"No," Miles said. "But I don't trust any First Captains from any House. They, like every First Captain, or Counsel, or any powerful position, only have the interests of their House at mind."

"Are you saying you don't trust me?" Charlotte asked in a mocking tone.

"If Drest told you to throw me out of this car . . ." Miles said.

"You'd be bouncing down the road behind us," Charlotte finished. "But you know that already."

All of the Houses—Great and Minor—had mostly the same aims: the betterment of vampire kind, and to ensure humans and vampires lived in peace. They were all akin to political parties who disagreed on how to get things done, but they had the Assembly there to make sure they all behaved. The hierarchy of loyalty went: House, Assembly, vampire kind, humans. Unfortunately, there were members from all of the Houses who placed their own personal betterment over that of anyone else. And some vampires believed that the vampire relationships with humans were too far in the benefit of humans.

Every year the vampires got together to discuss any problems they'd encountered as a species, any new technology the humans had worked on, and how to counter it. They talked about which members of which Houses were to be promoted, or demoted, and the general states of any Assembly projects or research that had been done and wasn't confidential.

That was the official stance, anyway; the unofficial one was that every year they got together so that the vampires could let loose without human eyes. No cameras or recording equipment were allowed at a Gathering of Houses, and anyone caught going against that rule would find themselves in the kinds of trouble that had centuries-long consequences.

"I do," Miles said. "Loyalty to the House first. So, while I may not trust Vedran because he places his House first, and I don't know what the aims of House Umbra are, I trust you for the exact same reason. I know that no matter what else, you will help the House before anyone else, even Drest. I also know that the aims of House Venator are as they have always been, to do what they can for vampire and humankind."

House Venator, the House of Justice, had once been the only vampire House to actively hunt vampires who had committed crimes against other vampires, or humans.

Charlotte raised an elegant eyebrow in quizzical fashion. "You're suggesting I would betray the head of our House?"

"No," Miles said. "And you know that."

Charlotte's mask broke and she smiled. "You are correct, of course. Can you say the same about all of the Houses?"

Miles considered the question, and the answer came easily to him. No, of course not. "I wouldn't like to say," he told her instead. Some things didn't need to be uttered in public.

Charlotte laughed. "You sound like a First Counsel," she said, making it sound like a genuine compliment.

The aims of each individual House were primarily to ensure their House maintained power and wealth over other Houses, and over humans. Many Minor Houses had been folded into the larger Great Houses over the centuries for that very reason. If one House found a way to gain an advantage over others, they would usually take it. So long as they didn't go against the Assembly, or provoke war against another House—or humans—the Houses were left to do whatever they wished.

Miles nodded his thanks. "You still haven't told me what's going on. Or where we're going. Or where I'm meant to be staying. Am I meant to be staying?"

"You are an Arbiter," Charlotte said. "Is there anywhere off limits to you?"

"Charlotte," Miles said softly. "Stop it. Just be honest with me. Please."

"Driver, stop the car and leave," Charlotte said.

The car pulled over to the side of the road, and the driver left without a word.

"Can you make him do tricks, too?" Miles asked when he was alone with the First Counsel.

"Yes," Charlotte said with a wicked gleam in her eyes. "Many."

Miles shook his head and chuckled. He'd known Charlotte for most of his vampire life, which was over four hundred years at that point. It turned out that they'd both become vampires around the same time, although Charlotte was a few years younger than him. She was one of the few people Miles had confided in over the years, and he knew that while her loyalties lay to the House first and foremost, he could trust her.

"Your investigation into the creation of illegal vampires has become more complicated than I believe you first realised," Charlotte said, a serious tone now in her voice. Any sense of the playfulness that Miles had known in her was gone.

"Which means?" Miles asked.

"House Umbra has had someone confess to the crime," Charlotte said. "This now means that the investigation falls under Umbra control. It means it will be taken from you, even as an Arbiter, and passed over to whomever Vedran deems worthy of it."

"Nonsense," Miles said, although he was fully aware that Charlotte's words were true. "This confessor was responsible for the deaths of humans. They turned humans. They fall under Assembly jurisdiction."

"Except House Umbra has already asked for a stay of Arbiter involvement while they investigate internally," Charlotte said.

"So it's House politics," Miles said, his words like venom to his ears. "I need to speak to Vedran. I want to see this confessor personally."

"Both things they will be ready for," Charlotte said. "I came here to meet you so that you could be warned of what has transpired. I do not know what will happen next, but whatever it is, it's not going to end well."

"Why else did you come to meet me?" Miles asked.

"Drest asked you to come here," Charlotte said. "He has been . . . distracted by something. He won't tell anyone what it is, but I think that's why you're here. Whether you are a member of the House or not, he trusts you. I will warn you that Gideon knows you're coming. He is less than happy about it."

Miles groaned slightly and rolled his eyes.

"Do not underestimate him," Charlotte said. "He is an arrogant bastard, but he's also a competent individual. And he hates you with the fires of a thousand suns. Probably not best to antagonise the little shit any further."

"Thanks for the warning," Miles said. "I feel underdressed for any party I'm meant to attend."

No ATOs, no Arbiters, no Inquisitors, beyond those the Assembly brought with them, were normally permitted to attend any House gatherings, although there were always exceptions. Assembly personnel tended to keep to themselves.

"You're not attending anything," Charlotte said with a laugh. "You'll be taken to one of the properties on the estate, where Drest will meet you tomorrow for breakfast. I think you've got a long day ahead of you tomorrow."

"It's not late," Miles said, looking at his watch. "I'd like to see Vedran tonight."

"I figured you might," Charlotte said. "He'll be at the party, so I'd give it a few hours, and I'll get him to meet you at the Umbra building. You can't miss it—it's the one with the banners outside the front entrance with the Umbra badge lit up by continuously burning fire pits."

"Fire pits?" Miles asked.

"Just . . . don't . . ." Charlotte said with a scowl.

"They always did like to push the limits of form," Miles said. "Not sure I'd want to be there when that pushing got to the point that Drest or one of the other Lords and Ladies had to step in."

"It'd be something to watch, though," Charlotte said with a slight giggle.

Charlotte stared at Miles for several seconds before leaning over and kissing him on the cheek. "I know why you left, I understand it. I do. And I support it. Still, Miles, I missed you."

"I missed you, too," Miles told her, feeling his heart hurt. Leaving the House had been the hardest thing he'd ever done, and everyone . . . well, most people, had been very understanding as to why, but he knew that everyone also expected him to come back. The longer that return to the fold went on, the more he hoped everyone realised he wasn't going to come back.

Charlotte beckoned the cold-looking driver back into the car and continued to Cannich, which, since it wasn't even nine PM, was busy with people going home from work or meeting up with friends. If you didn't know anything about the nearby vampire estate, you'd never know that Cannich was anything but a perfectly normal village. The fact that there were armed guards walking the streets put a slight spanner in that particular notion, Miles had to admit.

Once past the village, having been waved through a heavily manned checkpoint, the car drove on toward the expansive Affric estate. They stopped twice at two separate checkpoints before reaching the large metal gates that denoted the start of the estate proper. There were ten-foot-high stone walls either side of the gates, which were more for privacy than to actually try to keep anyone out. A vampire wouldn't even think twice about clearing such a small wall, although armed custodians—vampire guards—patrolling the area would give some pause about doing something stupid.

The gates were opened, and the car travelled slowly up the hill toward the mass of lights.

Along the half mile of driveway, Miles spotted more custodians in the trees that lined the drive, and as they got closer to the entrance of the main building of the estate, it was easy to spot the millions of pounds' worth of expensive vehicles that sat in front of the massive manor house that made up the living area for House Venator.

Miles spotted several custodians outside, each of them dressed in impeccable suits and thick coats. Their entire job was to ensure the smooth running of the day-to-day calendars of the various First members of each family. Most of them had been part of the family from birth, and they were loyal beyond reproach.

The car drove by the front of the house, which was lit up like a Christmas tree, with classical music pouring out of the open front entrance. Miles didn't know the composer; he'd never been one to remember one classical musician to another, which many other vampires his age considered some form of deviance on his part.

The car continued on, passed several large buildings that had been built a short distance from the manor house. One of the houses Miles knew was a large gym, with an indoor swimming pool, while the other was there to house those who worked at the estate.

Two minutes of slow driving later and the horseshoe of buildings came into view. Twelve in all, each one the size of a three-storey, five-bedroom barn house, all built to look into the centre, to see each other at all times. There was a large pit in the middle of the horseshoe where . . . disagreements could be resolved. There were dozens more cars dotted around the horseshoe, with custodians standing outside the front doors of the buildings. Fluttering banners showing the House sigils adorned five of the buildings, although only two of them had fire pits beneath them to show their House badge: House Umbra—a white background with a charcoal grey skull on it that appeared to be fading the further down the skull you went—and

House Phalanx—four circular golden shields interlocked against a midnight blue background.

Of the five Great Vampire Houses, Umbra, Venator, and Barbarous were the ones that Miles had had the most interactions with. All three had Firsts who were welcoming, although not always trustworthy. House Phalanx was tight-lipped and distrustful of outsiders, the House of One living up to its name. House Nix were considered to be . . . dark, even among other vampires. It wasn't called the House of Demons for nothing.

"I see Phalanx has followed suit with the fire pits," Miles said.

"You can expect the entire lot of them to have theirs dug tomorrow," Charlotte said, not bothering to hide her distaste. "But at least they asked."

The car stopped by the house on the furthest leftmost side of the horseshoe.

"This for me?" Miles asked.

"You can go," Charlotte told the driver while Miles and Church left the car. "I'll walk back."

"This is new," Miles said. "There were only a few houses the last time I was here."

The pair stood outside of the house and looked up at the second and third storeys. "So, you want me to show you around?" Charlotte asked, walking over to the front door, unlocking it with a key from a small clutch purse and pushing open the door. "After you."

CHAPTER NINE

The house was, Miles had to admit, lovely. The four bedrooms were all double in size, with king-sized beds in each of them. The kitchen was well stocked, the bathroom had a tub large enough for four, which was almost certainly not going to be big enough for some of the Houses, and there was a small study. The front room had a large TV, with a comfortable sofa and even a video game console, and there was an underground gym that had weight machines designed to be used by people who could bench-press a car.

"You thought of everything," Miles said after the tour was done.

"They still complain," Charlotte said, heaving a sigh and looking out of the window at the side of the house, which gave great views of the nearby loch. "*Incessantly.*"

"I'm sure you have a party to go back to," Miles said.

"Actually, I haven't been yet," Charlotte said.

"I'm honoured that you dressed up for me," Miles said with a laugh.

Charlotte did an overly exaggerated twirl. "You lucky bastard," she said with a curtsy.

"Go have fun," Miles told her. "Please. Or at least whatever passes for fun at one of those ridiculous parties."

"Blood, drugs, sex, and violence," Charlotte said. "Not necessarily in that order. Or any order. Honestly, the whole thing is quite tiresome."

"Who are the Lords or Ladies who have come from each family?" Miles asked. "Any chance you have a list?"

Charlotte pointed to a blue envelope on a circular dining room table. "All in there," she said.

"Church, go with Charlotte," Miles said.

"Seriously?" Charlotte asked him with a shake of her head.

"I have no doubt that there is nothing in a thousand miles that you can't deal with," Miles said. "But Church could use some time not cooped up."

Charlotte and Miles held each other's gaze for several seconds before Charlotte sighed and threw her arms in the air. "Fine," she said, conceding. "Church, come with me; maybe we can find you a nice rabbit to chase."

Church practically sprinted to the front door, her tail wagging enthusiastically.

He watched as she left the house with Church bounding out into the night for some well-earned exercise. He might not see the dog until morning if she found something interesting to run after or play with. It had originally surprised Miles just how soft and gentle Church was with animals that she could kill with ease, and he'd often spotted her running around with the deer and foxes that called the land where he lived home.

Miles did another circuit of the house before picking up the file and opening it, reading the list of names and Houses that they belonged to. Most were considered to be decent people, or at the very least not complete arseholes. No House wanted to send their more aggressive vampires to a gathering.

Miles made himself a sandwich and took out a few chocolate biscuits from a tin in the shape of the Count from Sesame Street, which he was pretty certain was meant to be a joke. There was a library of Blu-ray films in the shelves next to a large TV, and quite a few of them were old Hammer Horrors, most of which were beloved by a large part of the vampire community as comedies.

Before he'd become a vampire himself, he believed that vampires couldn't eat or drink. They were, after all, meant to be the dead, or undead. But vampires could eat and drink as they wished; they gave off heat, their hearts beat. It had been quite the revelation to discover that so many of the stories he'd heard were just that.

After he'd eaten and had a drink of water, Miles decided to go check out the surrounding area. He wrapped up warm in a large black fleece jacket and stepped outside onto the porch of the converted barn house. There were several men and women standing around the pit in the centre of the horseshoe, looking down on whatever was happening there.

Miles walked over, nodding toward several vampires from other Houses whom he recognised. He said hello to a few of them, though didn't stop to chat. Most vampires from the Houses didn't want to be seen chatting to an Assembly Arbiter. A level of paranoia there as to who might think they were giving away House secrets.

Inside the large pit—which was twenty meters long by thirty wide, was a man practising his martial arts with a pair of kali sticks against six others—four men and two women—who all carried a variety of blunt weapons. Miles immediately recognized Vedran and continued to watch with some amusement, guessing what the outcome was likely to be. Vedran had tanned skin and long black hair that flowed freely around him as he moved, as if it had a life of its own. He was also completely naked. His six-pack glistened in the low light, and his back was full of scars from before he'd become a vampire.

The House First Captain used one stick to block a strike from a female opponent using a quarterstaff, stepped aside, and brought the other kali stick around into the side of her head. The speed and ferocity of the attack was impressive, and the woman went down hard, next to four others who had met similar fates. Unlike Vedran, all were clothed, although most probably wished they'd worn a suit of armour.

The last fighter was a young man with long beard plaited with beads, which chimed together as he moved. He also used kali sticks, and the pair of them blocked and avoided strikes from the other in a fluid ballet.

Eventually, Vedran feinted with a strike to his opponent's head, then darted to the opposite side, and smashed his second stick into the knee of the man with a crunch, swiftly followed by a scream of pain.

Vedran soaked in the applause of the crowd as his opponents nursed their various states of injury.

"Miles," the man boomed, pointing at him. "Come, let's see what you're made of, old friend."

"I've had a long day, Vedran," Miles said.

"Do not make me beg," Vedran said with a beaming smile upon his perfectly smooth and chiselled features. Vedran had been born over five hundred years earlier, in what was now Croatia, although Miles couldn't remember if it had been considered part of the Hungarian empire at the time.

Miles sighed and dropped down into the pit, hearing the whispers of the onlookers as they realised an Arbiter was about to face one of the greatest warriors in any vampire House.

"Why are you naked?" Miles asked.

"I like to feel the cool air on my skin," Vedran said, flexing his large arms.

Miles sniffed the air. "All vampires?" he asked, nodding to the six who had now left the pit via the slope at the far end.

"I can't do this with humans," Vedran said and laughed, the sound booming around the pit. "They break far too easily."

"You have someone in your custody I need to talk to," Miles said.

Vedran nodded. "I do. The little weasel came and confessed his crimes." He walked over to Miles and whispered in his ear, "Illegal vampires. Sickening."

Miles looked the taller man in the eyes. They were a deep brown colour, and while they had always projected an air of warmth and easy-going, there was something behind them that Miles had only seen flashes of during his time having known Vedran. Something darker.

"You asked me to come talk to you. Any chance we can do that?" Miles said, before adding, "Please," in case it helped move things along.

"I am still full of vigour and adrenaline," Vedran said, walking away and raising his arms to the sounds of cheers from the dozens of vampires watching. "Fight me, Miles. No weapons. After which I will take you to our little prisoner and you may talk to him. No hurting him, though, can't be having that."

Miles sighed. He didn't want to do this. He didn't want to fight for the spectacle of it; he didn't want to fight to *prove* something. He fought because he had no choice. However, fighting Vedran was going to be the quickest way to get what he wanted.

"Fine," Miles said with another sigh.

"Are you going to strip naked?" Vedran asked.

"No," Miles said with a scowl. "The only time someone should be fighting naked is if you're bathing and someone attacks you. And even then, I'm iffy on it."

Vedran laughed again. "Fine—fists, feet, heads, elbows, and knees only. No biting, no eye gouging. I don't fancy having to regrow an eye again, it itches. No kicks to the bollocks, I know what you Arbiters are like." That last sentence gained a big laugh from his supporters.

Miles removed his coat and tossed it over to the corner of the pit. He knew that Vedran wasn't going to attack from behind; that would be beneath him. Vedran liked to look his opponents in the eyes when he beat them, as if it was the only way his honour could be satisfied.

"Ready?" Vedran asked Miles, who reluctantly nodded.

Vedran darted toward Miles, the former throwing punches to his opponent's head with speed, while keeping his power in check. Miles blocked or avoided the punches with ease, while trying to make it look as though he were having a hard time. He'd never been comfortable with people knowing *what* he could truly do, and letting people underestimate him was something he'd found worked well during his lifetime.

After the initial flurry of shots, the pair moved apart, with Vedran hopping from foot to foot, boxing in the air, and looking pleased with himself as people cheered his name.

Miles kept his eyes on his opponent, rolling his shoulders a little, trying to figure out how long he was meant to let this continue. It was true that Vedran could more than likely beat him in a one-on-one fight, but Miles knew if he could keep the combat going for a while, he could frustrate the larger man. Miles also knew he would rather get this finished. He just had to make sure that Vedran felt that he'd won fairly. A pouty vampire was not a helpful vampire.

Vedran moved back in to fight again, with the two men trading blows, blocking, and avoiding punches, elbows, and kicks. Testing one another. The whole time Vedran had the grin of someone who was so supremely confident in his abilities that he didn't need to worry about it.

The arrogance annoyed Miles. He didn't like being toyed with, or that Vedran's win was a foregone conclusion. On the other hand, Miles didn't want to go full vampire fighting mode. The cold, the loudness of the crowd, the adrenaline flowing through his body as his heart rate increased, the smell of blood in the air. These combined made the hunger inside of Miles rise, and control became a thing of necessity.

Miles's mind was elsewhere when a mean right hook smashed into his kidney, knocking the air out of him. He stepped away and took deep breaths as Vedran's eyes gleamed with enjoyment.

"Not submitting yet, my friend?" Vedran asked, stepping back toward Miles, his guard up, his movements more precise.

Miles blocked a kick to the knee, pushed a punch out of the way, and threw a punch that hit Vedran in the chest. As the larger vampire stepped back, his eyes opened wide in shock from being hit. From being hurt.

Vedran looked down at the red mark on his otherwise unblemished chest.

It took Miles a moment to realise the crowd had gone silent. "We done now?" he asked, knowing the answer, but hoping otherwise.

Vedran practically charged back toward Miles, throwing a flurry of kicks and punches, forcing the smaller vampire on the back foot as they moved across the width of the pit. Miles blocked a cross to his temple, a kick to his knee, but couldn't move fast enough to block the follow-up kick to his chest, which sent him sprawling on the ground.

Control. Control, Miles said to himself as he watched Vedran stalk toward him. *Do not give in to the fight.*

Miles rolled back onto his knees in time to block a knee from Vedran. Miles used the opportunity to grab his opponent's knee and twist himself and Vedran onto the floor, wrenching Vedran's knee in a painful direction it wasn't meant to go. This was getting out of hand.

Vedran moved fast and was back on his feet with a kick to Miles's head that the lesser blocked more out of reflex than any conscious decision.

The kicks came quickly as Vedran moved, driving Miles down the length of the pit, each kick putting more and more power into the blow. Vedran was becoming frustrated that Miles hadn't gone down as easily as he'd expected. Miles mentally cursed himself for putting up too much of a fight, even though it was pretty clear that he wasn't winning.

Miles blocked a kick with his knee, but Vedran had clearly been expecting it, and darted forward, smashing his elbow into Miles's exposed ribs with enough force to throw the vampire back across the pit.

Miles landed on his back, pain searing through his ribs, placed one hand on the pit surface, and vaulted himself up and onto the edge of the pit, where he landed in a crouched position next to several spectators.

"Enough," Miles said. "I submit."

There was a flash of anger in Vedran's eyes as the cheer went up from the crowd. He hadn't wanted Miles to submit; he'd wanted to *beat* him, to ensure that everyone knew that Vedran was better. Miles wondered if the Umbra vampire would hold a grudge against him for not giving the battle he wanted.

Miles dropped the ten feet back to the pit floor, landing lightly, and walking over to Vedran, where he offered his hand. "Good fight," Miles said, making sure the wince in his voice was easy to hear.

"You okay?" Vedran asked, suddenly concerned. "I apologise if I've broken a rib. I guess sometimes I get lost in the feeling of battle."

"I'm good," Miles assured him, rubbing his side for emphasis. "Nothing some ice and a drink won't make feel better quicker."

"Now, about that prisoner?" Vedran said. "Give me half an hour to shower and come to the cabin. You can meet him. However, he is *my* prisoner. You can't hurt him, clear?"

"Crystal," Miles said. "And thank you."

"No, thank you for the workout, my friend," Vedran said with a grin, and left the pit.

Miles remained alone as his bruised ribs healed. There would be a bruise in an hour, and by morning they'd be tender but fine. He could drink some blood to help with the healing, but right now his own blood was up, so smelling and tasting someone else's might cause him to lose more control that he was happy with.

"Interesting fight," a woman said as she lightly dropped down to the pit.

The woman was six feet tall, with black hair, olive skin, and several tattoos of skulls and snakes on her bare arms. Vampires could get tattoos, but they needed to be redrawn on a regular basis for them to maintain any kind of vibrancy. She wore a black trouser suit with matching strappy high heels.

Just as Vedran was an almost perfect representation of what many would think of when considering a male, Danica was what many would consider the perfect looking woman. She was, Miles would freely admit, beautiful. She was also quite possibly the most dangerous person Miles had ever met. She practically oozed danger. Her eyes were blood-red and sized Miles up as if he were her next snack.

If people had their perfect image of a dangerous and beautiful vampire, the High Lady of House Barbarous was what people would describe.

Miles bowed his head because he wasn't utterly stupid. House Barbarous was the strongest, fastest, most resilient, and potentially most dangerous of all the Houses. Their gifts of physical strength came at the cost of needing an almost constant supply of blood. Where Miles would probably need a few pints a week, a similarly aged Barbarous bloodline would drink a pint every other day.

There were some High Lords and Ladies that you could get away with being sarcastic around, or joking around with, and a few would even allow their people to question them openly without any physical recompense.

Not the Barbarous. You stepped out of line with them and they quite literally tore your limbs off.

"High Lady Danica," Miles said. "What a pleasure to see you again."

High Lady Danica stared at Miles for several seconds. "Liar," she said with a smile. "I'll let it go considering your place in the Assembly. An Arbiter, Miles. What an interesting career path you've taken."

Technically, an Arbiter could question anyone, even a High Lord or Lady. Technically, Miles would survive being thrown off a three-hundred-foot-high bridge. Didn't mean he wanted to try it.

"I'm honoured you've been keeping tabs on me," Miles said, wondering where this was going.

High Lady Danica stood in front of Miles and placed the palm of her hand against his chest. The hunger inside of him increased as just being near Lady Danica meant her power washed over him; it was her personal vampire gift. You wanted to be near her because her power lowered your inhibitions, made you fearless and emboldened. Being near Danica while she was using her power, was, quite literally, intoxicating. By which point, she'd torn open your throat to feed.

"Do you fear me?" she asked in a voice both seductive to the parts of Miles's brain that controlled another part of his body, and terrifying to the parts of his brain that wanted to stay in one piece.

Yes, I fucking do, Miles wanted to shout. Instead, he cleared his throat and tried not to look down at Danica's gaze. "I have a meeting to attend," he said.

"Shame," Danica whispered into his ear. "There are *important* things you and I should discuss."

Her voice made every part of Miles which was terrified scream at him, while the parts of him that were very happy about the current circumstance wanted to wait and see where things went.

"High Lady Danica," Charlotte said from atop the pit, Church sitting beside her. "Your people have been looking for you."

Danica sighed in irritation, patted Miles on his hip, and turned away to face Charlotte. "Ah, thank you for coming to find me," Danica said, meaning exactly none of those words. She turned back to Miles. "Maybe another time."

Miles made a noise that he wasn't sure he had any control over, and watched as Danica left the pit and Charlotte dropped down into it.

"She'd have bitten your cock off," Charlotte said once Danica had left the pit. "If you were lucky."

"She is still the scariest person I've ever met," Miles said as he sought to control the hunger inside him.

Charlotte looked down at Miles's hand, which had small pieces of orange lightning jumping from finger to finger.

"You were going to use your bloodline gift," Charlotte said.

"If she left me no choice," Miles said, looking down at his own hand as if he was shocked to see it.

"I'm honestly not sure how that would have ended," Charlotte told him.

"Not well," he said, flexing his fingers. "I thought you were going to the party, hence the dress."

"I decided I didn't want to," Charlotte said. "Figured I'd rather spend time with you and Church, and overheard someone talk about Vedran fighting an Arbiter in the pit."

"Ah, well, thank you for the timely intrusion," Miles said.

Charlotte performed an overly elaborate bow. "You're welcome—Vedran looked like he was enjoying himself far too much. Nothing he likes more than throwing a guy around in matters of combat, or in more . . . intimate situations."

"Are you gossiping?" Miles asked with a smile.

Charlotte grinned and winked at him.

Miles chuckled. "And now I have to go to see Vedran and his prisoner."

"Well, I'd better come along as your chaperone," Charlotte said with a smirk. "Just in case I can find something else to gossip about."

<h1 style="text-align:center">❦ CHAPTER TEN ❧</h1>

I can't say I'm looking forward to this," Miles said as he and Charlotte stood outside of the heavily guarded building for House Umbra.

"Illegal vampires," Charlotte said, as if reminding him. "The one thing I can say about the Houses is it's easy to be pulled back into their orbit. You remember that few years I took off in the eighteen hundreds? I came back here for a week and ended up back in charge of legal matters."

The door to the converted barn opened and a tall, thin man in a tuxedo stood in the doorway. He had a bald head, was clean-shaven, and had the smell of jasmine. "Master Vedran is expecting you in the basement," he said, motioning for Charlotte and Miles to enter the building.

It looked identical to the one that Miles was staying in. Same decorations, same layout; it was as if they'd all been made from identical plans to keep things simple and quick.

The custodian, which was what Miles guessed him to be, led them both through the house, which appeared to be completely empty. Everyone was either at the party, or outside the front guarding the house from . . . who knew. With House Umbra dealing in paranoia, spies, and manipulation, it wasn't difficult to understand that the people who worked for them tended to not be the most trusting bunch.

Charlotte and Miles were led down a set of stairs into the expansive basement where a, thankfully dressed, Vedran sat in the middle of a group of black gym mats, drinking green tea with honey. He looked up and smiled.

The gym smelled of sweat and blood, but there was also a plug-in air freshener fighting a losing battle to make everything smell like flowers. The mixture of scents was probably something those who lived in the house got used to; for an outsider coming in, it was quite the assault on the senses.

"You may leave us," Vedran said, neither thanking the custodian nor using his name. Miles wondered if the First Captain even *knew* the custodian's name at all.

"As you wish, sire," the custodian said with a bow, leaving the room without another word.

Vedran got to his feet, clapping his hands together with something approximating glee. "It's good to see you both," he said, giving Charlotte a hug and slapping Miles on the shoulder.

"You've come to see the prisoner," Vedran said. "As we agreed. The prisoner is down this hall. Only one door, at the end. Door will lock behind you; you'll have to call out to be let out. Charlotte will have to wait out here. Sorry, Charlotte, but you're not Assembly, and I can't allow you to ask questions to a House Umbra member, or indeed take any knowledge of their crimes back to your House. It's not that I don't trust you, it's just . . ."

"That you don't trust me," Charlotte said.

"Well, yes," Vedran admitted. "Please do continue, Miles. I will be in the viewing area next door. Call when you want to come out."

Miles looked back at Charlotte who gave him a thumbs-up. He opened the door and stepped into the dimly lit ten-foot-long hallway beyond.

There was nothing in the hallway except the metal door opposite the one he'd come through, so he walked over to it and, as it had no handle on the outside, pushed it open with an awful creak.

The roughly four hundred square foot room inside was lit via dozens of tiny lights in the ceiling. Considering none of the buildings were meant to have their own prison, it had the appearance of something hastily put together. The room was essentially a cell, with a cot bed at one end, a bedside table next to it, a sink, a shower cubicle in the corner opposite the bed, and a toilet next to it. There was a table in the middle with two metal chairs on opposite sides. A large mirror sat along the entirety of one wall. There was no privacy even in sleeping or going to the toilet.

With no windows and only a HVAC unit in the corner to recycle the air, someone had placed an incense burner on the bedside table, giving everything a more inviting, warm scent.

The door behind Miles clicked shut as it closed; there was no door handle on the inside either.

"You must be Miles," the lone occupant of the cell said, getting up from his bed. He had a Mancunian accent, with light brown skin and short dark hair. He was shorter than Miles by several inches, broad shouldered, and muscular. He wore a light grey set of tracksuit bottoms and a matching jumper. He had on no shoes, although he did have black slippers. The floor was stone, so Miles imagined it was probably not the warmest thing to stand on.

"I am," Miles said, taking a seat at the table. "I'm an Arbiter for the Assembly. I assume you're the man who drove from Islington to Scotland to confess your crimes."

"I am," the man said with a smile. "My name is Sajid Reza. And I confess to my crimes of creating illegal vampires for profit."

"Please do take a seat," Miles said, motioning to a chair on the opposite side of the table.

Sajid sat down, his smile still there. He had the appearance of someone who was exceptionally calm considering the seriousness of the accusations that had been levelled against him. In Miles's experience, the vast number of people who are calm and confident during an interrogation are either guilty as hell or they know something the interviewer doesn't.

"You have no power here, right?" Sajid asked.

"I'm sorry?" Miles asked.

"My crimes ensure that I fall under the law of House Umbra," Sajid said.

"No," Miles said, taking some enjoyment out of the flinch in Sajid's expression. "Your little enterprise resulted in the deaths of humans, and the creation of a desolate that then resulted in the deaths of vampires. The vampires are all up to House Umbra to punish you for, and they could push that the desolate falls under their purview, too, but you created vampires that killed humans. And that, my dear Sajid, means you're all mine."

"Wait, that can't be right," Sajid said, his mask of indifference slipping.

"Oh, it is," Miles told him. "You'll be handed over to the Inquisitor to have any intel . . . extracted from your memories. And then whatever's left of you will be given to House Umbra. Enjoy the torture; I've been told it's quite breathtaking. Literally."

"What do you want?" Sajid asked. Any confidence that he'd had when Miles had entered the room was completely gone. Funny how that happens when someone's best laid plans fall to pieces at the first hurdle.

"The names of the other vampires who died, the name of the desolate, and the name of your Boss," Miles said. "Not necessarily in that order."

"Who's to say I'm not the Boss?" Sajid asked confidently.

"Fuck off," Miles snapped. "There were five vampires who survived the attack. The one who ran to the Assembly. Someone by the name of Oliver. And three others. Two were killed by the Boss. Which makes you the lucky little prick who ran when it all went to shit. The Boss turned up, started clearing house, you legged it. Not sure why you'd want to come confess to the crime, but I assume it's because being here is safer than having your Boss find you."

Sajid stared at Miles. "You know what will happen to me?" he asked, his voice not quite a whisper.

"Yes," Miles said. "But you're responsible for several deaths. So I need to be sure. So you're going to try to tell me your Boss's name, even if you can't."

"His name is—" Sajid said and screamed in pain, falling off the chair onto the floor, clutching his head in both hands.

Miles walked over to the prone man and crouched beside him. "Do you need anything? Some water?"

Sajid shook his head. "I cannot give you the information you need."

"Yeah, I know," Miles said sadly. "I had to check you weren't just messing me around."

"You believe me now?" Sajid asked, with more than a little hope that he did.

Miles nodded and offered Sajid his hand. "You remember anything about what happened while you were making vampires?"

"I remember the day everyone died," Sajid said, taking Miles's hand and allowing himself to be helped off the floor. "The old man had come in; he was so excited. The vampires doing the creating didn't have names, just a designation that we'd drawn out of a hat. I was Gamma One. I only knew Tony, the vampire at the front desk. He dealt with the cash. And Oliver, who dealt with the security operations for the new vampires. The old man went to see Alpha One. It all went to shit after about day three. You ever seen a desolate?" Sajid sat back on his chair and let out one long breath.

"I've seen a few dozen or so," Miles said. "Killed some. One had infected others in his apartment building, hence the few dozen. It wasn't a good time."

"They're so strong, and they move so fast," Sajid said, the fear in his voice easy to hear. "They're not even anything close to human anymore.

They're . . . nightmares come real. I can still see the blood, I can hear the screams."

"You know who the old man was?" Miles asked.

Sajid shook his head. "I know he paid a lot of money to undergo the transformation. Tony would have known, but Tony's dead."

"What about Carla and Teresa?" Miles continued. "You know either of them?"

"Ah, shit," Sajid said. "They were just kids. They okay?"

"One is," Miles said. "One is dead."

"Fuck," Sajid whispered.

"Did you ever meet the Boss?" Miles asked.

"Met him twice; he wore a balaclava both times," Sajid said.

"Do you know where he might be now?" Miles asked.

Sajid shrugged. "No one knows," he said. "There's no structure in the company anymore. Danny took over, and Danny is about as useful as a glass hammer."

Miles smiled. "I've met Danny. Said he didn't know the names of any of those who turned the vampires."

"He didn't," Sajid confirmed. "We knew his, though. Gangster wannabe, that's all Danny is. I doubted he knew anything more than we did. Probably kept in the quiet by the Boss. So, do I still have to see the Inquisitor?"

Miles stared at Sajid for several seconds. "Arbiters give their recommendations, but the Assembly will ultimately be the people who assign you to a Judge or inquisitor. My recommendation is that you be handed over to House Umbra, and hopefully they can unfuck whatever was done to your brain. The Inquisitor might be psychic, too, but they'd only make it worse. Subtlety isn't exactly their forte." He got to his feet. "If I find out that you know more than you're telling me, House Umbra won't be able to keep you safe from what I'll do. I promise you that. If there's anything you've left out, let me know now."

"I don't know anything else," Sajid said, keeping Miles's gaze as he spoke. "I know I helped create illegal vampires, working for a criminal gang. I know I made money from it. I know it was wrong, and against Assembly law, and I have nothing to say that will make any of that different."

"Do you know who the old man was?" Miles asked him again.

Sajid shook his head. "I promise you, I don't. He was a big deal, though. Tony was freaking out about it, how we had to make everything run smoothly. I think he paid a lot of money."

"How many vampires did you turn?" Miles asked.

"Me personally?" Sajid asked. "Carla and four others. All were done to a high standard; all left the establishment in one piece."

"You will tell the Assembly their names," Miles said. "I assume you know them."

Sajid nodded. "What will happen to them?"

"They'll be investigated, probably given a stern talking to," Miles said. "Probably watched for a long time, but if they keep their noses clean, they'll be okay. You know any names of other clients?"

Sajid shook his head. "I don't, sorry. Who killed Teresa?"

"Danny," Miles told him. "With a broadsword. Apparently."

"Fucking weasel piece of shit," Sajid snapped. "And Carla, she okay?"

"She's in Assembly custody," Miles said. "She'll be fine. She's upset and angry, and more than a little freaked out about everything, but I think she'll be okay long term. Did Edge of Humanity know anything about the illegal vampires?"

"The club?" Sajid asked. "Not that I know of. Shit, the owners of that place would have nailed us up by our ears if they'd found out."

If they were lucky, Miles thought as he got to his feet. "Sajid, thank you for your help. I'm sure the Assembly will be in touch to explain how their punishment will be meted out. I imagine you'll know more what Umbra will do with you soon." He reached the door and paused, before looking back at the prisoner.

"Why confess?" Miles asked. "Why come all this way to confess in person?"

Sajid looked around the room as though something might jump out at him. "It was the right thing to do."

"We both know that's not it," Miles said. "You can tell me. You can trust me."

"It was my only choice," Sajid said softly. "Confess and hope for some semblance of safety, or spend my life running. The Assembly prisons are a better bet than a life always looking over your shoulder. I do what I'm told, I live."

The cell door swung open slightly, Miles walked through, and it closed automatically behind him as he walked along the hallway, through the door at the end, and back into the gym.

Charlotte sat against the mirrors that adorned one wall of the gym. "How did that go?" she asked Miles.

"Same as with everyone who works for this gang," Miles said. "Their minds are screwed around with to block out all memories of whoever the Boss is."

Vedran stepped into the gym, closing the door behind him. "So, was any of that useful?" he asked Miles.

"The Boss is still out there," Miles said. "But those creating the vampires are dead or in your custody. Whoever the Boss is, he's either got incredible psychic powers or someone he works closely with does."

"Are you suggesting he's a member of House Umbra?" Vedran asked, ever so slightly angered by the insinuation.

"No," Miles said quickly. "But he is powerful. I'll send my findings to the Assembly, and either they'll ask me to continue to investigate and find this Boss, who could be anywhere and anyone, or, as is more likely, they'll pass the investigation over to House Umbra. Good luck with that."

"You believe it to be a poisoned investigation?" Vedran asked.

"I believe it to be a gigantic pain in the arse," Miles said. "There's no evidence of who this Boss character is, where he is, and now that he's run away, how anyone can even find him? He seems to have wiped the minds of everyone who worked for him, so unless you can reverse that process, my guess is he's in the wind until he does something stupid."

"You might be right," Vedran said. "But hopefully this man will have learned his lessons and it'll be the last we see of him or his people for some time, yes?"

"Not sure how much of a help that would be to the families of the humans who died because of him," Charlotte said.

"We will deal with their families," Vedran said. "We are taking steps to find them. We'll do what we can to make things right."

"Any idea who the rich old man is?" Miles asked. "Danny said something about remembering an old club. You know, the gentlemen's clubs, with the wood panelled walls and expensive leather armchairs."

"We'll look into that, too," Vedran said. "We will get justice here, Miles. I assure you of that."

Miles offered Vedran his hand, which the older man shook enthusiastically. "Thanks for letting me see him," Miles said. "Take care."

"You too, my friend," Vedran said, before bowing his head slightly. "And also you, Lady Charlotte."

Charlotte rolled her eyes and left the gym with Miles, the pair going back outside and walking down the horseshoe in silence, neither one wanting to give voice to anything that someone might overhear.

The pair continued on past the house that Miles had been given, walking along a path that took them down to the Loch. The night had become colder, and the wind tore across the Loch as if it had a personal vendetta against it.

Charlotte and Miles stopped beside a jetty and small hut. There were spotlights dotted around the edge of the water, which lapped against the bank. Miles wondered how long he'd last if he fell into the icy darkness of the Loch. Not long, would be his guess. He'd survive—he could swim and hyperthermia wouldn't kill him—but he would surely lose all sense of who he was as the animalistic side of his hunger took over. He'd seen it happen several times. It never ended well.

"So," Charlotte said. "How much of what you learned tonight was complete bullshit?"

"Sajid's mind was Swiss cheese when it came to the Boss," Miles said. "You can't fake that."

"And Vedran?" Charlotte asked.

"He's a terrible liar," Miles said. "Always was. Still, I don't think he was actually lying about anything."

"Because he didn't say anything that wasn't already a known fact," Charlotte said.

"Exactly," Miles said. "He knows something more than he's letting on. I know that when I take this to the Assembly, they'll just pass it all over to House Umbra. Vedran knows that, too. Oh, I can shout and swear about the *human tragedy* and how the vampires need to be brought to account, but House Umbra has friends in high places who'll argue that every part of the investigation should be in one place. They're right; the investigation should be in one place with everyone working together instead of having me check one bit, and the Assembly another, and the Umbra another. They're just doing it for the wrong reasons. And it's fucking exhausting." Miles screamed the last few words into the night.

"Feel better?" Charlotte asked.

"No," Miles said. "I left the House because I was fed up of seeing Great Houses get away with whatever they liked. I wanted to make a difference. Instead, it feels like same shit, different day."

Charlotte laughed, which made Miles glare at her. "I'm sorry," she said. "It's just you either laugh at the frankly ludicrous nature of our lives, or you start to spiral out. I don't want to spiral anywhere, mostly because my job is already a nightmare of litigation, stagnation, and other words that end in *ation*. I hold my House to a greater standard than most. You wanted to hold all *Houses* to a greater standard, and I'm sorry to say, I'm not sure you can when half of them don't care."

"Great pep talk," Miles said. "Really, phenomenal stuff."

Charlotte kissed Miles on the cheek. "I'm going to leave you to stew. It's early. Go hunting, go for a run. Clear your head. Lots of deer nearby. Take the dog if you can find her. Enjoy yourself. Tomorrow, you'll see Drest in a better frame of mind."

Miles watched Charlotte walk away. His mood remained sour. She was right, as per usual; he would stew over everything. He would get annoyed and probably say something stupid. It was time to go get some exercise.

Miles ran as fast as he could, never stopping, never slowing. He moved quickly, vaulting over rocks and fallen branches, sprinting between herds of deer, causing them to scatter in all directions when they realised the smell of a predator was suddenly among them. Miles didn't hunt them, didn't touch them. He didn't need to; he just needed to run.

After hour an hour of heart-pounding sprinting, Miles stopped to survey where he was. He looked around and spotted the Loch, which meant he hadn't gone too far, but other than that, he didn't really know his exact location.

He found a large boulder and took a seat, his legs dangling over the side. He wished he'd put on better clothes for running, although the boots were comfortable. He unzipped his thick coat and was pretty sure he saw steam coming off him.

The lights of the Affric Estate were lost in the distance. He'd been gone from the estate for several decades since leaving as First Librarian of House Venator to become an Arbiter. The job wasn't actually that different, as a Librarian's job in one of the Houses is to acquire knowledge, which also meant investigating claims of crimes by members of the House against other House members. The First Captains were the ones who did the actual hunting and finding once the Librarian had decided if the case had merit.

The Librarians also monitored and cultivated the House libraries, cataloguing and collating information about the House members and ancestry.

Investigating crimes committed by or against members was only a relatively small part of the job, considering how few crimes House members actually committed. You didn't get to become a member of House Venator if you were problematic as a human. It was the House that prided itself on doing the right thing.

Miles pushed thoughts of his past out of his head and looked up at the multitude of stars above him. It was peaceful here, so far away from his responsibilities.

After some time with his own thoughts, and feeling better about having been for a run, Miles decided to make his way back. He jogged back to the Affric estate, enjoying the solitude, hearing owls out hunting and mice scurrying for cover. Fox kits played in the open, yipping excitedly. Miles found it endearing and stopped more than once to watch the creatures play.

Animals tended to be ambivalent toward vampires, so long as the latter didn't use their power near them. If that occurred, most animals scattered or turned to fight. Miles had been deep in the Canadian wilderness hunting when he'd met his first grey wolf pack. It had been a tense stand-off, and Miles remembered the concern about taking damage should the situation escalate. He was capable of feats of unbelievable strength and speed, and his healing was considerable, but no one in their right minds—vampire or otherwise—wanted to go one-on-all with a wolf pack. Thankfully, they'd all backed away from one another with no loss to pride or limbs.

Miles made it back to his guest house when the first flakes of snow began to fall. Church lay outside the house on a thick black duvet, although Miles had no idea where she'd found her new bed.

"You been stealing?" he asked, as he opened the door to the house.

Church looked up at him, yawned, and dragged her newly found sleeping arrangements into the house. Whoever it had belonged to, they were going to have a hell of a job getting it back.

Once inside, Miles closed and locked the door. It was five in the morning, and he had a feeling his meeting with Drest was going to be a long, awkward one. He took a pouch of blood from the fridge and drank it straight, savouring the rich taste, allowing the feeling of warmth and satisfaction to flow through him. He didn't normally need to drink so much in two days, but it was free blood and he'd had a long few days. Always a good idea to stay topped up, especially during winter.

He was going to shower and sleep, but his thoughts troubled him. It was true that House Umbra could take control of the investigation of the illegal vampire trade in London. And it was true there was nothing Miles could do about that. During his time as House Librarian, he also remembered a small bylaw about Arbiters and their cases leaving a country.

Miles put his coat back on. Time to go to the library.

❧ CHAPTER ELEVEN ❧

Gideon was a tall, thin man with dark wispy hair and an almost continuous facial expression of smug superiority. He was the current First Librarian of House Venator, and while he was unfriendly to everyone he met, he despised Miles.

"Do you know what time it is?" Gideon asked Miles outside the entrance to the library, a three-storey building a short walk from the main living accommodation at Glen Affric.

"Early or late, depends on your point of view," Miles said.

"Those are sun rays," Gideon said, pointing across the landscape behind Miles, who didn't bother to turn around. "I was about to go to sleep."

"Me too," Miles said. "I need access to the library."

Gideon couldn't refuse Miles for several reasons, all of which he knew. Mostly because no Librarian could refuse access to an Arbiter, but also because Drest would just order Gideon to allow him access, something Gideon seethed about internally. Outwardly, he sighed in an overly dramatic way and stepped aside.

Miles looked back down the dozen steps to the garden he'd only just walked through. The library had always been a beautiful building, one of Miles's favourites on the estate—made from white stone and large windows. It was full of books and documents, not only from House Venator, but from the Assembly, and went back to a time when the individual Houses had no one checking to make sure they were behaving.

As he stepped through the large dark wooden double doors and into the library itself, he paused, closed his eyes, and took a deep breath.

"You are smiling," Gideon said, although there was no admonishment in the words, which surprised Miles.

"I didn't realise how much I missed the smell," Miles told him. He opened his eyes and looked up to the roof three storeys above him. The second and third storeys were circular rings with a large opening in the middle, looking down on the entrance. The roof had sizeable glass panels all along it that were designed to cast rainbows of colour all around the wooden interior, bouncing off strategically placed polished surfaces.

"You can't come back," Gideon said, taking Miles out of his moment of tranquillity.

Miles laughed before he could stop himself. "You don't like me, and I don't care why. Just do me the common courtesy of pretending that my role as Arbiter means you really should behave like I care."

"No," Gideon said. "Why are you here?"

"There's a book of Assembly bylaws to do with investigations," Miles said. "I read it many years ago, before I left. I think it has something in it that will help me, and I'd like to check exactly what it says, so I don't get it wrong."

"Assembly law is at the back," Gideon said, removing a key from his pocket and passing to Miles.

"I know," Miles said, taking the key. He took a step forward, sighed, and turned back to Gideon. "Thank you. And I am sorry for disturbing you. I won't be long."

Gideon turned and walked away.

Miles had never liked Gideon. He'd always found him too keen to throw others under the bus if it meant he achieved something, always too happy to correct someone in as public a way as possible. He thrived in wanting everyone to know how clever he was, and while he was exceptionally smart, he had the people skills of a rabid honey badger.

He knew that Gideon hated him, but he honestly wasn't sure why. He'd never done anything to offend that he could be certain of; he'd never thrown his weight around when he was First Librarian and Gideon Second. He'd congratulated Gideon when he'd become First. Maybe that was the problem. He was First because Miles stepped down, not because he was given the job on merit.

Miles walked through the hall, moving by thousands of books detailing thousands of years of vampire and human history. The third floor even had a large selection of fiction books, and Miles used to take great delight in finding vampire authors and acquiring their work. He had no idea if Gideon continued the practise; it was no longer his place to ask.

He found the correct shelves with ease, and the system used by the library hadn't changed in two hundred years, so he found the book he was looking for soon after. All of the books were locked behind plexiglass windows, designed to ensure that the books stayed in good condition. The book in question was large, heavy, and bound in black leather, with *Bylaws of Investigations* written on the front in gold.

Closing the plexiglass behind him, Miles took the book over to one of the nearby wooden tables that were situated at the rear of the library and sat on a comfortable chair. He removed his pen and notepad from his satchel and got to work skimming through the book until he found the right passage.

The vast majority of people probably considered the idea of sitting alone in a library while researching barely used laws to be a less than thrilling way to spend time. To Miles it was as close to actual peace as he ever got.

Miles found the passage in question and copied it out, word for word, into his notebook, before taking a photo of it just in case. He closed the book, sat back in the chair, and sighed. It had taken him a little over thirty minutes.

"Find what you were looking for?" Gideon asked, his voice echoing in the empty building.

Miles nodded. "Thank you."

Gideon stared at Miles for a moment, before nodding once, scooping the book up, and walking away.

Miles stared at the writing in his notebook; *An Arbiter may continue an investigation passed to a House, if there is reason to believe the crimes are continued in another country.*

The word *may* was doing a lot of heavy lifting in that sentence, and Miles thought that most Arbiters would just allow the House to do the investigation in total, handing over all of their information. Any Arbiter using the bylaw wasn't going to be making themselves any friends in the House they were going against, and there would be, at some point, retaliation for it.

Fuck it, Miles thought, as he got to his feet.

"Are you done?" Gideon asked. "The great and wonderful Miles Watson is going to leave?"

Miles paused. "What's your problem, Gideon?"

Gideon crossed the floor and stood on the opposite side of the table to Miles, glaring at him. "If you don't know, you're not worthy to have it explained to you."

"The fact that you were Second Librarian beneath me for so long?" Miles asked. "Is that why you're so angry about? That you got this job because I left?"

Gideon laughed. "The arrogance that comes off you could be bottled up and used to power cities."

"Tell me then," Miles said, trying to keep calm. "Just goddamned tell me."

Gideon leaned over the table. "No," he sneered. "Die ignorant."

Miles shook his head and left the library. He had neither the time nor inclination to deal with Gideon. The sun was up, and in his haste to get away from Gideon, he hadn't checked the UV index. A rookie mistake. He was grateful it was the middle of winter, when the index barely rose above one. Even so, there was a tingling sensation on his exposed skin that made him hurry back to his temporary home.

Church was already asleep on the floor of the bedroom when Miles walked in. He showered, his need for sleep almost causing him to drift off as he did, and was barely dry by the time he got into bed and immediately fell asleep.

While sleep came easily to him, a peaceful sleep wasn't on the cards. Miles's dreams were full of violent imagery, of the pain and suffering of faceless people he felt he should know but didn't. More than once, he woke expecting to see some horrific visage in front of him, but found himself still alone in the dark bedroom.

Nightmares weren't a regular thing for vampires—most didn't dream— but when they did . . . well, that was usually a bad sign. Prophetic dreams were a thing in the vampire world, although the number of vampires who had them was limited to a handful, and usually only during great times of upheaval or stress. Miles couldn't say for sure that he was going through either. He wasn't overly stressed about the investigation, although he was irritated that House Umbra was going to swoop in and claim it for its own, and he doubted that anyone got prophetic dreams because they were a bit irritated.

Still, the memory of them lingered for longer than Miles would have liked.

Miles grabbed his phone from the bedside table and switched it on, bathing everything in a bright glow.

Contrary to popular belief, vampires had no real issue with technology. Vedran was set in his ways but in the minority, with generations happily using smartphones, iPads, and the internet with ease. Being hundreds of years old was no excuse to at least try to keep up with the technology that humans used. For self-preservation, if nothing more.

With a loud sigh, Miles got out of bed and tentatively looked behind the curtain. His phone said the UV level was low, so Miles opened the curtains fully, allowing himself to be basked in the meagre levels of sunlight.

It had snowed heavily since this morning and was continuing to snow. It would be several inches thick if it continued. The sky was a mixture of dark and light greys and shadowy blues, and the light reflecting off the snow gave everything an eerie blanket of warmth. Several vampires were out in the pit throwing snowballs at each other, because centuries old or not, snow is fun for the first thirty minutes of seeing it.

There were no vampire children, no vampires under the age of twenty-five, although why that age was chosen, Miles didn't really know. It just was, and everyone accepted it. Anyone trying to create vampires younger than that was . . . well, *executed* wasn't the right word. *Expunged* was probably more accurate. There were fates worse than death for those who lived centuries. And vampires had a lot of time to find them all.

Miles got dressed in a pair of jeans, a black T-shirt, and a black hoodie, and looked at himself in the mirror and sighed. "It's going to be a long day," he said to the reflection of himself. "Just don't punch anyone."

He left the bedroom and mentally prepared himself, heading downstairs to find Church sitting by the front door, a look of "you took your time" on her face. Miles opened the door to let her out, letting in a gust of snowy weather as Church bounded outside.

He closed the door then padded barefoot through to the kitchen, where he made himself a large mug of coffee. He paused before adding two spoonfuls of sugar and a splash of milk, then took the mug back through into the front room, where he enjoyed a moment of silence in the darkness. He had no idea what was going to happen in his meeting with Drest, or even what the ancient vampire wanted, but in Miles's experience, it was always best to make sure you were neither hungry nor caffeine deprived when meeting him.

After procrastinating on his phone for a while, Miles decided it was time to go. He pulled on his socks and boots, grabbed his thick coat, and left the building. His feet crunched under the fresh snow, and he pulled his collar around his neck to keep the chill out.

The space between the horseshoe of buildings was a blanket of fresh snow, with a few House members standing guard outside of their respective Houses. Mostly familiars and trusted humans, Miles thought to himself.

Church was playing in a bank of snow farther along, jumping high into the air and practically diving headfirst into it, throwing up a mass of snow as she exploded out of the bank, shook herself free of the largest pieces, and went to do it all over again. Sometimes Miles had to remind himself that despite her unnatural intelligence and size, she was still a dog.

"You staying or coming?" Miles asked as he walked by Church, who was on her back, all four legs in the air, rolling around in the snow.

Church rolled over, looked at Miles, snorted, and shook herself clear of snow, before following, nudging him in the leg with her huge head until he scratched her behind the ear.

"You're enjoying yourself?" Miles said looking down.

Church let out a small bark in the affirmative. One for yes, two for no.

"You made friends with the other dogs here?" Miles asked.

The two barks that followed made Miles's heart hurt. Despite Church trying to make friends with other dogs, most either shunned her, ran away as fast as possible, or were immediately aggressive. Church might look like a large dog to everyone else, but to another dog, she was something that wasn't meant to be. Something . . . abnormal. Every meeting with another dog reminded her and Miles of that.

"We need to find you some foxes and wolves," Miles said.

An enthusiastic bark.

For some reason that no one had ever been able to explain, foxes and wolves loved Church.

The pair continued on for a few minutes, as the main estate house loomed over them from a distance. Miles nodded hello to several Venator House guards and custodians who were out doing rounds, or checking for damage from the previous night's festivities.

Each person they passed nodded back to Miles, before looking down at Church and smiling at her. Some gave her a scratch or stroke, while some looked quite nervous about being near a dog so big.

They reached the steps up to the front door of the main house, where several guards stood. Miles showed them his Arbiter bracelet, and they let him through, telling him to have a good day.

The large foyer of House Venator's main building had two glass doors on each side of the varnished oak floor. Two of the doors were glass, and were open, while one was made from solid oak and contained the guard station for the building. The final door, which sat on Miles's immediate right, was made of metal. There was a fingerprint scanner just beside it, with a passcode keypad next to that.

The metal door opened and Charlotte stepped out. She'd changed from her glamourous but probably impractical dress into a navy trouser suit, with a cream blouse and white Nike trainers. Her hair was up in a bun, with a pen sticking out of the top of it.

"Good night?" Miles asked her.

"Want to guess how many arguments there were after I saw you last night?" Charlotte asked, walking over to Miles and hugging him.

"A dozen?" Miles asked, willing to bet it would be higher.

"Seventeen," Charlotte said. "I know that because our First Captain had to cite every single one of them so they'd piss off and go sober up, or calm down. Or both."

"And how is Halime?" Miles asked, imagining the First Captain becoming increasingly infuriated with the behaviour of vampires she would have normally crossed the road to avoid.

"Sleeping, I hope," Charlotte said. "Preferably before she murders someone. You went to see Gideon."

"I did," Miles said.

"He complained to Drest about you turning up and needing to use the library," Charlotte said. "You should have just called me if you needed legal expertise."

"I considered it," Miles said.

"And?" Charlotte asked, when Miles wasn't more forthcoming.

"Two things," Miles said. "One, I wanted to look for myself. I didn't want to disturb you with legal questions until I had done so. And two, I kind of missed the place. I wanted to see it while I was back. I just didn't realise Gideon would be there just as the sun rose."

"Did you find what you were looking for?" Charlotte asked. "Or at least enough to justify me getting a shitty call at sunrise?"

"I did," Miles said and explained what he'd discovered.

"You're going to make enemies," Charlotte told him. "New ones, I mean; you already have a lot of them."

"I like collecting stuff," Miles said with a smile. "You joining us for our meeting?"

Charlotte nodded. "I'm there in a legal capacity. I will not be answering questions for you or becoming involved in whatever the topic is."

"Do you know the topic?" Miles asked hopefully.

"Yes, of course," Charlotte said.

"Do I get a guess?" Miles asked.

"Absolutely fucking not," Charlotte told him, a beaming smile on her face.

"You're enjoying this far too much," Miles said.

"I know, it's great," Charlotte said, still smiling. She looked down at Church. "You coming?"

Church's tail wagged.

The hallway beyond the foyer had the same polished wood floor, but there were several thick red rugs placed along it. There were two doors down the ten-meter hallway, with one going out into a small balcony and garden, while the other was the destination of Miles, Charlotte, and Church.

The walls of the hallway were decorated with oil paintings of the Firsts of the House: Lord or Lady, Captain, Counsel, Authority, Librarian, and Custodian. Miles knew nearly all of them, although his personal thoughts on them ranged from enjoying their company very much to hoping they got kicked by a horse. Into a woodchipper.

Being part of the same House did not mean you had to like each other.

Miles reached the metal door at the end of the hallway and knocked twice, waiting until it was opened. He probably could have just opened it and walked through himself, but he was no longer a member of House Venator, and he felt weird just assuming that it would be okay.

The room beyond was spacious and set into two separate pieces, with five steps leading from one to the other. The lower part, where Miles stood, had the same wooden floor, although there was a large rug covering it with the pattern of an intricate map of the Scottish Highlands.

The wall opposite the entrance was covered in floor to ceiling book-cases, with a ladder that moved from the far end of the wall to the steps leading to the raised part of the room. There were hundreds of books there, and while it didn't quite match the splendour of the House Library, which was cavernous and easy enough to get lost in, it was still impressive.

At the far left-hand side of the room were a number of lockable metal cabinets next to a coffee table and a couple black leather sofas. To the right of the room, on the raised portion, was a set of large bay windows that overlooked the private garden. To the side of them was a huge desk made of dark wood. On top of the desk sat a forest green mat, a lamp in the shape of a globe, a notebook, a fountain pen and several bottles of coloured ink, and a computer. A swivel chair sat beside it, and a large number of comfortable looking cushions adorned the floor behind the chair, just in front of two blood-red leather armchairs, a glass coffee table between them.

Miles walked up the steps and looked out of the bay window at Church running around as Charlotte sat down on the sofa, with Church lying at her feet.

"You okay?" Charlotte asked.

Miles nodded, although he wasn't sure if he *could* actually speak. Being back felt odd. Not bad, just . . . odd.

There was a click from inside the room, and one of the bookcases slid silently out and across the floor on wheeled tracks. Miles didn't bother turning around; he knew it was Drest.

"It's been a long time," Drest said as he left his private room hidden behind the bookcases. "Charlotte, good to see you up and alert after last night's festivities."

"You say festivities, I say drunken debauchery," Charlotte said.

Miles turned to see that Drest hadn't aged a day in the decades that Miles had been away. He still looked about fifty, with long grey hair that fell over his shoulders, hair that had been grey the day he'd been turned into a vampire. He had a long beard that reached his chest. It was plaited down the centre with a golden ring just beyond his chin, and silver ringlets further down. He had piercing blue eyes, and his enormous, muscular hands were missing the little finger on one and the top of his index finger on the other. No one knew why. Drest was a tall, broad man, especially for the period of time when he'd been human, when Scotland was ruled by the Picts. Miles didn't know exactly how old Drest was, but the word thousands was used a lot.

Drest smiled; it was the kind of smile that made you think you were the only person in the room, the feeling was the same no matter the crowd around you.

"Still got the earrings," Miles said, pointing to the dangling silver crosses that hung from both ears.

"They're not going anywhere," Drest said in a thick Scottish accent. "I don't like people telling me what I can and can't do."

Miles wasn't sure if the Picts had similar accents, or if Drest had changed it over the years, and it wasn't something he felt the need to ask. "Yeah, we've met," Miles said.

Drest's laughter filled the room as he stepped up to Miles and hugged the smaller man, slapping him on his shoulder as he pulled away. "Nice beard," Drest said. "Maybe when puberty sets in, you'll get a proper one." He stroked his own beard and smiled warmly.

Miles laughed. "You're just in the middle of a midlife crisis," he said, making Drest laugh again.

"Your text said it was urgent," Drest said, sounding suddenly serious and taking a seat and motioning for Miles to sit beside him.

Miles sat down. Because when a Vampire First Lord suggests you sit down, you don't argue.

As a young man in the human army, Miles had been trained to hunt and kill people. He'd been good at it. Excellent at it. So good that when he left the military and joined a criminal gang, he'd started using his . . . talents to steal whatever needed to be stolen and end those who were a threat to the gang he was a member of. One such threat was Drest. No one knew that he was a vampire, let alone one of the most powerful to exist. Miles had been given the task of killing him.

Miles got close enough to stab him, without anyone noticing. Obviously, Drest didn't die, he didn't even get badly hurt, but the surprise of a human making it all the way to him without anyone finding out impressed the vampire First Lord. He'd offered Miles a job working for him. Not as an assassin, but as a protector, a hidden bodyguard. Miles spent the next several decades being trained to be even better than his already considerable talents. He investigated and removed threats to the Venator House before most people even knew there was a problem. Eventually, Miles became a vampire, and his ability to do his job increased exponentially. As did his desire to stop.

Drest made Miles First Librarian simply because of Miles's abilities as an investigator and his desire to be left to his own devices. He'd left that job because of his need to help more people, but seeing Drest again after years apart made him wish he'd kept in closer contact.

Drest looked over at Charlotte. "You need to say anything before we start?"

"He knows I'm here in a legal capacity," Charlotte said. "But also, what is said in this room is not to leave this room. Is that understood?"

Miles nodded. "Of course. You wanted to talk to me, too. I assume the two things are connected, considering the timing. What's going on?"

"You can come out," Drest said, taking a seat on the sofa next to Charlotte.

Danica walked out of the hidden room; she wore jeans and a light yellow T-shirt with a picture of Christopher Lee as Dracula on it. Miles had never seen the First Lady wearing anything other than elegant clothing, making her look as if she'd just stepped out of a photo shoot. She looked at ease, casual. She was also barefoot.

"You two," Miles said, motioning between the pair. "You're . . ."

"Yes," Drest said.

Miles turned to look at Charlotte. "You know about this?"

"Yes," Charlotte replied.

Miles looked back at Drest. "Right, how much shit are you in, and how do I help you get out of it?"

Danica crossed the room and kissed Drest on his forehead, before looking back to Miles.

"First of all, I need to apologise for my behaviour last night," she said softly. "It was unbecoming of me. I was . . . attempting to play a part. I'm always being watched, always being . . . it doesn't matter, but I shouldn't have involved you."

Miles blinked. Did the High Lady of House Barbarous just apologise to him? Was he dreaming? Had he hit his head a little too hard at some point?

"Thank you," he said eventually, not wanting to say anything else because he wasn't sure he could have said anything else. "What's going on?"

"We've got a big problem," Danica said. "And I'm hoping you can help."

Chapter Twelve

First of all, I'll make sure we're all up to date," Danica said. "A month ago there was an incident in Islington, London involving the deaths of several vampires. And it's possibly linked to a group of criminals who have been making illegal vampires for some time. Correct?"

Miles wondered what he was meant to say to that. He settled for "I assume you've been getting briefings from the Assembly?"

Drest nodded. "For the most part, it's only whatever you submit in your reports, but they are sent to us, yes."

There was nothing wrong with that; it was perfectly fine for any House to read the reports of any Arbiter that weren't marked *CONFIDENTIAL*, and nothing in the investigation that Miles had taken part in deemed that necessary. Even so, he felt as though they'd been keeping tabs on him, which was a bit weird, to put it mildly.

"Why did you want to contact me?" Drest asked.

"I originally wanted to talk to you because I needed to know if you knew of any House that has people in Fortress Falls, in Washington," Miles said, feeling as if he were wading into something with no idea when it was going to be too late to get back to shore. "I wanted to know if they'd talk to me when I got there. I know I could share that with one of the Assembly handlers, but I also know that if it got to the wrong person, my target could run. I figured talking to people I trust was the best way to get intel. And now you're telling me that's linked to why you wanted me to be here?"

"Yes," Danica said.

"Obviously, you have someone in Washington state," Miles said, asking anyone who felt like answering. "Seattle is a neutral city, so there's clearly going to be House members there. I mean, you literally have people in Fortress Falls?"

"Yes and sort of," Danica said.

"I know you've been blindsided by this," Charlotte said to Miles. "But I'd really just let them tell you, and then at the end you can yell at people."

"Superb," Miles said, making it sound anything but. "Please feel free. I'll keep my mouth shut."

"Two weeks ago, I was contacted by a man who works for me," Danica said. "That man's name is Oliver McCarthy."

Miles said nothing, but his inner voice said *fuck, fuck, fuck, fuck, fuck.*

"I think I might need more information than that," Miles said, trying to keep his concern out of his voice.

"Oliver is a spy for House Barbarous," Danica said. "He has been for several decades. Working within criminal organisations who might be a concern for vampires. He started to work for a man we can only identify as . . ."

"Boss," Miles finished.

"A month ago, Oliver's cover was blown," Danica said. "A desolate was created in an illegal vampire operation, and Oliver managed to rescue two new vampires. He went dark after that for two weeks. He contacted me and told me he was going to Fortress Falls."

"You were investigating this Boss the whole time?" Miles asked. "And no one thought to tell me that?"

"It's not much of a spy network if we tell everyone," Danica said. "Besides, the illegal vampires were not our main objective. The identity of this Boss is. He's someone who has been seemingly increasing his power and wealth. He's an unknown player, and we don't like unknown players."

"Okay, so Oliver is in Fortress Falls," Miles said. "I can go there, grab him, find out what he knows, and make sure his identity is secret."

"It's a bit more complicated than that," Drest said.

"Because of course it is," Miles replied.

"I have someone who works in Fortress Falls for me," Danica said. "Her name is Yvonne Dent. She used to work in Seattle, but . . . well, divorces can get complicated, and she wanted to move out of the city. She has a brother. By the name of Oliver McCarthy."

Miles looked between Drest and Danica. "I've never liked spy bullshit, and this is beginning to feel like the most bullshit of bullshit. Why would Oliver put his sister in danger like that?"

"Yvonne contacted me two weeks ago to say that her brother had arrived, said something had gone to shit in London, and he'd headed to her," Danica continued. "She didn't say what he'd been involved in. She did say that Oliver was concerned that with his cover blown, she might be in danger. He didn't have her number, so he needed to find out if she was safe in person."

"I assume you found out about the raid," Miles said. "That's why you know I was looking for Oliver. Some of the prisoners mentioned his name."

"Last night I got a call from an ATO who works with Megan Song," Drest said. "She mentioned that you were at the raid in London, an Arbiter looking for people dealing in the illegal vampire trade. The name Oliver was mentioned by some of those involved. We knew it wouldn't take long for you to figure out who Oliver is, and we needed to talk to you before you flew across the world with no knowledge of what you're walking into."

Miles nodded. "And I thank you for not making my life harder."

"You should know that one of the humans there ran off after you spoke to him," Danica said. "Kyle something or other. He's in the wind."

"He's just a scared kid," Miles said. "He'll fuck up something in another way at some point, and we'll get ahold of him again. Also, good to know that Megan has someone on her team who relays info to the Lord of House Venator. Which is probably grounds for dismissal, yes?"

"Oh yeah," Charlotte agreed.

"How was Oliver's identity found out?" Miles asked. "Sounds like he was good at his job for a long time."

"He's *excellent* at his job," Danica corrected. "He's actually a criminal, so it's easy for him to involve himself in their lives."

"We don't know yet," Drest said. "Oliver either doesn't know, or doesn't trust us enough to tell us."

"My investigation is getting a lot more complicated a lot quicker," Miles said.

"Except your investigation in London has been passed over to House Umbra," Danica said. "So it was already complicated."

"Aye, I already knew that was coming," Miles said.

"To make matters more complicated," Drest said, "Oliver's bloodline gift is telepathy."

"House Umbra?" Miles said.

"We believe that the Boss is from House Umbra," Danica said. "You might want to keep that information to yourself."

"That explains why they're so keen on getting involved in the investigation," Miles said and chuckled. "Umbra is not going to be happy after what I discovered last night."

"Ah, the angering of Gideon," Drest said.

Miles told everyone about his discovery in the library.

"You're not going to be making friends in House Umbra," Danica said.

"People assume I care about making friends," Miles replied, realising he was getting close to being a little too snippy. "I care about finding Oliver, finding who he worked for, and nailing them to something horrible. They killed people. Humans and vampires. Making friends is somewhere low down the list of things I give a shit about. Although, in hindsight, if you'd told me all of this when I'd arrived, I never would have needed to piss off Gideon."

"Everyone needs a hobby," Drest said with a wry smile.

"Even so, it would be wise to keep your newly learned information to yourself until it's needed," Charlotte said. "No sense in letting House Umbra know what's going on unless you need to."

"Good point," Miles agreed. "I assume there's more to this story."

"Yvonne mentioned something else concerning to us . . . we really don't need a repeat of the Maine situation," Drest said with a frown.

America had more than a dozen vampire cities spread throughout their states, but in the 1980s, there had been an incident in Maine that acted as a warning about what could happen when vampires take control. Some vampires decided to start experiments on humans who were dying, and ended up creating enough desolate that they overran the state in a matter of weeks. Dozens of ATOs had to go in and kill every one of them, at the cost of many of their own lives, but by that point, the desolate had spilled out into New Brunswick. Thankfully, the problem was stopped, but not before a lot of humans and vampires died. Those in charge of the experiments were hunted down and executed.

A wall was built around parts of Maine and New Brunswick, and large military installations were put in place around the edges of the two areas, with Nova Scotia becoming a land of refugees and military personnel for many years.

There had been such incidents before, but they'd taken place when there wasn't TV and news channels, and information could be downplayed or entirely hidden. It was the vampire equivalent of Chernobyl, and it played out live on TV for months. And once it was done, it forever altered how many humans viewed vampires.

Since then, a well-funded and government backed group calling themselves the Magistrate had appeared. Mostly they kept themselves to the non-vampire cities, and while their brand of investigating and arrest was little more than state sponsored assault, they had begun to worm their way into several vampire cities, when the Senator or Congressperson for that state decided to start listening to whoever shouted loudest. It was basically a Cold War between vampires and the Magistrate, and so far neither side was willing to blink first.

There had been attempts to take the Magistrate worldwide, but the European vampire community had been waiting for it and had done their best to limit the damage the influx of hate and fear had done. The Magistrate still managed to gain traction in a few countries like Russia and Belarus, but even there it didn't quite have the backing of its American incarnation.

Drest explained that there had been missing people from Fortress Falls—three humans taken, all found dead with their blood sucked dry in the last two weeks.

"Bollocks," Miles said, as the feeling of *what now* landed squarely in his gut. "You're thinking vampire serial killer."

"I don't know what to think," Drest said. "How many vampires do you know who'll willingly just leave their victims out for the public to see?" Drest asked. "The first body was found just before Yvonne contacted us about her brother."

"It doesn't matter if it's connected to what's happening there or just a coincidence," Charlotte said. "Serial murders by a vampire is bad press. And we do not need more bad press."

"Crap." Miles sighed. "So we either have a genuine, bona fide vampire serial killer—or something else on the loose."

"Yvonne was discretely looking into the missing people," Danica said. "She'd requested either House assistance or an Arbiter. Neither were allowed."

"Why?" Miles asked.

"The Magistrate took control of the investigation," Danica said.

"You have got to be kidding me," Miles said, feeling exasperated, as pieces of the puzzle fit together in his mind. "They can't do that; if it's a real vampire feeding off humans, then that's Assembly business. Why are they trying to keep it quiet? The Magistrate should be taking out adverts in the news about it."

"Exactly," Danica said.

The Magistrate could step in and take control of vampire on human crime so long as no House or the Assembly had already claimed the investigation. In that instance, they could work alongside the vampires, and often did without incident. Not all of the Magistrate wanted to subjugate the vampire community, but they were still a beacon for those humans who felt that the best vampire was a dead vampire. And that had been a problem in the past.

"So, I go to Fortress Falls and find Oliver before the Magistrate do, because if they get hold of him—I'll never get any leads on this Boss," Miles said. "What about the serial killer, any leads?"

"We don't know anything," Drest said slowly.

"Don't be cagey now," Miles said.

"The Magistrate's involvement makes information gathering on their case difficult," Danica said. "But we have a friend who has been feeding us information when she can."

Miles raised an eyebrow. "A friend?"

"Lauren Gibson," Drest said. "She works for the Magistrate in Seattle and is married to a police detective in Fortress Falls. She also works for us."

Miles looked around the room, unsure he'd heard right.

"What the actual fuck?" Miles asked after several seconds of silence. "You have a spy in the Magistrate. A spy who is married to a police detective. A human spy. A. Human. Spy."

"You look like you might have a stroke," Drest said.

"A. Human. Spy," Miles almost shouted. "Jesus fucking wept."

"You done?" Drest asked.

"No, I'm not fucking done," Miles said. "You put a human spy inside an organisation that would more often than not like to see us all dead. Or GPS tagged like we're bloody rhinos in some BBC production."

"That doesn't make sense," Drest said.

"I'm annoyed, it doesn't have to make sense," Miles said, getting to his feet, walking over to the bay window, and resting his forehead against the cool glass.

"It gets worse," Drest said.

"How?" Miles asked, genuinely wondering how it could be possible to get worse.

"She's missing," Drest said.

Yep, that would do it, Miles thought, but instead said, "Tell me everything."

"She contacted me a year ago," Danica said. "She was concerned that her brother was becoming more involved with the Magistrate in Seattle. She said she'd gone for a job interview with them, trying to figure out what was going on, and was horrified at what she learned. Torture, imprisonment, people having their lives destroyed by Magistrate members with no oversight."

"Why you?" Miles asked, turning back toward everyone in the room.

"We were in Seattle for an Assembly meeting," Danica said. "She saw me on the news, looked me up . . . online. Decided to approach me. She wanted advice, Miles. And that's all I gave her. Nothing more. She gave me a report of what she'd witnessed. No evidence, though, just her word against that of a powerful organisation. You want to guess how it would go if she went to the authorities?"

"What did she gather information for?" Miles asked. "Why not take it to the Feds, or the media?"

"Because we don't know who is and isn't friendly with the anti-vampire sentiment that many in the Magistrate like to peddle," Charlotte said.

"You knew about this?" Miles asked her.

"Of course. I wrote the legal deal for Lauren to sign," Charlotte said.

"Let me get everything straight in my head," Miles said, rubbing his temples. "My suspect, who works for House Barbarous, fled to America, where his sister also works for House Barbarous, and he's run to her little town right into the middle of a serial killer investigation, conducted by a group of people who would like us rounded up. And on top of that, you have a spy there feeding you intel about the Magistrate, who's currently missing. Why tell me that last part?"

"Because Lauren is why you're here," Drest explained. "I hadn't expected House Umbra to take the case away from you, but clearly they're hiding something and don't want an Arbiter searching into it. Last night, I tried to figure out how to get you there, and I came up with very little that was good, until Gideon told me you were in the library. I figured you'd have found something to help you. Now I'm asking you to help us."

Miles's mind settled on something. "Yvonne is Lauren's handler, right?" Danica nodded.

"If Oliver gets grabbed and they start poking their noses around his sister, Yvonne could get found out," Miles said. "And then you've got more than one *really* big problem, because the Magistrate and those who bankroll them are going to use their media people to say that vampires are putting spies in human law enforcement."

"That's the concern, yes," Drest said.

"And the Assembly in North America doesn't have the resources to send people to a small town called Fortress Falls to argue with the Magistrate about their investigation," Miles said. "Who's looking into Lauren's disappearance?"

"Officially, no one," Charlotte said. "She's not declared missing. I guess if she were, though, it would be local PD. Who her husband is a member of. From what I can tell, he believes she ran off with some other guy."

After what happened in Maine, a large part of Assembly resources went to monitoring the affected area, and so, while the East Coast and parts of the North grew a sizeable number of Assembly personnel, the West Coast branches, apart from California, were understaffed. Seattle was a neutral city, which meant that vampires were supposed to be free to come and go, and they were for the most part, but it also meant that the Assembly and Magistrate were always butting heads.

"So, I'm to find Oliver before the Magistrate do, and figure out where Lauren is?" Miles asked, wanting to make sure he had every single detail right.

"Yes," Danica said. "We cannot let Lauren's help come to light."

"What if it has already?" Miles asked.

"She's been missing for five days," Drest said. "If they knew that Lauren was . . . sorry, *is* a spy, I'd like to know why we haven't heard of any complaints."

"So, we're working off the idea that they don't know she's working for you?" Miles said.

"We are," Charlotte confirmed.

"Where were you going to take Oliver once you found him?" Drest asked.

Miles had considered it from the moment he realised he might have to go to America, and there was only one answer. "Vampire Island."

Vampire Island was the nickname for Vancouver Island. Victoria, on the southern tip of the island, was home to a huge vampire population, as well as one of the largest groups of Assembly personnel in the entire continent of North America. Getting Oliver there would give Miles the chance to get him anywhere, undocumented, and without trouble. That was the theory, anyway.

Miles hoped that Oliver was still in town, or at least that he hadn't gone too far. Further north of Victoria, on the Canadian mainland, were several vampire communities who most assuredly did not welcome humans, who even the Assembly stayed clear of. If Oliver had made his way to one of them, Miles was going to have a hell of a time getting to him.

"Good idea," Danica said. "I know Anya, the head Arbiter handler in Victoria, she's a good person. She'll help."

"I know Anya," Miles told everyone. He liked Anya; she was tough and determined and did not take shit from vampires or humans. She was also good at her job, and Miles ranked that above being personable. "I'd need to fly there first, anyway. Got to let them know I'm working in the area, seeing how they don't like it when you just call them up."

"Everything about Lauren remains between us," Drest said. "We don't leave people in the wind, Miles. We need to know what happened to her."

"Yeah, I get that," Miles told him. "I'll do everything in my power to find Lauren and Oliver. Her husband, the detective, what's he like?"

Drest and Danica shared a look.

"He's not great," Charlotte said. "Name is Reese Gibson. He's a detective, and he has some questionable friends from the Magistrate."

"Just to make things more complicated," Miles said. "And he's not worried about his missing wife?"

"It's a human disappearance, so he doesn't have to say anything to any of us," Charlotte said.

"So, are you asking me to officially take over her disappearance?" Miles asked.

"We're asking you to go and do what you were going to anyway," Drest said. "And while you're there, maybe make enquiries about Lauren. The second you take over her investigation, the Magistrate will link her disappearance to vampire involvement."

"If you have reason to believe she's in danger, take control of the situation," Danica said. "If she's found out, and she's alive, and the Magistrate don't know what she did, she could well be in serious danger should people question why a vampire is looking into her disappearance."

"Anything else?" Drest asked.

"You each have an entire House at your disposal—why me?" Miles asked.

"Two reasons," Drest said. "One, I can't ask a member of my House to get involved, and neither can Danica. And two, I trust you to do the right thing. Not the right thing that you think I'd like, the actual right thing. To you, the House or the Assembly comes second to actually doing the job."

Miles couldn't dispute that. "Yeah, we've had that discussion a few times. Mostly it involved shouting."

Drest's laugh had no humour to it, only sadness. "I wish I hadn't pushed you away, Miles."

"You didn't," Miles admitted. "I chose to leave. I chose to try something new. I want to make all of our lives better, not just my House. I don't want humans to fear us, to think that throwing garlic at us is going to do something other than make us wonder what the hell is going on."

"So, how's that going?" Drest asked.

"It's a work in progress," Miles admitted. "No one has thrown garlic at me for a while, though. No one has even tried to shove a crucifix in my face."

"I'd call that a win, then," Drest said.

Miles stared at Drest for several seconds. The mighty Drest, the man who had led armies, who had fought the Romans, the Vikings, the Irish, other Scots, the English, and who had bested them all. He looked . . . worried. It was more than that, something worse, as if something inside of him had deflated.

"I trust Drest," Danica said. "I was being watched by those who would use my relationship with Drest to further their own aims. There is a contingent of my House who expect me to behave like some seductress as it was how my predecessor behaved; occasionally I put on a show. Usually with those I believe I can trust, or need to test to see how they react. Drest told me I could trust you. I wanted to check for myself. I believe you are a good man, Miles Watson."

It wasn't forbidden for Ladies and Lords from different Houses to have relationships, but it often meant that someone in one of the Houses tried to advance themselves by finding dirt on their superior. It usually ended badly for someone.

"I'm still only interested in the illegal vampire operation," Miles said. "If the Magistrate are dealing with these murders, I can't just involve myself." Arbiters could go anywhere in pursuit of any investigation so long as it involved vampires, but they couldn't interject themselves into another investigation by a House, another Arbiter, or, in the US, the Magistrate.

"Okay, so I'll go to Fortress Falls and find Oliver, who will tell me what he knows about this Boss of his," Miles said. "And while I'm there, I can look into this missing human. At least try to figure out what happened to her, and hope it wasn't a vampire who did it. And absolutely nothing else."

"You want to track down this killer," Charlotte said.

"Vampires killing humans are bad for the business of vampires living," Miles said. "But if the Magistrate are dealing with it, I'd rather not get involved unless I have to."

"Do not make things more complicated than they need to be," Danica said. "If you think it's worth it, ask Anya to send an ATO team to do a projection sweep of the town. It's not interfering with the Magistrate, and it's doing something useful. There might need to be some circumventing to get it done, but the Magistrate can't complain about it."

"Yeah, I'll see how bad it is," Miles said. "We sure it's a vampire killer?"

"No," Charlotte said. "We're not sure about anything because they've been tight lipped about what they'd found. It's *their* investigation. US law means they don't have to tell any of us a damn thing. We can all thank the dickheads in Maine for that little piece of fun."

While what Charlotte said was true, Miles didn't want to add that they could also thank the billionaires who had tried to become vampires themselves and were told no by the Houses or Assembly. Becoming an illegal vampire wouldn't have been an option, as everyone would know they'd done it, and they couldn't blend into the average population. They were politicians, CEOs, billionaires, people who thought that becoming a vampire was a means to go on living forever. They didn't take the rejection well. Between them and those who believed that vampires were monsters and belonged back in the shadows, both groups had powerful friends, and they'd gotten the legislation passed to start the Magistrate project.

Not all states had a Magistrate branch. Most of the East Coast didn't, but among those who did, the Magistrate had gained more and more power over the decades, while removing more and more power from the Assembly.

A systematic long-term policy of making vampires feel uncomfortable to live in certain parts of the country.

"So, do you agree?" Danica asked.

"To find Oliver and get him out of that town before your spy games come crashing down around you and at least one human and one vampire are killed because of it?" Miles asked. "Yeah. I planned on going anyway, this is just extra incentive. You told me all of this so I didn't get there and fuck anything up for your people, and I thank you for that. I'll do my best to make sure they're both safe."

"Thank you," Danica said.

Miles stood and looked over at Church. "You ready?" he asked.

Church got to her feet and walked over to the door, waiting expectedly.

"I'll contact Anya," Charlotte said. "I don't think she'll wait long to call you."

"I didn't have Oliver's last name until you told me," Miles said. "Any chance you can get me information about him by the time I'm ready to leave?"

"I'll get it done," Charlotte promised with a thumbs-up.

"I'll have a car take you back to Inverness, where the private jet will be waiting to take you to Heathrow," Drest said. "Can you get tickets to America by the time you land?"

Miles nodded. There were always seats available for Arbiters and those working for the Assembly. Usually with vampire friendly airlines that had tinted windows and spaced out seating, like a whole jet of Business Class seats. They were popular with humans, too, which Miles used to find a little odd, but he realised that people would rather travel with an airplane full of vampires if they had reasonable legroom.

"It was good to see you," Drest said as Miles reached the door to his study.

Miles smiled. "It's been far too long," he admitted. "I'll make sure that it doesn't take years next time. Danica, it was a pleasure."

Miles left the building with Church beside him, only to hear Charlotte call after him. She caught up to him as he stepped onto the gravel driveway.

"Are you going to tell Umbra about your plans?" she asked him.

Miles shook his head and the pair set off toward his temporary accommodation. "Not unless I have to. I might not care about making friends, but I'd rather not make enemies unless necessary."

Charlotte and Miles stopped outside of the building he was staying in, and they hugged.

"Come back soon," Charlotte said. "It's been nice having you around again. Even if it was only a fleeting visit."

"I will do my best," Miles promised. He'd not really been looking forward to his return to Affric Estate, but it had turned out better than he'd hoped, even with his time spent in Gideon's company, and having to put up with Vedran's behaviour. He had a long flight ahead of him, into possibly dangerous territory. A possible serial killer he was under no illusions he wasn't to touch, a gangster who worked for someone who had the power to corrupt minds, and a human spy. Shitty things always did come in threes.

PART TWO

Liam Fricker *hated* vampires, and was happy to tell everyone he met that fact whether they'd asked or not.

He hadn't always hated them. When he'd been a young man in the early nineties, his dad had worked for a gang working out of Los Angeles. The gang—Mortis—had run the city's crime industry and his dad had been a valuable member of the gang. The gang was led by vampires, but most of the on the ground grunt work was carried out by humans like Liam's dad.

The LAPD, the Assembly, the FBI, and several other three-letter agencies had put together a task force designed to cripple the gang until it was extinct. Liam's dad had told him it would be fine, but it turned out that Liam's dad was either really naive, optimistic to an extreme level, or a moron. In Liam's mind, probably more the latter than the others.

The task force had broken the small guys and moved up the chain until one of the vampires at the top had flipped on everyone else. It had taken a few years, but the empire that Mortis had created was gone by the beginning of the new millennium. Those at the really low levels of the gang flipped on those higher up, and those at the top end flipped on everyone directly below them.

Those in the middle ground of the Mortis gang, a place where Liam's dad worked, were decimated. Almost a hundred percent of human employees were either arrested or killed in raids, and those who were arrested had the book thrown at them in court.

Any vampires behind the gang vanished, with most of the surviving gang members and their families thinking they had gotten away with it purely because they were vampires, and vampires keep their own safe.

In actuality, the vampires were found by the Assembly and either executed or placed in long-term stasis, but Liam hadn't known that at the time, and even when he'd discovered it years later, it hadn't mattered. By then Liam's dad had been sentenced to life in prison for the murders he'd been a part of, and twelve years after that, he'd been murdered himself in a prison riot. All of that, in Liam's mind, was the fault of the vampires.

Liam had wanted someone to blame, and blame he did, hating vampires with a passion for decades. His hate had only grown when his mom had died a decade later from a stroke. If pressed, that was the fault of vampires, too—although he had difficulty explaining it. Also the fault of vampires were his lack of wealth, his prison record, the fact that his wife had left him. Every bad thing in his life was, to his way of thinking, the fault of vampires, as though they'd cursed him and his family.

He'd met like-minded men and women, people who did what the government and law enforcement refused to do. He'd spent time online arguing with people who branded him a bigot, who said that the organisations he belonged to were just peddling hate and violence.

Of course they were peddling hate and violence—it was all the humans had left. The vampires controlled pretty much everything else. They ran the countries, they started and ended wars, they spread disease. They needed to control humans because humanity outnumbered them, and if they ever rose up, the vampires would be overthrown.

Fortress Falls was a town that had its fair share of vampires and their pets—a term his allies had come up with to describe those humans who willingly worked alongside vampires—but it had a rebellious core. The Red Demon bar was on the outskirts of town, a place where those who knew the truth could meet like-minded individuals to talk about the state of the world while having a few beers.

Sometimes it was just talk. Just a way to vent and let off steam at a system, a country, a world that appeared designed to ensure that people like them were always kept in their place. Sometimes, it went beyond talking.

There was a group in the bar whom Liam had known since his late teen years, when he'd met them at college, when they all realised how much their lives had been impacted by the vampire menace. They'd stayed friends throughout the years, all of them remaining in Washington state. Their bitterness had grown in leaps and bounds with every setback. And occasionally, that bitterness led them to drive to a vampire neighbourhood in Seattle, or

Newcastle, or any of the smaller towns and villages throughout the state, and exact . . . retribution. They weren't stupid enough to physically attack a vampire—that would leave evidence of them being there—but setting a vampire business alight or posting anti-vampire rhetoric around town, well, that was just getting even. Taking back—in Liam's mind—control of his streets, of his country.

Several weeks earlier, Liam had helped his friend deal with a problem. The problem hadn't involved vampires, but there was a good way to make people think vampires were involved. Sometimes it felt as if his little group of friends were the only right-minded people in the country. That the vampires had infested every part of humanity, chipping away at those parts that made them human.

The serial killer vampire was a godsend to the people of the Red Demon. Now they had tangible proof that the vampires were monsters. Not just hearsay and rumour, but an actual vampire murderer in their midst. A lot of them were almost giddy about the idea. Some were annoyed that the serial killer hadn't gone far enough, hadn't made a *show* of it. They hoped for more murders, for the victims to be found in increasingly horrific ways.

Some of the Red Demon members had wanted to turn vigilante, to hunt the monster down, but the moment they'd suggested it to members of the Magistrate who frequented the bar, they'd been forcefully shot down. Blake Summer, the leader of the Magistrate in Washington state, had made it very clear that any vigilante activity would be met with *severe* punishments.

Liam knew that it had annoyed some of the Red Demon regulars for some time after, and Liam had wanted to explain what was *really* going on, but he'd kept it to himself. Thankfully, they understood that Blake had a job to do to keep humans safe, and the last thing they needed was for anyone to start making that harder. Besides, the vampires didn't need the good publicity of someone getting hurt who had no involvement.

He'd worked with the Magistrate in secret and had done everything asked of him. It felt like humanity finally taking a stand against their oppressors. He'd been on a high for most of the day after the first killing, tinged with fear of someone knocking on his door. He'd slept with his shotgun at arm's reach for several days. And even now, a few weeks later, he was on his toes. He wasn't going to get caught out by any vampire-loving assholes.

He left the Red Demon early in the morning to the sounds of his fellow humans cheering him, as if he were their champion warrior. He felt like a warrior. It was a feeling he hadn't had since he'd played high school football, until he'd blown out his knee and had to settle for the life he found himself in.

It was just starting to get dark, and some of the bar's regulars had teased him about the vampire serial killer, but Liam wasn't worried. He was a big man at over six and a half feet and had maintained his bulk over the years. He'd done mixed martial arts—MMA— for many years, with only his temperament keeping him back, so people said, although Liam was pretty sure people were just jealous of his abilities.

He danced from foot to foot as he walked along the increasingly dark road toward his current home. The sun had almost set completely, and people had all run home, afraid of the 'serial killer' stalking their midst. Liam had almost laughed at the idea, but instead had just told the bar that he refused to be afraid of a single vampire. He lived close to the outskirts of town, in a small wooden cabin that he told people he'd helped build himself, though in reality he'd never made anything in his entire life. It had its own power and was far enough out of the way, with enough cameras and traps that he would know if anyone was sneaking up on him.

Liam had made it halfway into his two-kilometer walk when he'd passed by the old church that was long since in disrepair. Liam looked up at the church building. It was lit by a single streetlamp, and even in the dark you could tell it was not a place anyone should want to spend time.

He remembered when it had been struck by lightning, almost burned down, and become so damaged that it had to be abandoned. That had been what, fifteen years now? For a while it had been a haven for everyone who needed somewhere to go to misbehave. A little gang hideout, littered with the sellers and buyers of illicit materials. The cops had shut that down, and the dealers had found easier and frankly warmer places to deal than the dilapidated building.

"Liam." The voice was softly spoken.

Liam looked around at the darkness of the forest on either side of the road and saw nothing.

"Oh, Liam," the voice said again.

"Fuck you," Liam said, pulling a switchblade from his pocket, pressing the button and enjoying the sound of the blade flicking out. "Why don't you come over here and try to freak me out in person?"

There was a chuckle caught on the cold wind that swept along the dark road.

"That's right, motherfucker," Liam shouted.

He turned and the thing was right there, on him in a second, pulling him to the ground with arms that were far too strong for how little muscle they appeared to have. It wrapped itself around Liam, choking him out as Liam tried to thrash, tried to stab, until his vision went dark and the fight left him.

Liam woke with a start, looking around as his night vision took in his surroundings. He sat up against a wall in a room inside the church. He knew he was inside the church as the roof was partially missing, and he'd spent enough time in there smoking various substances to know what it looked like, even in the dark after so many years away.

"Hello, Liam," the voice from earlier said.

Two people walked into the room. One was male, and he walked in sniffing the air, looking around as if everything that was happening was perfectly normal.

Liam stared at the man's face. It was inhuman, its cheeks sunken, its eyes like two hot pits of burning red. A vampire.

"Keep that freak away from me," Liam said and tried to get away, but it was impossible. He couldn't move anything from the neck down.

"I won't kill you," the male vampire told him, crouching down beside Liam. "Just keep still."

"Fuck are you?" Liam shouted.

"Shush," the male vampire said. "You might learn something."

The second person wore a hooded cloak, shrouding their face in darkness. They placed a gloved hand on the head of the male vampire, their long fingers moving over the skull of the vampire, across his eyes. It was obvious to Liam that they were in charge, simply because of the presence they held.

"You are the guest of someone much more powerful than you can imagine," the crouched vampire said. "If you interrupt again, you might not learn why we came here."

Liam began to feel genuine fear as he knew there were two vampires before him. A master and servant.

"You're his master?" Liam snapped. "You don't talk yourself?"

The crouched vampire slapped Liam across the face, just hard enough to hurt but do no lasting damage. "Do you not understand how to shut up?" the vampire asked.

"Why am I here?" Liam demanded, blood trickling down from his split lip. "What do you want?"

"You did bad things, Liam," the crouched vampire continued. "I am here for your confession."

"Fuck you," Liam said, and spat at the vampire, the blood landing on his lapel.

The crouched down vampire wiped the blood away with the back of his hand. "I would listen and answer," he said. "It's better that way."

"Vampire scum," Liam barked.

The vampire sighed and moved away, toward the second, still silent. "I do not believe he understands his predicament."

The standing creature leaned back up against the wall, as if the act of standing was too much for it.

"Look down at your hands, Liam," the vampire said, his voice returning to the echoing creepiness.

Liam looked down at his hands but couldn't move them, couldn't see them in the light.

"Ah, I do apologise," the vampire said, removing a torch from his pocket and shining it on Liam's hands.

"See them now?" the creature asked, still using its servant to talk.

Liam looked down and for a moment couldn't comprehend what he was seeing. His hands were palms up, but they were covered in blood. It took his brain a second to figure out that he had no fingers. All of them had been torn off from the knuckle, leaving jagged lumps of bone and flesh where his digits had once been. Blood poured out of the horrific wounds.

"No, no, no, no, no," Liam said. "What did you do?"

"You are going to die here, Liam Fricker," an echo-like voice said. "I just wanted to hear you say sorry."

"You tore my fingers off," Liam said. "You tore them off. My fingers. Why?"

"I think you broke him," the crouched vampire said, looking up at the still hooded presence behind him, as Liam's sobs of horror tore through the still night.

The hooded creature chuckled to itself, walked over to Liam, and crouched beside him, the vampire following.

"You tore my fingers off," Liam said.

"And I made sure that you felt no pain," the creature said, its voice deep and echoing. "My blood ensured you felt no pain. You do not deserve to use those again."

"You fed me vampire blood?" Liam practically screamed.

The creature laughed. "I want you to know something, Liam. You should say sorry."

"For what?" Liam shouted through cries of anguish.

The creature pulled back its hood, and Liam's sobs increased as he looked upon its face.

"I'm so sorry," Liam said.

"Good," the creature said with a smile. "That's good."

Its arm shot forward faster than Liam could recognise, and the creature lifted Liam off the ground with one arm, the human's feet dragging against the ruined stonework of the church.

"It's late," the creature said to Liam. "You will be the first; you will be better in death than you ever could have been in life."

The creature increased the pressure around Liam's throat, tearing it out in one movement, watching the man crumble to the ground face first.

It crouched down beside Liam and watched the man die. It turned to the vampire standing nearby. "This is the start of it, Oliver. I am . . . I am tired. I should not have left my sleep to extract revenge. It was a risk I had to take, but you will have to do the rest alone for now. Is that okay? I can't do this without you, Oliver."

Oliver nodded. "They deserve what's going to happen to them," he said. "I will ensure that you are safe until the time comes for you to do what is needed."

"I had to balance myself earlier, my hand on your head," the creature said. "Thank you for that."

Oliver placed a hand on his master's shoulder. The creature wasn't *technically* Oliver's master, but it was easier for him to consider them that way. "Any time you need me," Oliver said.

The creature stood and looked down at the dead man, before slashing across his face with lightning speed, their razor-sharp talons cutting through flesh with ease. "We have much to do tonight before I can rest," they said. "We have much to prepare for. Are you ready, Oliver?"

"I will follow you into hell itself," Oliver said, and was surprised that he actually meant it.

The creature looked down at him and smiled. Oliver had helped save them when their life had been in jeopardy. He'd ensured they hadn't just lived, but thrived. They owed Oliver much, and they would ensure that when everything was done, he was given whatever reward he desired.

CHAPTER FOURTEEN

The ten-hour flight from London to Victoria was a pleasant one. It was quiet, the closed windows keeping the UV light out, while the warm lighting inside kept everyone relaxed. Miles had needed to buy one seat for himself and one for Church. Thankfully, his Arbiter credentials, and the fact that they were flying on a vampire airline, gave him a lot of leeway, although he'd still had to talk to the captain and promise that Church was used to flying.

Thankfully, Church's vampiric physiology—combined with Miles's status within the Assembly—meant that she bypassed all quarantine regulations for pretty much every country.

After takeoff, the flight crew had been more than happy to make a fuss over Church, and by extension Miles. Free drinks and food are never a bad thing.

It used to be that flying from the UK to Victoria meant you had to stop somewhere to change planes, but since Victoria was such an important destination for vampires, the vampire-friendly airlines flew from the UK to Victoria nonstop.

Charlotte had sent him a file on Oliver McCarthy—including a photo—although what was there wasn't exactly full of detail. Born just before World War Two, escaped France, moved to Amsterdam, escaped Amsterdam, and moved to America, before finally settling in California with his sister. He went to school, got a college education, and promptly vanished off the face of the earth. The next data Charlotte had found was forty years later, when a now vampire Oliver was arrested in Berlin for extortion. He was released without charge, although it sounded as though the German police had a good case. Whoever Oliver worked for had money or influence, quite possibly both. Which would explain why he'd run halfway across the globe to get away from them.

At some point, the weather had turned from cold with a sprinkling of snow to something much colder, with a large snow front moving in from the north. The captain of the plane had explained that it was unlikely to get to Victoria until a day or two, but that meant Miles had to get done in Victoria what needed doing, so he could continue on to Fortress Falls before he got snowed in.

The plane touched down, and after making his way through the airport terminal with Church beside him, Miles got into a cab and took the twenty-five-minute car ride into downtown Victoria.

The cab stopped outside of the Empress Hotel, which had been purchased by the Assembly a few decades earlier. A secondary building had been built onto the original, which was designed for vampires and their human companions to stay. The large number of security guards who resided around the interior of the hotel, and an equal number outside the front and rear entrances, made anyone think twice before starting trouble inside the hotel.

A conference centre had been built at the rear of the hotel, which was used mostly by the Assembly for activities within the community, bringing vampires and humans together. Vampire Island was run by vampires for the most part, but without human help it simply wouldn't work, and maintaining that level of balance between the two species was an important part of Assembly life.

"Miles," a voice shouted from the balcony above.

"Anya?" Miles asked, a little surprised to see her, considering that when he'd called her before getting on the plane, Anya had said she was going to be in meetings and might not be around when Miles arrived.

"Wait right there," Anya said and jogged down the stairs toward him.

Anya wore a teal salwar suit. The suit was covered in intricate silver embroidery, and she carried a matching silk dupatta, which was draped over one shoulder. She wore golden high heels, which meant she was a few inches over five feet in height, and her long dark hair curled down around her shoulders.

Miles bowed his head slightly. "It's a pleasure, as always," he said.

"Liar," Anya said with a warm smile, before hugging Miles tightly. "We need to talk. Where's that dog of yours?"

"She spent ten hours on a plane," Miles said.

"Ah, she can find us then. Come," Anya said, linking her arm through Miles's as the pair walked down the hallway. They stopped outside of a conference room. "This will do."

Anya opened the door, which activated the lights, bathing everything in a warm glow. There were desks inside the room, all positioned toward one direction, where a protector screen was set up.

"Meetings?" Miles asked.

"Who knows," Anya said. "I figured it best to talk to you before you head off to Fortress Falls and walk straight into trouble."

"What trouble?" Miles asked.

"There's a missing Magistrate member," Anya said. "Police report was filed about six hours ago. She's been missing five days, went running apparently and never came home. It was considered that she'd run off—extramarital affair perhaps—but now they're saying she might be a victim of this serial murderer."

"That is news to me," Miles said, lying through his teeth and trying to figure out why the husband would want to file a report *now*. Why wait five days?

Anya said, "You're not here to investigate that, right?"

Miles shook his head. "Looking for a criminal, not a human woman, although guess that may change if it turns out she's a victim of a vampire serial killer. Any news on that?"

"Right now, the Magistrate have sent people to Fortress Falls to investigate, but they're keeping whatever findings they have close to their vest," Anya said. "Weirdly close, if you get my meaning."

"You think something is going on?" Miles asked.

"Where the Magistrate are involved, I do," she told him. "Three bodies, all drained of blood, all on the main roads outside of the town itself. The wife of a police detective and someone who works for them goes missing, and if it turns out she's a victim of a vampire killing—we're all in deep shit. Whatever is going on, tread carefully; they hate us, and any excuse to make tensions between us increase will be jumped upon with gusto."

"Yeah, we've met," Miles said. "Are the House Umbra people in Seattle official?"

"Yes," Anya said. "However, we got word this morning that a number of House Umbra vampires are being sent to Seattle."

"They moved fast, considering they only got a confession two days ago," Miles said. "No idea why they'd think this Boss character is in Seattle, although I'm sure they know best."

"Whatever it is, Umbra really wants to find this Boss, but I doubt very much it's to find him and bring his crimes into the light for all to see," Anya said. "They're here to find him and make sure he stays shut up."

"You think this Boss is House Umbra?" Miles asked, voicing his own suspicions.

Anya nodded. "And I know you do, too. Bit too much of a coincidence that these crimes were committed, someone drives from London to Scotland to hand themselves in personally, and then House Umbra sends people to Seattle to look for this man when they have people already stationed in Victoria. My guess is whoever is coming isn't low down the pecking order. Be careful. The Assembly cannot be seen to overly attacking one of the Great Houses. That means if you have to subdue one, don't do it officially. And do it quietly."

"Anything else?" Miles asked.

"You're a gigantic pain in my arse," Anya said. "But don't get killed. Don't go to Seattle yet either. Although I'm going to assume you didn't plan to, anyway."

Miles smiled. "I do not. I'm searching for one Oliver McCarthy, who is, at best guess, in Fortress Falls. He may be involved in an illegal vampire creation operation; most of the gang affiliated with him are currently in Assembly custody. Anything else happening in that town has nothing to do with why I'm here. I will not be stepping on any toes, or getting into arguments about who can do what."

Anya nodded. "Translation: I don't want to know the whole story, do I?"

Miles shook his head. "Trust me on this. I didn't want to know."

"If whatever Drest told you bites you on the arse, it's just you. Right?" Anya said.

"It won't come back to you, I promise," Miles assured her. "I don't have to work with, or be involved with, the Magistrate's investigation at all. Nothing to do with me or why I'm there. Whatever murders they're looking into are all theirs."

"Why do I sense there's a *but* in all of that?" Anya asked.

"If I discover anything that takes my investigation into the same path as the Magistrate, I can step in, or if vampires are directly in danger, take over," Miles said. "Or if any desolate are created."

Anya nodded along as if running things through her head to see how often they might blow up in the face of the Assembly. When satisfied, she said, "I'll make sure that anyone trying to suggest you're interfering in House Umbra or Magistrate business is corrected. You're not going to Seattle, you're not involved in these murders. Everything should be fine. Just don't mention any desolate to anyone in Fortress Falls."

"You sure?" Miles asked sarcastically. "Because I figured they'd be thrilled to be told about it."

Anya pointed an elegant finger in Miles's direction. "No," she said. "Don't be a smart arse on this, Miles. Find this Oliver guy and get him out of that town before it turns into a pressure cooker."

"I'm on it, Boss," Miles said.

"And don't call me Boss," Anya said. "It sounds patronising when you say it."

Miles stood and walked to the door.

"Miles, one thing," Anya said.

Miles stopped at the doorway and turned back.

"Be careful," Anya said. "Taking out the fact that there's a Magistrate team in Fortress Falls, and taking out the fact that they got there awfully fast after the first body. Certainly faster than the Assembly could have, considering it wasn't even private knowledge that the body was killed by a vampire. Well, leaving all that aside, you're not immortal. I don't want a dead Arbiter on my conscience. And I definitely don't want to have to deal with your dog."

"I will," Miles assured her. "I'll contact you when I know something."

"The helicopter is waiting for you at the nearby heliport," Anya said. "Car is outside waiting for you."

Miles thanked Anya and left the hotel, finding Church sitting on the steps outside drinking from a bowl of water. With the dog alongside him, they walked down to the street level where a man in a dark suit waited with the door to a Bentley Continental already open.

Church jumped inside first, with Miles nodding a thanks to the driver, who closed the door behind him.

It didn't take long for the drive to the heliport, where a blue-and-white-striped Bell 430 sat on the tarmac waiting for them, and they were soon airborne.

"Whereabouts are we landing?" Miles asked through the microphone he wore on his headset.

"There's a big strip of land near the town," the pilot said. "It's not owned by anyone and isn't close to anything. There's a car dealership nearby, I believe your friends in the Assembly have already arranged you a ride. You just need to go pick it up. There's something in the pocket of the chair."

Miles removed the small envelope from the rear of the chair and opened it, removing a set of keys and an address: 21767 89th Street Northeast. There was a small map, and someone had written *10 minutes' drive from the dealership* in green pen beside it. Miles laughed to himself; Anya had been aware of everything well before he'd ever landed in Victoria.

The flight didn't take long, but it did allow Miles the chance to watch the incredible scenery below as they flew over the Canadian–US border in the Salish Sea. He logged into his closed Arbiter system, found the police report for the missing Lauren Gibson, and settled in to read.

It didn't take long. The report said that Lauren had been taken while running in the forest behind her house, which she did every day. According to the town website, there were paths through parts of the woodlands closest to the town that had trails for bike riders, runners, and hikers, and they were regularly used. There was no mention of why it had taken so long for a report to be filed, or what evidence they had to suggest she might be a victim of a serial killer, but the timing of the whole thing was off.

Miles put his phone away and resumed looking out of the window. He couldn't remember the names of all the places they flew over, but as they flew over deep forests with nothing even close to civilisation for miles around, he wondered if everyone could just take a break from kidnapping, killing, and generally committing crimes, so he could take a nice holiday.

True to the pilot's word, the helicopter landed in a field to the north of Fortress Falls just as the light outside dipped into dusk. Miles thanked the pilot and got out of the helicopter with Church beside him. The pair ran to the edge of the field and watched the helicopter take to the air.

"Right," Miles said, looking around. The field was large with buildings in the distance. Although from his vantage point it was difficult to make out what any of the buildings actually did, it was pretty obvious that none of them were residential in nature. One of the buildings had cars outside the front of it, which Miles figured was his best bet.

Church ran on ahead as they walked across the field to the nearest road, although *road* was probably pushing it a bit further than the dirt track deserved. The building with the cars was a dealership, so he was right about that, and there was a gun club nearby, along with several manufacturing facilities.

At the dealership, he spoke to a young woman at the front desk who removed a set of keys for a BMW from under the desk and passed them to him.

"It's in the parking lot out front," she said with a smile. "I'll take you. Oh, there's a note here, too."

Miles took the envelope and opened it, reading the note inside.

This is an Assembly owned car—do not break it. When you are done, drive back to Seattle and to our office there, and you will be able to hand it over. I repeat, do not break the car. Go to the local police precinct and ask to talk to Amber. Anya.

The Assembly finances were partially done through bookkeeping at a high government level, partially through funnelling money through other governmental agencies, and partially through a number of vampires who owned large swathes of land, and companies, in many countries.

The dealership woman took Miles out of the showroom with its half dozen mirror polished American muscle cars, and into the parking lot where a white BMW iX waited.

"An electric car?" Miles asked.

"It's the iX M60," she explained. "It's got a range of just under four hundred miles on a single charge."

"Any chance Fortress Falls has a lot of charging stations?" Miles asked.

"Several places do have them, yes," the woman said.

Miles removed the address he'd been given. "How about this?"

"Oh, they're all new builds; they all have solar panels and charging stations," she said.

"Well, thank you for your help," Miles said, putting the piece of paper away and pressing the unlock button on the key fob.

It took Miles a look at the handbook and five minutes to figure out how everything worked, before he set up the car how he liked it and set off. The city really was quite picturesque with a lot of large houses amid a large expanse of nature. The plane ride had given him the chance to read about the area.

It had been a small city for a long time, until early 2020, when it had become a big deal after a number of land developers did what land developers do. The incoming population over the next few years had gone from a little over five thousand to more than four times that. The town had grown in all directions, although mostly north, but it had meant that in five years the town had changed in ways that no one who had lived there in 2020 would have ever considered. Nor probably wanted.

Miles found the drive to be a useful one, purposefully taking the time to drive around the town to get the lie of the land. The hospital was only a few years old; it practically gleamed as he drove by.

There were the two local diners, good for food and as a local hub of information. Miles continued on to the police station. It too was new, created by the land developer, hopefully not run by it as well.

The final place on his list was the home of Lauren Gibson.

Miles parked the car and got out, letting Church out, who sat beside the car seemingly indifferent to everything. Miles scanned down the suburban street, looking at the near identical houses, as if the designer had just used control-C, control-V on the entire street. While it was still cold, the temperature had warmed enough to melt most of the snow in town, although with a forecast of an imminent snowstorm, that was likely to change quickly.

The road was quiet, with most driveways empty, presumably as the majority of people who lived in Fortress Falls didn't actually work there and had to commute from places like Seattle. Just close enough to a main town to get the amenities, but far enough away to not be bothered by the crush of people.

Each house was detached, with a drive and large garage. The Gibson residence had a pathway going along the side of the house with an eight-foot metal gate stopping anyone from being able to access the back garden.

As it wasn't officially a missing persons case until someone actually reported her missing, there was very little to go on where Lauren had been the day of her disappearance. Miles wondered if the town was full of good ol' boys covering for one another in the police force, and if they'd been involved in her disappearance. If someone had found something they couldn't keep quiet. The report was lacking detail, and considering one of the police was married to the missing woman, had no sense of urgency to it.

Miles walked the length of the street, Church happily trotting along in front, occasionally stopping to sniff. The end of the road banked to the left and continued on for several hundred meters, until it stopped at a small parking area next to a well-marked signpost indicating the trail for joggers and hikers. There were four cars parked and half a dozen people leaving the trail.

The sun had finished for the day, and with the darkness came a cold wind that whipped across the car park.

From having read the case report, Miles knew that Lauren had last been seen jogging at four in the afternoon. A few hours prior to the current time. Apparently, there were no witnesses of the crime; the only evidence was one of her shoes found on the trail. There wasn't even a name on the report of the person who had actually last seen her.

Church sat beside Miles and made a pitiful whining noise.

Miles looked down at her. "You hungry?" he asked.

Church nodded, snorted, and whined again.

"Yeah, okay, *very* hungry," Miles said, removing a dog chew from his pocket and tossing it to an appreciative Church. "Let's get a look at this trail, and we'll head back for food. We need to go find this Yvonne, too."

Miles and Church continued on along the trail into the forest. It was a pleasant walk, and after a few hundred meters there was a sign showing left for a more difficult trail or right for the easier one. Miles checked the notes that he'd been given on the case and discovered that Lauren ran the easier trail every day. It was in the report her detective husband had given to police. No indication that's where she was taken, just an inference.

The trail undulated with the land moving farther and farther north into ever increasingly dense woodland. The pair had been walking for several minutes, with Church bounding through the woodlands like a puppy, when she stopped running and sniffed the air. She sniffed again and looked back at Miles as he caught her up, and he immediately knew what she was smelling. Blood. Lots of blood. Human blood.

❧ CHAPTER FIFTEEN ❧

Miles and Church followed the scent of mostly stale blood, walking through dense woodland, ignoring the trail completely as the smell became increasingly overwhelming. The terrain was difficult and more than once it appeared that nature itself was trying to stop them from continuing, but Church ploughed through anything in her path at high speed, with Miles following a short distance behind, his night vision making sure he didn't fall over an errant tree root.

After a few minutes of walking, the pair reached a road. There were no lights on the road and only one building, which stood opposite where Miles and Church exited the woodlands. The building itself had been an old church, with emphasis on the word "had." The roof of the church was partially missing, and Miles could see the exposed wooden beams beneath it.

"Be careful," Miles told Church, who effortlessly leapt over the stone wall into the churchyard beyond.

Miles used the open gate, which creaked loudly as it was opened and sprang back into place the second he let go.

Miles looked around the land at the front of the church. There were several bushes and large trees littering the sides of the church ground, with most of them having become overgrown, and in the case of the trees, gangly. The closer Miles got to the church entrance, the stronger the smell of blood.

"Check the outside," Miles said to Church, who bounded off into the darkness surrounding the sorry state of the church.

The large wooden double doors were still in place, but the hinges were twisted and broken, leaving one door jutting out at an awkward angle. Most of the building's windows were broken, with only a few remaining.

Miles reached the front doors and pulled one back, which came away in his hand and fell to the ground with a crash. "Bollocks."

Stepping into the building, the smell of blood became almost overwhelming, and Miles took a deep breath to steady himself.

Religious imagery did nothing to vampires. No vampire recoiled from a cross, or anything else for that matter. Quite a few vampires still believed in their religion, still practised, still felt close to their beliefs. Miles didn't, but then he'd been raised by his grandparents who were God-fearing, which to Miles meant fear and/or hate of anything they didn't like or understand, which was pretty much everything. Miles had rebelled hard against that level of negativity in his life, so religion and belief were things he had little interest in.

The church entrance led into a nave, which was covered in the remains of wooden pews, bits of debris, and plant life. The windows on either side of the building were gone, with the plant life from outside making its way into the church. This building had been reclaimed by nature.

There was a door at the side of the nave which was missing, but that's where the blood came from, so that was where Miles headed. There was nothing of value inside the skeletal remains of the church. Miles noticed scorch marks on the floor and walls, and several of the destroyed pews were badly burned. He had no idea what had happened in the building, but it couldn't have been good.

Bloody footsteps led out of the door, across the nave, and out of a destroyed window on the opposite side. Miles bent down and touched one of the footsteps. The cold had stopped it from aging normally, but the smell alone suggested it had been a day since this had happened.

Miles sniffed the blood on his fingers. Definitely human. If he wanted to, he could taste the blood and find out rudimentary information about whoever it belonged to, but he wasn't entirely sure it was a wise first course of action. Seeing flashes of memory was disorienting at best.

He walked through the broken doorway and into what had presumably been a kitchen lounge at some point. There were old fixtures for a sink in the corner, and a wardrobe had been pulled down onto the ground; a large brown rat sat on it, looking at Miles as if daring him to say something.

"It's your home, buddy," Miles said to the rat, who darted off into the darkness of the room.

The only other door in the lounge was ajar, and the bloody footprints led into it.

Miles pushed open the door and . . . took a moment to figure out what he was seeing.

There was a lot of dark blood, some congealed and some dried. It covered almost every surface of the dilapidated room; even the ceiling was splattered with it. A large tree branch had, at some point, come through the only window in the room, decided it was happy, and continued to grow up and across the rear of the room.

Beneath the branch, lying on the floor in a pool of his own blood, were the remains of a human male. He was large—over six and a half feet, with a muscular physique that would have been imposing when he was alive, but with his body face down, it was impossible to say more. He wore jeans, no shoes, one sock, and a T-shirt that, whatever the original colour, was now red.

Miles ignored the gore splatter and stepped over a large pool of blood, kneeling down by the victim and turning him over.

He was maybe early forties. His throat had been . . . removed, torn out completely, right to the spine in places. There were slashes down either side of the man's face, some so deep that Miles could see bone, as his attacker had held on tightly. They'd removed one eye, and done enough damage to the features that Miles doubted the victim would be identifiable on look alone. Something had slashed across his face, removing his nose, lips, and large amounts of flesh. The victim had no fingers, just jagged lumps of bone and flesh where the tips had once been. Someone had taken the time to snap off each finger instead of just taking the hands.

The vampire who had killed him had allowed their power out, allowed their nails to grow into razor-sharp talons. All vampires could do it, although most only did so when fighting. Feeding in this way was . . . horrific. This was more about the violence perpetrated on the victim than any actual need for blood. Miles shuddered. He'd hunted his fair share of vampires who killed like this. He'd taken their lives and moved on without another thought. When someone was so . . . feral, there was little more to be done than put them down. The fingers, that was different. Was this to make identification difficult? Or was this just personal to them?

Miles quickly searched the room but found no belongings that identified the victim. He searched the man's pockets and found nothing there either. Was he a vagrant living in the church? Doubtful, as his jeans were an expensive designer pair, his hair and beard were well maintained, and they had a floral scent to them that Miles could make out, albeit faintly, considering there was so much blood.

There were tattoos covering the man's chest, both of his arms, the backs of his hands, and his neck. Most were just a mishmash of various tattoo styles: classic American, tribal, Japanese, and black and grey all made an appearance. So the face and fingers weren't to stop identification. They were for personal reasons.

At that moment Miles realised that despite his earlier introduction to the rats living in the shell of the building, none had come into the room. Not even after the body had been left alone. There were no insects either. Whatever had happened here had tainted the area badly enough to keep animals away.

There was a crash inside the nave, which Miles attributed to Church, and he left the body and the room just in time for a flashlight to be shone in his face.

"Hands up," a man shouted.

"I'm an Arbiter," Miles explained without putting his hands up.

"I said put your fucking hands up," the man shouted again, keeping the flashlight directly in Miles's eyes.

"You don't know what an Arbiter is, do you?" Miles asked.

"Do you know what being under arrest is?" a second man asked as he aimed his gun at Miles.

"Whatever happens, don't get involved," Miles said, knowing Church was just outside and could hear him. "Just follow to the police precinct. I do not want them trying to shoot you."

"Excuse me," one of the police officers asked as the flashlight was removed from trying to blind Miles. "Who are you talking to?"

The two officers were both male, both tall, both bald, and both looking as if they were wearing a shirt that was a size too small. One was black with a small beard, while the other was white with both arms covered in tattoos, including the Army Rangers insignia.

"Just surmising the awkward situation we find ourselves in," Miles said. "It's a bit of a coincidence that you've just arrived."

"We saw the car parked outside of the Gibson house," the black officer said. "Followed through the woods, heard noises in here."

"Well, then this has all been quite the good timing," Miles said. "Saves me a phone call."

"Is that blood on your hands, sir?" the black officer asked; his polished nameplate said his surname was Sheringham.

"Officer Sheringham," Miles said. "The victim is in the room behind me, young male, early forties; he's had his throat torn out." He looked at the name tag on the white officer: Shilton.

"Shilton and Sheringham," Miles said with a smile. He looked down at Officer Shilton's hand, which still rested on his holster. "You came here expecting trouble, didn't you?"

"Did you kill him?" Officer Shilton demanded to know.

"No, dumbass," Miles snapped.

"You're not from around here," Officer Shilton continued, irritation in his voice.

"I am an Arbiter from the Assembly," Miles explained. "I'm here because there's a vampire I'm tracking from London. He was last seen in town."

"Why were you at the Gibson house?" Officer Shilton asked.

"I wanted to drive around, get to know the place," Miles said. "I've been told you've had some murders in the area."

"The Magistrate are looking into it," Shilton said, with what Miles thought was a little more pride than he'd expect.

"I heard," Miles replied.

"You seem to know a lot," Officer Shilton said. "Move away from the door."

"You seem to know next to nothing," Miles replied, but stepped away.

Officer Sheringham walked up to the doorway and paused; he didn't look thrilled about what he was going to find.

"You seen a dead body before?" Miles asked.

"My partner didn't ask your opinion," Officer Shilton said.

"Look," Miles said, completely ignoring Shilton. "What's in there is bad. Real bad. Get people here who can process the room."

"Are you telling us our jobs?" Shilton snapped.

"Well, neither of you seem to have a clue what you're doing," Miles snapped back. He knew he shouldn't, but he didn't like being talked down to, and he definitely didn't like people pointing a gun at him.

"We're going to take you down to the precinct and we can run your name," Shilton said as Sheringham walked through to see the body. He didn't stay in there long.

"You okay?" Miles asked.

"Whoever did that was an animal," Sheringham said.

"And this asshole has blood on his hands," Shilton said. "Looks like we've got our murderer."

"I can't believe that neither of you know what an Arbiter is," Miles said with a sigh, and showed his bracelet. "No, nothing?"

"You could tell us anything," Shilton said. "I don't have to believe you."

"Fine," Miles said. "Take me in, let's have a chat with the Assembly and see how quickly we can get you guys fired."

"Excuse me?" Officer Shilton said, his tone immediately aggressive. "Did you just give me an order, boy?"

"*Boy?*" Miles asked. "Fuck you."

Miles allowed himself to be arrested, his hands cuffed behind his back, after which he was marched outside of the building and put in the back of the police car, a black Dodge Durango with FFPD written down the side in big blue letters.

"This is a nice welcome to the town," Miles said when both officers were back in their patrol car.

"Shut up," Shilton snapped. "We're taking you to the station; you can do your talking there."

"My pleasure," Miles said with a barely suppressed smile.

Miles was taken into the police station, which beyond the reception area and its key code secured door was open plan with the detective's offices in one corner—all three of them, from what Miles could see—and everyone else between the entrance and where they sat. A captain's office was halfway down the bullpen, next to a hallway with the word *Interviews* written above it. Presumably the officers needed reminding.

"Caught this one in the vicinity of a possible murder victim," Sheringham said as Shilton applied pressure to Miles's shoulder, attempting to force him down into an uncomfortable metal chair. Miles allowed himself to be pushed down; he wanted to know if his suspicions were correct before he announced himself. You can tell a lot about someone if they don't have any idea who you are, nor that you know people who could have the whole station shut down and turned into a Starbucks with one phone call.

Apart from the dynamic duo, there were two others, one male and one female, a detective, who was on the phone in her office, and a lady at the reception desk.

"Quiet night?" Miles asked.

"Shut up," Shilton snapped and walked off to the detective's office, knocking twice before going inside and closing the door behind him.

"Can you take these cuffs off?" Miles asked.

"Not yet," Sheringham said without looking up from his computer screen. "We're going to talk about why you were in that church."

"Out here?" Miles asked. "Not in an interview room? Do I get a phone call? Do I get a lawyer? Seriously, what backward, dumbass level of fuckery is going on here?"

"You did what?" The shout came from the detective's office. A second later the door was flung open and a woman walked out. She was five and a half feet tall, with light brown skin, dark brown shoulder-length hair, and several earrings in each ear. She wore jeans, a white T-shirt, and dark brown boots, and her police badge hung around her neck. She radiated anger.

"Sir, are you an Assembly Arbiter?" she asked Miles.

"I am," Miles said.

"My name is Detective Amber Lambert." Amber looked to Officer Shilton with a mixture of disbelief and outright rage. "Get the cuffs off him. Now."

"I did ask nicely," Miles said, snapping the cuffs with a little pressure and holding out his arms in front of him, the two dangling pieces of cuff still attached.

Shilton's eyes went wide, and he unlocked the remains of the cuffs, removing them from Miles's wrists while trying to also keep one eye on Miles.

"I want to give a heartfelt apology from all of us at Fortress Falls PD," Officer Shilton said, keeping his eyes low. "We're all under a lot of pressure at the moment, but that's no excuse."

"Apology accepted," Miles said with a smile, before turning to Amber. "I am not here to get into any investigations you have ongoing. I'm looking into a vampire who might be in the area. I decided to check out the area first and wandered into a horror show."

"Would you like to wash your hands?" Amber asked.

Miles looked down at the dried blood on his hands. "Yeah," he said. "Back in one second." Miles walked back across the floor, through the door to reception, and opened the front door to let Church in, who had been waiting in the shadows at the side of the precinct.

The receptionist let Miles and Church back into the bullpen, and Church went and found a corner to lie down in.

Amber stared at her.

"She's friendly," Miles assured her.

"She's gigantic," Amber said.

"Long story, but she won't bite anyone," Miles said, looking over at Shilton, who was staring at Church with genuine fear. "Don't like dogs, officer?"

"She's just real big," Shilton said without taking his eyes off Church, who was presently ignoring the officer as the receptionist brought over a bowl of water and some treats, both of which were graciously accepted.

"I figured there'd be more of you," Miles said, looking around the bull-pen. "Possible serial killer, etcetera."

"The day shift has more people working here," Amber said. "We don't have anyone working on those cases. They've been taken over."

"The Magistrate," Miles said. "The level of fuckery is high, then."

"They help humans more than your kind do," Shilton snapped.

"Sure they do," Miles said.

"Shilton, go do your job," Amber said, before turning back to Miles. "A word, please."

Miles followed the detective into her office, where she closed the door and motioned for him to take a seat.

The office had two chairs next to each other in front of a large wooden desk, where another more comfortable looking chair sat behind. There was one large window against the wall opposite the door, and two bookshelves next to it. It was about as nice as a detective's office could be.

"You didn't need to break the cuffs," Amber said as she took a seat, and Miles did the same.

"I did not," Miles admitted. "I told both of them more than once who I was, and Shilton drew his gun on me, cuffed me, and was more interested in my humiliation than in actually doing his job. My guess, after his little outburst, that he's a paid-up member of the *we hate vampires club*. How many vampires do you have living in town?"

"The construction crew making the new buildings out of town has vampires to work the nights," Amber said. "And there are a few dozen who live in town full-time, but they tend to keep to themselves."

"Any vampire cops?" Miles asked.

"No," Amber admitted. "We did try to ask for Assembly assistance in this case, but the Magistrate arrived and took control of the investigation."

"Arrived real fast, if I heard correctly," Miles said, wanting to test how much Amber was going to be an asset while he was in town.

"*Real* fast," Amber said. "Precognition levels of fast. The body wasn't even in the morgue."

"What's the lead investigator for the Magistrate like?" Miles asked.

Amber laughed, although it wasn't with any humour. "The lead Magistrate hates vampires. And I mean, just on a personal level. I've met some Magistrate people who just feel like they should have human checks and balances, but Blake Summers straight up *hates* you all. It's made actually getting anywhere in the case a little more complex than I'd like. I've been removed from it, if I'm honest."

"I'm sorry," Miles said. "That sucks. What happened to Lauren? Someone mentioned it earlier. Missing woman, detective's wife, but someone said she ran off with some fancy man."

"Lauren Gibson has never run off with a fancy man her whole life," Amber said, checking back to the door to make sure it was closed. "No idea what's going on there, not my case. She wasn't even a missing person until six hours ago, and now there's talk that she might be the killer's next victim, but with no body, we don't know."

"Her house is awfully close to where that dead body I found is," Miles said. "You want me to take a look into it? I assume the Magistrate aren't linking the two cases."

"Not yet," Amber said. "Can you look into it? I'm not allowed to; it's been made *very* clear to me it's not my case."

Miles remembered that he'd been told not to get *officially* involved in the case unless it was necessary. However, considering how dodgy everything sounded, and how close the Gibson residence was to the body he'd discovered, it was looking as if he was going to have to get involved before the Magistrate did. Which was weird in itself. Why had a report been filed, but the Magistrate not actually taken control of the investigation?

"What's the condition of the other bodies found?" Miles asked. "I assume you know, officially or otherwise."

"No damage to the bodies," Amber said. "Drained completely, but otherwise fine."

"The body in the church was torn to shreds," Miles said. "They're not the same killer."

"We have another killer?" Amber asked.

"Maybe," Miles said. "Who filed the missing person report? There was no name mentioned."

Amber shook her head. "I'm not sure, but can find out for you."

"You going to get in trouble for that?" Miles asked her.

"I'll cross that bridge when I come to it," she said. "Lauren is missing. That's more important. Can you help us find her?"

"Anything else?" Miles asked.

"The Magistrate have suggested that the police here keep an eye out for one Oliver McCarthy," Amber said, moving her monitor to show Miles a picture, which appeared to have been taken from a CCTV camera. "He's a person of interest in Lauren's disappearance, apparently."

Well, ain't that a kick in the nuts, Miles thought to himself. "Any idea why him?" he asked.

"They've not been shy in thinking she's having an affair and run off," Amber said. "And now that they're saying some vampire named Oliver is involved, I don't think it'll be long before they link him to their murders. I think we need to find this Oliver character before they do."

"One second," Miles said, removing his phone from his pocket. He sent an email to Anya, blind copying in Charlotte, saying that he was officially taking control of the Lauren missing person case due to the proximity of the body found that night in the church, which showed signs of a vampire attack, and the fact that rumours were mounting that Lauren was likely to be a victim of the same vampire serial killer.

Miles stopped, read it back, and added, *If it is linked to the Magistrate investigation, I will be happy to share all intel I find with them, and would expect all intel they have to be shared with me. Please let the relevant parties know this change.* He hit *send,* fully aware that at some point, someone in the Magistrate was going to get that email and scream at the screen they read it on.

He sent a second message just to Charlotte: *The Magistrate named Oliver as a person of interest in Lauren's disappearance. This whole thing stinks to high heaven.*

"Okay, I'm now in charge of the Lauren missing person case," Miles said, offering his hand to Amber, which she shook. "I need your help on this case, so as of now, you're my human liaison."

"You work fast," Amber said.

"Missing person cases aren't meant to be tardy," Miles said. He passed her his phone so she could read the email.

"The Magistrate aren't going to like you getting involved," Amber said. "I mean, it's not their case, but I get the feeling they're not going to like you being here at all."

"I know," Miles said. "It's going to be brilliant. How's Officer Dipshit going to take it?"

"Officer Shilton is going to do his job or he can leave," Amber said. "So, do you have a plan of action?"

"I'm going to get some sleep, and a shower, and probably something to eat," Miles said. "Tomorrow afternoon, I'd like to talk to Reese Gibson. Can you arrange that?"

Amber nodded.

"Okay, I have two questions," Miles said. "One, any chance there are people in your town who might take matters into their own hands when they see a vampire walking around?"

"There's a bar in town," Amber said. "It's called the Red Demon; it's an anti-vampire bar. They have a UV light built into the doorframe."

"Which is illegal," Miles said.

"Yes, it is," Amber said. "But any vampire going in there is doing so knowing full well what those people are. There are multiple signs on the front door, there's a mural of a vampire's decapitated head lying next to its body. The only way I'm getting that lighting system out of there is with a SWAT team and some people are going to get hurt on both sides."

"At least you know where the awful people are," Miles said.

"Exactly that," Amber said. "What's the second thing?"

"I'd like to see the details of the murder victims," Miles said. "I assume the Magistrate isn't going to let me just ask for them unless I can say with evidence that Lauren is the killer's next victim. Any chance you can get ahold of copies? Maybe a morgue attendant who owes you?"

"I can do that," Amber said with a smile.

"Good," Miles said, getting to his feet.

Amber wrote something in her notebook and looked back up at Miles. "I've been a cop for twelve years and never encountered this. This is a quiet town."

"And hopefully it will be again," Miles said. "I'm going to need people I can trust, and honestly, you seem to be the most competent person I've met since I arrived here."

"I'm not sure how to take that," Amber said.

"Fair enough," Miles admitted. "Look, I just need help here. Cops I can trust, who don't have a friendship going on with the Magistrate. Something weird is happening in this town, and frankly I think I'm going to have a lot more to do than I'd first considered."

"I would definitely count on that part," Amber said. "You're going to have to deal with them soon, though."

"Aye, but let's cross that especially shitty bridge when we come to it," Miles said. "In the meantime, I'd appreciate a lift back to my car at the Gibson house. I'd really like to go to whatever the Assembly got me as a place to stay so I can get my body clock onto the right time zone. Tomorrow morning, I think we should go talk to a husband who still hasn't bothered to report that his wife is missing."

Chapter Sixteen

The building that Miles had been left to stay in by the Assembly was a little more lavish than he'd been expecting.

It was a ten-minute drive out of town, in a secluded neighbourhood of similarly styled large houses, all with some land between them. Some of the houses were still being built, and there were construction crews still working even late into the night. Miles figured they were probably the vampires that Amber had been talking about, but they were far enough away from his property that noise was limited.

Miles pulled up outside the dark house and opened the front door, finding a basket waiting inside with instructions for the alarm, the garage door, and even the large TV in the living room. Anya had thought of everything.

After a quick tour of the house, and discovering that it had five bedrooms, a library, and an indoor swimming pool, Miles opened the garage and drove the BMW inside, relieved to see that it already had a charging port for an electric vehicle.

When Miles was born, people had used a horse, or horse and cart. It had been several centuries before the combustion engine had been created, and several decades more before cars were little more than a death traps on wheels. Plugging the car into the house just felt like another in a long list of things that he'd never even considered a possibility as a human.

The rear of the property overlooked more forest, which was definitely the theme of the town, but the garden was large enough for Church to run around in, something she was keen to try out.

Miles let Church run laps and continued on through the house, finding a well-stocked gym with weights and punch bags, which were designed for vampire use. He got changed and worked out for an hour.

When he was done, instead of showering, he left the house—making sure to lock up and set the alarm as per the instructions—and went for a run through the forest, pushing himself as the elevation increased, until he started up a hiking trail of a mountain. He stopped about halfway up, overlooking the beautiful vista before him, and took a moment to calm his heart rate.

Arriving back at the house, he found Church waiting for him on the decking in the garden.

Miles showered and just about managed to make it to his bed before falling into a deep sleep.

His dreams were more of the same violent imagery as before, but this time they were of a multitude of dead and dying, of Miles fighting for his life against a mass of overwhelming power. A suffocating, crushing power that had no form, just . . . darkness.

Miles sat up, his dreams staying with him as he went downstairs, filled the expensive-looking coffee percolator with beans and water, removed some butter and milk from a fridge large enough for a grown man to live in, and put some bread in the toaster.

Once everything was made, he called Charlotte. She answered on the third ring, and Miles linked the call to the house speaker system.

"How's Washington state?" Charlotte asked.

"Cold," Miles told her. "And I don't just mean the weather."

"People not keen on vampire help there?" She asked.

"Most of the town isn't. Thankfully, Anya has really put on quite the hospitality," he told her, drinking from his mug of fresh coffee. "I rang because I have a question."

"I got your email," she said. "You didn't exactly stick to the *officially stay out of it* phrase of the investigation."

"Hard to when things have gotten this complicated," Miles said with some exasperation. "A serial killer vampire who just bleeds people dry should put the investigation firmly into Assembly territory. Yet the Magistrate don't want to share information with anyone about it. I found another body last night. Doesn't look like the same MO as the previous victims—so do we have two killers running around a very small town? Whatever is going on—it's not something I can just sit out of. And then there's them naming Oliver as a person of interest in Lauren's disappearance. They'll link him back to the other murders if they can, despite him having been in the UK when the first bodies were found."

"If Oliver is involved in what happened to Lauren, finding one finds the other," Charlotte said. "You seen Yvonne yet?"

"No, I needed sleep," he told her. "But even I'm starting to question the coincidence of her brother turning up here two weeks ago, and suddenly people start dying."

"You think Oliver is the killer?" Charlotte asked. "Or at least working with the killer?"

"I don't know what I think yet," Miles told her. "It's doubtful, considering the first one died before he arrived, but I'm not ruling anything out right now. Getting back to the legalities of my involvement . . ."

"Ask away," Charlotte said.

"What happens if Lauren turns up as a victim of our vampire serial killer?" Miles asked. "That would throw their idea about Oliver out, and I'm presuming the case will fall firmly under the Assembly, and therefore my remit."

"The Magistrate can either help or get the fuck out of your way," Charlotte said. "The Magistrate is one of those things I hope doesn't leave America. They're the Crystal Pepsi of hate groups. There might have been good people involved in its creation, but ultimately the people in charge are assholes who just want to see us die."

"I don't think a soda company thinks about us that much," Miles pointed out.

"You know I'm glaring at the phone, right now, yes?" Charlotte asked.

Miles tried not to laugh. "Yeah, I figured as much."

"Oh, before I become overwhelmed with rage at your voice and forget, I got a call from an ATO member by the name of Megan Song," Charlotte said. "You two go way back, yes?"

"We do; what did she want?" Miles asked, finishing off his coffee.

"She said Danny was released," Charlotte said. "No more info than that. She just wanted you to know."

Miles considered the information and wondered just how in the hell Danny had gotten out. Someone, somewhere, with immense power and influence must have pulled strings.

"Any news on Kyle?" Miles asked. "The one who did a runner from a highly trained ATO team."

Charlotte was quiet for a moment. "Are you suggesting that someone let him go?"

"He's a human who escaped ATO custody," Miles said. "I thought about it after I left Drest's and wondered how that might happen."

"I'll look into that more," Charlotte said.

Everything about the last few days stinks, Miles thought to himself.

"You should know that House Umbra found out you're in America," Charlotte told him. "Vedran was not impressed. He marched into the Assembly staff building here and demanded to speak, to know why you were still involved in *his* investigation. He was even more pissy after I explained, in extreme detail, how the law works, and why the Assembly is still in charge of the investigation while it's ongoing outside of London."

"I'm sure you took no joy in that," Miles said.

"I loved every single second of it," Charlotte said. "The little shit isn't going to let it go, though. You know what he's like."

"He never was one to leave things," Miles agreed. "Can I ask you something else?"

Charlotte chuckled. "Of course."

"Ah, you know what, it's not important," Miles said.

"Miles." Charlotte's tone was both friendly and telling him not to screw around and just tell her.

"I've been having nightmares," Miles said. "Violence, death, a crushing weight of . . . darkness."

"You ever had prophetic dreams before?" Charlotte asked.

"No," Miles told her. "Not ever, and I'm not even sure that's what it is. It's been a few days now, and it's every dream. Something is bothering me and I don't know what it is, or . . ."

"Or you're having visions," Charlotte said. "Your power is telekinesis, so it's not psychic power leaking out into your dreams like the House Umbra vampires get. You ask Drest?"

"No because I didn't think they were important," Miles admitted. "I'm still not sure they are, but I also know that you're not going to mock me for telling you about them. You ever had them?"

"Prophetic dreams, no," Charlotte said, her mind clearly considering something. "You know, it's possible that your dreams are because you're in close proximity to a threat, even an unknown one. Or maybe you're being taken into a threat, that would explain it. A sort of vampire proximity to danger alert. Or maybe you ate too much cheese. I'm sorry I'm not much help."

"It's okay, it's just weird and uncomfortable," Miles said. "Dreams could just be dreams, right?"

"But they don't feel like dreams," Charlotte said.

"No," Miles said. "No, they don't. Anyway, I better go. Killers to hunt. Missing spies to find. Suspect husband to go question. Busy day."

"If I think of anything for your dream issue, I'll let you know," Charlotte said. "I can ask a few people I trust, see what they think. No names mentioned."

"Thank you," Miles said, feeling a little relieved that he'd been able to talk to someone about it all.

"Be careful, Miles," Charlotte said.

"Always," Miles told her and hung up.

By the time he'd finished his toast, washed up, and walked upstairs to get dressed, it was almost ten in the morning. Miles decided to put on a suit, considering he was probably going to have to talk to official people, and at least try to look like he was an official person himself. The Arbiters didn't have a dress code, and while Miles was happier in jeans and a T-shirt, sometimes it paid to look the part.

Getting dressed in a black suit, white shirt, and black boots, he decided to forgo the tie. That was the one garment that Miles had never been able to wear. They felt constricting and could easily be used as a weapon against someone, and it was weird that people chose to wear them.

"You ready, Church?" Miles called from the back door, and the large dog bounded in from outside, letting Miles close the door and lock up before going to the garage, opening the door, and getting in the car.

The drive to the Gibson residence was a short one, and there were three cars outside of the house. One parked opposite the house was a grey Hyundai Santa Fe, which had been Amber's car from the previous night. He got the feeling she was more interested in catching bad guys than in playing games and was happy to have her on his side. Hopefully, anyway.

The other two cars were a black Mercedes-Benz G-Wagen with Magistrate written across the back in white letters, which was parked directly outside the house, and a silver Ford F-150 parked in the driveway.

Interesting.

"Church, stay out here by the car," Miles said.

Church tapped the dashboard once with her paw.

"Anyone comes to look at the car, make sure they know they're not welcome," Miles added as he opened the car door, holding it open for Church to jump out of the car. She walked to a nearby verge and sat down.

"Good girl," Miles said, tossing her a treat from his pocket, which she caught in mid-air.

Miles crossed the road and walked up the driveway, stopping beside the Ford to give it a cursory glance, before continuing on up the half dozen steps to the red front door, which opened as he stepped up to it.

"You're early," Amber said, looking as though she'd gotten very little sleep.

"All nighter?" Miles asked.

"I'm sustained by caffeine and rage at this point," Amber said, stepping outside. "Reese Gibson called in the Magistrate."

"Ah, well, it's good to see we all know who's working with who," Miles said. "You seem off about it."

"That a detective called in the Magistrate for an interview about his missing wife who he hasn't even reported missing?" Amber said. "Yeah, can't imagine what's weird about that!"

Miles nodded, wondering just how much the Magistrate knew about Lauren's disappearance. If they'd found out about her betraying them—just what would they be capable of? She either was a victim of a vampire serial killer, had had her position within the Magistrate compromised, or had just done a runner—none of which boded well for her.

Amber pushed open the door and they stepped inside the Gibson residence.

Directly behind the front door was a reception room with baby blue painted walls, dark brown wooden floorboards with a white rug over part of them, and a coffee table in the middle of the room next to the charcoal grey corner sofa. Two large men sat on the sofa, each of them carrying a Colt AR-15.

Both men had dark goatees and military style hair. They wore black tactical gear, with a secondary weapon holstered against their hip. Neither of them looked all that happy about Miles entering the house.

"Vampire is here," one of the two men shouted.

"Thanks very much," Miles asked. "Do you take coats here, or do I check them with someone else in military cosplay?"

The men ignored Miles, although he could tell neither of them wanted to let his words rest. That was the thing that Miles had discovered about the Magistrate—a lot of its members were really thin-skinned.

Next to the reception room was an archway that led to a set of stairs going to the floor above, and a large open plan kitchen, dining, and living room area. All of the walls were painted a slightly off-white colour, with more dark brown floorboards, more white rugs, and a general coldness to everything. Someone was taking minimalism to a whole new level; this was not a home that felt lived in.

The kitchen had granite-coloured cabinets and fixtures, and the large dining table was made of granite, with six wooden chairs around it. The living area, with its cream sofa and two wooden chairs with fur throws over them, cemented the look of a show house rather than an actual home. Either that, or the designer had just copied a picture from a home decor magazine.

The entire space was occupied by six people—four men and two women—all in the same tactical gear as the two in the reception room, although at least these six didn't look as if they'd been cloned in a tank like the two previously. None looked happy that Miles was there.

"Through there," one of the men said, pointing to around the kitchen where there was a patio with sliding doors that led to a good sized, immaculately kept garden. There were flower beds down either side of the lawn that sat in the middle, although even if it had been the height of summer and the flowers were in bloom, Miles couldn't have said what any of the flowers were.

Two men sat in comfortable seats inside the patio. They sat beside each other and neither got to their feet nor offered their hands to be shaken. One was in tactical gear. He was white with blond hair, a full beard, and tattoos of several dragons on his bare arms. The other man was in a black T-shirt, jeans, and white trainers. He was also white, with long brown hair tied back in a ponytail, and he kept looking out of the patio window as Miles sat down in front of them.

"Blake Summers and Reese Gibson, I presume?" Miles said.

"Reese, let me talk to the vampire for a moment," Blake said, and the man in the T-shirt and jeans got up and walked away.

"I'll check on him," Amber said, leaving Blake and Miles alone.

"I'm fully aware that you're going to take over this case," Blake said with a frown. "But I also know that there's a missing human woman who worked for us, and you couldn't give two shits about that, so I'm going to be watching to make sure you don't let your vampire killer run out before justice can be served."

Miles stared at Blake for a while, feeling a little bit of happiness at how uncomfortable it clearly made him. "You hate me," Miles said eventually. "You've never met me, though, so I'm going to guess you just hate all vampires, yes?"

"Your kind are responsible for deaths and misery on a scale almost unimaginable," Blake said bitterly.

"You want to give me a single piece of evidence for that?" Miles asked. "Or maybe pick up a history book. Because humanity does not need our help to fuck up. Besides, this is more than protecting humanity, this is personal to you, isn't it? Do you know Oliver McCarthy?"

"Why?" Blake asked.

"You named him as a suspect in Lauren's disappearance," Amber said. "How did you find that name?"

"We don't have to share our sources," Blake said, sounding sure of himself.

"You don't want to share how you found the name of a possible kidnapper?" Miles asked. "Bit weird."

"You are here to talk to Reese," Blake said, seething with every word. "I suggest you do so and then leave, vampire."

"Okay, well, you and your friends can all leave so I can talk to him," Miles said.

"No," Blake replied with a slight sneer. "The law . . ."

"The law says I'm in charge," Miles snapped. "Lauren Gibson has been missing for five days. And wasn't actually declared missing until yesterday. Not by her husband, by the way. I didn't want to actually take charge of the investigation, but it seems that we have a vampire serial killer on the loose, and the presenting scenario is that she's become a victim. You've also named someone as a person of interest, but have given no information on how you came to that name. Though until we find her body—I'm keeping *all* avenues of investigation open." He cast a look towards the door that Reese Gibson had just walked out of and Blake scowled at him.

Miles heaved a sigh. "Like it or not, I'm your best chance at stopping any more deaths. If you like, I can get an actual lawyer on the phone to tell you what the law says. I'll tell you what that lawyer told me earlier today: you can either help me or fuck off. Pick one. Until then, I get to interview Lauren's husband alone. I'll even let Amber stay so the big bad vampire doesn't intimidate your *friend*. We both know you have no legal standing while I'm here, and while I can't stop you running your own investigation, I can stop you from interfering in mine."

The colour of Blake's skin around his neck and jaw went beetroot red, and Miles wasn't sure if he was about to have a heart attack. Instead, Blake got to his feet and marched out of the room, with his squad following behind.

Amber reappeared a few seconds later with Reese in tow, the latter of whom retook his seat, while Amber took Blake's.

"So," Miles said, hoping that Reese didn't share Blake's viewpoint on vampires, if only because it would make things so much more arduous than not. "Why don't we start at the beginning."

CHAPTER SEVENTEEN

Reese and Lauren had met ten years ago on a blind date, when they'd been set up by mutual friends. They'd immediately hit it off and were dating a week later, moving in together six months after that, and married three years later.

Lauren was a doctor at the local hospital working at the ER, and Reese a local officer. After a few years, Lauren was promoted in work, and Reese became a detective. Everything was rosy, at least according to Reese. She'd left her job as a doctor and gone to work for the Magistrate, and was well liked there.

"We tried to have a baby," Reese said, obviously upset by the topic. "It didn't work out, but we got past that and it felt as if we were both heading in the same direction. Now she's run off with someone, and everyone thinks she's been abducted."

"What makes you think she's just run off?" Miles asked.

"I found messages between her and some other guy," Reese said. "They were . . . intimate. On her phone. We argued. Next I know she's left."

"Who's the other guy?" Miles asked.

"Oliver McCarthy," Reese said.

"So, you think Oliver was having an affair with your wife," Amber said.

"Do you have those messages?" Miles asked.

"She took her phone with her," Reese said. "I didn't think she was abducted. I thought she'd just run off. That she was in no danger."

"Someone thought that she was in danger enough to file a report of a missing person," Amber said.

"Well, they clearly don't know my wife," Reese snapped. "I thought she was just shacked up with some other guy, and that they were both laughing at my expense."

"The Magistrate are suggesting she's a victim of a vampire abduction and possible serial killer," Amber said. "Do you not think that's the case?"

"Just covering all their bases, I guess," Reese said. "I don't know what to think anymore."

"Has she contacted her family?" Miles asked.

"No, and neither have I," Reese said. "I was never good enough for them, so they're going to be in on it."

"Is there an office in the house?" Miles asked.

"Upstairs," Reese said. "You're welcome to go check. The sooner you all understand she's left, the better for all of us. Not sure why a vampire even needs to be involved."

"Well, your house is pretty close to a dead body I found last night," Miles said. "Not the best first impression ever. Anyway, the body was . . . attacked. From what I understand, these serial killer cases are pretty clean."

Reese looked between Amber and Miles. "Are you serious?" he asked, sounding emotional for the first time. "No one told me."

"We've been trying to get ahold of you for the last two days," Amber said grimly. "The Captain said you're on leave."

"Your wife has run off so you decided to switch your phone off and go hide somewhere?" Miles asked.

"I needed some time to myself," Reese said.

"Where?" Miles asked.

"I have a cabin," Reese told him. "I spend time there when I need to clear my head, or just get away. Everyone kept saying that they'll find Lauren soon, and I got fed up of telling people she's not dead, just fucking someone else."

With repeated assertions that they were wasting their time, Miles left Amber to continue questioning Reese while he looked around the house, which gave the impression of being lived in more so than the front downstairs.

The large bedroom overlooking the driveway had several colourful paintings on the light grey walls, but no pictures of either Reese or Lauren. There was a large bed, a huge TV, and a smattering of wooden furniture. A games machine sat next to the TVs, game cases lying beside it, along with several Blu-rays. Miles went through the drawers, opening the cupboard up to check everything. It felt invasive, but that was the point.

The guest bedroom was similarly decorated, but the office, overlooking the rear garden, had a dozen photos on the walls. Every photo was the same pose: Reese stood behind Lauren, holding her around the waist. Both smiling, both looking like a happy couple.

The office contained a locked metal filing cabinet, a black wooden desk with a PC on top, an office chair, and that was it. Miles clicked on the PC, but found it was password protected.

Miles considered the stark difference between the two floors, and he returned to Reese and Amber, to find that Reese had left.

Miles leaned up against the wall, while Amber continued to sit in the patio chair. "So," he said. "This is not what I was expecting."

"Lots of couples don't have photos of themselves all over their walls," Amber said.

"What's he like to work with?" Miles asked.

"He's a good detective in a cases closed way," Amber said. "But an asshole. There have been rumours about him having affairs for a long time."

"Any possibility that Lauren was having an affair?" Miles asked.

"I know people who know Lauren well," Amber said. "I don't care what Reese said, Lauren wasn't having an affair. She worked all hours she could, she did nothing for herself. I think she was lonely, I think she was hurting, but that's about it. They might have been an unhappy couple, but we found no evidence of her playing away from home."

"You ever met Lauren?" Miles asked, looking around. Something was bothering him, but he couldn't quite put his finger on it.

"Yeah, a few times," Amber said. "She's quiet, keeps to herself mostly, although she's always at the local department picnic and any fundraising done in town. She likes knitting. She's learning to speak French, and likes cooking. She's nice."

"Okay, we have nothing to go on," Miles said. "Something isn't right, though. Who filed the report? I want an actual name."

"Yvonne Dent," Amber said.

Miles laughed. "Okay, something *really* weird is going on here."

"You know Yvonne?" Amber asked.

Miles decided that if he was going to have Amber trusting him, he needed to trust her. At the same time, she didn't need to know about Drest and how Lauren was a spy for the vampires. "I'm here to see Yvonne. She has a brother who is in some trouble."

"Assembly trouble?" Amber asked.

Miles nodded. "A separate investigation; he's not got the profile of a killer, let alone a serial killer—but the timings sure as hell looks suspect. Could be that the first killing was someone else, and Oliver has been doing it since. Could be he's involved somehow. Need to find him and get to the bottom of it."

"Can you track her blood or something?" Amber asked.

"Even if I tasted her blood, probably not," Miles said. "It's been days since Lauren went missing, so that would get me nowhere, and besides, where would I even get her blood? I think the best option is to talk to Yvonne. Maybe she's got some information she's not telling you. Lauren's missing, but we have no idea where to start."

He stared around the room and sniffed.

"You feel like there's something else," Amber said.

"This whole room is bothering me. It feels too fresh, too new, and there's a faint smell of fresh paint," Miles said, stepping away from the wall.

"How new?" Amber asked.

"Days," Miles said.

"I'll go check with Reese," she said and left Miles to go through the downstairs. He opened every cupboard and drawer in the downstairs, but while he found several films and videogames, even a learn to speak French book, there was nothing that might help locate her.

Amber came back into the room. "Reese said that Amber redecorated a few weeks ago."

"He's talkin' out his arse there," Miles said. "This is a few days old, at most."

"To hide something?" Amber said. "Like a fight?"

Miles scanned the sea of cardboard and considered possibilities about Lauren's disappearance being linked to her spying. "Let's say for one second that Lauren wasn't grabbed by some bogeyman vampire out there? What if she found something she shouldn't have? What if Reese and his Magistrate friends are involved in something they shouldn't be? What if she didn't go missing out there, but whatever happened happened in this house?"

"And they cleaned it up?" Amber asked, looking around. "You think Reese did something to Lauren?"

Miles nodded. "How many times are husbands responsible for something that happens to their wives?"

There wasn't even a second of pause before Amber answered, "Too many."

"There you go," Miles said. "And now she's hurt, in her house, and Reese needs help. He calls his Magistrate buddies, who are only too happy to come help him. There's a new problem. The Magistrate can't just say the serial killer vampire did it; there would be no bite marks. So they stage her having run away."

"We have zero evidence to say that's what happened," Amber said.

"I know, I'm just thinking out loud," Miles said.

"And what would the long-term plan be?" Amber asked. "Just dump her body somewhere?"

"If it were me, I'd incinerate it," Miles said. "Toss the ashes somewhere. What's the old saying, 'No body, no crime?'"

"That's genuinely terrifying," Amber said.

"I get that a lot," Miles told her. "You know any cops who won't squeal to the Magistrate if we ask to look into Reese?"

"Squeal?" Amber asked. "Seriously?"

"It the boot fits," Miles said.

Amber sighed. "Fine. Yes, I know some cops who are not fans of the Magistrate, but there is no way a judge is going to sign off on this. No way. One call from Reese's union rep and we get nothing. He's not a suspect. There's no crime to be a suspect of."

"He's the only person I've met who *is* an actual suspect," Miles said. "Just because he's a colleague doesn't mean he gets off without investigation first."

"I'm not about to give anyone a free ride, cop or not, but we need to make sure we have evidence linking him before we tear his house upside down looking for something," Amber said, sounding more irritated. "Do you really believe that he's kidnapped or killed his own wife?"

Miles shrugged. "Like we agreed, most murders are by the partner," he said.

"You didn't answer the question," Amber said.

"I don't know if he did it or not," Miles said. "But there's something off about this place. I don't like off."

They replaced the ladder and attic hatch before leaving the house to find Blake Summers and three of his people standing beside their G-Wagen at the bottom of the drive. Reese's car was gone, which was a little premature on his part, but Miles knew he could always find him again.

One of the two men from the reception room stepped in Miles's path.

"Don't do that," Amber said.

Miles looked up at the Magistrate member and smiled. The young man stepped aside, and Miles turned to Blake. "What is it we did? Did a vampire kill your family?" Miles read the man's reaction. "No, not that. Did they eat your pet?"

No not that either, Miles thought.

"Did you catch one fucking your wife?" Miles asked and laughed, before catching sight of Blake, whose eyes burned with rage.

Blake stepped up to Miles who didn't move. "Fuck you, vampire."

"Look, Blake," Miles said. "I don't care if your wife had an affair with a vampire. It wasn't me. Lauren is missing, and her home is close to a murder scene that probably involved a vampire. If she's run off with this Oliver person Reese told me about, then I'll consider the matter closed and I'll move on. My guess is that you figured you'd name him a suspect so you can hope to tie a nice little bow between the murders you're investigating and Lauren's disappearance. Either Lauren ran off with this Oliver and you're naming him for revenge, or he did kidnap her and you naming him just muddies the water of my investigation into what happened. So, you go do your job with your military cosplay friends, and I'll do mine, and we'll all be fine."

Miles didn't want to tell Blake that he knew for certainty that Oliver *couldn't* have been the killer of the bodies the Magistrate were investigating. He already knew they were corrupt, and he wanted to see what they'd do next.

"Are you threatening me, vampire?" Blake asked.

"Let's not do this," Amber said, the voice of reason in what was rapidly becoming a tense situation.

"I'm not threatening anyone," Miles said, holding up his hands. "I'm merely suggesting that you don't interfere in an official Assembly investigation. Because there are actual laws making sure you don't. I wouldn't want to see any of these . . . fine officers of yours going to jail for a looonng time just because they couldn't stop themselves from doing something stupid."

"My people will behave," Blake said. "Just make sure your vampires do the same."

"Only one of me," Miles pointed out.

"There's never only one of you," Blake said as he opened the car door. "You're like cockroaches."

"Nice to meet you, too," Miles called after the car as it drove off at speed into the distance.

"Do you enjoy pissing people off?" Amber asked.

"Depends on the person," Miles admitted. "In Blake's case, yes, it was quite entertaining. Any chance you know who the victim was I found in the church last night?"

"We're running dental records," Amber said as her phone went off. "Speaking of which, I need to take this."

Church padded over to Miles and nuzzled his hand until he scratched her behind the ear. "No trouble for you, then," Miles said as Church let out a low rumble of contentment. "Two vampire murderers in the same place at the same time isn't unheard of, but it does little to ease the fears of anyone who was already concerned about us being here."

"Doc Hammond wants to see you," Amber said. "About the body last night."

"Okay, I really need to go talk to Yvonne," Miles said. "Considering she's a good part of the reason I'm here. Can I meet you at the hospital after?"

Amber nodded. "Yeah, eight okay? There's a park next to the hospital. Should have fewer eyes and ears. I'll meet you there."

Miles checked his watch. "Good idea. I'll see you then."

The library was a two-story building made of concrete and glass. The concrete had been painted over in blue and white, giving it a much more inviting appearance than it would have had otherwise. It had a slanting slate grey roof with a small terrace at the far end. The whole building was about the size of four football pitches situated two-by-two. There was a small parking area to the side of the building and next to a community centre.

There was no note on the library door, but it was locked, so Miles knocked.

A young woman approached the doors with a look of concern on her face. She appeared to be in her thirties, with pale skin and long blonde hair partially dyed deep blue, and she wore a pair of faded blue jeans, white Converse shoes, and a black hooded top with a picture of Ripley from *Alien* on it. She had multiple bangles of a variety of colours and styles on each wrist and several rings on her fingers, as well as earrings in both ears and a nose ring.

"Are you with the police?" she asked, her accent placing her as a local, although Miles knew differently.

"I'm an Arbiter," Miles told her.

"And your dog?" the woman asked.

"This is Church, and I'm Miles Watson," he said.

"Church?" the young woman asked. "You named your dog Church?"

Miles shrugged. "I hadn't considered being asked that question as many times as I have over the years. She seems pretty happy about it, so I'll manage. You're Yvonne Dent, yes?"

"Yes," she said, unlocking the door but still not opening it.

"I'm here to talk to you about your brother, Oliver," Miles said. "I'd rather do that inside. If possible."

Yvonne appeared to wrestle with whether she should open the door but eventually settled on letting Miles and Church inside.

"Will your dog be okay?" Yvonne asked.

"Church will be fine," Miles said. "She's not exactly your average pooch."

"She's about the size of a pony," Yvonne said. "I assume she's the offspring of a vampire dog or something?"

"Something like that," Miles said as he looked around the small foyer, with several chairs—all blue with metal legs and a plastic seat—and flyers on the walls. The windows down one wall, next to the only other door out of the room, showed the library beyond.

"Astonishing," Yvonne said, crouching down and stroking Church's head. "She's quite beautiful."

That got Yvonne a lick on the face from Church, causing the vampire Librarian to giggle. Yvonne stood and looked over at Miles. "Did Danica tell you I work for House Barbarous?"

Miles nodded. "Do you know where Oliver is?"

"That's a complicated question," Yvonne said.

"Can we make it less complicated?" Miles asked as they stepped into the library itself, and he found himself smiling as he took a moment to savour the smell.

Yvonne, having realised that Miles wasn't following her anymore, turned back to see where he'd gotten to. "You like libraries?" she asked with a warm smile.

"I was the First Librarian of House Venator," Miles said.

"Which is why you're now an Arbiter?" Yvonne asked, making it sound like a much more perfectly natural career progression than Miles felt it was.

"Something like that, yes," Miles said. "I find libraries to be peaceful places. Somewhere I can go and relax and lose myself. Somewhere I can hide, too, if I'm honest."

"I hang out by the microfiche when I want to be alone," Yvonne said. "It's downstairs in the basement, and no one ever uses it. I don't even think most people in town know how to use it. Actually, I doubt anyone under the age of twenty even knows what microfiche is. We had a class of schoolkids come in the other month, and we showed them a rotary phone. Blew their minds. Obviously, that was before everyone started to side-eye the vampire." There was a genuine sadness to Yvonne's voice that made Miles wonder just how quickly the human inhabitants of Fortress Falls had returned to being distrustful of vampires as a whole.

Miles and Church followed Yvonne through the library to a door at the opposite side of the floor to the entrance, stopping by a selection of books on the desolate.

Yvonne stopped and turned back. "Oh, the desolate interest me. We don't actually know much about them, except that they're monsters who destroy everything in their path. Obviously we know about Maine and the other places like it, but very few people have ever gotten close enough to the desolate to catalogue their behaviour."

"Because they tend to kill everyone," Miles said, removing a book that said *Desolate: Myth and Legend*. The cover had a picture of a slouching desolate on the front, and Miles wondered if it was a photo or artwork; if the former, he hoped the photographer got out alive.

"Yes, well, that's true, but not entirely the whole story," Yvonne said. "I'm reading a book on desolate queens and kings at the moment. It's fascinating."

"They're meant to be practically mythological," Miles said.

"There's evidence to suggest they have existed before, and may do so again," she said, clearly excited by the topic. "Anyway, we should continue."

Miles returned the book and followed Yvonne to a nearby door, which was marked *STAFF ONLY*. Yvonne opened the door, revealing a good-sized staff room, with a comfortable looking, if worn, couch, a desk with computer, a small kitchen, and a coffee table. There were flyers and leaflets affixed to one wall, most of which were homemade and signalled various activities taking place over the next few months in the community centre.

"Tea?" Yvonne asked, as Miles tried to place her accent and failed.

"Milk, one sugar, please," he said.

Yvonne smiled and removed two mugs from a cupboard, and set about making the drinks. "My brother was always a problem," she said without looking back at Miles. "He came here two weeks ago. Terrified. He said he was being hunted. Managed to use a fake passport to get out of the UK."

She poured the hot water into the empty mugs and let the tea brew, returning to her seat.

"Where's your brother?" Miles asked.

"In town somewhere," Yvonne said sadly.

"Do you know what happened to Lauren?" Miles asked. "You put in a police report for her being missing."

Yvonne nodded slowly. "Her husband certainly didn't seem to care too much. Someone had to." She got up and made the tea, bringing the two mugs back and passing one to Miles. "Things are going to get bad in town."

"Aren't they already?" Miles asked her.

Yvonne shook her head. "Not even close."

CHAPTER EIGHTEEN

Two weeks ago, my brother arrived saying he was running from some-one," Yvonne said. "I called Danica."

"House above blood," Miles said, almost instinctively.

"House above blood," Yvonne repeated. "My brother belongs to no House. I tried to get him an in with Barbarous, but he wasn't having it."

"Who's his bloodline?" Miles asked, wondering if Yvonne knew that her brother did actually work for House Barbarous too, but deciding to keep that information to himself for now.

"I have no idea," Yvonne said. "He was turned in the sixties in San Francisco. I don't know who turned him, or what House they belonged to, or what bloodline they are. The last time I saw my brother, I told him to fuck off and die."

"Not a close family then?" Miles asked.

"My parents were murdered by Nazis," Yvonne said, a hardness to her tone. "Not these jumped-up privileged pricks you see on the TV who are sad that the world is moving on without them, actual fucking Nazis. My brother and I never really saw eye to eye on a lot of stuff after they were gone. He moved to America. I stayed and killed Nazis. Our paths never really came back together after that."

"Why'd you tell him to fuck off and die?" Miles asked.

"Because he's a criminal," Yvonne said. "Mostly because of that, anyway. He works in a gang, or for a gang, or some shit. They're vampires who just want to get rich and don't much care how."

"And he came here to see you," Miles said.

"Fleeing trouble again," Yvonne explained. "I asked him what had hap-pened, but he wasn't too keen on talking about it. I asked him why he came to me. He said I was the only safe person he could think of. Do you know what happened to him?"

Miles considered keeping the information to himself, but Yvonne probably deserved to know. "He worked for an illegal vampire creation operation," he said. "They turned some old guy into a desolate, who got free and killed a bunch of other vampires, and their Boss figured the best way to deal with it was to murder the lot of them."

Yvonne closed her eyes and shook her head sadly. "Fucking hell," she whispered.

"Aye, it's not great," Miles said, his mind going back to the fact that Danny had been released from custody. "Someone with power is running the show. I want to find Oliver so he can hopefully tell me. Everyone else has had their brains scrambled. If Oliver can't say, then I'm not sure how I'm going to find who's behind it."

"You came all this way to find my shitty brother?" Yvonne asked.

"Okay, I think we can put aside whatever this is," Miles said, and took a sip of tea.

"Meaning what?" Yvonne said.

"For a start, I know that Oliver was working for Danica as an undercover spy in a particular London gang," Miles said. "I know that he came here to see you two weeks ago. Presumably either to escape himself or to check that you were safe. I'm thinking a little of both.

"Your brother's identity got found out, and he ran. He saved some lives first, though. I want to know *how* his identity was discovered, and who he's running from. House Umbra took over the investigation officially, as someone came and confessed, in a move I can only describe as bullshit, and both Drest and Danica told me that you were also working for them and wanted me to do them a favour."

"What's the favour?" Yvonne asked, drinking her own tea.

"Where's Lauren?" Miles asked. "They told me you were her handler."

Yvonne held the mug close to her lips, without drinking it. "Missing," she said without looking at Miles.

"Her husband didn't think so," Miles said. "Her husband thinks she's shagging the handyman or something. Actually, that's not quite true; he thinks she's shagging Oliver."

Yvonne laughed. "Reese is a moron. An abusive moron at that."

"He hit her?" Miles asked, hoping to keep the anger he felt out of his voice.

"Never," Yvonne said. "He kept tabs on her, monitored her phone, monitored who she spoke to. They have a social media account that has both of their names on it so he can keep an eye on it."

"That is pretty creepy," Miles admitted. "You think he *could* have hurt her?"

Yvonne considered it for a moment before saying, "Yes."

"Any chance she's been grabbed by this killer the Magistrate are investigating?" Miles asked.

"Oh God, no," Yvonne said. "I'm pretty sure there's no vampire serial killer. I don't know what's going on, but it ain't that. Vampires don't just leave their victims lying around, staged. If it was a real vampire, they'd have hidden them—they wouldn't want the Assembly or Houses hunting them down."

Miles nodded in agreement. She was voicing the same suspicions he'd had himself.

Yvonne continued, "If there was genuine evidence of a vampire serial killer, they'd be shouting from the rooftops of every building in the land. There'd be news articles on the front page of every Magistrate friendly rag of a newspaper. They're keeping it all under wraps for a reason, I just don't know what that reason is."

"Any chance you brother is involved?" Miles asked, finishing his tea. "The Magistrate have named your brother as a person of interest in Lauren's disappearance."

"What?" Yvonne asked. "That's insane."

"I don't disagree," Miles said. "You never answered my question, though. Any chance your brother is involved in whatever is going on here? Not that he's murdering people, or kidnapping humans, but that he's involved somehow."

"Yes, always," Yvonne said. "If there's something shitty going on and Oliver is around, it's almost certain he's involved somewhere. He's a magnet for crime and criminal activity. He arrived after the first body was found, so in this instance I doubt he's killing people."

"Where would he hide in town?" Miles asked.

"No clue," Yvonne said. "There's loads of old abandoned factories and buildings in the forest northeast, outside of town. There used to be big companies working out there, logging or mining or whatever the hell they were doing. They stopped and cleared off a while back, though."

"You been to look yourself?" Miles asked.

Yvonne shook her head. "My brother can take care of himself. He's not a murderer, or not that I remember, but he's more than capable of keeping himself safe. You got any family?"

"Not for a long time," Miles admitted.

"Yeah, well, it's really hard to have a family member who just won't stop screwing up," Yvonne said. "You give them chance after chance to sort themselves out, to show the world that they're better than that, and they just keep taking that opportunity and pissing it up the nearest wall. I've long since realised that while he was my brother for the first part of his life, he's just a stranger who shares my DNA now."

"Did you give him any money?" Miles asked, feeling sorry for Yvonne, and understanding how hard it was to have family who are meant to be there for you, meant to do what's right, but only really care about themselves.

"I gave him food, coffee, and somewhere to sleep for just over a week," Yvonne said. "Then four days ago, I get a call saying he has to deal with something, and that was the last I heard of him."

"That's it?" Miles asked. "He didn't say anything else?"

"He said sorry," Yvonne said. "He said he knew he always got into trouble, and that he was worried about me, which is why he came here, but that he had to do something. He had to help someone. He said I shouldn't know more because it would put me in danger. I haven't seen or heard from him since."

"Do you know where he is?" Miles asked. "The Magistrate are clearly interested in him for something. I don't think they genuinely believe he ran off with Lauren. I think, from what you've told me, he might have involved himself in something really bad. If Blake finds him before I do . . . we both know that won't be good."

"You've met Blake then," Yvonne said. "He's a real piece of work. Lauren hates him."

"Why?" Miles asked.

"Because he's a terrible human being," Yvonne said as if that explained everything.

"Are he and Reese friends?" Miles asked.

Yvonne nodded. "I think so, they seem to get on well. Lauren used to say that she was worried Reese was being dragged down a dark road, but then I always thought that Reese was a dick, so I don't assume it took much convincing."

"Any chance Oliver and Lauren are connected?" Miles asked.

Yvonne paused then. "Not that I'm aware of."

Church let out a long whine.

"She okay?" Yvonne asked.

"She knows you're lying," Miles said.

Yvonne's expression hardened as she looked between Miles and Church, as if she was trying to figure out if Miles was telling the truth.

"I saw her talking to him," Yvonne said. "A few days before she went missing. Out by the church."

"Where I found a dead person?" Miles asked yesterday.

"They're not killers," Yvonne snapped. "My brother is a lot of things, but he's not a murderer. And Lauren is the sweetest woman on earth. I'm not sure she's capable of killing anyone. Look, I don't know where my brother is, and I don't know where Lauren is. I hope you find them both before something bad happens to them. If it hasn't already. Can your dog really tell when someone is lying?"

Miles looked down at Church. "Nah," he said. "Danica said you were looking into the victims. What'd you find?"

Yvonne's eyes narrowed for a moment, and Miles wasn't sure if she was going to tell him they were done. But she worked for Danica, and Danica would not be happy to discover that a member of her House hadn't helped out on an investigation she wanted.

"Three victims, all three were from Seattle," Yvonne said. "All three were attacked in secluded spots close to the far north end of Fortress Falls. All three were drained of blood. Magistrate were on the scene before anyone even knew what was going on with the first victim. They let Doc Hammond see the bodies but refused to allow the details to go to the local PD. Refused help from the Assembly. Just being shady as usual."

"You know anything else about the victims?" Miles asked.

"One was a drifter on the run from the law for burglary, one was a police officer who had recently been diagnosed with stage four lung cancer, one was a teacher who had recently left his job due to stage four pancreatic cancer," Yvonne said. "The latter two had no reason to be anywhere away from home. Both were due to have chemotherapy within the next week; all three were estranged from their families."

"Weird," Miles said.

"Yeah, little bit," Yvonne agreed.

"I'm meant to see Doc Hammond later," Miles said. "You've spoken to her about this?"

Yvonne nodded. "She's how I know about it all. Before you ask, she doesn't know about Lauren working for Danica, and she definitely doesn't know about Oliver. I don't exactly like to tell the world about my brother."

Miles considered the three threads. Three bodies found. First one just before Oliver arrived in town. Two within ten days after. None after Lauren went missing. Excluding the one he found last night.

"What is it?" Yvonne asked.

"This killer took the lives of three humans in two weeks," Miles said. "But none since Lauren went missing. They drained three people dry in a short period of time; a lot, even for the most voracious blood feeder among vampires, and then what, they were just full?"

"You're thinking it's all bullshit, aren't you?" Yvonne said, not making it sound like a question.

Miles exhaled slowly and nodded. "Aye."

"You think the Magistrate are killing people to make it look like vampires?" Yvonne asked.

"I doubt it," Miles said. "Draining a human dry is *really* hard. Doing it so that it *looks* like vampires is even more difficult. There's definitely more to it than I first thought, though. I need to find your brother; do you know if there's a way I can contact him? Or where he might have run off to? Am I going to need to go wandering in the frozen wilderness of Canada?"

"He doesn't know anyone but me," Yvonne said. "He has money, but not a huge amount, and people are hunting him. He might have stormed out of here and vanished, but he won't have gone far. He'll be in the forests, or at some motel out on an interstate. I don't even have a phone number. Even if I wanted to find him, I couldn't."

"I was going to come here to find one criminal," Miles said, getting to his feet. "And I've walked into a clusterfuck. Thanks for your help. If I find your brother, I'll let you know."

"Go easy on him," Yvonne said. "I know, I'm not his biggest fan, but I also don't want to see someone kick seven shades of shit out of him."

"I'll do my best," Miles said as he left the room, Church following. Miles removed his phone from his pocket. "What's your number in case I need to contact you? Please."

Yvonne told him as he typed the number and saved it in his phone, before sending her a text.

"That's my number," he told her. "Call me if you hear anything, or if you just want to chat, that's fine, too."

"He's not a fighter," Yvonne called after him.

Miles looked back at her.

"He never was," Yvonne said sadly. "He's just an idiot."

"Could he have killed the man in the church last night?" Miles asked. "If forced to. If his life was in danger."

Yvonne said nothing for a moment, but eventually nodded once. "Yeah, he's still a vampire."

Miles nodded that he understood and left the library. "What do you think?" he asked Church as they reached the BMW hire car.

Church barked, and Miles opened the passenger door for her to get in.

"Aye, me too," Miles said, looking back at the library. He removed his phone; he didn't have long before he was meant to see Doc Hammond. Hopefully her information about the dead victims might shed some light on the investigation. As to finding Oliver and Lauren . . . that would have to wait until after.

Miles drove through the dark city. Considering it was getting late, and the fact that people had died and gone missing in the last few weeks, Fortress Falls was still busy, with lots of people going about their daily lives. He wondered how many people were truly afraid of a possible murderous vampire in their midst. He imagined that there was probably a surge of sales of UV lights, which was probably sensible. When you're human and a vampire attacks you, you need every advantage you can get.

He drove by a large park on the way to the hospital, and spotted Amber's car, pulling over next to it and parking. It was close to eight; he'd been at the library for longer than he'd expected. He opened the car and stepped out. It had started to snow, and the frigid air caused Miles to zip up his jacket as he exited the car.

"You can come run around if you like, but you'll have to stay close by," Miles said to Church, who nodded and jumped out of the car, staying by Miles as the pair walked over to Amber, who sat on a park bench close to the parking area but overlooking the floodlit park, where a large number of kids played baseball. Adults stood around watching the game, cheering the kids on.

"Amber," Miles said, taking a seat beside her.

"You ever play?" Amber asked, nodding toward the park.

"I've hit a ball with a bat," Miles said. "I don't think we called it baseball, though."

"Doc Hammond is running a little late," she said.

"Anything I should know about her?" Miles whispered.

"Don't piss her off," Amber said out the side of her mouth.

They sat for a short while as Miles told Amber his suspicions about a "vampire" serial killer in their midst.

"Okay, so you just think, what? The Magistrate are killing people?" Amber asked and laughed for a moment, before seeing Miles's expression. "Oh, shit, you *do* think that."

"I don't know how, but I'm hoping the doc can give me a sense of what's happened with the bodies as to whether it's a traditional vampire kill or something else," Miles said.

"That's the Doc," Amber said, nodding toward a woman running toward them.

Doctor Beatrice Hammond was in her early fifties but looked ten years younger. Her long dark hair with a streak of grey running through it was tied up in a ponytail. She had pale skin and a tattoo of a phoenix on the side of her neck, just below her ear. She was five foot seven and wore running gear: light grey leggings, a turquoise jacket, and black-and-blue-striped trainers. She tapped the fitness watch on her wrist several times as she jogged across the field. She carried a black rucksack, dropping it at Amber's feet before the pair hugged.

"Aren't you cold?" Amber asked.

"Need to keep fit," Doc said. "Also, I go running at this time every night, and didn't want to give people any ideas to think I was changing my routine. Doing something out of the ordinary."

"You think you're being spied on?" Miles asked.

"I think with the way things are, it's prudent to be cautious," Doc Hammond said. "You must be Miles, and this must be Church."

Church sat up at the mention of her name, receiving her expected attention.

"Pleasure," he said, offering her his hand. She looked down at it and shook her head.

"Don't do handshakes," Doc Hammond said. "Nothing personal."

"I get it," Miles said. "So, you want to talk out here? It's becoming a bit of a snowstorm."

"You warm enough?" Amber asked Miles, a little concern in her voice.

"I'll be fine," Miles told her. "What about you?"

"I'm good," Doc Hammond said, as she started to hope from foot to foot.

Amber opened the bag and removed several files. "These the three victims?"

"And the victim from the church," Doc Hammond said. "First of all, as you probably know, the previous victims were all drained but otherwise unharmed. No broken bones, no physical trauma of any kind except for the being dead part. Definitely vampire bites. I've seen them before."

"And the one at the church?" Miles asked.

"That's a problem," she said. "No vampire bites. Just major blood loss through physical trauma. And he had the tattoo of the Mortis gang." She removed her phone from her bag and activated it, scrolling through the pictures to find the right one before showing Miles.

"Never heard of them," he said, as Amber took a look and shook her head.

"The Mortis gang was a biker drug cartel back in the 1980s," Doc Hammond said. "Worked mostly out of LA and down to southern California. At some point, they decided to branch out into contract killings. Their leader was a man by the name of Frank Duke. He was a vampire. His upper three lieutenants were also vampires. Beneath them were a dozen high-ranking familiars, who weren't vampires but were a giant pain in the ass. At last count, the gang had over a hundred members spread out all across the western United States, going as far east as Denver. We know, for a fact, over three hundred murders they personally carried out. Mostly other gangs, people who got in their way, occasionally cops who wouldn't take a bribe, threat, or hint."

"Not exactly surprising they're bad, considering the name they picked for themselves," Amber said. "That doesn't sound like something we want in our town."

"They broke people for pleasure," Doc Hammond said. "They killed anyone in their way, and it took the task force and Assembly to work together to bring them down."

"Okay, and then what?" Miles asked.

"They scattered before we could get them all," Doc Hammond said. "Frank Duke and his lieutenants were killed by Arbiters in a fight that left several Assembly personnel dead, along with a dozen humans. It was . . . it was bad. Really bad."

Miles thought back to anything he might have heard about Arbiter deaths in America, and something moved free. "I wasn't an Arbiter in the 1980s," he said. "But I remember being told about a human-vampire task force in L.A during that time. Lots of arrests, lots of deaths. Lots of vampires quickly and quietly being taken care of."

"And our deceased victim was one of them?" Amber asked.

"No," Doc Hammond said. "Our victim is forty-four years old. He'd have been a child when the gang was in its heyday. Which could mean it had reformed. I got a DNA hit on our victim because his father was a member. He did time up until his death in the early noughties. My concern is that we have people wanting to recreate this gang, living in town. And also, that when people find out who the victim was, it's going to get bad. Worse."

"Who's the victim?" Amber asked.

"Liam Fricker," Doc Hammond said.

Miles looked between Amber and Doc Hammond as neither of them looked happy about the information. "Why is that bad?" He asked.

"Liam was a regular at the Red Demon," Amber said. "And along with his best friend Travis, and Travis' brother Cody, and a bunch of others who drink there, he was as anti-vampire as they come. And seems like he was murdered by a vampire. If that gets out, we're going to have problems in this town. More problems."

Amber passed the victim reports to Miles.

"Are those at the Red Demon likely to do something stupid?" Miles asked as he flicked through the reports on the victims.

"Yes," Amber and the Doc said in unison.

"This Liam guy hated vampires, yes?" Miles asked, throwing a stick for Church to run after.

"Blamed them for his life," Amber said. "Repeatedly. To anyone who would listen."

"Whoever killed this Liam guy didn't kill the others," Miles said. "The MOs are completely different."

"Can you be sure?" Amber asked.

"Let's go somewhere quiet and indoors to talk this through?" Miles asked, looking around to check if anyone was nearby. The snow was getting heavier, and the temperature was dropping quickly. It would be well below freezing soon. "Doc is turning into an icicle, and I don't need to let my core temp drop and start getting hungry. Let's go to my place and look through all of this horror in genuine warmth."

"I'm not exactly used to this subterfuge and sneaking around," Doc Hammond said, clearly welcoming the chance to start moving again.

Amber and Doc Hammond took the former's car and followed Miles and Church through town to his temporary accommodation.

"You vampires sure don't live a poor life," Doc Hammond said as she got out of Amber's car, after they'd parked behind Miles.

"One of the perks of being an Arbiter," Miles said, opening the front door and welcoming everyone inside.

Miles brewed coffee and brought it through to the dining room, where the files of the deceased had been placed. He'd also found a packet of cantucci that had been half dipped in chocolate.

"Okay, where were we?" Miles asked, dunking a cantucci in his coffee.

"You were about to tell us why the Magistrate isn't screaming headlines searching for a vampire killing people," Doc Hammond said.

"Aye, because, for one, we just don't drink that much blood," Miles said. "I mean, even House Barbarous doesn't need enough blood that they'll drain three people dry in two weeks. It's overkill. It's a Hollywood movie version of a vampire. I need maybe a pint a week, but I'm average age in centuries. A new vampire would need two pints a week, and even a brand new House Barbarous vampire would need a pint a day. And there's no way a new vampire cleanly murdered three people and drank them dry."

Miles stabbed a finger at the files. "Yes, like you said, Doc, there are definitely vampire fangs involved, but seriously, no hair, no fibres, no fingerprints, no CCTV, no evidence of any kind that a vampire was actually there? There's no way to say how many vampires might have been involved. These are the cleanest crime scenes on earth. The bodies were killed elsewhere and dumped there, I'm certain of it." He removed his phone from his pocket and took photos of all the victims' personal details.

"I agree," Doc Hammond said, taking a cantucci of her own. "So if the Magistrate are lying?" she asked.

"Then we have a problem," Miles said. "Because it goes way beyond politics, and if they're trying to set vampires up for this, they'll start a war. I need to find Lauren, and I need to find Oliver. We need to find out what the hell is going on here."

"You said you think Lauren was hurt at her home," Amber said. "I think you're right. I think something happened, and she got hurt, and the Magistrate are covering for Reese."

"Why, though?" Miles asked.

"I dug into that," Amber said. "Reese and Blake went to college together. You got a computer?"

Miles retrieved his laptop and passed it to her.

Amber logged in, found Lauren and Blake's joint social media page. She went straight to the photos. She scrolled through the myriad of pictures of landscapes, of Lauren and Reese together, until she found one with Blake and Reese.

Miles read the title of the picture: *College Days*. Reese stood beside Blake and two other men, all four facing the camera, smiling, their arms around one another's shoulders.

"That's Travis Sharpe," Amber said, pointing to one of the men.

"Who's the last man?" Miles asked, moving closer to the screen.

"That would be an alive Liam Fricker," she said.

"Can you bring up Blake's page?" Miles asked.

It took Yvonne less than a second to find Blake's page, which was open to the world to see. She scrolled through it, showing a mass of anti-vampire rhetoric, most of which was based on myths and propaganda.

"I feel ill just looking at this stuff," Doc Hammond said as she scrolled by one post which said that vampires kidnapped children. It was liked by a hundred and six people.

"Some people only have hate in them," Miles said. "If it wasn't vampires, they'd just need someone else to blame for whatever shitty excuse for a life they ended up with. Stop."

Amber stopped scrolling on a shirtless Blake as he flexed for the camera.

"Can you zoom in on that?" Miles asked, pointing to the screen.

Amber clicked on the photo and used the keyboard to zoom in where Miles had pointed.

"Fucking hell," Miles whispered.

"It's a tattoo," Amber said.

"Of the Mortis gang," Doc Hammond said.

"That's how some of them know each other," Miles said. "Family of Mortis gang members. Can you check to see if Reese or Travis are also affiliated?"

"I can look into it," Amber said. "You think these guys killed Lauren, don't you?"

Miles nodded slowly, wondering whether he should tell her of his suspicions that Lauren's double-crossing had got her killed. That would expose both Drest and Danica to trouble. "I'm sorry, but I think she's dead. I think her husband killed her and had his Magistrate friends cover it up."

"And Oliver?" Amber asked.

"I don't know," Miles said. "But if they find him before we do, they'll pin her murder, and the murders of those three others, on him."

"Could Oliver have killed Liam last night?" Doc Hammond asked.

Yvonne had said she couldn't believe that he'd kill anyone, that he wasn't a murderer. However, as Miles had discovered many times over his long life, vampires forced into a corner will react to save themselves first. And Oliver was a criminal. A criminal who had worked with a gang capable of violence, so the likelihood was that he wasn't shy about using it when needed. If Oliver felt that he was being hunted by the Magistrate, then there was always a possibility that he would want to even the odds a bit.

"Yes," Miles said. "He might have just taken Liam to get information, but it got out of hand. Maybe Oliver lost control. I don't know. Yvonne said he might be staying in the forest around town, but if he's in town, he's going to need blood. Unless he's surviving on rats, and I can tell you, he won't want to do that. Any chance you can check the CCTV of any local emporiums for purchases?"

"You want to go search now?" Amber asked.

Miles nodded. "Yeah. Doc, you're welcome to stay. There's food, there's drink, and you've been exceptionally helpful. Or we can drop you off, your call."

"I need to get back to the hospital and get my stuff," Doc Hammond said. "You think there's going to be more deaths?"

"If these murders are Magistrate arranged, how and why are they doing it?" Miles asked. "It's not for publicity; they've been trying to keep everything quiet. So it's for something else. They haven't explicitly said Oliver is the killer either. They've labelled him a person of interest."

"You look like something is on your mind," Doc Hammond said.

"Someone told me that the gang I was investigating had a Boss who was gaining in power and influence," Miles said, thinking back to the meeting with Danica and Drest. "What if the Magistrate knows that Oliver couldn't have killed those people, because they already know that he wasn't here?"

"You think someone from that gang is working with the Magistrate?" Amber asked.

"I think we need to find Oliver," Miles said. "And really fast."

CHAPTER NINETEEN

The three left Miles's accommodation, taking the cars they'd arrived in, although Miles followed Amber until they arrived at the park. Miles and Amber thanked Doc Hammond and watched as she walked to the hospital.

Miles watched Amber as she opened the boot to her own car, removed a shotgun and black holdall, and returned to Miles's BMW, opening the passenger door and rear passenger door to let Church switch to being on the rear seats.

"My car can stay here," Amber said by way of explanation. "You do know we drive on the other side of the road here?"

Miles pretended to chuckle. "You are a witty detective," he said sarcastically, getting into the driver's seat.

"Hey, I just don't want to get driven into oncoming traffic," she said, sitting down and buckling up.

"How about thrown out of a moving vehicle?" Miles asked as they set off.

"You threatening a detective of the law?" Amber said. "That's low."

Miles laughed and looked back at Church, and stroked her behind the ear as she settled down. She almost immediately fell asleep behind Miles's seat.

"So, to the emporium first?" Miles asked.

Amber gave directions and Miles was soon outside of a small shop just off the Main Street that ran through town. The neon sign was red, but otherwise it looked like every emporium that Miles had ever been to.

"I'll go in and talk," Amber said. "I figure an Arbiter might . . . spook people."

"Please feel free," Miles said, keeping the car heater on while Amber ran over to the emporium.

She appeared ten minutes later carrying a piece of paper and looking quite pleased with herself.

"Ta da," she said as soon as she'd opened the car door, and passed Miles the paper.

"That's a picture of Oliver," Miles said. "CCTV is good in there. Little surprised they let you have this."

"I suggested they either helped me or talked to an Arbiter," Amber said.

"Well, it worked," Miles said, staring at the picture, hoping to get something from it. Oliver was centre frame, wearing dark clothing and holding a white and red polystyrene box. "He's holding a crate of blood."

"He is," Amber said, removing a second piece of paper from her pocket and passing it over to him.

Miles unfolded the small piece of paper, which had a series of numbers and letters on it like a serial number.

"This is the tracking number for the crate," Amber said, using her phone's map app to show somewhere outside of town, surrounded by forest.

"Oliver stole a newly delivered blood crate," Miles surmised. "And all new blood crates have a tracking chip in them in case idiots steal them. I assume that spot on the map is where the chip was found."

"The crate, but otherwise you would be correct," Amber said. "Why would someone need a crate of blood?"

"It's twenty-four pints," Miles said. "It's why they're tracked. There's no good reason to need that much blood. So he figured out it was tracked and dumped the crate."

"So where is that?" Miles asked, pointing to Amber's phone.

"That is where there are quite a few disused cabins, used by the loggers while they were working. They were going to build houses, but the deals fell through. There's a quarry to the north that's still in use, lots of people around there, some mining stuff further northwest, but that's all long disused. No development for years, until those rich people purchased the land you're staying on."

"We start there, then," Miles said, putting the car in Drive and setting off.

"There's a lot of land to search," Amber said.

"When was this taken?" Miles asked.

"Four days ago," Amber said.

"Did they spot a car?" Miles asked.

"No car," Amber said. "I looked; he either parked it a long way and walked or just walked the whole distance."

"Stolen cars lead to police," Miles said. "And hired cars need ID. He's on foot. He can get away into the forest quicker that way."

"So," Amber said, "you're the vampire. Is there somewhere a vampire would stay that is out in the forest?"

"Somewhere safe from the sunshine," Miles said. "Somewhere we could sleep and not worry about being woken. We sleep pretty deeply, so there's always a concern that someone would sneak up on us. Oliver has to know that at the very least his old Boss is after him. Probably that the Magistrate are too, even if he wasn't involved in Liam's death."

"And if he wasn't?" Amber asked.

"We have a *really* dangerous vampire out here," Miles replied. "I'd like to think we're not that unlucky. We have a vampire who is desperate enough to steal twenty-four packs of blood from an emporium. I think he'll be in some decrepit place in the forest."

The turnoff to where the crate had been found was a few miles outside of town. It was nearly another mile down a dirt road, and once they'd stopped and everyone had gotten out into the night, Amber had to turn on her flashlight to be able to see. Miles was thankful that vampire and Church's eyes had no such issues.

While there were half a dozen metal sheet cabins, all were so dilapidated that the fact they remained standing was probably a miracle. There was no way a vampire was staying there.

"No one is living here," Miles said, looking through the partially rusted away wall of one cabin into the insect-infested interior. "There's no roof on two of them, and even the most desperate of vampires would be hard pressed to hide here. The first day the UV gets above one, they're going to have a shitty time."

"There are two good ones," Amber said. "And by good, I mean they have all four walls and a roof. It won't surprise you to find that those two are full of drug paraphernalia."

"Church, you got anything?" Miles asked.

Church had been sniffing everything she could find, and she whined slightly, pawing at the ground and kicking up snow.

"Too many animals come through here," Miles said. "Even this late into winter, it's all muddled up."

Church walked back to the car, sat down beside the back wheel, and made it known she did not want to smell any more cabins.

"Okay, so where to next?" Miles asked as they stood by the car, scratching Church behind the ear. "No car tracks here, so he didn't drive down this way. He carried the crate all the way down here and dumped it. He would have been freaked out, scared that he'd been found. If he's got a place to stay, it's somewhere he would consider safe. Good exits in case of emergency, and somewhere he can see or hear or smell people coming."

"There's an old factory; it's not far from here," Amber said. "These cabins were put here because the people who owned the factory wanted some of their staff to live close by. This was meant to be the start of a new phase of the town. It lasted a few years."

"How far to the factory?" Miles asked.

"Half a mile, maybe," Amber said. "You can drive right up to it. We have to get kids out of there quite a lot, although not since the rumours started of a serial killing vampire. People don't really like coming up here when there's a possibility they won't be coming back."

"What happens if we find Oliver at night?" Amber asked.

"He might need to be subdued," Miles said. "You got any incendiary rounds or electric baton?"

"I've got an electric baton," Amber said. "Never had to use it."

"Let's make sure we don't have to make tonight your first time," Miles said with a smile.

"Can you drive around that way?" Miles asked. "Keep your lights on. I'll take Church through the forest; if we spook him, he might run right into us. Save us the bother of hunting him. Which way, exactly?"

Amber pointed out the direction. "Head that way, you can't miss it; it's massive. There's a signpost about halfway between here and there. Some kids nailed it to a tree; it's got a massive drawing of a cock and balls on it. It's practically a town landmark."

Miles looked over the way that Amber had pointed and nodded as if it was fine. "Drive down slowly to the entrance to the mill and wait for us."

Miles and Church were already on the move when Amber drove away. They ran through the forest, not going all out, but still making good time until Miles spotted the faded signpost with the crude drawing.

He'd taken only a few more steps when the scent reached him. Church looked back at Miles.

There was no point in asking if she smelled it, too. There was no mistaking the smell of blood.

They met Amber up the road from the mill. "There's blood here," he told her. "If Oliver is here and I can find his scent, I can track him should he run off."

"Can you track via scent?" Amber asked.

"Some can," Miles said. "Some can track via heat signature. Some can sense vampires nearby. All vampires can track via blood if they've tasted it. The older the vampire, the more they can do more than one."

"And you?" Amber asked.

"My sense of smell is much better than a human's, probably not as good as Church's, though," Miles said. "If I had the vampire's blood, I could track them for miles."

"So what you're smelling is a fresh kill?" Amber asked.

"Just blood at the moment," Miles said. "But it doesn't bode well, does it? This could be dangerous, Amber."

"I'm a cop, Miles," Amber said. "Humans are plenty dangerous enough."

"On that, we agree," Miles told her.

"You want me to drive the car down to the mill entrance?" Amber asked.

"No sirens, but keep your light on," Miles said. "If you're okay with that."

"Will he notice it?" Amber asked.

"If he's there, probably, aye," Miles said. "I don't plan on making you bait, if you're worried." He opened the passenger car door and removed a holdall in the footwell. "No normal bullets; they won't do anything but irritate him unless you get a head shot."

Miles removed a stun baton and a tranquilliser gun, placing them on the passenger seat. "This works if they get in close," he told Amber, picking up the baton. "Do not let him get in close. Do these tranquillisers work on vampires?"

"They're Assembly rounds," Amber said, picking up the gun, removing the cartridge of small needlelike projectiles, and making sure it was loaded. "They'll put him down. Don't you need a weapon?"

"No," Miles said by way of explanation. "Stay safe."

"You too," Amber called after him as he ran into the forest with Church taking the lead.

Miles ran as quickly as he dared, considering he didn't know the terrain or area and the last thing he wanted to do was slip down an embankment and hit a tree.

Church had no such compunction and ran with a freedom that only dogs seem to possess, and Miles had to increase his own speed just to keep up with her.

It didn't take them long to reach a rocky ridge that overlooked the disused factory. Church sat beside Miles, the pair of them watching the front entrance to the factory as his loaned BMW pulled up and the engine was switched off. Amber got out of the vehicle, the tranquilliser gun in one hand, and walked up to the locked gate, peering through the chain-link fence at the disused property before her, her flashlight illuminating parts of the building. Just a police detective doing her job.

Miles looked over at the factory again. No lights inside, which was to be expected; Oliver was a vampire, after all. He removed his phone from his pocket and called Amber, who picked up on the first ring.

"I can't see you," she said.

"I see you fine," he told her. "I'm going to send Church to come stand with you. The fence is locked up, yes?" Miles patted Church on the head and pointed to Amber.

The dog snorted and ran off toward her destination.

"Yes, we've had trouble with kids here before," Amber said. "A few years back one got really hurt, and the owners—a big conglomerate— made a big show about how we have to ask permission to be let in. It's company property, apparently. They've added some heavy-duty locks, but that's about it. You can still get in from the massive bloody gap down by the stream."

"Take Church to the stream," Miles said. "Have a look around. Make a lot of noise."

"We're trying to spook someone, yes?" Amber asked, her voice now a whisper.

"He's a vampire, not Superman," Miles said. "No need to whisper unless he's about twenty feet away. And there's at least double that from you to the factory entrance. Just don't shout."

"What if he's in the woods around me?" Amber asked, quickly looking around, the light flicking between trees.

"He's not," Miles said. "The scent is coming from the building. Church is with you anyway; she'd have smelled someone if they were in the forest with you."

Miles watched Church arrive and a happy-looking Amber greet her. "I feel like I'm being watched," she said.

There was an aura of unpleasantness about the whole place, and Miles wondered if something really was lurking just out of range of his senses. He dropped down from his perch on the rocky alcove, landing softly on the leaf-covered parking area of a factory well past its best days, and remained motionless for a second. It wasn't quite dark yet, but he activated his night vision, checking for heat trails, and found thousands of them. Mostly small animals and birds. It would be impossible to track someone here, even more than it was back in London. Miles went back to his normal vision, walked across the parking lot to the locked gate, and ripped the chain and padlock free, tossing them aside and pulling the gate open. If there needed to be a quick egress, he wanted to make sure Amber was able to get back to the car as quickly as possible.

The sounds of footsteps from the side of the factory took Miles's attention, and he turned to see Amber walking up a steep bank toward him, with Church at her side.

"There's an old grate down there," she said. "Looks like it's been used recently; there are drag marks on the metal of the tunnel. Also, Church barked and pawed at the ground."

"You smell something?" Amber asked Church, who barked one time again.

"Someone has been staying here," Miles said. "The smell of blood is stronger in here; there's a scent of at least two people, too. It's just a question if that someone is our prey."

"Oliver and someone else?" Amber asked. "Lauren?"

"I guess we're about to find out," Miles said.

"Also, you probably shouldn't use the word *prey* around humans," Amber said. "Even when it's not meaning us, it's . . . off-putting."

Miles considered the request. He'd never really thought about it before. "I'll try not to use it." He looked around. "How far are we from the main part of town?"

"Seven or eight miles maybe," Amber said. "You broke the gate; someone is going to yell at us about that."

"They can yell at me," Miles said, looking over the factory.

Church stayed with Amber, while Miles took point and the three of them made their way across the parking lot and through the partially open factory shop floor entrance.

There wasn't much to find inside the cavernous room beyond, apart from the occasional scurrying critter and cobweb. The gantries above looked ancient and unsafe, but Miles quickly scaled the side of the wall and leapt onto one.

"Church, you got anything new?" Miles called down. The further into the mill they went, the stronger the smell of blood. It led to the far end of the mill.

Church barked, followed by a long whine.

"What does that mean?" Amber asked.

"Lots of scents," Miles said. "If we find Oliver's, she can track him, but as exposed as this part of the mill is, there's going to be birds, rats, bigger animals. It also depends on whether or not he used this part of the factory. If there are tunnels below, he may have stayed there. It would explain why there's no scents up here for him; he's not using it."

"Too many scents up here?" Amber asked Church.

Church barked.

"I'll check out up here," he called down, before walking to the rooms at the end of the gantry, only to find more critters, more mess, and a general lack of anyone trying to kill him. He returned to the gantry.

"No joy?" Amber asked.

Miles dropped over the metal railing and landed near Amber and Church. "Nope," he said. "If this is where Oliver is living, he's not using the rooms up there for anything."

The three had walked only a few paces across the factory floor when Church began to whine and paw at the floor.

"The scent of blood is strong here," Miles said as Church crossed the floor and stood beside a metal door with a circular lock in the middle, like those found on ships. The door was sealed shut. Amber followed as Miles took a deep breath, while Church pawed softly at the door.

"What does that mean?" Amber asked.

"Nothing good," Miles said, placing one hand on the door. He turned back to Amber and Church. "Ready?" he asked.

Both nodded.

Miles turned the wheel and there was a hiss as the seal broke. The smell of blood made him take a step back as it overpowered his senses. He continued on as Church took several steps away, toward the open entrance, her eyes firmly on the doorway, her hackles up, making a low threatening growl.

"You okay?" Amber asked.

"So much blood," he said, raising his hand to give him a minute as he continued to open the door. "Fresh blood, too. It's just overpowered my senses. It's all I can smell."

"I'll call it in," Amber said.

"Yes, take Church with you outside," Miles said, pulling open the unlocked door and breathing through the stench until his senses had settled. A newer vampire might have lost control with that much blood. If this was where Oliver was hiding, Miles wondered what the hell he'd been doing.

"Called it in," Amber said. "Captain told me not to do anything stupid."

"Would walking down those stairs be considered stupid?" Miles asked.

Amber shone her torch over the steps. "Yes," she said. "We should go down anyway."

"Church, you take up the rear," Miles said, and took his first step onto the stairs. He told himself it was to check they were sturdy enough to take his weight, but in reality it was because he needed to steady himself in case the scents below threatened to overwhelm him.

The basement was huge. Easily the length of the entire floor above, but it was mostly empty apart from filing cabinets, old metal shelving units, and a pile consisting of dozens of dead rats.

"What killed all the rats?" Amber asked.

Miles picked up one rat by its tail, noticing the bites around its neck. "Something *really* hungry," he said, dropping the carcass back to the ground and wiping his hands on his jeans. "We can survive on the blood of other animals easily, but we'd need more than one rat could give us. A dozen would keep the cravings at bay for a while, hence the rat mountain here. Although if he killed all these rats, why steal so much blood?"

"There must be more than a hundred rats," Amber said as they walked by them.

"Better pest control than a cat," Miles said, as he continued on along the basement.

"Was that the smell?" Amber asked.

"They're all dry," Miles said. "The smell is over this way. Not just blood, but . . . death."

With every step, Miles's anxiety increased. What was making that smell? How many bodies would they find? Was he wrong, was Oliver killing people? Would Lauren be among his victims? The questions tumbled through his mind, and he welcomed them if it meant he didn't think about blood.

At the halfway point of the basement, with plenty of nothing ahead of them, there was a door standing ajar, which when pushed open revealed a storage room with high ceilings that sat under one of the rooms adjacent to the main floor above.

Amber gasped as the light from her torch fell over the body that had been affixed to the wall at the far side of the room. Just as it had in the church, blood covered every surface. The smell of blood, shit, and death was horrific, and Amber had to cover her mouth with her jacket sleeve as she turned away from the scene before them.

"Stay there a second," Miles said, stepping farther into the room. He walked slowly over to the body, the scent of blood in the windowless room more potent than it had been in the church with its ventilation. He stayed a dozen feet back, partly because he had no wish to get closer, and partly because of the mess. The man had been nailed to pieces of wood that were in the shape of a cross, although they hadn't been created with any real skill. His throat was missing, torn out like the previous victim's, and his entire abdomen was ripped open, the contents all over the floor where a second body lay, partially obscured by the filth and gore created by the crucified man. The second body was positioned to look up at the crucified man, their legs under the body above them.

"Jesus fucking Christ," Amber said from behind Miles, while Church let out a low, unhappy growl.

"Easy," Miles said, looking back at Church, who turned and walked out of the room.

"Is that a second body?" Amber asked, pointing to the person on the ground. "And where are his organs?"

Apart from the blood and muck, the second victim was covered in bits of detritus from around the factory, almost as if whoever had done this had tried to partially bury them.

Miles reached out and removed a piece of the cardboard with one hand, dragging it away with an accompanying sound he'd rather have never heard again.

"Oh fuck," Amber gasped. "That's Lauren Gibson."

Lauren was covered in blood to the point where Miles couldn't actually see what colour her clothes had been. Everything was various shades of dark red, her hair matted to her crimson face, her eyes closed, almost serenely.

"What happened here?" Amber asked.

Miles shrugged. "Not a clue. Blood is powerful stuff, and there are things out there that can use it to control, to gain power. This is all crude, though. Her body was placed here, and his body was torn apart, although what happened to the bits that fell out, I have no idea."

"I need fresh air," Amber said. "Don't move anything. They're going to need photos and . . . holy shit, that's bad."

"I'll meet up with you in a second," Miles said as Amber bid a hasty exit. "Church, go with her."

Church didn't need to be told twice, and Miles was soon left alone.

Judging from the . . . consistency and smell, the blood was hours old, maybe six at the most. Miles reached out tentatively with a finger and touched the blood. It felt like blood. He raised his hand to his nose; it smelled like blood, too. He decided that tasting it was a step further than he was willing to go, and he removed a piece of tissue from his pocket, wiping his fingers clean.

It was dark in the storage room, and even with a torch, it would have been difficult to make out who the male victim was, but the female victim was definitely Lauren Gibson. She was easy to identify, if not from her face then from the Super Mario Brothers mushroom tattooed on her shoulder.

Being in such close quarters with so much blood had messed with Miles's senses, but he took a deep breath and reached out, closing his eyes and trying to block out the stimuli in front of him. He opened his eyes, hoping to find a heat signature that might say where Oliver—if it was him—went, even if it was freezing cold.

Besides his own, there were no trails except Amber's and Church's. No rat trails either. In fact, no animals of any kind had been inside the basement room, as though they had known to stay away.

Miles sighed. It was time to go see what was happening upstairs and hopefully get a lead on where the resident murderer might have run off to. He looked over at the dead man. "I'm sorry this happened to you," he said softly, before looking down at Lauren at the exact moment he registered her heartbeat. "Holy shit," Miles shouted. "She's alive."

CHAPTER TWENTY

A lot happened in a very short space of time.

Miles shouted for Church to get Amber and ran over to Lauren. He ignored the overwhelming scents of blood and death as he knelt beside the woman, using some old rags he'd found to try and wipe the majority of the blood off her face, while checking that she didn't have any wounds of her own.

He slowly turned her to the side, and she let out a slight groan as he examined her back for anything that might cause her serious damage. While he found nothing, he didn't want to move her and risk any internal injuries.

Amber returned to explain that she'd called the ambulance and Doc Hammond, along with her station, all of whom were coming en masse.

Miles left Amber and Church to keep an eye on Lauren, while he traversed the tunnels beneath the factory, searching for any signs of Oliver or anyone else who might have been involved. He found nothing and returned to Amber as she was going to meet the paramedics.

"You know the name of the man nailed up like that?" Miles asked.

"Travis Sharpe," Amber said grimly. "The Magistrate will have a field day with this; that's two of their supporters massacred."

"Better find out where Reese is," Miles said. "Just in case all this death is catching. Besides, he'll want to know his wife is alive, won't he?"

Amber nodded and left, returning a few minutes later with three paramedics who took over, as Miles explained that Lauren was alive. They thanked him while ushering a bloodstained Miles out of the room as they got to work.

Miles and Church followed Amber out of the basement and up into the factory where Doc Hammond and six police officers waited. The car headlights were left on, illuminating the entire front of the factory.

Doc Hammond pointed at me. "Is that yours?" Several of the officers looked troubled by the sight of a blood-drenched vampire.

"No, it's Lauren Gibson's," Miles told her, knowing that wasn't going to be a great explanation, but he was tired and that's what he had.

"Is she . . . ?" One of the police officers asked, leaving the last word hanging.

"She's alive," Miles assured him. "This isn't her blood. It belongs to the body that was crucified above her."

Doc Hammond stopped walking toward the factory and turned back to Miles. "Crucified?"

"Yes," Miles said with a nod. "Before his belly was slit open and its contents allowed to fall out on top of her. Whoever did it gathered all of the bits and removed them. Which was nice of them, I guess. I didn't do a full examination, so I can't say more."

"You need to get cleaned up," Amber told Miles.

"Yes, you really do," Doc Hammond agreed. "There's a nearby stream that should be able to get rid of the most of it, but I think your clothes might need stronger stuff."

There was a bark from somewhere in the darkness of the forest beyond.

"That's Church," Miles said. "I'll go find out what she wants."

"You need backup?" Amber asked.

Miles shook his head. "I'll call if I do." He set off after Church, her occasional barks making sure he went the right way, until he found her further down the stream nearby.

Church stood on the bank of the stream, her gaze fixated on a nearby large rock. She looked back at Miles, whined, and returned her glare to the rock.

The smell of blood was obvious from several feet back, even upwind as he was. "What did you find?" he asked her, jumping over the stream and crouching down by the large rock in question where a bloody handprint sat.

Church barked.

"He slipped here," Miles said. "He put his hand out to steady himself. You think you can track him?"

Church barked again, leapt over the stream, and set off at a fast pace through increasingly dense woodland, with Miles following as closely as possible. Church stopped every few hundred meters as she found another blood mark on a tree or rock. They were headed in the right direction.

After stopping half a dozen times, they found themselves at least a mile away from the factory, but they continued on, moving farther and farther up a slight incline, until they stopped once more and Miles looked back.

"We've gone high and not even realised," he said, looking down over the treetops that littered the side of the ridge they were on.

Church whined and sat in front of a sheer cliff face which loomed over a hundred feet high. She looked back at Miles and snorted.

"Yeah, I guess you're not going to be climbing that," Miles agreed. He walked over to the cliff face and saw blood smeared across parts of it. He looked up at the summit. There were no overhangs or anything that made it look like an overly complicated climb. Plenty of handholds, although it wasn't as if he needed them. The biggest problem would be if someone was waiting right at the top and the second Miles reached it, he was kicked off. A hundred-foot fall onto hard soil wouldn't kill him, but it wouldn't feel good either.

Miles looked around. There were large trees close to the edge of the cliff, the top branches almost lightly tickling the summit of the cliff face.

"I have a plan," Miles told Church, who sat waiting. "I'll go look, you stay here."

Church's whine was not one Miles felt was full of confidence.

"I never said it was a great plan," Miles agreed. "But it's what we have unless you want to backtrack and go around this cliff to where it slopes back down." He pointed off into the moonlit tree line in the distance and Church followed with her eyes.

Church huffed and stood.

"Okay, how about you head that way, I'll go up, and we'll get this runner in between us," Miles suggested.

Church set off at a sprint, moving much faster than she had when she was making sure that Miles could keep up.

"Show-off," Miles whispered. He turned to the cliff face and launched himself at it, landing twenty feet up, his fingers now talons.

Moving up the cliff face was easy, his talons making sure he had purchase as he moved at speed to the top. There were multiple bloody smears along the face of the cliff, and just before he reached the summit, Miles stopped. The idea of someone waiting for him was foremost in his mind. He moved across the face of the cliff, coming up at the far side closer to the tree. He reached the top, pulling himself up with a jump and landing on the edge in a crouched position.

Miles sniffed the air. Blood. Again. Less so than there had been, and it was tinged with sweat, but it was still unmistakably blood.

The top of the cliff consisted of a large clearing surrounded by thick trees and bunches, as well as several large boulders sitting to the side closest to Miles. The clearing had an inch of fresh snow across it, and footsteps that looked as if someone had been running in circles. An owl hooted from somewhere in the distance, followed by the howl of a . . . possibly a wolf. There were wolves in the area, not something he was concerned about, although he didn't need Church to return with half a dozen new friends.

Miles stood and walked out into the clearing, sniffing the air and trying to figure out exactly where the runner had gone next. The bloody smear on one of the trees gave away the direction, but as Miles stepped toward it, he was greeted with the low growl of a vampire.

The vampire dropped down from one of the trees, landing on all fours twenty feet in front of Miles. It was covered in blood, and had already changed into its vampire form. Its burning red eyes, evident even beneath all of the blood and grime. The vampire wore a simple T-shirt and jeans, but no shoes or socks.

"Oliver, I assume," Miles said as he stepped in front of one of the boulders. "Any chance we can sort this out like adults?"

The vampire roared in response, propelling itself forward with incredible speed, forcing Miles to throw himself to the side as the vampire smashed into the boulder, unable to stop itself in time.

Miles rolled along the pine needle-covered ground, coming back to his feet in front of a large tree just in time to dodge one of the boulders that had been picked up and thrown at him like a tennis ball. The boulder smashed into the tree, splintering a chunk of it from the force and making it list to the side.

The vampire launched itself across the clearing, its hands outstretched, dark talons prepared to rend flesh from bone, but Miles pushed out his hand in front, forming a telekinetic shield that the vampire smashed into face first. Miles twisted the power and forced it outward, throwing the vampire back across the clearing into a tree trunk, the impact accompanied by the sounds of breaking bones. The vampire fell into the thick bushes around the clearing and disappeared from sight.

Miles didn't have to wait long for the vampire to return as it sprinted out of the darkness, its arms flailing wildly in front of it. Miles pushed away its legs with a telekinetic strike, but as the vampire fell forward, it sprang forward, clawing at Miles as he tried to put some distance between them.

"I don't want to hurt you, Oliver," Miles said. "I just want answers."

Oliver was faster than Miles had expected, and he was soon dodging and blocking blow after blow, as his attacker sought to cleave him apart. Miles blocked a swipe of the vampire's arm, bringing his own elbow down on the joint, breaking it, only for the vampire to ignore it and swipe across with his good arm. Miles blocked and smashed the palm of his hand into the vampire's chest, unleashing a telekinesis blast at point-blank range, which threw the vampire into the partially destroyed tree.

Blood trickled down Miles's face, and he found that the vampire had cut along one of his arms and his left side, drawing blood with both, but thankfully neither wound was deep enough to bother him.

Miles's hands changed in a heartbeat, his fingers elongating, his nails becoming steel-hard talons. His face became sunken, his nose partially flattening, his skin hardening over his body, his fangs pushing their way out of his gums with a twinge of pain, his eyes turning bright red as he shrugged off his jacket and tossed it aside. The vampire before him was little more than a blazing vision of heat and blood in a dark forest.

"Enough," Miles shouted. "You need to calm down."

Oliver had lost control. Maybe it was all the blood, or the cold, or a combination of the two, but whatever had happened to him had caused him to ignore all reason. He was reacting on instinct, and that instinct said to run and kill anyone in the way.

More detritus was thrown Miles's way, but it was easily avoided even without the telekinesis, as he waited for the vampire to return. He didn't have to wait long as the almost feral creature sprinted out of the wood, leaping at Miles with an incandescent howl of rage.

Miles jumped back to avoid the attack, and immediately darted in, smashing his hands into the vampire's chest and unleashing his bloodline gift. The power rolled through Miles's body and out into Oliver, who screamed in pain, blinked, and fell to the ground.

"Bollocks," Miles whispered. "Are we done now?"

Oliver wept softly on the ground. He got up onto his knees and looked up at Miles, now back to his human-looking self. "You have to let me go. She's in danger."

"Lauren?" Miles asked. "Why is Lauren in danger? What's going on, Oliver?"

"I won't hand her over to those thugs," Oliver said. "I won't have her hurt anymore."

"Oliver," Miles said softly, trying to make sure that Oliver didn't snap again the moment he was able to. "You do know I'm a vampire, yes? Did you hit your head, or something? I'm with the Assembly. I'm an Arbiter. I'm here for you. Your Boss in London, you ran from him. He was making illegal vampires, you remember?"

"You're here for that?" Oliver asked. "Why?"

"Why?" Miles repeated, feeling his irritation grow. "Because people died, dipshit. Some old guy got turned into a desolate, and a bunch of vampires were killed. And more executed by your Boss when he turned up." Miles took a moment and forced himself to calm. "On top of that, Danica told me you worked for her. She asked me to come find you."

"Danica did?" Oliver asked.

Miles nodded. "A lot of people are worried about you."

"Carla and Teresa?" Oliver asked. "Are they okay?"

"Teresa was killed," Miles said. "Carla is safe. She's with the ATO."

"Teresa died?" Oliver asked. "How? Why?"

"Danny killed her," Miles told him. "She started hurting people. He didn't want the heat."

"Danny," Oliver said, a low growl in his voice. "Is he okay?"

Miles nodded. "I think so. He, Kyle, and the others were handed over to the ATO."

"Who's Kyle?" Oliver asked.

"Human. Your Boss brought him in," Miles said.

"Not *my* Boss," Oliver snapped. "He would never bring in a human who wasn't a familiar. I might not be able to remember his name, but I know that."

"And you don't know a Kyle?" Miles asked. He was concerned that whoever Kyle was, he'd never been taken in by the ATO. It had stuck in his mind, and he knew that there was something not right there. He described to Oliver what Kyle had looked like.

"Yeah, I know him," Oliver said. "Don't know his name, though. Not his real name."

"And he's not human?" Miles asked.

"He *told* you he's a human?" Oliver asked with a laugh, which turned into a barking cough. "I don't know his name, but he's two hundred years old at least. He's the Boss's familiar, so I guess *technically* he is human. He's a fucking murderer for hire, though. Because he's a familiar, the Boss's brain fuzzing never worked on him. He knows everything. It's why he was the Boss's right hand."

And he was never taken into custody, Miles thought to himself. "Bollocks."

"You can't take me in. I need to get to Lauren, I need to keep her safe," Oliver said, trying to get to his feet.

Miles placed a hand on Oliver's shoulder and pushed him back down. "Wait," he said. "What's going on with Lauren? You crucified someone over her, and then disembowelled him."

"You don't understand," Oliver said, panic creeping back into his voice. "They're going to come for her. People are going to die."

"Who is *they?*" Miles asked. "The Magistrate?"

Oliver shrugged and took a deep breath. "I don't know who they were. I was looking into those vampire murders; I wanted to show Yvonne I wasn't useless," he said. "The Magistrate were involved, and I read my sister's notes about them. Something didn't feel right. I tracked the Magistrate for days but arrived too late to save the third victim. The Magistrate were right there, though, I don't know how they got there so quickly. Liam Fricker was there, but it was getting to daylight, and I needed to rest."

"What happened next?" Miles asked, wanting to know everything that Oliver knew before he had to take him in officially.

Oliver took a deep breath, letting it out slowly. "The next night, I followed Liam to the Red Demon, and he met up with three men who had a van. I followed the van into the forest but lost them. I found them just as they were taking a woman out of the van, throwing her down a steep hill. They were laughing. I got down the hill before them, and scooped her away. She wasn't moving. She was hurt. I heard them shouting about how she was meant to be dead, but I just kept running. I brought Lauren here. If they find her, they'll kill her."

"Did you see who hurt her?" Miles asked. "Or why they hurt her?"

Oliver shook his head. "I only saw them try to dump the body. You need to let me go."

"I can't," Miles said. "Did you kill Liam Fricker and Travis Sharpe because they were involved?"

"They deserved it," Oliver snapped and shoved Miles as he sprang to his feet, but Miles grabbed his shoulder and tripped him, dragging him back and dumping him on the ground.

"I said I need to go," Oliver said.

"You can't," Miles told him. "You need to come with me. We'll figure out what's going on with Lauren. We'll get her help. We'll get her security. Whatever you . . ."

Miles heard something in the forest behind him and turned just as something blasted him in the chest. A second blast dropped him to his knees as his torso felt as if it were on fire.

Two people stepped out of the forest; both wore black tactical armour that covered their entire bodies. One of the men carried a shotgun that was held directly at Miles, whose entire body screamed in pain at the pellets of incendiary rounds that littered his torso. Down inside of him, a deep burning anger raged.

Oliver tried to run by Miles, but he was hit by the second attacker who had large metal gauntlets on his fists. He had a faint purple glow around his knuckles. Oliver's legs buckled, and he dropped to the ground as the attacker punched him in the head. There was a flash of purple as the gauntlets struck flesh, and Oliver went out cold.

"UV gauntlets," Miles said, spitting blood onto the floor. "Classy."

There was a bark from somewhere in the darkness of the woods; Church was on her way.

The attacker with the shotgun walked over to Miles, picked him up by his throat, and threw him across the clearing, where he impacted with a large boulder. "Take the vampire," the shotgun user told his friend. "This one is mine."

Miles watched as Oliver was dragged away into the dense forest, and the attacker using the shotgun stalked toward him.

"A vampire who uses a gun," Miles said. "How pathetic."

The shotgun user looked down at his weapon and replaced it in the holster on his back before charging toward Miles. Miles grabbed a boulder and smashed it into the vampire's head, knocking him back. The vampire shook his head from the blow, allowing Miles to follow up with a telekinetic blast that threw the vampire back into a tree, rending it in half. The larger part of the tree crashed to the ground and tumbled over the side of the cliff with a cacophony of noise that echoed around the forest.

The top of the tree came out of the darkness like a javelin, forcing Miles to dive under it and roll back to his feet, only to be met by the feral vampire who had sprinted toward him at a speed Miles had barely the time to react to. Miles managed to block the first punch, but couldn't manage the rake along his ribs.

Pain flared along Miles's side as he tried to put distance between himself and his attacker. Miles's bloodline gift wouldn't be usable for a while.

The vampire continued to move quicker and quicker, with each blow taking more strength, driving Miles back toward the cliff edge. The vampire got inside Miles's guard and grabbed him by the throat, lifting him off the ground. Miles kneed him in the face, which caused the vampire to stagger back. He wrapped his legs around the shoulder and pulled back, wrenching the arm until he heard a tear and felt the shoulder pop, but the vampire kept hold of Miles.

Miles kicked the vampire in the face, shattering the mask, and revealing the face behind it to belong to someone Miles recognised. He couldn't remember where, though.

The vampire went for his shotgun, and Miles reached out with his telekinesis, wrapping it around a boulder and throwing it with everything he had at the vampire. Instead of jumping away, the vampire leapt feet first toward Miles, catching him in the chest and sending him flying back off the cliff into the tree behind him. Miles hit what felt like every single branch on the way down. He used his talons to slow his descent, but the bark came away and he pinballed between more thick branches until he hit the ground back first, the air driven out of him as something howled in victory high above.

"Church," Miles said, rolling onto his side, as more pain erupted through him. His arm was pointing the wrong direction, and the gash in his ribs was bone deep. He couldn't take a deep breath and coughed up blood. Punctured lung, maybe? Broken ribs, almost definitely.

Miles made it to the tree he'd become acquainted with on his way down, as his arm reset itself, causing him to cry out in pain and slump down onto the cold, hard ground.

"Church," he screamed. He was exhausted, hurt, and needed blood. And rest. There was no time for either.

He was about to scramble up the tree when a bark from the side of where he stood was quickly accompanied by Church sprinting toward him, her legs covered in little nicks and cuts as she'd run flat out through whatever vegetation had been in her way.

Miles crashed to his knees, overjoyed at seeing Church in one piece as the dog ran up to him, licking his face and hands, nuzzling against his neck.

"I'm okay," Miles assured her. "Bloody, battered, and more than a little bruised, but I'll live."

Church lay down beside Miles as he removed his phone and called Amber, who answered on the second ring. "I hope you're having a better day than I am," she said.

"Define better," Miles replied. "Found Oliver. Unfortunately, two vampires found us."

Amber paused for a second. "You okay?" Her tone was sombre, concerned.

"I'll explain when you get here," Miles told her. "I need you to go into the boot . . . damn it, the trunk of my car. Bring me a blood pack. Church will come get blood. You give it to her."

"Miles, do you need medical attention?" Amber asked.

"I'm a vampire," Miles said with a slight wince that he'd tried to keep out of his voice and failed. "I need blood. Church won't be long." He hung up because he wasn't sure he could continue having a conversation while his body knit itself back together.

Church was on her feet. She stood in front of Miles.

"Go, I'll be fine," he told her.

She turned and sprinted off into the darkness of the forest.

Miles enjoyed the silence for a few minutes, punctuated with occasional pangs of pain as his ribs started to reset themselves in the correct place. He dialled Charlotte.

"I know I hadn't spoken to you in a long time until a few days ago," she said cheerfully. "But this is a lot more contact than I'd expected."

"Found Oliver," Miles said. "Something is going on in this town, Charlotte. Two vampires arrived. At least, I think both were vampires. One was, I know that. I recognised him, broke his mask before he kicked me off a cliff."

"Off a cliff?" Charlotte almost shouted. "Are you okay?"

"I broke some stuff," Miles said. "I know who the vampire who kicked me is. I recognised him."

"Who was it?" Charlotte asked.

"He's one of two Inquisitors who was outside my hotel in London a few days ago," Miles told her. "They informed me about Vedran having someone confess. And now they're here, in America, trying to kill me."

"The Inquisitors are trying to kill Arbiters," Charlotte said, letting out a low whistle. "You think there's a takeover in the Assembly?"

"No, I think the Inquisitors I just saw work for House Umbra," Miles said. "Oliver's gift is telepathy. I think House Umbra are involved in the illegal vampire trade and are cleaning house, so to speak."

"And using Inquisitors to do it," Charlotte said.

"Masked Inquisitors," Miles told her. "I don't think I was meant to see his face. Can you look into whoever they might have been? Quietly."

"I'll get information to you soon," Charlotte said. "Stay safe, Miles."

"One last thing," Miles said. "Kyle is technically human, but he's this Boss's familiar. It's why I didn't know he was anything other than human. He's an assassin. Try to get ahold of Danny; he's probably in danger as he knows too much."

"Will do," she said.

Charlotte ended the call, and Miles gingerly moved away from the tree. The Inquisitor hadn't jumped down the cliff to end him, so either killing him wasn't the end goal or the Inquisitor just hadn't the time to deal with him. They wanted Oliver; Miles just happened to be there.

By the time Church made it back, Miles's body was craving the blood that she dropped at his feet, and he dropped to his knees, tearing open the pouch and drinking the cool liquid down in one go. Once sated, Miles leaned up against the tree he was closest to and sighed, only then noticing that Church had darted back off into the forest.

A short time later, Church returned with Amber in tow.

"How bad is it?" Amber asked.

"My injuries or Oliver?" Miles replied.

Amber shrugged. "Both?"

"Injuries are fine, I'll be sore in the morning, but if I was human I'd be dead, so I can't complain," Miles said, getting to his feet and stretching. "As for Oliver. It's really bad. We need to go talk to Lauren if she ever wakes up. First, I need a shower, a change of clothes, and a cup of coffee. I'll fill you in on what I know on the way. And when I'm done, I'm going to go see your local Librarian.

CHAPTER TWENTY-ONE

The walk back through the forest had done Miles a world of good, and by the time they reached the factory, greeted by Doc Hammond and looking as if he'd seen enough for one lifetime, he felt vaguely like his exceptionally old self.

"What happened?" Doc Hammond asked.

The factory was swamped with police and forensics, including several dogs.

Miles took the Doc to one side, away from prying ears, and told her exactly what had happened.

"So, we still have Oliver out there," Doc Hammond said, sounding exhausted.

"Yeah, and at least one Inquisitor who has travelled the globe to find him," Miles said. "I'm going to assume on orders from House Umbra."

"Why would they do that?" Doc asked.

"Making sure no one finds out that they're linked to an illegal vampire trade worth millions," Miles said. "They're risking their lives to do this. If they're caught and the Assembly find out, they're dead. Their names and faces are going to be passed to every Arbiter and ATO team on the planet. The Inquisitors would come under special investigation. I can't imagine any Inquisitor throwing away their lives and their profession for some extra cash from a House."

"Would a House protect them?" Doc Hammond asked.

"Maybe," Miles said. "But it's more likely they'd make them disappear. Give them something to do somewhere far away. I don't think I was meant to see their faces, but I also don't think they were able to finish the job while they had to deal with Oliver. I imagine I'm now on their list of targets."

"You going to be safe?" Doc asked.

Miles shrugged. "Who knows. Lauren, she okay?"

"She's been taken to the local hospital," she said. "She's alive, but in some kind of deep sleep. Police have people there watching her, I've put in a no-visitors order, unless accompanied by me, Amber, or yourself. Not really sure what happened to her, or what being covered in the gore of a local idiot was meant to do."

"Travis Sharpe?" Miles asked. "Amber recognised him."

"Amber arranged someone to sit on the Red Demon," Doc said.

"She mentioned it on the way here," Miles said. "That going to become a problem?"

Doc Hammond looked back over at the crime scene. "It's not public knowledge yet. I've spoken to the Captain, I trust him, and he's not anti-vampire, so it should be out of the media for now. We can't keep it to ourselves forever."

"Officer Shilton?" Miles asked.

"He's a big part of why, yes," Doc said. "He's been stood down for the time being, given other duties."

"Two members of that group of four are dead," Miles said as Amber rejoined them. "What're the chances of Reese and/or Blake being next?"

"We'll look into finding them both," Amber said. "Oliver is still out there, after all."

"Aye," Miles said softly, turning back toward the forest. "But I don't think he'll be causing us any trouble." He took his phone out of his pocket and called Anya.

"How much is a pain in the ass is this going to be?" Anya asked.

"Nice to speak to you, too," Miles said before relaying what had happened and what he needed.

"You want an ATO team?" Anya asked.

"Preferably, yes," Miles said and told her about Lauren, Oliver, and the Inquisitors.

"You want to protect a human woman from her own kind?" Anya asked.

"I do," Miles said. "The Inquisitors took Oliver, and I need to know why. Oliver was with Lauren, and Lauren was going to be dumped in the forest by people who have ties to the Magistrate. It's all fucking linked, Anya, and I walked right into the goddamned middle of it."

"You know a bunch of House Umbra people arrived here about an hour ago?" Anya asked.

"Yeah, I figured they might," Miles said, wishing he'd been wrong. "This Boss is making sure that anyone who knows anything disappears, or ends up dead. House Umbra are concerned because whoever this Boss is, if they get found it's going to blow up in their face. I think whoever is behind this is in bed with the Inquisition, too. Or at least with several members of them."

"You think," Anya added.

"No actual proof, no," Miles said. "Just my recognising one of my attackers."

"I'll get the ATO people there ASAP," Anya said. "They'll be trustworthy. And they'll be damned good at their jobs. Stay safe until then."

Miles looked over at Amber as she directed his people. "The cops here are unprepared for any shit a vampire House will bring in to find a problem. Tell the ATO agent in charge to let me know when they get here, I'll go brief them."

"Will do," Anya said. "And I reiterate, be careful, Miles."

Anya hung up and Miles looked down at his bloodstained hands. "I need a shower and change. Can we go back to my place so I can do both?"

Amber nodded. "I'll drive," she said, opening the rear passenger door for Church to jump into.

Miles settled into the passenger seat, switched on the seat warmer, turned up the heating, and drifted off to sleep, waking when the car pulled to a stop.

"I didn't think vampires slept at night," Amber said as Miles looked around to figure out where they were.

"Got hurt, got cold, needed blood," he said, his brain not entirely in gear yet.

"You need a minute?" Amber asked.

Miles nodded, and Amber left the car, taking Church with her.

Alone in the car, Miles rubbed his eyes and realised they were outside his temporary home. The snow was coming down heavily now, and several inches had fallen on the ground since the last time he'd been here.

He opened the car door, stepping out into the frigid weather, and jogged across the driveway to the front door, his footsteps crunching all the way. He unlocked the front door, switched off the alarm, and turned on the lights.

"Make yourself at home," Miles told Amber. "Church might want some food. Actual food, not blood."

Church took Amber's hand in her mouth and led her toward the kitchen before Amber could even say anything.

Miles went to his room, showered, and changed into fresh jeans, a new white T-shirt, a thick navy jumper, and extra thick socks. He picked up some tough hiking boots and put them on, too, before grabbing a clean coat and leaving his bedroom.

He found Amber and Church in the kitchen, the latter tucking into whatever had been found edible.

"There's not much in the fridge," Amber said. "Found a tin of beef, which honestly wasn't something I realised came in tins. Church seems to like it. Look, it's early in the morning. I think we should head to my house to get some actual food. It doesn't look like you're going to be able to go shopping anytime soon."

"Will your boyfriend, girlfriend, husband, significant other be okay with me turning up?" Miles asked.

Amber laughed. "Wife," she said. "She works part-time at the library with Yvonne. I've texted her and she's up. She's a bit of a night owl."

"Human?" Miles asked.

"Pam is human," Amber said with another laugh. "I'm sure we've got something better to eat than tinned offal, too."

Church snorted, pushed the bowl away with her paw, and walked out of the kitchen.

"I think she agrees," Miles said. "Let's go meet your wife."

Amber drove through Fortress Falls to a quiet suburb about a mile away from the centre of town. The houses on the street were all detached, with their own driveways and small gardens out front, although considering the amount of snow, it was hard to tell where the drive ended and the garden began.

Amber's house had a red door under a porch, where two chairs and a table were now partially buried in increasing levels of snow. It was beginning to look like a winter wonderland.

Amber unlocked the door and went inside, the lights in the large room beyond already on. The entire downstairs was open plan, with the door leading into a large living area that took up the length of the house. Bare wood stairs sat beside the living area, with an archway next to them that led into a dining room. A set of glass sliding doors sat at the far end of the living area, which Miles could see led to a deck and garden outside.

"Pam," Amber called out. "I have company."

Pam's head appeared at the top of the staircase, looking down. "Be right down," she said.

"Food?" Amber asked Church, who barked.

"Is there a dog down there?" Pam asked.

"Get down here and find out," Amber said, taking Church and Miles across the length of the living area, past a set of burgundy leather couches, a large TV on the wall, several dozen bookshelves that appeared to be groaning under their own weight, and a glass cabinet full of photos.

"I assume that's you and Pam," Miles asked, pointing to one photo of Amber and another woman standing in front of the pyramids of Egypt.

"It is," Amber said, removing a plastic container from the fridge. The kitchen was in a horseshoe shape, with a glass door closed on one side and everything else around a counter in the middle of the room, with four chairs around it. Amber removed the lid, revealing some roast pork, potatoes, and vegetables, all covered in gravy. "Church be okay with it?"

"Church would be okay eating a car door," Miles said, taking a seat at the centre counter.

Church glowered as best she could at Miles, licked Amber's hand, and tucked in as Amber placed the container on the floor for her, along with a bowl of water.

Amber watched Church eat and smiled. "You two been together long?" She asked. "Wait, rephrase that so it doesn't sound weird."

Miles laughed and accepted a plastic bowl full of more roast meat, veg, and several types of potato. "Twenty something years now," he said as Amber slid a fork along the counter to him. "How about you and Pam?"

"We've been together since college," Amber said. "I was there doing American history, and Pam was studying psychology. We hit it off, and here we are. Been married ten years now."

"Although I promise not to psychoanalyse anyone," Pam said as she entered the kitchen and kissed Amber.

Pam was a few inches taller than Amber, with dark skin, long black hair, and half a dozen rings in each ear. She shook Miles's hand. "So, you're a vampire," she said.

"I am," Miles said.

"Not American," Pam said. "Scottish?"

Miles nodded. "Aye. You're not from Seattle. I'm not great with accents, but Georgia?"

"I am," Pam said. "Born and raised in Atlanta. Went to a West Coast university, met my lovely wife, and decided to stay here for a few years. Then we got jobs, and now here we are."

"You like living here?" Miles asked, having another mouthful of delicious food.

"A lot," Pam said. "Apart from the cold. The cold is something I feel in my bones. Meant to be going back to Georgia for the holiday season, but life got in the way."

"By *life* she means my job," Amber said. "Or at least, she means our killer."

"Ah," Miles said. "Which one of you is the cook?"

"We both cook," Amber said. "That's my roast pork. Pam's food tends to include more chillis."

Pam kissed Amber on the shoulder. "So, Miles. How much danger is my wife in?"

"Pam," Amber almost shouted. "I have a gun. I'm not some newbie at all this."

"I know, honey, but with some psychopath out there, I'm worried," Pam said softly.

"We'll find whoever is behind all of this," Miles said.

"And is your dog safe?" Pam asked, looking down at Church before crouching down and making a fuss of her.

"Safe with good people," Miles said.

"Have you spoken to Yvonne yet?" Pam asked Amber. "She might know something about Lauren. Shame what happened to her. Nice lady."

"Ah, you need to keep this between us," Amber said. "But we found Lauren. She's not in a good way, but she's alive."

"Oh, thank the Lord," Pam said. "You should still talk to Yvonne. She knew her more than I do."

"Yeah, we've met," Miles said. "In fact, I need to talk to her again tonight." He removed his phone and texted Yvonne's number: *You at the library? Need to talk.*

The three talked for a while as Church continued to be fed, decided a lie-down was in order, and promptly fell asleep under the dining room table.

"Can I ask you a vampire question?" Pam asked.

"Pam," Amber said, her voice practically pleading not to say anything that might be considered upsetting or offensive.

"It's fine," Miles told them. "What do you want to know?"

"Can you do the whole wings thing?" Pam asked. "I've heard that's a pretty big deal."

Miles smiled. "No, I'm not old enough, or strong enough, depending on your point of view," he told them. "Besides, not every vampire can turn into a form with wings. Some are just big creatures with huge claws for hands, and some look like they'd belong in a horror film. Depends on the vampire."

"Do you know which one you'll be?" Pam asked, continuing unabated.

"Not until it happens," Miles said. "If ever."

"Can I ask another question?" Pam asked, clearly in her stride as question master.

"Sure thing," Miles said, taking a drink of water from a glass supplied by Amber, who mouthed an apology.

"I've spoken to a few vampires in my time, and some of them have issues with blood packs instead of . . . well, you know . . ." Pam trailed off.

"A live person?" Miles finished for her.

"Yeah, that," Pam said.

"A live person comes with risks," Miles said. "There are no human diseases that bother us, so that's not an issue, and while taking a small amount from a living being brings no risks, actually feeding can be problematic. I don't feel the memories of a blood pack. I don't have a blood pack in my head. There's no emotional or physical connection. It's quick and easy. And a synthetic blood pack is infinite and can be easily obtained, and now with new flavours. It's the future."

"I'd have preferred flying cars," Amber said.

"You and me both," Miles said with a laugh. "Is taking from a person better? Yes. A thousand percent. And we all have to do it at some point, the blood packs aren't a complete substitute, but they stop us from having to deal with the memories of a different human every time we need to properly feed. The blood packs are like having a fast-food meal, while a living person is like having a gourmet chef cook a special meal meant for just the two of you."

Pam and Amber stared at Miles for a while.

"How often do you need a person?" Amber asked.

"If I take blood packs regularly enough, probably once a year," Miles said. "There are places we can go that are regulated, that are clean and safe, and, well, it's not like it was in the old days when you took someone to an alleyway."

"That's a real thing?" Pam asked. "That really happened?"

"Not for nearly a century now," Miles explained. "Or, should I say, it still happens, but there are places that are designed for such proclivities. Places that let humans and vampires . . . mingle. Usually repeatedly. Humans who are fed on usually have increased healing for several days after. And vampire blood has changed human medicine for the better."

"Human drugs, too," Pam said.

"Yes, those too," Miles said with a smile. "Humans and vampires benefit one another. We don't need to feed on humans all the time. And very few vampires would want to."

Pam leaned over the kitchen counter toward Miles and whispered, "Those places where humans and vampires . . . mingle. Is there one in Fortress Falls?"

"I don't know," Miles whispered back. "There will be a few in Seattle; there's like something in the region of forty in LA. Most big towns will have at least half a dozen, all competing for the best time, trying to get big name vampires to go and enjoy themselves."

"Wow," Pam said. "You learn something new every day."

Miles's phone vibrated and he read the message from Yvonne: *At library. Be right there*, he replied.

"I'm going to go talk to Yvonne," Miles said. "Hopefully by morning we might have heard something about Lauren's condition. Thank you for a pleasant evening. It was lovely to meet you, Pam."

"You too," Pam said with a smile.

"Go sleep," Amber said, kissing her wife. "I'll be back before dawn, I hope."

"Keep her safe," Pam said to Miles.

"I will do all I can to make sure she stays safe," Miles assured her. "And Church will help."

Church yawned and clambered out from under the dining room table, moving a few chairs in the process. Miles wasn't even sure how she'd managed to cram herself under there in the first place.

Miles left with Church behind him, allowing Pam and Amber some time to themselves. The snow outside appeared to have increased in its continuing assault on the city. It would be well over a foot thick in some places by morning, and there was a cold wind that whipped through the street as if to remind everyone of their place in the pecking order of life. Miles pulled his coat collar up around his neck and walked over to the car, opening the rear door to let Church in before getting onto the driver's seat. He started the engine, switched on the heaters, and checked the range before it needed to be charged. Deciding he had enough power to keep the car going for a week based on the day's usage, he turned up the heater.

Amber emerged from the house, jogged over to the car, and got in through the passenger side door, warming her hands on the heater as she rubbed them together. "They said the storm was going to be bad, but this is getting to become apocalyptic. We'll be using snowmobiles by the end of the week."

Miles hoped he wouldn't be in town long enough to worry about apocalyptic levels of snow and pulled out of the drive.

"Library?" Amber asked.

Miles nodded. "Yvonne needs to know about Oliver. And I'm not sure, but I think she knew more than she was letting on."

"Lauren may never wake up," Amber said. "What about using the House Umbra to psychically probe her brain? Or you could bite her and take her memories."

"The biting one doesn't work like that," Miles said as the windscreen wipers earned their pay. "I might get a memory about her attack, or I might get a memory about the time she passed her driving test, or how she painted a wall in her house. You have no control over what you see, or the level of crushing emotion that can come with it. And that's even beginning on the ethical and moral implications of me drinking the blood of someone who can't consent to it."

"And the psychic Umbra vampires?" Amber asked.

"They can't dig through minds of people who aren't at least awake without serious injury," Miles said. "It does weird things to them. I was once told it was like grabbing hold of an electric fence and you can't let go, as a horse on the opposite side tries to kick you off."

"That's quite the image," Amber said.

"He was an odd vampire," Miles said. "So our best bet is she wakes up. Otherwise we're going into a grey area. There are vampires that have a gift and can go into people's dreams, into their subconscious and just walk around, but it's rare. I haven't heard of one in about a century. They tend to lose their minds if they use it too much."

"Not many great options," Amber said.

"Well, we could give Lauren vampire blood intravenously," Miles said as he continued down Main Street toward the library a few minutes' distance away. "That would almost certainly wake her up."

"Let's try that, then," Amber suggested.

"That brings its own issues," Miles pointed out. "Mostly that they're going to wake up, confused, hurt, possibly fearful, and with vampire blood in their system, which could make them stronger and more dangerous, or just melt their brain. Like you said, not many great options."

Miles's phone vibrated again. He read another message from Yvonne: *I think there are people walking around outside.*

It was probably nothing, but if it got out that two anti-vampire proponents had been killed, their friends may see the library as an easy target for their ire. "We need to hurry," Miles said.

Amber drove down Main Street as fast as she could, and an orange glow lit up in the distance. Even through the snow, Miles knew what it was.

Amber was on her radio immediately. "Officer needs assistance," she said. "We've got a fire at the library."

CHAPTER TWENTY-TWO

The fire was nowhere as bad as it could have been. Someone, presumably with a single digit IQ, had set a bin on fire. The bin had exploded, covering burning debris all over a nearby pine tree, which went up like a bonfire, even in the cold snowy conditions. There was a small parking area to the side of the building and next to a community centre, which had thankfully been left alone. The stench of the accelerant used was obvious to Miles, even mixed among the smell of burning trash.

The Fire Department turned up and set about putting everything out, and Miles left Amber to talk to them while he examined the area with Church, who occasionally sneezed as the smell of burning bothered her nose.

Miles knocked on one of the two glass doors that had *Entrance* written above them in green lighting. Someone had spray painted *Humans not Leeches* on the doors in red.

Yvonne answered the door and motioned for Miles and Church to come inside. "I hope you've had a warmer reception being here than I've had tonight," she said, irritated.

"Did you see any of the people who set fire to the front of your library?" Miles asked.

"No, sorry," she said. "We have CCTV, but I haven't checked it yet."

"Can I see the footage?" Miles asked as they stepped into the library itself.

"Sure," Yvonne said.

"Why are you open at three in the morning?" Miles asked as they walked through the library.

"I come here to work," she said without looking back. "I write reports that need to go back to Danica, I read, I do whatever needs to be done for the morning. Also, there are vampires in town, so I like to make sure they know the library is open should they need somewhere to come and chill out. The community centre has a few nights a week when all the vampires in town come over. It's not many, but it's nice to feel like everyone belongs, you know?"

"That the same community centre where Lauren worked?" Miles asked Yvonne, before he looked out of the window at the small snow-covered playground behind the library. He wondered if those who had started the fire were standing somewhere in the darkness beyond, watching.

"You wanted to see the CCTV, right?" Yvonne asked, bringing Miles back to the present.

Miles stared at the computer screen as Yvonne brought up the CCTV footage of the arson attack. The footage was of good quality, although the heaviness of the falling snow occasionally made it look as if there was static.

A dark van drove by at high speed, and a few seconds later two men in black wearing masks stood guard as a third person ran past the CCTV footage to spray on the door. After only a few seconds, two more masked men threw Molotov cocktails into the bin, which exploded, showering the nearby plant life in fire.

"You know any of them?" Miles asked.

"Yes," Yvonne said. She moved the footage back several seconds and stopped it, showing the man who had gone to spray on the doors of the library. He had a visible tattoo on his forearm.

"What the hell is that?" Miles asked.

"It's a bobcat," Yvonne said. "The local high school football team."

"That guy is at school?" Miles asked.

"That guy is the dad of the school football running back," Yvonne said. "He played himself twenty years ago. He's a bully, a drunk, and someone whose best days were those few years when he was someone at school. His son, who is a delight by the way, volunteers here to read to kids once a week."

"The apple was dropkicked away from the tree then," Miles said. "What's his name?"

"Cody Sharpe," Yvonne said.

"Oh shit," Miles whispered, staring at the tattoo on the screen. "His brother was found murdered today. And however bad you think the word *murdered* sounds, I assure you the reality was worse. I'm going to take a guess and say that these idiots all hang out at the Red Demon."

"Cody and Travis did," Yvonne said. "Cody did not like his son reading here. He separated from his wife about five years ago, and his son lives with her."

"Any chance that separation has anything to do with vampires?" Miles asked.

"I may have helped her get out," Yvonne said.

"Did you help Lauren get out, too?" Miles continued.

"No," Yvonne said. "She wanted to, a lot. Several times she had her bags packed, in the car, ready to go."

Miles took a seat on the nearby couch. "Why'd she stay?"

"Reese is a cop," Yvonne said. "That pretty much sums it up. He had buddies on the force in town, but also in Seattle. He's friends with Magistrate members, so she figured they'd find her, force her back here. Or kill her."

"I found out that Reese, Blake, Travis, and Liam were all friends," Miles said. "At least two of them were the offspring of ex-members of a biker gang called Mortis. There's more. Liam and Travis were killed, possibly by the same person."

"Vampire?" Yvonne asked.

"Oliver," Miles said.

Yvonne stared at Miles for several seconds. She blinked once and looked away. "No way," she whispered.

"I saw Oliver tonight," Miles said. "He tried to tell me something about what happened to Lauren. I asked him if he'd killed them and he said they deserved to die. Not exactly a confession, I know, but not a denial either. I'm not sure why he killed those two men, but they were trying to dump her body in the forest. They must have thought she was dead, but she wasn't."

"Where's Oliver now?" Yvonne asked, a frantic tone in her voice.

"With two Inquisitors, who I think are working for House Umbra," Miles told her. "They took him, nearly killed me in the process. Any chance there's something you're not telling me about Oliver's associations with criminals?"

"Why wouldn't I tell you if I knew?" Yvonne snapped, getting to her feet and walking over to the window, looking out. "My brother is out there with Inquisitors."

Miles nodded. "He's a telepath, did you know that?"

Yvonne's shoulders sagged, and she nodded.

"So you knew his bloodline gift was probably House Umbra," Miles said.

Yvonne nodded again. "He made me swear I wouldn't say. He was scared the House would send someone after him if they knew. My brother is a walking, talking problem, and we haven't spoken in a long time since a few weeks ago, but he's still my little brother."

"I think they've sent people after him now," Miles said.

Yvonne looked back at Miles accusingly. "How'd they know he was here?"

Miles had been considering that question since the encounter with the Inquisition and could come up with only one answer. "They followed me," he told her. "I think."

"You *think?*" Yvonne snapped.

"House Umbra took control of the investigation. I didn't tell House Umbra that I was coming here, because I don't trust them, but I assume they'd want to keep an eye on me, so they probably tailed me," Miles explained. "Your brother is one of five gang members who were at the building when the desolate was created. One is in Assembly custody and knows nothing, one is in Umbra custody and I'm pretty sure is terrified, and two are dead. Your brother is the only one out there unaccounted for."

"The House is afraid of losing face," Yvonne said. "You think Oliver is dead?"

Miles shook his head. "No, I think they'll take him somewhere and keep him alive until the people in charge get here. And then, once they know everything he knew, they'll kill him."

"Any idea who?" Yvonne asked.

"Someone high up in House Umbra," Miles said. "Someone who would be concerned about their involvement coming out. Someone who could get Inquisitors to work with them. Inquisitors notified me of House Umbra having someone arrive and confess. One of those Inquisitors just tried to kill me. All points in one direction. Vedran."

"Shit," Yvonne whispered.

"I need to make a call," Miles said. "Church, stay here."

Miles ran out of the library, motioning to Amber and the officers that they would be one minute as he removed his phone, calling Charlotte.

"Am I the only person you call now?" she asked.

"Yes," Miles said. "The vampire who fled the desolate, who went to the Assembly in London, his name was Alex Richards. Find out if he's alive.

Danny Mortimer from the raid the other day. Clara, too. And Sajid, the vampire in House Umbra custody. Him, too."

"You think they're not?" Charlotte asked.

"House Umbra is cleaning up after someone," Miles said, in a hurry. "Those vampires and Oliver are the only living beings who were there when the desolate was created."

"On it," Charlotte said and hung up, aware of how quickly she needed to move.

Miles didn't feel better about getting Charlotte to check, and he was pretty sure that something bad was going to happen to everyone who had been at that building at the same time as the desolate. He knew he could call Anya and lodge a complaint about House Umbra and their possible involvement in making people disappear, but he didn't have any actual *evidence* they'd done anything. Despite knowing in his gut it was them.

He walked back to the front of the library and found Amber. "Yvonne identified one of her attackers as Cody Sharpe," he told her. "Don't put it through officially, though. Let them think they got away with it."

"Okay, I'll get a patrol to stay on the Red Demon," Amber said. "I don't think they'd talk to us even if we did go inside. They're going to keep quiet about wherever Cody is. It won't be easy to get information from them."

"I didn't think it would," Miles agreed. "We'll go see them tomorrow night. I want them to think they got away with it."

"Why?" Amber asked.

"Because they're going into hiding tonight," Miles said. "They'll be drunk on victory, but then they'll wonder if the police are about to come knocking. When none do, I imagine they're stupid enough for at least one of them to return to that bar."

"You know it's an anti-vampire bar," Amber said. "You turning up could start a fight."

"They attacked one of my own," Miles said. "They're going to be getting a visit from me one way or another."

"But not tonight?" Amber asked, a slight question of hope in her voice.

Miles shook his head.

"In the meantime, Lauren has woken up," Amber said. "She's apparently disoriented and scared, but okay. She doesn't remember anything from about a week or so, though."

"Okay, make sure Reese and Blake don't get anywhere near her," Miles said. "Oliver didn't name them as being the ones who hurt her, but he did say the Magistrate were involved."

"We're going to need more than the word of Oliver to go after Magistrate members," Amber pointed out.

"Aye," Miles agreed. "I know the Doc said she'd asked to get protection there to only let certain people in to see Lauren, but just to be safe."

"You think someone will try to finish the job?" Amber asked.

"I have no idea," Miles said. "We still don't know what happened to get Lauren from her house, to have Oliver find her in the forest being dumped by Travis and Liam."

"Hopefully she has answers," Amber said with a yawn. "Sorry."

"Okay, I'm going to take Yvonne home and get some sleep," Miles said. "It's almost dawn. You need to rest, too, it's been a long night."

"I will. I'll see you in the afternoon," Amber said, tossing Miles his car keys. "Be careful."

Amber walked away and got into the rear seats of a patrol car, which drove off into the night.

He looked over at the front of the library, at the spray-painted words that had been placed there. Words he disliked. *Leeches*. It was a popular, if uninspired, slur on vampires. Miles had always found it to be a weird way to try and hurt the feelings of people who were quite possibly hundreds of years old. He'd seen people use vampires as the reason for all of the problems in the world before, and he'd see it again. He'd hoped that humanity had moved on, but while they outwardly said they had, too many of them retained those old fears and hates. They kept them warm on cold nights.

Yvonne stood in the doorway of the church, looking down at the scorched earth where the fire had taken root. The bin was destroyed; the plants would need to be worked on to see if they could be saved.

"Senseless," Yvonne said with a tut. "In all my years on this earth, I'm never surprised by the stupidity of man."

"I've got several centuries on you," Miles told her. "Trust me when I tell you, it doesn't get better. Will they come back?"

"Travis was the meaner of the two brothers," Yvonne said. "Cody is just a whiny little dick."

"You want to inform the police it was him and his friends?" Miles asked.

"Why bother? Officer Shilton is their drinking buddy, and Reese is the drinking buddy of those Magistrate assholes," Yvonne said, a snap to her voice as she let her anger out. "Do you know where the Magistrate comes from?"

"Yes," Miles said softly.

"The fucking vampire hunters and Inquisitions of the world reborn," Yvonne continued as if Miles hadn't said anything. "I know the Assembly used the name Inquisitors mostly to take the word back and give it to the vampires, but I don't think that helped matters. The Spanish Inquisition used to murder vampires in their beds for the crime of possibly biting someone. Barbarism was the name of their game, and I don't think the Magistrate is any different. It might have been Cody and his dipshit friends who did this, but it was Magistrate strings being pulled from on high. I'm certain of it."

Church padded out by Yvonne, stopping to get a stroke before she continued on to Miles.

"Are you going to be okay?" Miles asked.

Yvonne smiled and looked at the dark, cloud covered sky. "I was wondering if you'd be able to give me a ride home, please. I'm . . . I would rather not have to deal with any more humans tonight."

"You lock up, and I'll take you home" Miles said, watching Yvonne go back into the library as Church licked his hand and made a whining noise.

Yvonne emerged from the library a few moments later, wearing a thick black coat that stretched down to her knees. Along with Church, the pair of them walked back through the early morning to Miles's car, where they all got in.

"So, where to?" Miles asked.

Yvonne gave directions, which took Miles to a house close to where he was staying, although Yvonne's was at the far end of the neighbourhood, after turning down an unlit road where seven more houses sat in darkness.

"Vampire neighbourhood," Yvonne said as she pointed to her house. "This whole area is going to become a vampire district when it's done, I hope."

"I thought there were more than seven vampires living in town," Miles said as he stopped the car outside the detached house that belonged to Yvonne.

"A few more, but some don't live in town itself, and some live on Main Street," Yvonne said. "I think they believe that if they live closer to the humans, they'll be integrated more with them. It never occurs to them that it doesn't work like that." She got out of the car and looked back at Miles. "Come on in; we can talk about Lauren."

Miles nodded toward the back seat. "Church okay to come, too?"

Yvonne smiled. "Of course. I've got a big garden."

Considering the whining noise that left Church, Miles was pretty sure he wouldn't have had a choice, and it was nearly dawn, so any further investigation would have to be after he'd gotten some sleep. He was fully healed from his earlier encounter, and the blood he'd taken ensured that he wouldn't need more for several days, but he still needed rest. Spending an hour or so talking to a fellow vampire about work was probably the best use of his time.

Miles left the car, opening the back door for a far too exuberant Church to bounce out, run around the car, throw herself into a massive pile of snow on the side of Yvonne's front garden, and explode out, raining more snow down around her as she ran around, snapping her mouth at the falling snow.

"She not seen snow before?" Yvonne asked as she walked up the pathway from the sidewalk to her front door.

"She's seen plenty," Miles said. "She's just a lunatic."

Church walked over to Miles and shook herself clean of snow, smiling at him as he brushed himself clean.

Yvonne's home was an exact image of the layout of where Miles was staying, although hers was less sparse and more Librarian at home. As Miles followed Yvonne through the front of the house to the living area at the rear, there were a dozen bookshelves lined up against one wall, with a large dark red leather armchair next to them, positioned in front of a bay window that overlooked the back garden.

"I take my work home," Yvonne said after spotting Miles looking through the bookshelves.

"You like the classics," he said. "And historical fiction. Ancient Rome, Troy, Greece, Egypt. You've got an era, too."

"Ah, I do love the time period," she said, putting water in the kettle and switching it on.

"And a proper kettle," Miles said.

"It was a gift," Yvonne said with a smile. "I don't know how I managed beforehand. Tea, coffee, hot chocolate? I'm sorry, I don't drink alcohol, so really strong coffee is about as hardcore as it gets."

"Whatever you're having is fine," Miles said.

"Pot of tea, seeing how you're British," Yvonne said, opening the back door and letting Church run out into the garden. "A small piece of home. Milk and sugar?"

"Yes and yes," Miles told her as he continued to search the mass of books. "Lots of vampire fiction books."

"I like to see what they're saying about us," Yvonne said. "I read *Dracula* as a little girl and fell in love with vampires. Didn't expect to become one. That was not on the cards."

Miles looked over at her. "What was on the cards? If that's okay to ask?"

"Ah, well, I was going to marry a rich man, have children, and be a lady of leisure," Yvonne said. "Then I realised they weren't really my dreams, just the dreams others had forced on me. When I was old enough to know better, I decided I wanted to go to university and study classical literature, to become a teacher. Didn't work out that way either."

The kettle clicked to signify the water had boiled. A short time later, Yvonne brought over two mugs of tea, placing one in front of Miles.

"Have you told Danica about all of this?" Miles asked.

Yvonne nodded. "Most of it. I called her when you were out on your own call."

Miles had suspected as much. It was the life of someone who worked for a High Lord or Lady of a House. You did as you were told, and you did your job well.

"Can I ask you something?" Miles asked.

Yvonne nodded, although it was tentative.

"Why would Oliver see Lauren getting dumped in the forest and hunt down and kill two people responsible?" Miles asked. "When I spoke to him, he said they deserved to die, not that he killed them. Maybe he was just there to watch someone else do it?"

"He's working with someone else?" Yvonne asked.

Miles considered it for a moment. "Lauren is in hospital. Oliver said he was too late to stop the deaths of the people the Magistrate are investigating. Maybe Oliver caught up to this supposed serial killing vampire, and they worked together. Or, maybe the Inquisition got here early, started to remove problems their way. Which leads to the question of, why would they care about Lauren? Or the Magistrate? I don't know what's going on in this town, but something doesn't fit." He yawned.

"You can stay here if you like," Yvonne said. "I've got a spare room."

Miles wasn't sure that was the best idea ever. He didn't know Yvonne well, and she clearly worked for Barbarous House, whom he had been in conflict with once or twice over the years, but if she wished him harm, she was going about it a really strange way. On top of that, Miles was also concerned that the people who firebombed the library might not stop there.

Dawn was coming. Miles could feel it edging ever so slightly over the horizon.

"I'm going to put on a movie in my games room and if you want to stay and watch, you can," Yvonne said.

"I'd love to stay, thank you," Miles said. "What are we watching?"

"I haven't decided that bit," Yvonne said with a smile.

Miles followed her through the house to the opposite side of the front door. He peered through the open doorway of what looked like an office and found Church curled up on the floor, snoring softly.

"I guess my decision was made for me," Miles said to Yvonne.

"She's a wonderful dog," Yvonne said. "You're lucky to have a loyal companion like her."

"I am," Miles agreed.

"What happened to the person who made her?" Yvonne asked. "Did you kill him?"

"Yes," Miles said softly. "I did not want to. Apart from using vampire blood to create a genetically enhanced dog, he'd also tried to find a way to stop his wife from dying. He had done . . . awful things out of grief. She hadn't known about any of them, and she died in ignorance. He continued his research nonetheless, becoming obsessed. He killed a lot of people. A lot. He was pretty much gone by the time I arrived, his mind a mass of rancid thoughts and visions."

"You were friends?" Yvonne asked.

Miles took a deep breath and let it out slowly. "Yes," he said eventually. "We were friends. I mourned his wife. I sat with him as we buried her, I told him I would help him if he needed it. He told me it would be fine. I had no indications of the horrors he'd inflicted throughout Eastern Europe. There are always vampires who decide that humans are just too tasty not to feast on, so the Assembly would hunt one down and attribute more deaths to them than they'd actually admitted. I offered to kill my friend myself. I don't think he would have let anyone else do it without a fight."

The conversation flowed for a time, until the pair moved to an adjacent room. It had a five-person corner couch at one end and a projector set up above it, while one entire wall had floor to ceiling bookshelves full of movies in their cases.

Miles picked out several old VHS seventies Golden Harvest films that did not appear to be translated into English. "This is original," he said. "You speak Cantonese?"

"I speak fifteen languages," Yvonne said, selecting *Aliens* and starting the film.

They sat on a comfortable sofa ready to watch, and both of them were asleep before the half hour mark.

Chapter Twenty-Three

Miles walked through a dark place. There was an overwhelming feeling of being watched from all angles as the darkness all around him slowly moved in. Of being watched. Of being constricted by things he couldn't see. It was overwhelming.

He struggled to see anything around him as he moved from a walk to a flat-out sprint, but the feeling of oppression only increased. A chattering sound filled the space. A never-ending cacophony of noise. He dropped to his knees, his hands over his ears.

A shrouded figure walked slowly toward him, a hundred meters away, the darkness parting in its wake. Miles couldn't tell if the figure was male, female, human, vampire, or anything else. Waves of power radiated from the figure as the ground turned to liquid, but Miles remained knelt atop it. Ripples of water washed by him as the shrouded figure continued its march, the darkness tearing itself apart and snapping together behind it.

The figure stopped before Miles, crouched down before him, and touched his face with a bone-chillingly cold hand.

The sound had stopped; the darkness receded.

"You just have to do nothing," the shrouded figure said, its voice echoing all around. "Do nothing. Let them die."

Miles looked up at the nothingness inside the hood. He wanted to nod, to agree, to tell the figure whatever it wanted to hear if it would just go away. Instead, he said, "No."

The figure snapped upright and screamed in incandescent rage. "Then you will die."

"No," Miles said again and struck the figure in its chest with the flat of his palm, as he leapt to his feet.

The figure flew back, hitting the ground, liquid cascading over it.

Miles stood defiant, staring at the shrouded figure as it got back to its feet. "I will not be commanded." He took a step toward the figure, which radiated hate.

"You will die," the figure repeated.

Miles ran at the figure, ducking below a swipe of its outstretched hand. "You first," Miles said, smashing his palm into the figure's chest, and unleashing his bloodline power.

Miles woke to the sounds of screams in his ears. He jolted upright, expecting something to attack him, but he was in the same room he'd been in when he'd fallen asleep. The long, thick curtains, ever so slightly not shut together, allowing a stream of light into the darkness. The VCR had long since switched itself off.

"Are you okay?" Yvonne asked as she walked into the room carrying a blood pack in one hand while she drank from a second. "I thought I'd let you sleep."

Miles was mortified. "Oh, I'm sorry," he said. "Just a bad dream."

Yvonne sat on the sofa. "We don't get *bad dreams* that cause us to wake up and jump out of a sleeping position, Miles. This the first time?"

"No," he admitted. "The last few nights I've had visions of blood, violence, pain, but this . . . this was a figure. A . . . thing. It told me to do nothing. That's it. When I said no, it got angry. I hurt it, I think. I'm not sure. It's all a jumble. I don't know what it means."

"Nothing good, I would imagine," Yvonne said.

"I need to go shower and change," Miles said. "Thank you for your help. And for your hospitality. I really appreciate it. I promise we'll find Oliver."

Yvonne nodded as sadness swept over her face. "I know Oliver and I have had issues over the years, but he's my brother, and the thought of him being in the custody of Inquisitors makes my skin crawl. I'm meant to protect him, and honestly, it feels like I was never able to do that."

"We'll find him," Miles assured her.

Yvonne forced a smile. "You know, I asked you to stay partly because I was still freaked out by what had happened, but also because there aren't a lot of vampires in town who want to be seen with other vampires right now. Most of them are either in denial that humans are looking at them differently, so they've moved away from the town for now, or they've banded together in some kind of doomsday prepper cult. Not an actual cult, just vampires who think the end of times is coming. None of those groups are great at conversation. It was nice to have an actual interaction with someone who understands what it's like to be a vampire."

Miles knew what it was like to feel alone in a city, even if you technically had people around you. "Let me know if you hear anything. We can go for a coffee if you like."

"How about you come over tomorrow morning and I'll cook?" Yvonne asked. "We could actually watch the film we were going to watch."

"I'd like that," Miles said.

The job of an Arbiter could easily become one of loneliness. Other vampires were either mistrustful that they were in some kind of trouble, or they were actually in some kind of trouble and wanted to be somewhere else. Miles had done a lot of good work over the years, making sure that vampires and humans were safer, but that came at a cost of moving from place to place, never really making connections with people on more than a superficial level. Seeing Charlotte and Drest, no matter the reason why, had made him realise that he needed to be more open to new people.

Miles and Church went back to his home, where he put the car onto charge, got a shower, changed, and had something to eat. It was light out, being only two in the afternoon, but it wouldn't be for long, and the UV index was zero, so Miles wasn't particularly worried about the sunshine. He had just made himself a cup of coffee to go, using a travel mug he'd found in the cupboard, when his phone rang.

Unknown Number.

"If you're trying to sell me something, I'm going to be upset," Miles said as he answered.

"My name is Henry Shaw," he said, his voice a deep baritone. "I'm the ATO Commander in charge of the team that arrived in town. I hear you have a vampire problem."

"That's a bit of an understatement," Miles said.

"You should know that a House Umbra delegation arrived in Seattle late last night," Henry said. "Led by Vedran Vinko."

It was a surprise to Miles. "Vedran actually came himself."

"I'm not sure what they're looking into, but they held a meeting with the Magistrate," Henry said.

That was a much bigger surprise. "Seriously? What the hell do House Umbra want with the Magistrate?"

"Your guess is as good as mine," Henry said. "I would have liked to have had ears on that conversation."

"Me too," Miles admitted. "Any chance we can meet?"

There was a pause before Henry said, "Why yes, Arbiter Watson, we do have information regarding the issue you asked us to look into. I think it would be wise for you to come to our HQ. We've set up at the community centre."

"Is there a problem?" Miles asked.

"That's very true," Henry said. "It has been a long night."

Miles wracked his mind, thinking of and discarding a dozen problems that might have arisen. The one that stuck in his mind the most was the one he hoped would happen the least. "There's another Arbiter there?"

"I don't believe that's the case, no sir," Henry said. "It is close, though."

"House members are there," Miles guessed.

"That would be an accurate representation of the issue at hand, yes," Henry said.

"Umbra," Miles said, hoping it wasn't, but knowing full well he wasn't that lucky.

"Yes, sir," Henry said. "I will see you shortly and we'll have a full report of the situation."

"Fucking hell," Miles said. "I'll get there now."

"My sentiments exactly, sir," Henry said and ended the call.

Before Miles was even out of the building, his phone rang again.

Amber.

"Anything horrific happen in the last few hours?" Miles asked, hoping his joke wasn't about to bite him in the arse.

"Lauren is talking," Amber said. "You want to know what she said?"

"The CliffsNotes version would be great," Miles said. "I'd like to ask her myself, though."

"Okay, husband is an asshole, doesn't remember anything, hopes the vampire who took her is okay," Amber said. "All direct quotes. She's on medication and is quite chatty. I think she's a mess emotionally if not physically, but then can you blame her?"

"Not really. She hopes that Oliver is okay?" Miles asked.

"Yep," Amber said. "She was concerned about him, said he helped look after her. I didn't tell her what happened to him, I didn't want to cause her any stress. I said we were looking for him, which is close enough to the truth. How's Yvonne?"

"She's good," Miles said. "I'd like to go have a chat with the arseholes responsible."

"Tonight, yes?" Amber asked. "I remember you saying you want to wait."

"I'm not going to be running around town throwing people through windows, if that's what you're worried about," Miles said. "I'd rather not give the humans in this place more reasons to distrust us. In the meantime, I'd like to see Lauren."

"Okay, you want to meet me at the hospital?" Amber asked.

"I have to go see the ATO who arrived," Miles said. "Sounds like we've got uninvited House Umbra members. I'll come see you once I'm done."

"How bad are we talking?" Amber asked.

"On a scale of one to ten? About thirty-six," Miles said. "I'll tell you everything once I've figured out what's going on."

"Be safe," Amber said, ending the call.

"You want to bite some House Umbra people?" Miles asked Church, who yawned.

The drive to the community centre was done with trepidation as Miles was pretty sure he knew who was waiting for him at the other end.

He parked his BMW next to the two ATO modified military JLTVs—Joint Light Tactical Vehicles—painted black. The JLTV was a vehicle used by the Assembly throughout the United States. Beside them were four Mercedes G-Wagons, which were all an identical in their black paint, black rims, and tinted windows.

"You don't have to come in," Miles said to Church, who followed him nevertheless.

The community centre had a dozen meeting rooms of various sizes, and one large room that could seat several hundred people. According to the leaflets in the empty reception area, it could be hired out for parties.

Just beyond the small reception was a long open corridor with doors on either side. Halfway down was a tall woman in black tactical gear. She had dark skin, a bald head, and a revolver at her hip, and she held a Remington 870 shotgun in her hands. She looked over at Miles and nodded once.

"They in there?" Miles asked, pointing to the door beside her and noticing the ATO badge on her left lapel.

"I am to tell you that they are," the woman said. "I am also to tell you that Henry did not know they were coming. He wants you to understand that."

"I'm not mad," Miles said. "Or disappointed. I don't blame any of you for a House turning up and making a nuisance of themselves. Anything I need to know before I go in there?"

"First Captain Vinko is here," the woman said with a smile that never reached her eyes.

Miles nodded that he understood. "I get it, thanks." He opened the door and stepped into a large, wooden-floored room, with rows of stacked chairs along one side under windows that stretched up to the ceiling high above. There was a hook on the end of a long stick that was used to open the windows, most of which were closed, the lighting above artificial and harsh.

There were a dozen people at one end of the room, in front of a large stage. Several stood off to the side, while the rest stood around a table with various pieces of paper strewn across it. Of the dozen, most were from the ATO team that Miles had seen the previous night. They were the ones standing off to the side, occasionally glancing at those around the table with a mixture of unpleasant expressions.

"You must be Miles," one said, walking over and shaking his hand. He was taller than Miles by several inches, broader too, with dark skin and a bald head. He had a large beard and his voice was deep and commanding. "Name's Henry."

"Good to meet you," Miles said.

At the table, along with three Assembly Inquisitors, was Vedran Vinko, who wore a dark green tailored suit and black polished shoes that had a mirror shine. A chain for a pocket watch hung from his suit jacket pocket. He looked over at Miles and smiled.

"Miles, my friend," Vedran said, walking over to him and slapping him on the shoulder.

"Vedran," Miles said. "Why are there Inquisitors here?"

"I left my House Umbra guard in Seattle to do their job," Vedran said. "But I wanted to bridge any gaps between my House and the Assembly, so I agreed to bring three Inquisitors with me to ensure that there were people from both sides helping."

Miles turned to stare at the Inquisitors, and all three of them bowed their heads in unison.

"You were in Seattle to talk to the Magistrate," Miles said to Vedran. "Any problems?"

Vedran smiled broadly. It was fake, and Miles knew it. "No problems," Vedran said. "Just needed to ensure that their investigation into the deaths of three innocent humans didn't need assistance. Do *you* need any assistance, Miles?"

Miles considered whether or not to mention that he'd recognised the face of the Inquisitor from the previous night, but he decided to keep it to himself. No need to let Vedran know anything that he didn't need to, especially if Vedran was involved with the kidnapping of Oliver, as Miles suspected. And if Vedran was involved, the three Inquisitors with him were involved.

"Thank you for the kind offer," Miles said, doing everything in his power to keep his temper in check. "But I'm good. I hear one of the criminals in London was released from ATO custody."

"Thank you for the information," Vedran said. "I will look into it."

"Anytime," Miles told him.

"I will take them to their new roles in town," Vedran said. "They'll be assisting the police in any investigation they have. And then I must leave, as I have work to attend to in Seattle. We will find this *Boss*, you have my word. After all the hard work you did before House Umbra took over, I won't let this matter die. You should have come to me and said you needed help, though."

"I wasn't sure if Oliver was actually involved in what happened with the desolate in London," Miles said. "No point in wasting your time."

Vedran's smile faltered just a little bit. "Anything I can do to help the Arbiters is never a waste of time."

He made it sound as if he was doing Miles a massive favour, which Miles bristled at, but he remained quiet. There was no point in taking the obvious bait, for one, but also the quicker Vedran left the town, the happier Miles would be.

"So long, ladies and gentlemen, it was an honour," Vedran said with a flourish before leaving the room, the Inquisitor in tow.

"What the hell just happened?" Henry asked when the ATO team and Miles were alone.

"House Umbra is making sure there's nothing to get back to them after what happened in London," Miles explained. "Not sure why they're talking to the Magistrate, though.

"I have no idea," Miles said. "When did Vedran turn up?"

"About an hour ago," one of Henry's people—a woman with dark hair and a scar across her cheek—said.

"Everyone out," Henry said.

Everyone did exactly what they were told, leaving Henry and Miles alone.

"I don't trust him," Henry told Miles.

"Then we're working from the same page," Miles said. "There were two Inquisitors who attacked me and kidnapped Oliver. And now three more are with Vedran. Pretty sure all five are working together. I don't want those Inquisitors anywhere near Lauren, just in case."

"I'll post my own people at the hospital," Henry said. "What about Oliver?"

Miles wasn't sure how to answer that. "Look into it. They'll have taken him somewhere in town. Somewhere quiet. If Vedran is working with the Magistrate, maybe they've given him somewhere to stash Oliver. The Inquisition helping the police is concerning. Start looking into Officer Shilton. He's friends with the Magistrate."

"I don't understand why the Magistrate are keeping quiet about the three dead murder victims," Henry said. "If they were trying to create a panic about vampire murders, they've gone about it the wrong way. Keeping everything silent isn't their usual style."

"Can you check into the victims?" Miles asked, opening his phone and showing the photos of the victims' details to Henry. "I want to know if any money was transferred into their banks in the last month. Large amounts. Check their families, too."

"You're thinking they're being paid to die," Henry said, transferring the files from Miles's phone to his own.

"Right now, nothing is out," Miles said. "Whatever is happening, Lauren may have more information. Oliver said that he saw Liam and Travis take Lauren's body and dump it. Said he heard about a phone call. If she found out something she wasn't meant to, that might be a reason to kill her."

"How does House Umbra fit in?" Henry asked.

Miles didn't have a good answer for that. "Let's hope we figure that out before anyone else dies."

The ATO team left and Miles called Amber and told her about Vedran and the Inquisitors.

"They going to be a problem?" Amber asked.

Miles thought for a moment. *Almost certainly* was his first thought, but instead he said, "We'll see."

"Oh, I forgot," Amber said. "Ignore the protest outside of the hospital."

"The what?" Miles asked.

"It got out that Travis was a victim," Amber said. "Some of his friends from the Red Demon and the Magistrate took it upon themselves to protest the precinct and hospital. The Magistrate are currently trying to frame it that Oliver is some kind of vampire mass serial killer, and that they rushed in and saved the day."

"They're lying, you mean?" Miles said.

"Absolutely," Amber replied.

"Thanks for the warning." Miles ended the call, looked up at the ceiling, and mentally cursed ever coming to America.

CHAPTER TWENTY-FOUR

The large field outside the front of the hospital, where Miles had met Doc Hammond, had three dozen people in it with placards and banners, marching around, chanting about how they weren't safe from vampires. The placards were mostly *VAMPIRES = EVIL* or on that theme. The person who wielded the placard with a misspelling of the word *vampires* made Miles chuckle.

There were also several news outlet vans in the parking area, with some of the reporters recording the protests or interviewing protestors. Miles didn't need to be anywhere close enough to hear them to know that they were going to spout the same lies they always did, and that the reporters wouldn't tell them they were wrong or fact check; they'd just run the report of humans being angry at vampires over and over. A never-ending cycle of lies and misery made to look like news.

The sun was on its last legs for the day and the snow was beginning to fall in earnest, giving Miles the hope that the protestors would give up and go home when it got too cold.

Miles parked in the hospital parking lot, got out into the cool air, and walked toward the hospital, Church by his side. The pair stopped under the shade of some trees to watch as Blake Summers of the Magistrate climbed onto a small podium in front of the hospital main entrance, while several of the news outlets stood before him.

"I would just like to thank my Magistrate brothers and sisters, and the people of this town who worked with them to end this terrifying threat that besieged this beautiful part of the country," Blake said. "The victim, Lauren Gibson, the wife of a local detective, was found held prisoner by a monstrous vampire. She is thankfully alive and well, but we must never forget what could have happened if not for the timely intervention of those working by our side.

"By working together, the vampire menace has been ended, but it will not be long before there's another, and another. Until more humans are taken by their savagery. Their need to feed and hunt. They are little more than animals, watching us like a tiger watches its prey. It may not pounce the first day, it may not pounce the second, but at some point, the need to feed will take over and that human who thought the vampire was their friend, or just out there minding their own business, will show their true colours. And it will end in tragedy."

"Did he just imply his Magistrate idiots did a damn thing?" Miles asked Church, who whined in response.

"This must never happen again," Blake Summers said. "And to that end, I will be petitioning the Governor to ensure that every town in Washington has a Magistrate office. That we can take our streets back from the monsters who would prey upon us."

"Fuck you," someone shouted from the street as they walked by between Miles and Blake.

"Bigot," someone else shouted.

"Liar," a third person said.

Blake looked flustered for a moment. "It's okay, my friends," he said eventually. "You have been told that the vampires are like us, that they are our allies. There are too many of them who wish us harm. And we need to know who is a threat to our lives, our liberty, and our freedoms. Thank you, and God bless a human America."

"Am I meant to applaud?" Miles asked Church, who huffed in response. Miles watched as Blake was taken into the hospital by two large men as the reporters threw questions at him like bullets.

There was a sizeable counterprotest going on in the field next to the hospital now, and some of it was spilling out to the parking area, resulting in a few scuffles. Miles pushed himself away from the tree and walked by the reporters who were heading back to find something else to record or question, and entered the hospital through the large glass double doors.

Amber sat just inside on one of a dozen seats along the large bright hallway. There were doors on either side, and occasionally someone walked out of one door, crossed the hallway, and walked into another.

There were a few people in the hallway, with most watching Blake practically skip up the hallway and disappear behind a corner. Several of the people looked unimpressed with Blake, with a few shaking their heads in disgust, but Amber was the only one who looked as if she might follow Blake and beat his piss out of him.

"Did you fucking hear that shit?" Amber practically shouted. "God bless a human America? I should arrest him for inciting a riot."

Miles smiled. "People who have lived pointless, petty lives often need someone to blame for their own misfortune. Blake's core demographic is going to eat that shit up; that's all he cares about."

"He took credit for stopping a serial killer who seemingly doesn't exist," Amber said, more than one person turning to watch her. "But even if Oliver had been a serial killer, Blake didn't do a damn thing. The Magistrate didn't do anything."

"That is true," Miles said, trying not to make eye contact with the others in the hallway, who were all fully invested at this point. "But technically, he didn't say he or the Magistrate did anything. He just thanked people for helping end it."

Amber opened her mouth, closed it, and let out a deep breath. "He's still an asshole."

"Aye," Miles said. "He's a mighty shitehawk of a man, but he's not our main issue right now. You okay to see Lauren?"

"Yeah," she said and got to her feet.

Miles and Church followed Amber down the hall, through a set of double doors, and down a second identical hall to several sets of lifts.

"Need to take the elevator up," Amber said. "We can take the stairs, if you'd prefer."

"I'm fine," Miles said as Amber pressed the call button a little too furiously. "Are you okay?"

"No," Amber said curtly. "I am angry that people like him . . . like Blake can just make things worse with seemingly no consequences."

"The Magistrate are bankrolled by people with serious wealth and power," Miles said. "Makes them hard to get at. I know it sucks, but people with both don't always get their comeuppance. Sometimes bad people do bad things and get away with it. And it sucks, and I try to make sure it doesn't happen, but it still sucks."

The lift arrived and Amber stepped inside, using her police ID badge to swipe across a card reader. "You're very calm about it," she said when the doors had closed after Miles had stepped into the lift.

"I've been doing this a long time," he said. "I've seen bad people get away with shit for centuries. Sometimes I got to go after them. Sometimes I got to make an example of them. Or someone else did. But there was always another arsehole waiting to spring up and continue where the last one left off. Blake Summers is worthy neither of my time nor my brain space."

"Pam said you were charming," Amber said, with the first smile that Miles had seen since he'd arrived to meet her.

"Your wife is a lovely lady," Miles said. "And she's wrong."

"Oh really?" Amber asked.

"I'm both charming and dashing," Miles said with a grin.

Amber was still laughing as the lift doors opened and they stepped out into the hallway beyond. Miles followed Amber through the hospital, ignoring the occasional loudspeaker announcement and avoiding any nurses, doctors, or other members of staff who were trying to do their jobs.

The west wing of the hospital was the new build, and you had to walk over a short, glass-covered bridge to get to it from the main hospital building. The night had settled in, bringing more bad weather. Not a good night to be out and about for vampires. Or humans, for that matter, although thankfully they tended not to start needing to drink blood because they had a bit of a chill.

"Is there a direct method to get in here?" Miles asked as they walked along the empty corridor of the west wing.

"Yep, door below," Amber said. "Stairs or elevators to get up here. It's not officially opened yet, as there's still some work being done on the top floor. It's good enough to keep Lauren safe, though."

The ATO were stationed at the end of the corridor, with the Inquisitor nowhere to be seen.

"Aren't you meant to have company, Henry?" Miles asked.

"Pretty sure there were meant to be cops here, too," Amber agreed.

Henry stood, nodded to Miles, introduced himself to Amber, shook her hand, patted Church, called her the best girl, and looked around before speaking to Miles. "They're downstairs in the break room. They did not like us taking positions here. They wanted to be inside the room with Lauren. I didn't think any human would like that. Or any vampires, for that matter. There's a possibility your people might be sulking."

"Thank you for doing this," Miles said.

Henry waved away the comment. "We've set up in the rooms on this hallway, two-person four-hour shifts. We'll be here for as long as you need us. I assume you're here to talk to Lauren?"

Miles nodded. "You've spoken to her?"

"Only to say hello," Henry said. "Told her why we were here, she appeared to understand."

"Any visitors?" Amber asked.

"Only people who have come to see her are doctors, nurses, Doc Hammond, and you," Henry said. "I assume we won't be seeing her husband."

"I imagine Reese is off somewhere shitting himself with fear of what his wife will tell everyone," Miles said, before looking down at Church. "You want to stay here?

Church's answer consisted of her walking over to a nearby room and lying down in front of it.

"Back soon," Miles told Henry, and with Amber beside him, they went to see Lauren Gibson.

Considering all of the horrific things Lauren had gone through, she looked in pretty good health. She had pale skin, several tattoos on her arms of various pop culture items, her blonde hair cut short. Lauren sat in bed with a punnet of grapes beside her, while she alternated between eating and drinking from a glass of water.

"Hi, Lauren," Miles said as he entered the room. There was a bed and a large window; the blinds were pulled shut, and a door standing ajar led to the bathroom. A TV sat on a stand nailed to the wall in front of the bed. The only light in the room came from the lights above the bed, which were warm and pleasant.

"Miles Watson and Amber Lambert," Lauren said with a smile. "I did wonder when I'd get a visit from you, Mister Watson. I hear you've done quite a lot to find me."

"You doing okay?" Amber asked.

"Well, I don't remember anything from the past week, give or take," Lauren said. "I've been told the vampire who had me has gone missing. That true?"

"Oliver McCarthy," Amber said. "We're searching for him now; you're safe."

"I don't think he was going to hurt me," Lauren said. "He helped me. I guess that sounds weird."

Amber and Miles shared a concerned expression.

"You're worried about me," Lauren said. "How sweet. I'm a bit out of it on drugs right now, so my manner might be a little more forthright and skittish than usual."

"So you're not doing okay, then," Miles said.

"I really am fine," Lauren said.

"I know you've answered plenty of questions from my colleagues," Amber said. "But I think Miles would like to hear it all firsthand from you, if that's okay?"

Lauren took a deep breath, letting it out slowly before beginning. "I don't remember the day I was taken. I don't remember what happened to me while I was in the custody of that vampire. I don't remember being found. The last thing I remember is a few days before I was taken. I was in Seattle. I work for the Magistrate. I'm sure you know that, Mister Watson."

Miles nodded.

"I don't hate vampires," Lauren said quickly. "I don't even dislike them, but I have my reasons why I had to work there."

"You want to share them?" Amber asked.

"No," Lauren said, her gaze never leaving Miles.

"I already know," Miles said.

That got a look of surprise from Lauren. "How?"

"While I'm an Arbiter with the Assembly now, I used to be First Librarian of House Venator," Miles explained. "I have friends in several of the Great Houses."

"So?" Lauren asked with a shrug.

"I had a very nice chat with First Lady Danica," Miles said. "She sends her best."

"Danica told you?" Lauren asked, choosing her words carefully.

"She did," Miles said. "She also told me that Yvonne was your handler. And I know that Oliver didn't kidnap you. So, shall we start again?"

"I went to the Magistrate to keep an eye on my brother, Robby," Lauren said. "Reese was always talking about his Magistrate friends; it's one of the reasons I think he's a piece of shit. I figured I could use that. I got an inter-view; I got accepted in the Seattle office. Eight months later, my brother went missing."

"Did you find him?" Amber asked.

"He's dead," Lauren said. She closed her eyes and bit her lip.

"I'm sorry," Amber said.

"What happened?" Miles asked.

"Robby was found in a slum apartment with vampire bite marks all over his body," Lauren said. "Blake told me that Robby was undercover and had been found out. That's bullshit. My brother couldn't go undercover as anything other than the geek he was. He joined the Magistrate because he got caught with enough drugs on him that the judge gave him a choice, jail or Magistrate. He hated the fuckers just as much as I do."

"How long ago was he found?" Miles asked.

Lauren closed her eyes and took a deep breath, letting it out slowly before continuing. "Two months ago. A year ago, I knew something was going on, so I joined the Magistrate. I had to get him out, and when there was some vampire conference in town, I went to Danica for help. She agreed to help me and my brother get out of Washington, away from everything here, if I helped her find out what the Magistrate were up to. And then he went missing, and then he was found dead. And I knew those bastards had done it."

"The Magistrate," Miles said. "Three dead bodies. Any ideas?"

"There are a lot more than three," Lauren said. "I found out that they took humans who were dying, or on the run, stuff like that. They paid a lot of money to them on the promise to do an experiment that would turn them into a human-vampire hybrid."

"No such thing," Miles said.

"Desperate people do desperate things, Mister Watson," Lauren said.

"The Magistrate are killing humans," Miles said, thinking it through as he said each word. "Why? Are they trying to make loyal vampires or something? Wait, they have a vampire prisoner; that's how they're draining them dry."

Lauren nodded. "At least one. I have no idea who."

"Do you have proof?" Amber asked.

"On a USB drive," Lauren said. "Which Reese took after he attacked me."

"You remember?" Miles asked.

"He found out what I was doing," Lauren said. "He . . . he confronted me. Called me a vampire's whore. Took the USB drive. He . . . he was always a bastard, but I had no idea he was going to hurt me. I remember Blake and those two thugs, Liam and Travis, coming in. I thankfully remember nothing else. They hate you, Miles, hate all vampires, but they *really* hate humans who don't hate like they do."

"Blake Summers in particular," Miles said.

"He's an evil piece of shit," Lauren said. "Always was a little too quick to blame others for his misdeeds. Reese told me about how someone played a prank on him in college, made him look foolish, so he beat the kid with an iron bar outside the campus one night. Left him deaf in one ear. Blake waited a year to get that revenge. The man is patient, but he's a monster."

"How about those he employs?" Miles asked.

"They've bought into the vampires are evil bullshit, too," Lauren said. "You know what's funny? What's really fucking funny? Blake caught his wife getting absolutely railed by a vampire. And when he walked in on them, his wife saw him and just kept going. He was a bully, a thug, and I saw that woman after he'd been displeased about something. She tried to leave him. He told her he'd kill her."

"That why you didn't leave Reese?" Amber asked.

"They would come after me anywhere," Lauren said. "He used to be sweet, and I ignored those red flags. The raised voice, the mean-spirited jibe. He told me once that if I ever left him, he'd find me. He knew how to find me. He wasn't lying."

Miles watched Lauren for a moment before saying, "You told everyone you didn't remember what he'd done? That's your official statement?"

Lauren nodded. "I don't want him to know I remember," she said softly. "Not until I can get out of here. Can get a lawyer, can get away. You think Danica will help now?"

"If she doesn't, I will," Miles said.

"You think Reese is worried what you might know?" Amber asked.

"He should be fucking worried," Lauren shouted. "The piece of shit made my life miserable for years. He fucking hated me. Said I held him back, said every bad thing that happened to him was my fault. Accused me of fucking his friends, of fucking the mailman, for Christ's sake. If I'd been fucking around as much as he accused me, I'd be unable to walk straight."

"What was Oliver trying to do?" Miles asked her.

"I don't know," Lauren said. "He found me before they could kill me. He took me, I guess to the factory. He helped me, fed me vampire blood. I don't know why he killed Travis and Liam like he did. I'm not sorry they're dead, though. Honestly, good riddance. Travis was always a piece of shit. He was always . . ."

"Always what?" Amber asked.

"He stared at me," Lauren said with an exasperated sigh. "He was friends with Reese, and whenever I saw Travis, he would stare. He was creepy. I told Reese I didn't like him, but Reese just laughed. What a guy my husband is."

"Do you know where Reese is now?" Amber asked.

"I'd make a guess, he's at his cabin," Lauren said.

"Do you know where that is?" Miles asked.

Lauren shook her head. "Wasn't allowed to. Another red flag in a fucking parade of them. Officer Shilton knows. Blake. Travis and Liam would have known. Cody, Travis's brother. A few others."

"A real who's who of arseholes," Miles said.

"I can go talk to Shilton," Amber said. "If the Magistrate are hiding Reese, we might be able to get them on obstruction."

"Except Lauren doesn't want people to know she remembers," Miles said. "I think that's wise. We don't want people scattering to the wind. We *want* them to think they've gotten away with it."

"For now," Lauren said, menace in her voice for the first time.

"The cabin," Miles said. "Would they have taken Oliver there? If the Magistrate and Vedran are working together, it stands to reason they might need something out of the way and quiet to do whatever they needed to."

"We need to find that cabin," Amber said. "I'll go make a call."

After Amber had left, Miles said. "You heard anything about House Umbra?" As a question, he knew it was a little clutching at straws.

"That would have been way above my pay grade," Lauren said. "The higher ups in the office are true believers in the cause, and they don't let outsiders in."

"The cause?" Miles asked, unsure he actually wanted to know.

"Eradication of threats to humans," Lauren said. "That's a direct quote, by the way. Blake said it to me. They believe. It's like they're a cult or something. Always trying to figure out ways to remove rights from vampires, to create new weapons to hurt vampires. They've been working on exoskeletons that make them stronger, and UV knuckle-dusters."

Miles remembered the UV gauntlets. "I've seen those knuckle-dusters in action," he said. "Exoskeletons? Seriously?"

"I laughed, too," Lauren said. "But then I saw the look of seriousness on the face of Blake and it didn't seem so funny. If they could come up with a suit of armour that would make humans as strong as vampires, wouldn't you be concerned?"

Miles considered it for a moment. The idea of humans wearing armour that made them stronger sounded straight out of some 1980s action film, but if they had created new weapons to fight vampires, to kill vampires—silly or not, that was a concern.

"I'd really like some rest," Lauren said. "Are we done here?"

Miles stood and nodded. "Thank you for your time. I hope you can put all of this behind you and find some peace and happiness."

Sadness crossed over Lauren's face. "I'm not sure I'll ever be able to do either. Too much has happened. Can you do me a favour?"

"Sure," Miles said.

"Can you tell Yvonne and Pam that I enjoyed their friendships?" Lauren said. "I'm not sure when I'm going to get the chance to speak to either of them. The local cops want me to stay here awhile, and that kind ATO agent said he's not going anywhere, and I got the feeling he wasn't letting in visitors."

"Not yet," Miles confirmed. "And yes, I can do that. Take care, Lauren. I'll let Danica know that you've been found safe and well . . . as safe and well as possible."

"Take care, Miles," Lauren said.

Miles left Lauren to rest and nodded a greeting to the ATO members guarding the corridor that her room was in. He continued on until he'd left the hospital and sat on a bench next to a small, snow-covered garden. He breathed in deeply and let it out slowly, watching the cloud of breath leave his mouth like a plume of smoke.

Miles's phone rang. It was Charlotte. He immediately answered it, wondering what terrible thing was about to befall them all next.

"Before you speak, listen," Charlotte said quickly. "It's all gone to shit, Miles. All of it."

CHAPTER TWENTY-FIVE

You want to maybe explain a bit more?" Miles asked.

"The criminal that came to House Umbra to confess is dead," Charlotte said. "He tried to escape from custody and was executed by House Umbra guards. And Alex Richards, who came to the Assembly. He's dead, too. They're thinking an assassin did it last night."

"How?" Miles asked.

"They gained access to him while in custody and detonated a heavily modified UV explosive in his cell," Charlotte said. "Turned him to ash."

"Any CCTV?" Miles asked.

"It was disabled," Charlotte said. "During the daytime. No one saw anything. Those cells are underground, Miles. They have no access to the outside. Each one is a large, dark box. There are human guards in that building. No one knows anything."

"Paid to look the other way?" Miles asked.

"Someone was," Charlotte said. "I'm not allowed to investigate, it's not a House Venator case, but I've passed everything to Drest to see how to proceed."

"And Danny Mortimer?" Miles asked.

"He was decapitated in his own living room," Charlotte said.

"Carla?" Miles asked, almost not wanting to know.

"She's fine," Charlotte said. "Megan brought her to us under the pretence of Carla being a witness to an internal matter, and we've got her in protective custody. There's something you should know, though. I asked a few favours from a House Umbra Second Librarian, though. She knows of a familiar, says he comes across as this kind, sweet kid, but in reality he's a creepy dude. Doesn't know his name."

"Kyle," I said. "Oliver said that Kyle was a familiar."

"That's what I figured," Charlotte said. "But here's the good bit, you want to guess whose familiar he is, and what he unofficially does?"

"Vedran," Miles said immediately. "And I'm going to guess he's a problem solver of some kind."

Charlotte made a *ding, ding, ding* sound. "Excellent guess."

"Not much of a guess," Miles explained. "I just picked whichever role would cause me the most irritation."

"Irritation?" Charlotte almost snapped. "Mon ami, this is dangerous. He's a killer. A professionally trained killer."

"The Boss, sorry, Vedran put him there a week before the desolate happened," Miles said. "He was there to keep an eye on the gang until they became a problem. Presumably, Vedran got wind of something that wasn't right. Or he wanted his people watched if he was going to have a big deal human come in to be made into a vampire. Either way, it's why he hadn't killed Carla or the rest of them. He was waiting on orders, probably reporting back as he tried to find Oliver."

"You know this how?" Charlotte asked.

"It's what I'd do," Miles said. "You keep quiet and listen, see if anyone knows anything they shouldn't. Relay that intel to your boss and wait to be told what to do next."

"Turns up?" Charlotte asked. "I don't think you understand how dangerous a highly trained murderer is."

"I know," Miles said with a smile. "I'll be fine. Thank you for letting me know."

"Miles," Charlotte said, sounding irritated that he wasn't as concerned as she felt he should be. "Take this seriously. You were a scholar, a librarian. You're an excellent investigator. Yes, I know you were a soldier, but that was a long time ago. Kyle is a *killer*."

"I'll be fine," Miles repeated.

"Fine isn't going to keep you alive," Charlotte said. "I would be very angry with you if you get killed by this shithead."

"I promise you, I have no intention of being killed by anyone," Miles told her.

"Just be safe, Miles," she said. "This is all getting dangerous."

Charlotte ended the call and Miles phoned Anya, putting her on video. He told her everything he'd discovered since arriving in America, even if she already knew it. She said nothing until he'd finished.

"I assume there's no reason for me to ask if you're sure," Anya said, rubbing her eyes.

"I have no firm evidence that the Magistrate are killing humans in some kind of strange experiments," Miles said. "I have no evidence that they're keeping vampires prisoner without informing the Assembly."

"Which goes against every agreement we have with them," Anya said. "You're going to need firm proof. And I mean so firm it's like a wall. A literal wall of proof. Can you get it?"

"I may have to do some things you won't like," Miles said. "And by you, I mean the Assembly. Any chance you've ever heard of anything like this?"

Anya said nothing for long enough that Miles thought his connection had glitched. Eventually, she blinked. "You're asking if I've heard anything about what could be a complete disaster in Magistrate-vampire relations, and could potentially get House Umbra investigated by the Inquisitors? Because the answer is no. If the answer was anything else, I'd currently be standing on top of a tall building, while I screamed into the void."

Miles decided not to make things worse by replying.

"Fuck," Anya shouted after a few seconds. "House Umbra and the Magistrate working together is bad enough, but if everything you say is true, it's . . . it's bad, Miles."

"I don't know why House Umbra would be working with the Magistrate, though," Miles admitted. "Or if it's just Vedran specifically."

"Before you do anything rash, find out," Anya said. She swore loudly for several seconds, including a few words that Miles hadn't even heard before. "If there is something going on, Miles, find proof, bring me the proof, and then end it. Quietly. If Umbra and the Magistrate are in bed, we need to know. If the Magistrate is kidnapping our people, we definitely need to know. If they're officially trying to stoke up anti-vampire sentiment and by extension are emboldening morons to hurt vampires, we can use that to keep them off our backs. I'll make some calls; maybe we can get some sort of official investigation of the Seattle branch. Be safe, Miles."

Miles stared at the dark screen on his phone for a second after Anya ended the call. He got up from his seat and walked around to the front of the hospital, where both Amber and Church were waiting for him. Amber was hugging herself tightly, while stamping from foot to foot, while Church was trying to catch snowflakes in her mouth.

"Everything okay?" Amber asked.

"Nope," Miles said. "We need to go to the Red Demon. We need to find Cody, find Reese's cabin, and . . ." He didn't want to say that there was a good chance Oliver was already dead.

They took separate cars to the Red Demon and both parked on the opposite side of the street, in the parking area next to an old 7/11 that was long since closed down and boarded up. There was CCTV on the building, but it pointed only at the car park, which Miles made sure to mentally note.

The Red Demon's sign was, unsurprisingly, neon red, written under a similarly coloured demon that looked as if it was out of a 1940s cartoon, complete with pitchfork. There was a parking area outside the front entrance, which was taken up by a number of cars and motorbikes. And a few people milled around near the entrance. Most were either smoking or on their phones, but there was a group of six at the far right side of the building where they were shrouded in darkness. One of them kept looking around, and Miles got the impression he was nervous.

Another man turned to look at whatever his companion was searching for and gave him a playful punch on the arm, followed by several of the group laughing.

"Officer Shilton," one of them said. "You are a bad police officer."

Miles watched the front of the bar for a few seconds and came to the conclusion that the establishment was a shithole.

There was a tapping on the passenger side window, and the door opened, letting in a lot of frozen air from outside. Amber dropped into the passenger seat and rubbed her hands.

"You'd think I'd be used to winter here having lived here my whole life," Amber said.

Two police cruisers pulled up outside the bar, and several officers got out, including Officer Sheringham.

"My time to shine," Amber said. "Stay here; don't do anything that will get people shot at."

"Can't promise anything," Miles called out as Amber got out of the car.

He knew that Amber was right, that going into the bar was a bad idea. He'd also been interested in the group of six men who had run off into the night the moment the police arrived. Officer Shilton included.

"I'm going for a walk," Miles told Church. "You coming?"

Church licked Miles's hand, and he scratched her behind the ear before opening the car door and getting out, with Church following soon after.

Miles's night vision was all but useless considering the amount of lights around the bar. His car was shrouded in darkness, so he was certain he wouldn't be seen as he jogged along the side of the road, crossing it farther up, away from the bar as the police entered, making a lot of noise in the process.

"I'm going to look up top," Miles told Church. "I'll be back soon."

Church walked off to keep herself hidden in the darkness as Miles quickly scaled the fifty-foot exterior wall of the bar, pulling himself up and over the summit onto the roof.

Miles walked along the flat-top roof with loud HVACs humming away and a number of footlocker style black boxes covered in dark netting. He lifted the netting and found that the boxes were locked with padlocks that required a number to open. He weighed up the pros and cons and tore the padlock off one box, dropping it to the floor as he pushed open the lid.

"Oh shit," he whispered, as the contents of the box were revealed.

It was a box of vampire killing equipment. UV knuckle-dusters, UV and electric shock batons, tasers, and worst of all, a few dozen rounds of incendiary ammo. He lifted one of the cases of nine-millimeter bullets out of the box and opened it, letting them spill onto his hand. Someone was gearing up to kill vampires.

Miles tore the lock off a second box and opened it. Empty.

Fuck, Miles thought as he removed his phone from his pocket and took photos of everything, while his anger threatened to bubble over. He kept a box of incendiary ammo with him, walked over to the edge of the roof, and stepped off, landing softly on the ground.

There were two police officers outside the bar, neither of whom tried to stop him as he walked through the front door.

"Goddamn it," Miles shouted as he stepped through the entrance, passing the UV lamps that surrounded the inside of the doorway. He felt his exposed skin tighten and burn.

There were a few dozen people inside the bar, with most sitting at various tables on a sizeable raised platform to the left of the entrance. To the right was the bar itself, behind which scowled a large bald man.

Between the two was a path that led around to the right of the bar and down onto a dance floor, where Miles spotted several police officers talking to the patrons.

Amber rushed over to Miles. "You're on fire," she said, tapping him on the head to put out the smoke.

Miles passed Amber the box of bullets. "They were on the roof, along with a lot of other vampire killing shit."

"Fuck off, vampire," someone shouted from the throng of people on the raised portion of the bar.

"We don't take kindly to your kind," someone else yelled.

"I don't know what I'm angrier about," Miles said softly. "The weapons concealed on the roof, the UV lamps around the door, or the fact that everyone in this room's combined IQ is about the same as wet bread."

Miles picked up a stool from beside the bar, turned and launched it at the UV lamps surrounding the door, which exploded from the force, showering pieces of glass and wood all over the floor.

"You can't do that," the bartender shouted.

Miles raised his arm to show his bracelet. "This says otherwise. While you are more than welcome to have anti-vampire gatherings, it's illegal to have UV lamps in a place of business, and it's definitely illegal to have Assembly technology hidden on your roof."

"I'm not saying shit," the barman said.

Amber emptied the box of bullets onto the bar and lifted one to show the barman. "This one bullet means a jail term for those who own and run this establishment. The fact that there are thirty of these means federal prison for you. Hope you enjoy your new home."

Officer Sheringham cuffed the barman while reading him his rights, before marching him out of the bar.

Amber turned around to the others, most of whom radiated hate.

"If I find out that any of you were involved in what happened at the library yesterday, I'm going to make it my life's mission to put you in jail for a long time," she said. "We have enough shit to deal with without having to keep a constant eye on people who want to make it worse."

"They need to leave," a man shouted from the rear of the raised area. "Fucking bloodsuckers. They murder us in our beds, they steal our children to make slaves of them, they spread disease, they spread death."

"I'm done here," Miles said.

"I'm going to be a while," Amber told him.

He found the barman outside, sitting in the back of a patrol car with Officer Sheringham standing beside it.

"I'd like a moment with him," Miles said to Sheringham, who looked nervous. "I'm not going to kill him," Miles assured the officer.

Sheringham nodded and stepped away.

"You can't leave me with him," the barman shouted as Miles opened the door and crouched beside him.

Miles had considered just pushing the barman's mind, opening it enough to get the answers he wanted, but he'd rather use that as a worst-case scenario. He didn't want anyone to say that the things these idiots said about vampires were even close to accurate.

"Whose weapons were they?" Miles asked calmly. "I'm pretty sure they weren't yours; I saw the look of surprise on your face when I gave the bullets to Amber. I get that you hate me, and I don't care, but I'm also pretty sure you don't want to go to federal prison. Or Assembly jail. I will petition for that. And I will get that. You'll spend the next ten years in an Assembly prison. With vampires. Lots of vampires. I'll make it known exactly what you're in there for."

"You can't do that," the barman said, a shake to his voice.

"I can," Miles said. "I can have you put in with the worst vampires imaginable. The people who were too evil to even be allowed to spend their prison time in stasis. Those hardcore arseholes who think that humans are little more than cattle. They will love you. Their new human toy to break slowly and savour it. Or they'll just tear your arms off and watch you flounder around on the floor. It'll be one of the two."

"They belong to Cody," the barman said quickly.

"He owns the bar?" Miles asked.

"Blake Summers owns the bar," he said. "It's not official or anything, but he's the one paying the bills. If anyone is putting stuff up there, he knows about it."

"Where's Reese's cabin?" Miles asked.

"Never been," the bartender said. "Only those close to the group get to go. Like Blake."

"And Cody?" Miles asked. "He close to the group?"

"Look, Travis was a believer," the barman said. "But he kept Cody in line. Cody is nuts. He's fucking gone. He wanted to firebomb the library. He wanted to kill every vampire in town."

"Where is he?" Miles asked.

"I don't know," the barman said.

"Where. Is. He?" Miles repeated, pushing his power onto the barman, making sure his words went right into the barman's mind.

The barman clamped his hands over his head. "I don't know," he practically screamed.

Miles stopped pushing his power and stood, turning to Sheringham. "We need to find Cody Sharpe," he said. "As a matter of urgency."

Amber left the bar and motioned for Miles to join her.

"You find anything out?" she asked when they were alone.

Miles told her everything the barman had told him.

"So Blake owns this place," Amber said. "We did wonder, but his name isn't on anything. We'll search for Cody."

"I saw Shilton here earlier," Miles said. "He looked to be in deep conversation with a bunch of others. Maybe he knows where Cody is."

"We'll fin—" Amber started, but her phone rang.

"We've got a situation here—get Miles to the hospital now!" Doc Hammond shouted.

Amber stared at her phone again. "Did you hear that?"

Miles nodded.

"I'll meet you there," Amber said. "I'll finish up here and get everyone to join."

Miles ran over to his car with Church close behind, who jumped into the front seat of the car the second the door was open. Miles set off toward the hospital, cursing the winter conditions, which made driving more hazardous than he'd have liked.

There was no one outside the hospital; whatever protestors had been there had long since gone home, or more likely to the Red Demon to congratulate themselves.

Miles parked the car, let Church out, and ran over to the entrance as his phone rang. He answered, looking around to check that he wasn't about to be jumped or something equally stupid.

"It's Henry," he said. "The Inquisitors demanded to interview Lauren. They've threatened to open fire on anyone who comes close to her room."

Miles set off at a sprint, jumping over a six-foot hedge as though it were only a few inches high and continuing on at full speed, practically bursting through the double doors that signified the entrance to the wing. He continued down the hallway, the lighting occasionally flickering, and ran through the stairwell door, taking the stairs five at a time, using the bannisters to move between sets of stairs, until he reached Lauren's floor.

He opened the stairwell door and stepped out into a cacophony of shouting as Henry's ATO team, along with Doc Hammond, were huddled at the end of the hallway. Henry shouted down the hall and was met with shouts coming back. There were bullet holes in the wall at end of the hallway, a tight cluster of five shots. They'd been the only warning the Inquisitors were going to give.

"Miles," Henry said. "They've gone mad. They ordered us all to leave, said it was Inquisitor business, and barricaded themselves into the room with Lauren. They hurt a human cop, took him with them."

"Anyone else hurt?" Miles asked.

"Not yet," Doc Hammond said. "But honestly, it feels like a miracle at this point."

"Church stay here," Miles said.

Church sat, although every part of her practically vibrated with a need to disobey that order and go with Miles.

"This is Arbiter Miles Watson," he shouted at the corner of the hallway. He risked a glance down at the two Inquisition agents who stood guard outside of Lauren's room. Two men, both wearing black hooded jackets, black combats, and dark boots. Both carrying a silenced MP5.

"You will not come closer," one of the Inquisition shouted.

"I just want to know why you're doing this," Miles said.

"That is not your concern," the guard shouted.

"Any of you the same arsehole who attacked me and Oliver the other night?" Miles shouted.

No reply.

Miles took a shot at something. "How long have you worked for House Umbra?"

Silence.

"Or is it just Vedran you're working for?" Miles continued. "He brought you here to do this, didn't he? What does Lauren know that he's so scared of?"

Silence.

A muffled scream rang throughout the stillness that followed.

"What was that?" Henry asked.

A second scream. Louder. More urgent.

The two Inquisition guards ran into Lauren's room, followed by gunfire and more screams.

"Stay here," Miles said to everyone.

"Absolutely fucking not," Henry said.

"What he said," another member of Henry's team said.

Miles had no time to argue and ran up the hallway as another bloodcurdling scream rang out.

He kicked open the door to Lauren's room and found Lauren standing in the middle of the floor, with three Inquisition agents on the ground at her bare feet. She had her foot placed down on the chest of one agent and held his wrists, forcing his arms upright, pointing toward the ceiling.

Lauren looked up at Miles. Blood drenched her face and chest, turning her hospital gown crimson in the process. She smiled.

"Don't," he said.

Lauren shrugged and ripped the Inquisition guard's arms off. She tossed one away, and held the other over her mouth, which elongated like a snake, allowing more of his blood to flow down into her maw. She drank it down, as blood continued to spray out from the body of the now screaming Inquisition guard.

"Stay back," Miles shouted. "No one gets in here. No one."

Lauren removed her foot, placed it on the screaming guard's head, and pushed down. His skull popped like a water balloon.

"Okay, you've made your point," Miles said. He had no idea what that point was, but he was pretty sure it had been made.

"These vampires were unkind," Lauren said. "They wanted to hurt me. They wanted answers I refused to give them. They wanted to know what I'd discovered about House Umbra First Captain Vedran Vinko. They're working for him, you know. The Magistrate are, too. They made a deal. Vedran and Blake. I was so close to figuring it out when my dipshit of a husband found me."

"You killed Liam Fricker and Travis Sharpe?" Miles said.

"Liam, yes," Lauren said. "I woke up too early, had to sleep. Needed to feed. Oliver made sure I had blood. He tried to drink my blood. He tried to save me, but . . . well, it didn't work quite as Oliver had planned. He's not a bad guy."

"Why kill Travis and Liam?" Miles asked, wanting to keep Lauren talking, wanting to figure out what she actually was. Not vampire. Not desolate. Something . . . else.

"Ah, that's a long story, and I don't think we'll have time for it," Lauren said. "Just know they both deserved what happened to them. Actually, they deserved more." She dragged the curtains free from the window and lifted one of the Inquisition bodies up with ease, throwing him one handed through the window with a smash that sounded louder than it probably was.

Miles stepped into the room. "What are you?" he asked.

"You don't know?" Lauren asked. "Actually, I didn't know either. Oliver helped me search for all the information I needed."

"You don't have to do this," Miles said, taking another step forward. "You're not desolate. They're mindless."

"Not true," Lauren said. "They just need a queen."

Three of the bodies of the Inquisitors started to twitch. Miles took that as a bad sign.

The next time he looked up, Lauren was perched on the edge of the windowsill. "We can talk about this," he said.

Lauren shook her head sadly. "I'm afraid we can't. I tried. I tried to talk. I tried to run. I tried so many times over the years, but this is where it all led. There's no talking now. Please don't get in my way; I'd hate to have to kill you."

"You have a choice," Miles said.

"So you do, Miles," she replied. "Do nothing. Let Blake and his friends die. You have a choice to come after me or stop what's about to happen here and in the morgue. Once killed by a Desolate Royal, they just lie and wait until activated. The desolate just need their queen." She dropped out of the window without another word.

Miles froze as the words from his dream slammed into his mind. The darkness he'd felt in his dreams was Lauren. He turned back to the ATO. "Get to the morgue, now. There are desolate there about to wake up. Kill them all. I've got these ones."

Henry and his team nodded and ran off as three of the Inquisitors shakily got to their feet.

"Probably got these ones," Miles corrected.

❧ Chapter Twenty-Six ❧

The largest of the Inquisitors, one of the two who had been in London what felt like a lifetime ago, got to his feet before his three companions. He was the same one who had kidnapped Oliver. The same one who had hurt Miles in the forest. And now he was undead at Lauren's hands, and soon to be *very* dead at Miles's. Miles smiled; he was going to enjoy this.

Miles backed out into the hallway. He needed more space.

He used his telekinesis to close the door as he backed down the hallway, but the desolate tore the door apart as it exited. There was a deep red gash around the throat area of the desolate, and his head lolled at an odd angle. It charged Miles with an ear-splitting scream.

Miles blasted the desolate with telekinesis, bouncing the creature down the hallway, but a second desolate ran out of the room, moving faster than the first had, and threw herself at Miles, her clawlike hands trying to tear into the flesh of his neck. She wrapped her hands around his neck and squeezed tightly.

"Church," Miles shouted, twisting away from the desolate and smashing her headfirst into the wall.

He scrambled back as desolate number three lurched out of the room, saw Miles, and screamed in rage.

"Off the leash," Miles shouted.

There was a low rumbling growl, like the sound of thunder in the distance, before Church barrelled into the female desolate, taking her off her feet. Church grabbed the desolate around the torso and bit down, snapping ribs and sternum, before tossing the desolate to one side and pouncing on the creature.

Miles used his telekinesis to throw the newest desolate back down the hallway, where it collided with the first, and both went back over onto the floor.

Church wasn't done with the desolate she'd injured, and with her jaws wrapped around the Inquisitor's head, she crunched down. One desolate down, two to go.

He noticed Doc Hammond and one of the ATO agents at the end of the hall. "You two, with Church," he shouted. "Get to the morgue in case those two humans she killed wake up. These are mine."

"Do you want a weapon?" The ATO agent asked.

"No, I'm good," Miles said, turning back to the now standing desolate.

Miles allowed the change of the vampire to flow through him. His hands grew longer, his nails became razor sharp talons, and his fangs elongated as his body changed to become the predator he kept locked up.

The desolate roared in anger and charged at Miles, who smiled. It had been a while. He had some frustrations to work out.

Miles dodged the first desolate and ripped the face off the second, kicking it back into the closed room behind it with enough force to destroy the door in the process. He spun back to the first desolate, dodging its lunge, smoothly moving around it, and ripping out the Achilles on both its heels.

The desolate made no sound as it fell like a tree to the floor, crashing into the tiles. Its body no longer able to remain upright. Miles clamped his hands around the head of the desolate, digging his talons into its skull, and wrenched back with everything he had, tearing the desolate's head in half as he decapitated the creature.

Miles got to his feet as the last desolate stumbled back out of the hospital room, its face a ruined mess. He stepped over the body, pushed aside an attempted swipe from the remaining desolate, and punched his talons through the throat of the creature, twisting and ripping them clear through the side of its neck. The desolate took a step forward and its head detached, rolling off as the body hit the ground.

He looked down at the carnage he'd caused and forced his body to calm, to return to its normal, more human-looking state. He was covered in the dark ichor of the desolate, and he needed to change, but it would have to wait.

Miles spotted a large dagger sheathed on the hip of the desolate whose head he'd ripped in half, and removed it. There was a small button on the side of the dagger's hilt, and he pressed it. The blade crackled with electrical energy.

He kept the dagger and ran into Lauren's room, jumping out of the window and landing on the ground sixty feet below with a graceful roll through the soft snow, coming up into a sprint.

Two police cars, lights still flashing, were both outside of the hospital, but there was no one around. Miles pushed on, reaching the hospital front entrance, the doors of which opened for him as he continued on into the foyer. Doc Hammond and five police officers stood near the entrance, some of the latter occasionally glancing over at Church who sat beside them, now back to normal size, keeping guard.

"The ATO and officers went down to the morgue. There are more of those . . . things down there," Doc Hammond said, throwing her ID to Miles. "They're trying to contain it all."

"Church, stay here," Miles said, catching Doc's ID. "If any of those things gets up here, you know what to do."

Church barked, the noise echoing around the large open space.

"What's she going to do?" one of the officers, a young, nervous man, asked.

"She's going to tear their throats out," Miles said. "Don't worry, it won't come to that."

Miles ran off toward the morgue, taking the stairs as they were quicker, and using Doc Hammond's ID to get into the morgue area, where the sounds of gunfire erupted around the floor.

An ATO agent, her face a bloody mask, sat outside the elevator, her gun aimed at it.

Miles crouched beside her. "You okay?" he asked.

She nodded. "I'll live," she said, her fangs showing as she smiled. "It was their claws, not teeth."

More gunshots.

Miles gripped the knife tightly and ran down the hallway to the sounds of screams and shouts above.

A bloody and battered Travis staggered out of the morgue. He saw Miles and shrieked an ear-piecing, inhuman noise that sent a shiver up Miles's spine. The desolate charged forward and was dead on a more permanent basis a second later, when Miles drove the dagger into his skull and activated the electrical current. The smell of cooked flesh and hair filled the hallway.

Miles removed the dagger from the desolate's skull, stepped into the morgue, and killed the next desolate with the same dagger. The remaining ATO opened fire on a desolate Liam who just didn't want to fall down dead, even with the incendiary rounds the ATO were using.

Miles drove his dagger into Liam's skull, until the charge in the battery burned out and he had to change back into his vampiric form, tearing apart anything that remained.

When it was over, the ATO had lost no one, but three of them had wounds that would need looking at, with Henry's face receiving a horrific claw mark that cut down across his left eye and almost removed his nose. Officer Sheringham was breathing heavily, but was otherwise unharmed, with one of the ATO having stayed with him and the three Officers who'd accompanied him. All had survived the attack.

"Everyone okay?" Miles asked, fully aware of the horror show he portrayed at the moment.

Henry and his people nodded.

"You've got one out in the hall," Miles said. "She's hurt, but alive."

"Goddamn it," Sheringham said, looking down at his injured friends. "God fucking damn it."

"It's done," Miles told Sheringham, who stared at him blankly.

"You sure?" a seated officer asked, a young man who looked as if he might throw up or pass out, possibly both.

Miles nodded. "Are you okay?" he asked the other officer. "Any bites?"

The man shook and practically sprinted from the room.

"What happened here?" Sheringham asked.

"Did any of you get bitten?" Miles asked.

"They weren't using their teeth," Sheringham said. "Just claws. Is that weird?"

Miles looked around the room at the bodies of the dead desolate. There were a dozen incendiary rounds fired into the chest of one, and it had only dropped when Miles had punctured his brain with his dagger. He crouched down beside one body, turning it over. "That's odd," he said, more to himself than anything else.

"What's going on here?" Sheringham asked again, a panic to his voice.

"Lauren is . . ." Miles stopped and looked up at Officer's Sheringham's fear filled face. "A Desolate Queen. I don't understand how she can be so good with her powers, though; she's only been one for at most a few days. Amber still at the Red Demon?"

Sheringham nodded as he left the morgue, with Miles helping him when he stumbled. "Amber sent us on to check on everything."

"We'll stay here and help," Henry said as a medic attended to his face. "Do you know what that thing upstairs was?"

"Lauren?" Miles asked.

Henry nodded.

"Yeah," Miles said softly. "They're meant to be a myth. I've never actually seen one in person."

"She looked pretty goddamned real," Henry said, wincing as the medic held his nose in place so it would heal properly.

"She's a Desolate Queen," Miles said.

"She make those desolate stronger?" Henry asked. "I've killed desolate with incendiary rounds before, never had one take twelve. How are Desolate Queens made?"

Miles shrugged. "I'm going to find that out. Yvonne has a collection of books on them, and she said she's interested in reading them, so she's my next stop."

"They gonna wake up again?" a second ATO agent asked.

"I checked over the bodies of the desolate downstairs," Miles said. "I think they were under Lauren's control. She didn't want us dead, or to make more desolate, just to keep us busy. That's why they didn't use their teeth. I need to make a phone call and figure out what we're meant to do to stop her."

"She's going after Reese," Officer Sheringham said. "Right?"

"He abused her for years," Miles said. "What would you do?"

"We didn't know," Sheringham said softly. "If we had, we might have . . ." Sheringham's voice trailed off, unsure how to finish that sentence.

"He's probably at his cabin; you got any idea where that is?" Miles asked.

Sheringham shook his head slightly.

"Cody Sharpe or Shilton," Miles said. "Any idea where they are?"

"No idea, but Shilton has a house out past the city limits," Sheringham said. "It's on Bolder Road. They're new developments, but most aren't done yet. There's rumours that it's Magistrate money building them as a retaliation for those where you're staying."

Miles checked the street on his phone and memorised the destination.

"I thought he was a good guy. He just . . ." Sheringham said, his voice trailing off.

"Hated vampires," Miles finished for him. "A great guy, except that one gigantic flaw of hating an entire group."

"It used to be different," Sheringham said. "He used to just sound off about vampires and stuff, but the last year, he went all in on it. He started spouting nonsense, easily disproven stuff, but I called him out on it, and it stopped. Then you showed up and, well, he got real angry."

"That I was here?" Miles asked.

Sheringham nodded. "Said you'd spoil everything. Said vampires need to learn their place. That was the last thing he said to me. You're going to have to bring him in, aren't you?"

Miles looked away. At best, Shilton was friendly with people who wanted to murder vampires and had played a part in killing at least three humans, along with the kidnap and attempted murder of Lauren. At worst, he was completely involved and would need to be dealt with like any enemy of vampires. Permanently.

"We need to go," Miles said, although not to anyone in particular. "Keep everyone safe, Henry."

"Will do," he said with a thumbs-up.

He left the hospital and removed his phone, calling Yvonne, but there was no answer. He looked down at Church who walked beside him. "I'm sure that's nothing to be concerned about," he said, not believing his own words as he started to jog toward his car. He called Amber.

"We need to get to Yvonne," he said when she picked up. "Lauren's a Desolate Queen, and that's *really* bad for everyone."

"How bad?" Amber asked.

"On a scale I can't even begin to count the number of," Miles said.

"You think Yvonne knows about them?" Amber asked.

"She's reading a book about them," Miles said. "I could call Drest, but he might want to get a battalion of vampires here to hunt her down. And if I tell the Assembly, they'll burn the state to the ground to find her. I want to know what a Desolate Queen actually is. I've never encountered one before, and honestly I could use the help. The ATO are still at the hospital. Lauren didn't behave like a normal desolate, and she could have had those desolate murder everyone in the morgue, but I'm pretty sure she was controlling them to just keep everyone busy.."

"I'll head over to the hospital," Amber said. "You think the ATO will help me round up people like Shilton? I don't want him running around out there, helping his buddies."

"I'm sure they'll be only too happy to help," Miles said. "I'll call you with what I've found out."

He set off, stopping his car outside of Yvonne's home, and got out, letting Church follow. They walked up to the front garden of her house as the downstairs exploded in a fireball.

The front door to Yvonne's home blew back toward him. It threw him back onto the snow-covered garden, just as the kitchen window exploded, sending a fireball over Miles's head.

Miles got back to his feet and removed his phone to call the Fire Department when Church barrelled into him, knocking him to the ground. His phone skittered out of his hand, as a lash of blood-red power smashed into Church, throwing her back against Miles's rental car with a sickening thud.

"Church," Miles shouted, throwing himself toward her, only to have the same power slam into him, driving him back. Blood poured from a wound across his chest. He refused to give up and got back to his feet, staggering toward Church and collapsing beside her.

Church's fur was slick with blood from a wound across her ribs.

"It's okay," Miles said softly. It would heal, but the sight of someone having hurt Church burned inside of him.

He rubbed his hand on the wound against his chest and held it down beside Church's mouth, and she licked his hand. His blood would help her heal more quickly.

Miles looked back at the house. Whoever had attacked them was still inside. He got to his feet, his vampire form having taken over. Someone was going to die for what they'd done to Church.

The fire continued to consume the house, as two people in black tactical gear and masks walked out. One carried a shotgun and moved to the side, keeping it pointed at Miles. The second attacker removed a pistol and pointed it at Church. Church growled, low and angry.

"You move, she dies," the pistol holder said.

"Which one of you threw that power at me?" Miles asked. Being able to lash vampiric power like that was an old bloodline gift, from a House that was no longer considered one of the Great Houses.

"Hurts doesn't it?" the attacker with the pistol said. "You want some more, or you want to do as you're told?"

It didn't matter how long it was going to take, or how far he had to go, Miles was going to kill him for what he'd done to Church.

"Where's Yvonne?" Miles asked, looking over at the fire-ravaged house.

The masked attacker still holding the shotgun stepped forward and smashed it into the side of Miles's face, knocking him to the ground. A nasty cut just above his eye began to bleed heavily.

A black van pulled up and a side door slid open.

"Get in," the attacker who'd hit Miles said.

Miles looked between the two attackers.

"We've been told to bring you alive," one of the attackers said. "We need to know what you know, and who you've spoken to. Now get in."

While the attacker had confirmed that they needed Miles alive, he doubted they were concerned about how much pain he was in, but there was no way they were taking Church. They were going to kill her the second he got into the van.

"On your feet," the shotgun user shouted.

Miles got slowly to his feet, his hands raised.

"Now move," the shotgun user ordered.

Miles pushed out a blast of telekinetic energy directly in front of him, throwing both attackers back across the garden.

"Church, run," Miles said.

Church was up on her feet in an instant, narrowly avoiding a bullet shot from the attacker's pistol. Miles threw himself toward the shotgun user, colliding with them. The attacker punched him in the chest, where the power had hit him, and Miles yelled out in pain. He fought through the agony in his chest and wrenched the shotgun free, smashing his forearm into the visor of his attacker's mask, shattering it. He moved to the side, wrapped his legs around the attacker's arm, and snapped the elbow at the joint, before pulling hard and wrenching the arm out of its socket. The attacker screamed in pain, but Miles refused to let go. He was going to make sure this attacker was no longer a problem.

Miles knew that Church was gone, but that was fine—there was no way the attackers would be able to deal with him and get her.

Pain erupted through Miles's side, and he suddenly couldn't breathe. He touched his ribs and found blood and rolled away from the masked attacker.

"Enough," a familiar male voice said as Miles was lifted up and practically thrown to his side, landing on the snow-covered ground.

Miles saw the man he knew as Kyle get out of the rear of the truck. He pulled Yvonne by her hair, forcing her down to a kneeling position, pointing a gun at her head. She had a gag in her mouth, and a set of UV light cuffs were on her wrists.

"Incendiary rounds," he said. "This will either kill her or turn her into a vegetable. Want to find out which?"

"Church would have liked to say hi again," Miles said, through gritted teeth, raising his hands to surrender.

"Get in the van, Miles," Kyle said.

One of his masked attackers kicked Miles in the ribs hard enough for them to break, and he winced as he was forced up to a kneeling position and a pair of UV cuffs were attached to his wrists.

The attacker switched the cuffs on, and Miles screamed out in pain as he dropped to all fours, his arms turning bright red.

"Enough," Kyle commanded. "Get him in the car alive, you fucking idiots."

"He hurt me," one of the attackers said.

"I don't care," Kyle snapped.

Yvonne was practically thrown into the back of the van and Miles was dragged up to it and thrown in beside her as his attackers climbed in, their guns aimed at the two vampires. They removed their masks, revealing them to be the female Inquisitor from London and one of the Inquisitors with Vedran earlier in the day.

The rear of the van had two seats facing away from the driver and passenger, and nothing else. They'd put down some tarpaulin on the bare metal of the van, but there was nothing by the way of comfort.

"You okay?" Miles asked Yvonne, who nodded. "Why is she gagged?"

"She's a biter," Kyle snapped.

Miles looked back at Yvonne. "Nice."

Yvonne snorted and the van set off. Miles sat quietly for a few seconds before he started to laugh.

"What's funny?" Kyle asked from the front passenger seat.

"Vedran's behind all this shit," he said. "He's the Boss. You're Vedran's underling. You were what, the House assassin? And now you're Vedran's errand boy. That's some serious downgrading in the job department."

The female Inquisitor punched Miles in the jaw, snapping his head aside and sending him to the rear of the van.

"That wasn't nice," Miles said.

"You should keep your energy," Kyle said. "You're going to need it."

PART THREE

Chapter Twenty-Seven

Lauren hadn't wanted to be found and taken to hospital. That had never been the plan. She'd wanted to rest, to heal, and then to finish what she'd set out to do. To end Blake and Reese.

At first she'd been terrified of what she had become, but the more she slept, the more her brain understood what she was and how her newfound powers worked. Oliver explained to her what had happened. He'd been forced to let her feed on him. It had saved her life, but instead of turning her into a vampire, it had turned her into a Desolate Queen.

At first he'd been scared of her, but he'd quickly realised she wasn't a monster, and he had helped her feed, helped her practise her abilities, become a sounding board for her. Lauren hoped he was okay. She'd asked if they could tell Yvonne, but Oliver had said no. He'd told Lauren that his sister worked for one of the vampire Houses, that she would be honour bound to inform them of what had happened. That an extermination team, or whatever they actually called themselves, would arrive and hunt her down.

She'd had to spend the day after she'd been found in her hospital room, sleeping until it became night. Desolate Queens couldn't function during the daylight hours, and being outdoors in the daylight killed them quickly. Both things Lauren had known the second she'd woken for the first time.

The Inquisitors came to her hospital bedroom intent on hurting her, on getting information she didn't want to give. They wanted to know how much she knew about Vedran. They asked her again and again about him, about House Umbra, and when she refused to answer, they'd set about tearing it from her mind. It hadn't worked out well for them. And drinking their blood had ensured she had a small measure of control over them.

She'd hoped the Arbiter and those with him hadn't been badly hurt by the desolate Inquisitors. She'd felt a tiny stab of pain in her chest as each of the Inquisitors died, and she was glad the Arbiter was still alive.

She was glad she hadn't had to kill the Arbiter. She got the impression that the Arbiter was a good man, and while she might be considered a monster by some, it didn't mean she was a monster. She was still Lauren Gibson . . . she hoped.

Lauren had lied to the Arbiter when she said she hadn't known about Vedran's relationship with the Magistrate. She hadn't wanted him to talk to his superiors, to take away her chance at vengeance. It was all she had left. The Magistrate were responsible for taking away her life, her freedom, her brother, every hope and dream she'd ever had. They would pay for that. She'd planned to run that night, to escape into the darkness, find Reese, find Blake, and end them both.

Desolate Queens could control the desolate that they made, but they also had control over vampires whose blood they drank, or who drank their blood. She was new to everything, practically a babe in her new life, but she could control vampires to a rudimentary degree. She'd been practising on Oliver, and it had been a tiring experience, but the blood helped. She *craved* the blood, and she was okay with it. She wondered if that was her new state of mind. Had her need to hurt those who wronged her always been there, just under the surface, or was it another aspect of what she'd become?

Lauren had read about how her scent wouldn't change from its normal human one until she had created and risen desolate of her own. Even so, she'd still been concerned that the Arbiter's dog would be able to tell her apart. That she would know that Lauren wasn't human. It had been a great relief to know that the dog hadn't discovered the truth about her.

Lauren ran from the hospital as fast as she was able, reaching the nearby forest in what felt like no time at all. She slumped to the ground, her bare feet cold and wounded. She needed to feed again. She wondered if she would ever have that part under complete control. She'd been given synthetic blood and had thrown it all up. Apparently, Desolate Royals only drank the real stuff.

She sat on a tree stump and thought back to everything that had happened in the last few days. It felt as if months had gone by since she'd been attacked by Reese. Since he'd discovered that she'd been working with the vampire Houses to gather intel on Magistrate activities. That they were working with Vedran from House Umbra, although she still wasn't entirely sure why.

Lauren remembered being barely conscious as Reese called Blake, and she'd passed out, only waking up when Travis, Cody, and Liam arrived to deal with her. Travis had stood above her semiconscious form, unzipped, and pissed on her, laughing the whole time. He'd died hard because of that. They'd both died hard. Both had deserved worse.

She needed to find Blake. Wherever Blake was, Reese would be. She needed justice for what had been done to her, what had been done to her brother. She would need allies to help her get inside the Magistrate building in Seattle.

She started running again, this time with a destination in mind.

She stood in the shadows of the trees across the road from the Red Demon and watched as patrons came and went. It was early in the morning now, and she was about to walk across to the bar when she spotted Amber leave while on the radio. She tried to listen in, but the wind ripping across made her unable to catch what Amber was saying. It was obvious from her expression that she was upset, and she practically sped out of the parking lot into the night.

Lauren watched the taillights of the car disappear around a corner before crossing the road and walking through the parking lot to a number of stares that she ignored.

She entered the bar, stepping over the remains of a UV lamp, and looked back at the doorframe. She was glad the light was broken, or it might well have killed her.

Lauren smiled, happy for a bit of luck for a change, and walked over to the bar, only then realising she was barefoot. And in a hospital gown. The bar patrons were silent as every eye was on her.

"Hello, beautiful," a man said from a table behind her. He patted his thigh. "I got a seat for you, right here."

Lauren ignored him. "I'm looking for Blake," she said to the barman.

"Aren't you Reese's wife?" the barman asked.

"Hey, I was just playing," the man at the table said. "Didn't know you were Reese's."

"I'm not Reese's anything," Lauren said sharply.

"Yeah, I heard you're a vampire lover," someone shouted. "Reese told us all you ran off with some vampire, but you got a little more than you counted on. That's what you get."

Lauren turned to find out who had spoken. There were twenty-one people in the bar, not including the barman and Lauren. She could hear the heartbeats of every one of them. No one on the dance floor.

"We're not open," the barman said. "Order of the Police Department. You need to leave."

"Then why is everyone here having a drink?" Lauren asked.

"I haven't sold them anything," the barman said. "They just appeared out of thin air. We're in the middle of a support group. Pick the one you think works best."

Lauren looked around the bar. "I'd like a drink. And I'd like to know where Blake is."

"Why can't Reese tell you?" the barman asked.

"Because my husband has run away," Lauren said. "Because my husband is a gutless coward."

"He told us about you and your vampire friends," someone said, and this time Lauren turned to catch the speaker. A middle-aged blonde lady with a constant look of disgust on her face.

"Did he now?" Lauren asked.

"He was sickened," she said, practically spitting the words. "You should be ashamed of yourself."

Lauren nodded slowly and turned back to the barman. "Not very good service in here, is it?"

The barman leaned over close to Lauren, and hissed, "We don't serve vampire lovers." His breath smelled like stale cigarettes and cheap whisky.

Lauren grabbed his ears and tore them off, tossing them to the floor as the barman screamed in agony. His shock stopped him from moving in time to avoid her jumping up into the bar and smashing his head into the wood as people behind her screamed and shouted.

She looked back at the people in the bar, licked her bloody fingers, and dropped down from the bar. Like vampires, when feeding her fingers elongated, ending with talons, but unlike vampires, her hands and arms grew longer, too, and her jaw split open around each side of her mouth, allowing it to unhinge. Her ears grew into something resembling that of a wolf, and her eyes turned to a bronze colour, with black pupils like an owl. Her teeth, now piranha-like, were capable of rending flesh from bone. Desolate didn't feel like vampires, leaving small marks; they tore and rent flesh, drinking and gorging themselves.

The man who had been seated sprang up, smashing a bottle and coming at Lauren, who grabbed his arm mid-swing with one hand and ripped his arm off from the elbow as though she were snapping a fried chicken wing.

She tossed his arm aside and kicked him in the chest, collapsing his ribs, puncturing his lungs, and all but destroying his sternum, as he flew back through the wooden banister behind him and impacted with the brick wall at the far end of the bar with a sickening thud.

Lauren grabbed the woman who had been seated with him and bit into her throat, feeling the warmth of her blood as it spilled into her mouth. She dropped the woman to the ground and sighed as her victim convulsed at her feet.

"Next," Lauren said.

She moved through the bar, killing and maiming as she needed, but simply feeding on most, taking a bite, and moving on to the next as they scrambled for the exit, be it the door or one of the windows. A few removed concealed guns and started shooting, the bullets slamming into her flesh only for the round to be ejected from her body a few seconds later, spilling to the ground amongst the dead and hurt.

A few managed to make it outside, but Lauren ran after them, throwing them back inside, through one of the windows with a crash or the now broken door. A few people outside saw what was happening, and Lauren quickly went after them, too, killing them quickly before returning to the bar to find five people all trying to get through the door to the apartment above.

Lauren stepped over the bodies of those in the doorway and launched herself at the group, tearing into them with her teeth and throwing them around the bar when she was finished so she could move on to the next terrified victim.

When she was done, Lauren was drenched in blood, and it took a great will to turn back into her human form. She tore her hospital gown off and tossed it aside, walking naked over the carnage she'd created. The barman was still on the ground behind the bar, whimpering softly, his face a bloody pulp. She reached down, pulled him upright, and tore his throat open with her teeth, taking a deep drink before casually dropping him back to the floor.

Lauren searched him, removing the keys for the apartment upstairs, tossing them in the air, and catching them as she looked around. There was no one alive. Combining those in the bar when she'd arrived with those who had turned up, thirty-three humans had been killed in a matter of minutes. She felt an itch in the side of her neck and dug her fingers into the flesh, pulling out the round of a bullet and throwing it aside.

She walked over to the doorway, switched off the lights to the bar, picked up the door, and forced it back into its place, pulling a large table behind it with one hand to make sure it didn't fall down again.

Satisfied that it would have to do, Lauren stepped back over the bodies and used the key on the door, going upstairs to the empty apartment to shower, watching the blood swirl down the plug hole and laughing. Once clean, she changed into an ill-fitting pair of jeans and red hooded top. She would need better clothes, but they could be acquired from elsewhere.

She made herself cheese, chicken, and ham sandwiches using half a loaf bread, before grabbing a six-pack of soda and a bag of tortillas. She needed fuel, and she wanted to remove the taste of blood that lingered on her lips.

Lauren wondered if she would get stronger over time, or if as she was already as strong and fast as she would ever get. A number of drunk humans wasn't exactly a good test, but more would come.

Feeling full, and not wanting to stay too long, she returned to the bar. No one knew where Blake or her husband were, she saw from the memories of many of those she'd bitten. They were terrible people, with thoughts of nothing but hate. They blamed everyone for their own shitty lives, and wanted others to feel the pain they felt. Trying to fill a hole in their soul with only bile. Lauren would have felt sorry for them if they weren't so insufferably awful.

She walked behind the bar, stepped over the barman, and retrieved a cold beer from the fridge, drinking it down in one gulp. She got a second, repeating the action, and then a third and fourth. There was no drunken buzz, but the cool liquid was pleasant.

Lauren removed a bottle of bourbon from the wall and drank from the spout, almost finishing half the bottle before she felt the alcohol have even the slightest effect.

"Goddamn it," Lauren shouted, throwing the bottle at the wall where it smashed. She jumped back over the bar, kicked the body of a man out of his chair, where he'd been when she'd fed on him, and sat down to wait.

She wished she had a watch and had taken her phone with her, but there hadn't been time when the Inquisitors had arrived. Lauren knew that they were working with Vedran. A vampire of great importance. Their minds were weird, though, and she was unable to get much out of them, as though they'd created walls around their memories. The word Seattle was evident, though, along with images of the Magistrate Headquarters—her old place of work—and she knew that was her next destination.

It didn't take long for the first gasp of air to leave the mouth of one of the patrons of the Red Demon. Then another, and another, and soon a dozen people were relearning how to breathe. Lauren sat and waited. She'd seen how quickly the Inquisitors had turned into desolate, but with so many in the bar, she wasn't sure how long it would take.

She'd been able to delay the desolate versions of Liam and Travis because she hadn't remained with them. Putting them in the cold storage of the morgue had further delayed their creation until the time was right. Being so close to so many new desolate threatened to overwhelm her. She couldn't have delayed so many so close to her, even if she'd wanted to.

After only a few minutes, twenty-five of the not so long ago dead humans were back on their feet. They were covered in blood and had ragged wounds around their necks where Lauren had bitten, but those would heal. They would have no minds of their own, bar the need to feed, Lauren knew that much, but she didn't need companions; she needed bodies who would do as they were told.

"So, ladies and gentlemen," Lauren said, fully aware she didn't need to talk to them, but feeling odd about just leaving. "Welcome to the revolution. I hope you're all hungry. Enough flesh and blood as you can gorge yourselves on."

The desolate made noises that Lauren took as agreement.

She moved aside the table, pushed the door, and stepped outside. They would need to find shelter before the morning, but she knew a place they could stay. A set of caves outside of town.

"We've got a long run ahead of us," Lauren said to no one in particular. "Let's go visit my husband."

With the twenty-five desolate keeping pace behind her, Lauren sprinted off into the night.

CHAPTER TWENTY-EIGHT

Miles wasn't entirely sure when he'd been injected with whatever had knocked him out. One minute he'd been in the van, with no windows to see where he was going, and the next thing he knew, he'd woken up in a cell. He remained on his back to check everything was in working order and slowly sat up. He didn't feel ill or have any adverse effect from whatever was used on him. The cuffs were no longer on his wrists, presumably because the Magistrate felt he was no longer a threat in his cell.

The cell itself was fifteen feet by fifteen feet in size. There was a single bed, a toilet, and a sink between them. There were no windows, which Miles surmised was because they were probably underground. The cell was made with thick metal bars that had UV lights on all sides. The lighting in the block was dim, the purple UV light creating an eerie glow throughout.

There were eight cells in the huge room, each one identical, all next to one another in a nice long row. The cell next to him had Yvonne, who sat upright on the ground beside the sink. She held her legs tight against her, her chin rested on her knees, her eyes closed.

"Yvonne," Miles said softly.

Yvonne opened her eyes and looked over at Miles. "You're okay?" she asked. Her eyes were red and puffy; she'd been crying.

"What happened?" he asked.

"They knocked you out," Yvonne said. "Brought us in here. They've been coming in every few hours to check on us. They injected you with more of whatever it was they used. They injected me, too, but once I woke up, they let me be."

"How long have we been here?" Miles asked.

"Twelve hours, maybe," Yvonne said. "I felt the sun rise, even as far under the ground as we are."

Miles heard footsteps coming from outside the cell block. "Where are we?" he asked.

"Seattle," Yvonne said. "The Magistrate building. One of the guards bragged that there was no escaping this place."

Miles knew where that was. The Magistrate Headquarters was built partially on the old Gas Works Park. He remembered reading about it a few years earlier because there was a big row due to the fact that the park was a family place. The Magistrate allowed the actual park to stay but took over about half of the land beside it and build a skyscraper. Miles had seen pictures of the whole area after the Magistrate built a dock on the rear of it. He hoped Church was okay.

"How many guards?" Miles asked.

"Fifteen, twenty?" Yvonne asked. "I'm sorry, I don't remember. We were taken in here. Oliver was here, they dragged him away. He hasn't been back since."

"That's okay," Miles said. "All humans, or some vampires, like Danny?"

"A mix," Yvonne said. "I found that odd. We're in the Magistrate building and there are vampires here. And, I don't know if you've noticed, but Blake and his people *hate* us."

"It's come up once or twice," Miles admitted. "They must both be getting something out of this."

"Any ideas what?" Yvonne asked.

Miles shook his head. "I'll ask when I get the chance."

The door to the cell block opened and a light was switched on. The light was cool and harsh, and Miles had to blink twice to get his eyes used to their new surroundings.

"Miles Watson," Blake said from outside the cell.

"Hey, look everyone, it's the hate-filled twat," Miles said with a smile as he clapped. "Why don't you come in here, and we'll have a nice talk?"

"I have a better idea," Blake said, motioning toward the door.

Oliver was dragged into the cell block by two human men. Both wore black tactical gear, the same as he'd seen other Magistrate members wear when he'd gone to the Gibson residence. However, they had high collars, presumably to stop bites from vampires. Not that it would stop a vampire from tearing someone's head off, but Miles wasn't going to be the one to help his enemies have better protection.

One of the two men was tall and had short hair and a permanent snarl on his face, and the other looked like a skinnier version of Travis Sharpe.

"Cody," Miles said. "I've been looking for you."

The two men ignored Miles and opened Yvonne's cell. The two men dragged Oliver inside, dumping him on the floor, while Blake watched on, a gun in his hand. Yvonne didn't move, just stared wide-eyed as her brother lay on the bare concrete ground, his face a puffy mass of burned flesh. He'd been worked over good.

"You used UV gauntlets on him," Miles said. "Not very sporting."

"We needed answers as to what you know," Blake said. "Vedran wants to talk to you, too. He asked us to keep you company until he gets here."

"Ah, your Boss keeps you on a tight leash," Miles said.

"Fuck you, vampire," Blake snapped, spitting at Miles. "You have no idea what's going on."

"Vedran gets you to do his dirty work," Miles said. "I mean, that's what's going on. Oliver there worked for Vedran in London, making illegal vampires. I'm not sure why, though. I'll have to ask him when I see him. I do know that Vedran scrambled their brains, but if they ever became unscrambled, well, he's royally fucked. I guess that's why he has Oliver still alive. He wanted to know what Oliver knows and who he's told. *You* want to know what Lauren knows and where she is. Because you know she's coming for you."

"Smart little vampire," Blake said.

"You, on the other hand," Miles continued, "are paying humans to do experiments on them, kill them, and dump them in the forests. Although I don't know why. Whatever the plan is, I'm guessing Lauren figured at least part of it out, got caught before she could tell everyone, and you were shit scared of killing more humans in case she could out you all. You decided that hunting her was your best way forward, but she was hunting you. She killed Liam and Travis. Did you know that, Cody?"

Cody paused at the door and looked back at Miles, his face contorted with hate.

"Your brother died because he was a dipshit," Miles said. "Complete and utter moron who played fuck around and find out with a Desolate Queen. And oh boy, did he find out."

Cody snarled and almost threw himself at the cell, but Blake intercepted as Miles sat back and smiled. "I'm going to kill you, vampire," Cody shouted. "I'm going to carve your heart out!"

"With a spoon?" Miles asked, and when no one replied, he said, "Not a fan of that film, no?"

"What did you do to my brother?" Yvonne shouted. She'd turned to her vampire side and stood over a motionless Oliver, rage coming off her in waves. If she was older, more powerful, there was a good chance that Cody and Blake would be forced back by it.

Blake laughed, guided Cody out of the room, and shut the door, leaving the unpleasant lighting in place.

"Yvonne," Miles said.

Yvonne's glare snapped toward Miles. "What?" she practically roared.

"Check your brother," Miles said, keeping his tone even and soft. No need to anger a rage-filled vampire.

Yvonne blinked, looked down at Oliver, and gently lifted him off the floor, laying him on the bed. "I can hear him breathing," she said. "It's . . . laboured."

"Okay," Miles said.

Yvonne held her wrist a few inches above Miles's mouth. She grew one nail and slashed it up her wrist, blood spilling out immediately, falling onto the swollen mouth of Oliver.

After a minute of blood loss, Yvonne's wrist had healed, and Oliver's face looked considerably more normal, although Miles could still hear the wheezing sound in his chest. That would take longer to heal, and considerably more blood.

"Hey, sis," Oliver said weakly, looking up at Yvonne's sad face. "You always said I'd get into trouble I couldn't get out of."

"What did they do this for?" Yvonne asked. "My little brother. Why did they hurt you?"

"They needed to know what I knew," Oliver said, looking over at Miles. "Arbiter."

"Miles," he said.

Oliver nodded, although it looked painful. "I worked for Vedran because he offered me a lot of money. I also worked for Danica. Figured I could inform on them to her and make some cash at the same time. She wanted me to figure out who the Boss was. Every time I was with him, I couldn't remember his name. No phones allowed, that would have been a giveaway. I couldn't remember his name until they started battering my head around. He was here, scared I'd be able to say to everyone what he did. That he ran a crime syndicate. He wanted money. Still does. More importantly, he wanted people in positions of power."

"The old man who died in London?" Miles asked. "The one who became a desolate."

"He's a High Court Judge," Oliver said. "He had a lot of friends in high places. Including several of those who fund the Magistrate. People who had been officially turned down by the Assembly when they'd asked to become vampires. Vedran wanted to turn him and start turning his friends. And then he would have people on his side when he killed the First Lord of Umbra. And more importantly, he'd have the Magistrate in his pocket."

"He's already turned people, I assume?" Miles asked.

Oliver nodded. "Judges here and there, people at various political levels. A network of people designed to get him more power when he becomes First Lord."

"Ah, that's what this was all about," Miles said. "Vedran wants a promotion. Those Inquisitors who work for him, I assume they have done for a long time."

"I don't know," Oliver said. "Vedran has money and power, and wants more. He wants House Umbra to be *the* Great Vampire House."

"Did you see him?" Miles asked.

Oliver shook his head. "He's not in the building. I had to talk to him through his tablet. I don't understand why Blake would willingly work with a vampire? Any vampire? He hates us."

"People put aside their beliefs when it means they can get what they want," Yvonne said. "There are politicians and media people who do it all the time. They rant and rave when their opponent behaves in a certain way, but dismiss it when it's the behaviour of their own guy. Blake is just a hypocrite like them."

Oliver moved and winced again. "So this Kyle is here, too? He was sent to find me after I went missing. To kill everyone once I was found."

"People like Kyle are trained in infiltration," Miles said. "They excel at hiding in plain sight until they're needed to remove people. He killed everyone who worked in the building when the desolate was created. Danny included."

"Damn it," Oliver said. "He wasn't a bad guy. Not by Vedran standards." Yvonne helped her brother sit up.

"I think they've broken a few ribs," Oliver said.

"Why didn't you tell Danica about the plot?" Miles asked.

"I didn't figure it out until I came here," Oliver said. "After I found Lauren, she told me about the Magistrate, about Vedran's involvement. It's . . . a lot. I started to put things together then. Couldn't contact Danica in case someone working with Vedran intercepted it. Couldn't contact Yvonne in case it put her in danger. Besides, I couldn't leave Lauren; she was too weak to feed herself. She slept a lot. I made notes of what she told me, of what I saw when she fed on me."

"You turned her into a Desolate Queen," Miles said, putting more pieces together.

Oliver nodded. "Didn't mean to. She's not a monster. She's not evil. She's just hurt and angry. How'd you figure it out?"

"It came up when she brutally murdered three Inquisitors with her bare hands, reanimated them, and set them on me," Miles said.

"There's a Desolate Queen out there?" Yvonne asked. "Seriously?"

"There is, but Lauren is not our enemy," Oliver said.

"Do you know anything about them?" Yvonne asked no one in particular.

"Sunlight kills them," Miles said. "It's partly why they're so rare; the sunlight usually kills them before anyone else can."

"Yes, but while we are capable of walking through the sunlight, we live mostly in the darkness," Yvonne said. "They *dwell* in darkness on a permanent basis. They are incapable of doing anything while the sun is out. Their body shuts down and they sleep, almost like a coma. There are tales of hunters going after one only to find a cave system with hundreds of desolate all sleeping around the queen or king. They are dangerous on a level most vampires can only dream of."

"Anything else?" Miles asked.

"There are tales of Desolate Royalty living long lives and never once becoming a threat to humans," Yvonne said. "And there are tales of those who live decades without incident, but then they lose control of their desolate and all hell breaks loose. The problem with Desolate Royalty is that they need to have desolate to control. And those desolate need to feed. So, either they feed, and someone goes behind and beheads the corpse to make sure they don't rise, or you get more and more desolate. The queen or king becomes more powerful. And in the end, we're all fucked. If they can keep control over their desolate and make sure there's nothing left of the people they eat, or at least that they're properly disposed of, there's nothing saying they can't live a long and untroubled life."

"They are, at the end of the day, just a different species of vampire, then," Oliver said. "I read that in one of the books at the library."

"I wouldn't say that out loud too often," Miles said before he could stop himself.

"You stole books from my library?" Yvonne asked, making it sound as if a terrible crime had been committed.

"I think in the scheme of things, the Desolate Queen is more of an issue," Miles said, not wanting the conversation to descend into bickering between siblings. "What more do you know?"

Yvonne shook her head slightly and tuned back to Miles. "If you find Desolate Royalty, do not bring in large numbers of vampires to kill them. One taste of their blood, and they could control them. One bite, and it's quite possible that one would try to bite them, and they belong to the king or queen. Small teams kill Desolate Royalty. Large teams become meals and bolster their army."

"That's happened before," Miles said. "Poland, I think. A group of knights, a hundred strong, hunted a Desolate King. Those knights included several vampires from Great Houses. Not one of them survived the encounter. There's a book on it in the library at House Venator."

"What happened to the Desolate King?" Oliver asked.

"From what I remember, a three-man squad found him, killed him," Miles said. "This happened way before my time, something like 970 AD. After the king was killed, the rest of the desolate died quickly. Desolates without a king or queen are feral, as Maine can attest. If they have a head and you remove it, they quickly descend into murdering one another in a frenzy. The three warriors who killed the king watched as their old friends were torn apart by their desolate brothers. All three joined a monastery on their return. None ever spoke about what they saw in that place. Even when writing down their story, they left out pieces of what happened."

"She's not a monster," Oliver repeated.

"Yet," Yvonne said, "Desolate Royalty control their desolate, but what happens when Lauren loses that control, or heaven forbid, she dies? If that happens in a city like Seattle, there would be hundreds, thousands dead. It would be like Maine, only much worse."

"Lauren is not going to lose control," Oliver said. "I've been helping her keep control, learn how to use her powers. While she slept, her subconscious seemed to know what she can do. It's like it's written in the genes of the Desolate Queen. She got tired quickly, but she never once lost control."

"How many desolate did she have with her?" Miles asked.

"None; we practised on rats," Oliver said. "I know it's not the same thing, but she had dozens of rats under her control all at once. She's not a monster."

"Oh yeah, controlling dozens of rats is perfectly normal non-monster behaviour," Miles said, hoping that even in Oliver's injured state, he still managed to get the sarcasm.

"Is she coming here?" Yvonne asked.

Oliver looked between Miles and Yvonne. "Yes," he whispered. "She wants revenge on the Magistrate for killing her brother. For all the shit she saw them do. She's not going to come alone."

"Desolate," Miles said feeling weary. "Okay, we needed to get out of here before, but now we *really* need to get out of here. When is the assassination of the Umbra First Lord planned?"

"Not yet," Oliver said. "They need to make sure everything is ready for when he's in control. I think that's partly why he needs me to tell him what I know and who I spoke to."

"Why kidnap Yvonne?" Miles asked.

"They don't know who I spoke to," Oliver said. "They couldn't do it with you looking around; it would be too suspicious, especially after you became friendly. Taking you meant they could get my sister at the same time. They *really* want to find Lauren, too. Although I doubt they'll be happy with that when they do."

"Do you have a plan?" Yvonne asked.

Miles glanced over at the light switch next to the door. He reached out with his telekinesis and flicked it off. "Maybe," he said, flicking the light back on again. He looked around the cell block and spotted the two CCTV cameras, one at each end. He reached out with his telekinesis again and crushed the first one, before repeating the action with the second.

Now that no one was watching, Miles dropped to the ground, crawled under the metal-framed bed, and using more telekinesis, slowly unscrewed three screws from the slats holding the springs to the frame. He was going to get more, when the sounds of footsteps from behind the door reached his ears. He put the screws in his pocket and moved back out into the middle of the cell.

An Inquisitor stormed into the cell block, marching straight over to Miles's cell. She was the woman from London. Cody stepped into the room behind her, a set of UV gauntlets on his hands. He had eyes only for Miles, and those eyes said he wanted to do horrible things to the vampire.

"Hey, Cody," Miles said with a wave. "How's being an only child?"

Cody rushed toward the cell, with the Inquisitor intercepting. "He's trying to goad you into doing something stupid," she told him.

"Oh, Cody is far too smart for that," Miles said. "Say, how's your son and ex-wife? You see them often?"

"That . . . *bitch,*" Cody said, pointing at Yvonne. "She helped my wife take my boy from me."

"You're a thug and a bully," Yvonne snapped.

"Vampire whore," Cody shouted.

The Inquisitor looked between Cody and Miles. "What was your plan here?" she asked the latter. "You want to wind Cody up so he comes in there and tries to kill you?"

"I mean, it's not a terrible idea," Miles said. "As far as ideas go."

"And then what?" the vampire asked, taking a step toward the cell door. "How do you plan on escaping this place?"

"I don't," Miles told her, removing a screw from his pocket, and keeping it in his fist as he walked over to the cell door, looking up at the UV light that cascaded down between him and the Inquisitor, blocking him from touching the cell door on his side.

"You don't plan on escaping?" the Inquisitor asked.

"I plan on walking out the front door," Miles said. "No escape necessary."

"And why's that?" The Inquisitor asked. She looked down at his hand. "You plan on killing me with a screw?"

Miles smiled and pushed the screw forward with incredible power, slamming it into the eye of the Inquisitor, who screamed in pain as blood poured out of the wound.

She fell to the floor, one hand over her damaged eye, and scurried away, blood seeping through her fingers until she was out of the room.

"Hey, Cody," Miles said.

Cody's face had gone ashen, all hints of the anger now replaced with fear.

"Don't you want to have a go with those gauntlets of yours?" Miles asked.

Cody looked down at the gauntlets and back up at Miles, and ran from the room.

"How does that help us get out of here?" Yvonne asked.

"Oh, that was just the preliminary," Miles said. "Now we wait for the main event."

CHAPTER TWENTY-NINE

The main event started several hours later.

The cell block was dark, and Miles knew that the sun was up outside. He could just *feel* it. His body needed sleep, craved it, and through the darkness Miles could hear the gentle snoring of Oliver as his body continued to repair itself.

Miles, however, was not asleep. He lay down on his bed, his eyes closed, and he waited. He knew it was going to be a long wait, but when the door to the cell block opened, he was not disappointed.

He stayed still, his eyes still closed as he felt the flash of light over his face. A flashlight, just to check he was asleep. More footsteps. A key in the cell door. A slight squeak as it opened. It took every ounce of will for Miles to not smile as his quarry crossed the cell floor. He stood above the prone Miles, his breath full of alcohol. He'd clearly needed the courage.

"Fuck you, vampire," Cody whispered.

Miles's eyes opened just as the dagger was plunged down toward his chest. He caught Cody's hand and held it steady as he got to his feet, letting his vampire side out as he moved. The scent of terror was pungent as Cody's idiotic brain realised, far too late, that he was utterly fucked.

"You should know something, Cody," Miles said, enjoying the dawning spread of fear on the human's face. "When we feed on someone, we can inject a euphoric drug into the system of the person we feed on. It means they feel no pain. They enjoy it quite a lot, in fact. We can choose to do this. On the other hand, you will feel all of this."

Cody turned to run, but Miles was on him in a second, pulling his right arm behind his back with one hand, and sinking his teeth into the human's neck. Miles drank deeply, feeling the memories of Cody flood his mind.

Cody had been there when Travis and Liam had attacked Lauren. Miles saw Cody drive the van with Lauren's body in the back, unaware she was still alive. He listened to Blake laugh about it, about how a vampire sympathiser deserved everything she got.

Memories of Cody's life flashed through Miles's mind. Of his childhood at the hands of abusive parents, of his own abuse of his wife and child, of his beating a man to death in a bar because the man bumped into him. How Travis had helped. How they'd laughed about it.

Finally, memories of Cody in Seattle. In Magistrate Headquarters. He was with Blake; they were talking about the vampire in the basement. About using it to further Blake's aims. About paying humans to let them be fed to the vampire, about trying to create a desolate. Trying to recreate what happened in Maine. Blake showed Cody around, taking him into a large tunnel. There was a keypad, and Blake tried to shield the number as Cody watched: *111876*.

The memories moved on to Blake talking about wanting to eradicate vampires at some kind of event. He spoke about his ancestry, about being one of the vampire hunters; people who had hunted once great vampire bloodlines to extinction because of fear and hate.

Miles pulled away before Cody died, letting his semiconscious body fall to the floor. He crouched beside Cody, and the younger man blinked at him. "No one is ever going to miss you," Miles said in a conversational tone. "Reese is with Vedran. Blake is upstairs. I'm going to find them all and kill them. I'm going to kill every single one of the bastards who helped you. You had a shitty life, and you turned into a shitty adult because you wanted to."

"Please," Cody said softly. "Don't."

Miles lifted Cody up off the ground by his skull. "Fuck you," he said and extended his nails into talons, punching them into his skull and brain, killing him instantly.

He removed the set of keys from Cody's pocket and unlocked Oliver and Yvonne's cell. "This was your plan?" Yvonne asked.

"It's close enough," Miles said. "Stay behind me, don't get hurt."

Miles led the way out of the cell block, taking the stairwell beyond up a single door. Miles pushed it open, revealing a small room. There were computers and terminals on one side, and monitors on the wall above them. Most of the monitors showed nothing but a black screen. A chair sat in front of the computers, but there was no one here. Had Cody been alone? Had they trusted him that much? If so, they were morons.

Yvonne and Oliver joined him in the room.

"Nothing is working," Miles told them, as he tried to get any of the monitors to show him something. "No internal CCTV. No radio, no anything. Cody was left here alone."

"Lauren is in the building," Oliver said.

"You think Lauren by herself took out an entire building's comms system?" Yvonne asked.

"She's not by herself," Oliver said. "We have a link."

"*A link?*" Yvonne asked.

"I think she could control me if she wanted to," Oliver said.

Miles took a step back from Oliver. "What?"

"I mean, if I died, she could bring me back as a desolate," Oliver said. "But it means we have a sort of . . . a link. It's the only right word for it. I can tell when she's near. She's in the building. She's not alone."

"Desolate," Miles said. "How many?"

"I have no idea," Oliver said.

The lights in the room went out, plunging the three into darkness for a moment, before blue lighting kicked in.

"Emergency generator," Miles said. "Probably. That Lauren, too?"

"Yes," Oliver said.

Miles exited the room through the only other door and ended up in an L-shaped hall with the blue lighting from earlier, and a single door on either end. He opened the door into a large circular room, with a sixty-foot-high ceiling and glass viewing platform forty feet above the pale, sand-covered floor. The walls were bare concrete and pockmarked with blood, both old and new. The floor itself sloped up slightly, stopping at a mound in the middle, like a very gentle hill.

They'd made a mini coliseum. A mini coliseum that stank of disinfectant, shit, and blood.

There were a dozen doors dotted around the room, all of which were closed, except two. They were single doors, all dark metal, except one that was a set of double doors with another keypad beside it.

Miles crossed the room and looked up at the glass viewing platform. The glass had been cracked by something. So it was strong enough to take a blow and not shatter. Miles filed that information away just in case. On either side of the viewing platform was a set of walnut-coloured wooden doors.

A vampire moved out of one of the open doors, walking on all fours like an animal. Its face was contorted with rage and thirst. Whatever was left of the human he'd once been was long gone now. It was completely naked, its pallid flesh covered in open wounds.

The vampire was joined by a second which came in through a door ten feet away. He had light brown skin but looked no less unhealthy. An open wound on his muscular right shoulder wept down his arm. Both vampires were bald, both naked, both nothing even close to whoever they'd been before being brought to this place.

The pair of them snapped and snarled at one another, before turning their attention to the three newcomers.

"Oliver, keep safe," Miles said without taking his eyes off the vampires. "Yvonne, one on the left. You good?"

Yvonne wordlessly went left, charging into the vampire and dodging a swipe of the creature's clawed hands. She grabbed the vampire by the Achilles and tore through the tendon, which made a noise like the cracking of a whip.

The second vampire leapt at Miles, who caught it in a telekinesis bubble in mid-air, using the vampire's own momentum to slingshot it across the floor into the double doors at the end, which buckled from the force of the impact.

The first vampire tried to get back to its feet, but one of them was several inches away from the rest of its body, and it slipped on its own blood, smashing into the floor, where Yvonne slammed her claws into its skull.

"You probably don't deserve this," Miles said as he casually strolled toward the vampire he'd thrown across the room. The vampire's arm was twisted in an unnatural position, but it ignored it and screamed at Miles, charging at him.

The vampire was feral, but it was also young, and therefore had nowhere near the level of power needed that Miles would have been concerned about. Even so, he wanted this done, and then he wanted to find the person who had brought this on others and explain to them the error of their ways.

Miles waited until the last moment to draw the blade, ignite the electrical current, and drive it into the eye of the vampire, killing it the instant the blade punctured the brain and cooked it. He removed the dagger, letting the body of the vampire fall to the ground.

"You good?" he asked Yvonne, who despite having some blood on her looked no worse for wear.

"Been better," Yvonne admitted.

Miles walked over to the door, which had buckled from the impact of the vampire, and kicked it with every bit of strength he had, breaking the lock and sending pieces of it showering around the landing outside.

There were stairs that went up to his left and down to his right, with the small landing between. A door was open on the landing, revealing some kind of medical suite, although it was devoid of anyone he could question.

Miles took the stairs three at a time up to the floor above and pulled open the golden handle on the door, stepping into a luxurious room with sofas, a bar, a pool table, and a long dining room in the middle. The door to the right of the room was closed, but the door in front of Miles was open, leading to the viewing platform.

"There's no one here," Miles said to Yvonne and Oliver as they followed. "You think down the stairs?"

He wanted to set the whole place on fire. Maybe if he had time later. He left the room, settling for snapping off one of the door handles, and followed the siblings through the door to the right.

The stairwell beyond was lit in the same blue light as everything else had been, and after five flights of stairs, Church and Miles reached a small empty landing with a single metal door.

He pushed it open, revealing a large floor with a number of offices with glass windows on either side. A set of large double doors was on the opposite end of the door the group had just walked through. Miles opened his mouth to speak but gasped in pain as he felt the pressure hit his chest. He crashed to his knees and looked down at the bullet hole in his chest as Yvonne and Oliver pulled him back into the nearest room.

"I wanted this to be easy," Kyle said, from further down the floor, stepping out from a hall between two of the offices. "But you deserve what's going to happen to you."

Miles tried to talk, but his chest hurt, his lungs burning inside. He spat dark blood on the ground and looked up as a lift arrived halfway down the floor, and Blake Summers stepped out, along with a dozen armed Magistrate personnel.

"We really don't have time to be dealing with you," Blake screamed, easy to hear with the office door still open. He wore UV gauntlets, but they were connected to a set of armour on his torso that let off a faint purple glow.

Pain surged through Miles's body, the incendiary bullets doing their job. It wasn't going to kill him, but it was going to make being able to defend himself difficult.

"Where's your mutt?" Blake called out.

"You two need to go," Miles told Yvonne and Oliver, as they all crouched down by a thick oak desk that Yvonne had overturned to use as cover. "I'll keep them busy."

'They'll kill you," Yvonne said.

"I'll be fine," Miles said and winced as he moved. "Mostly fine."

"You come out and surrender and your friends live," Kyle said. "I'd rather not kill vampires I don't have to."

"They all die," Blake snapped, as another lift arrived and more armed Magistrate got out. "We don't have time for this."

"Sir," one of the Magistrate said. "We're being overrun."

"Where's your master?" Blake screamed at Kyle.

"Maybe they'll just kill each other?" Oliver asked.

"We're not that lucky," Miles said, risking a look around the side of the desk, only to feel disheartened at how many Magistrate members stood just beyond the office. "Ever heard of Butch Cassidy and Sundance Kid, because this might be similar?"

"What are they waiting for?" Yvonne asked.

"Something is coming," Oliver said. "Lauren is here."

"Don't move," Miles said. "No matter what happens next. Both of you stay here and keep each other safe."

There was a low rumble from somewhere within the building, which built up over several seconds.

"She's here," one of the Magistrate screamed, as the doors at the end burst open like a dam, a flood of desolate tearing through them into the room as the Magistrate opened fire.

Miles stayed low and watched through the glass window with part fascination and part horror as the desolate charged toward the waiting Magistrate, who used incendiary rounds at the rapidly approaching hoard. Until it was too late.

The desolate swept into the crowd of Magistrate like a tsunami, tearing anything in their way apart. Some died, some were badly wounded, and one UV grenade went off, vaporising four desolate where they stood, but the rest continued on.

Lauren appeared in the doorway as her minions murdered everything that moved. She wore a red T-shirt, jeans, and black boots. Her hair was now much shorter and appeared to have been done herself. "It is safe," she said.

Oliver was the first to his feet, practically running over to Lauren and hugging her as the Desolate Queen smiled. "It is good to see you safe," Lauren said with genuine warmth while the last of the Magistrate were torn to pieces.

"I don't know where Reese is," Miles said, hoping to preempt the question, while keeping one eye on the gore covered members of the desolate, many of whom he had vague recollections of from his time in the Red Demon.

"And who knows?" Lauren asked.

"Maybe Blake," Oliver said, looking over at the mass of bodies as the desolate fed. "He's not here."

"Anyone else?" Lauren asked, her tone even. Scary.

"Kyle," Miles said. "I assume you haven't eaten him."

"No," Lauren said. "Blake fled. He is a coward, and we will kill him."

"We find him, then," Miles said.

"Lauren," Yvonne said softly from behind Miles. "I'm so sorry."

Tears fell from down Lauren's cheeks. "Me too," she said softly.

"You doing okay?" Miles asked her, his body healing itself, putting his recent feeding to good use.

"You know, I always thought that being a vampire meant you were just the same as you were when you were human," Lauren said to Miles. "That some people just couldn't handle the power it gave you, that they were bad people when they were human, but they just hid it well. Is that true?"

Miles shrugged. "Somewhat. People who hide their true self from others are emboldened to let it out when they have the power to act on it. A person who wants to hurt people but is afraid to as a human has no such fear as a vampire. It's why we select people carefully."

"I never wanted to hurt people," Lauren said sadly. "When I was human, I just wanted to be happy. To be free. To be free of all this." Lauren placed her foot on the back of a still-alive Magistrate member's back. She pressed down, forcing the crawling man to stop and gasp in pain. "But as a

Desolate Queen, I feel differently. I want to hurt these people. I want them to suffer for their misdeeds. Does that mean I was a bad person when I was human?"

Miles shrugged again. "It means you have the power to do what you need to do. You have the power to make things right, or make things worse. You could use that power to bring justice to those who would never see it otherwise, or you could use it to bring terror to them. The desolate are little more than animals. Beings of pure chaos. You are not that. The decision you make to be the kind of person you are is the same when you are a vampire or a Desolate Queen. What kind of Desolate Queen do you want to be?"

"These people need to be punished for their crimes," Lauren said. "I do not feel anything for their deaths. As a human, I think I would have been mortified by what I have done here. My sense of right and wrong is the same as it ever was, but I care little for their worthless lives. They do not deserve to breathe the same air as good people." She lifted one of the Magistrate up by the back of his neck and tore out his throat, drinking deeply from the blood that erupted.

The four were halfway along the floor, with several of the desolate having finished feeding and following behind, when Oliver quickly darted in front of Lauren, shoving her to the side as a cloud of blood left his head.

"Shit," Kyle said, but the desolate were already running toward him, putting themselves between him and their queen. Kyle ran over to the lift, practically throwing himself through the open doors, which closed just as several desolate reached them.

Lauren knelt by Oliver, a bullet hole in his head, burn marks all around the wound. Despite the horrific wound, he wasn't quite dead. An incendiary bullet to the head would be quite capable of killing a vampire of his age, and considering the brutality he'd endured during his time in the care of the Magistrate, his body was already doing all it could to keep him going.

"I'm sorry," he said softly, although it wasn't clear who he was talking to.

"My brave brother," Yvonne said, dropping to her knees and holding Oliver's hand as he died.

The wound in Miles's chest was all but closed, the bullet having been pushed out at some point. The wound still hurt, though, the pain feeding his anger. Would an incendiary bullet to his head have killed him? Probably not, but it would put him out of commission for some time.

"He took that bullet for me," Lauren said. "I didn't ask him to do that."

"He said you weren't a monster," Yvonne said. "He believed you were . . . good."

Lauren stood, holding Miles's hand in hers. "Help me kill them all," she whispered.

Miles turned toward her. "It would be my pleasure."

CHAPTER THIRTY

Miles knelt inside the lift that Kyle had taken to escape and turned into his vampire form. He blinked and his vision changed, allowing him to see heat. More importantly, allowing him to see which button had last been pressed.

The heat was faint on floor twenty-seven, but there was definitely a difference in colour between that button and the rest. There were no buttons higher up than twenty-seven, and Miles wondered what was on that floor that Kyle would want to get to.

"You coming?" Miles asked Lauren and Yvonne.

Yvonne and Lauren ran over, a half dozen desolate behind them, all cramming into one lift.

"What about the rest?" Miles asked, watching the other two dozen desolate in the room beyond.

"They'll take the stairs," Lauren said, and with a wave of her hand, her desolate tore through the door to the stairs beyond, clearing out of the room in seconds.

"I'll come back for you, brother," Yvonne said softly as the lift doors closed.

It was, by some margin, the most uncomfortable lift journey that Miles had ever been on. The low rumbles from the desolate as they breathed in the tiny space were disconcerting. The simple fact that until not long ago, Miles had considered all desolate to be little more than feral monsters who needed to be killed. Not to mention the smell of them, which in such an enclosed area was somewhat overwhelming.

"When we stop, I'll send them out first," Lauren said, motioning to her desolate.

Yvonne had picked up a pair of UV knuckles from one of the dead Magistrates and was staring at them as they glowed purple.

"You good?" Miles asked, more than a little worried about where her head was.

"Yes," Yvonne said, that one word making it clear she was done talking.

The lift stopped and the doors slowly opened, revealing a dark floor beyond. The desolate ran out without a word, with Lauren following a few seconds later.

The floor was open plan, with multiple workstations all around, everything bathed in the same blue light as below.

Miles looked out of the windows giving a view of the nighttime across the city of Seattle. He looked back at Lauren and her desolate. He had no idea what was going to happen to them once this was over. He shouldn't let desolate live; they were capable of spreading their death among human populations at frighting speed. But Lauren probably wasn't going to let her desolate just be destroyed. He pushed the thought aside; it was a problem for later.

He continued on through the floor, following the desolate as they stopped and sniffed doors and tables and chairs, before moving on. To Miles's mind, it was like being led by a gang of especially monstrous bloodhounds.

At the end of the floor was another lift next to a door that required a numerical code to open.

Yvonne pressed the button to the lift, but nothing happened. She pulled the lift doors open, showing the empty lift shelf beyond.

Miles looked down the shaft but saw nothing in the darkness. He looked up and saw the lift a few floors above him. He brought his head back in as Lauren kicked the locked door, causing it to make a horrible noise but not bust open.

"Private lift and staircase," Yvonne said. "Who wants to guess where Blake is?"

Miles placed his hand against the door and used his telekinesis to push with everything he had, but the door didn't budge. "Reinforced with something," he said. "I think we could probably get it open eventually, but . . ."

There was a familiar noise in the darkness of the floor.

"Down," Miles shouted, throwing Lauren to the ground as bullets smashed into the door behind where he'd been.

"Everyone okay?" Lauren asked as she scrambled behind a nearby office wall.

"Yvonne?" Miles said.

"I'm good," she called out from inside the lift shaft.

"My desolate," Lauren said with a smile that bordered on wicked.

There was more gunfire, accompanied by the sounds of howls from the desolate farther along the floor, and crashes of glass as bullets hit the windows.

"You will not take this from me," Blake screamed from farther down the floor.

"Where did they come from?" Miles asked, as a UV grenade detonated and Lauren cried out in pain.

"Deal with Kyle," Lauren said. "Blake is mine."

"I'll help," Yvonne said, pulling herself back onto the floor.

Miles didn't bother to argue and ran at the open lift, jumping through and catching hold of the metal railings on the opposite side of the door. He glanced back to see the desolate fighting several heavily armed Magistrate, the occasional flash of purple lighting up the brawl.

He moved along the metal side of the lift shaft until he reached a maintenance ladder, and used it to quickly scale the rest of the fifty feet of emptiness between him and the lift above. The ladder took him up and beyond the stationary lift. As he held on to the ladder twenty feet above the lift, there was no obvious way to get onto the desired floor without going through the lift. Miles dropped the twenty feet down on top of it, making more noise than he was comfortable with. He tore open the hatch, waited a few seconds for anyone to start shooting, and when no one did, dropped inside.

The control panel of the lift was set to keep the lift stationary, so after pressing the button to open the door, and once again stepping to the side of the lift to make sure he avoided bullets, he stepped outside. Miles leaned back in, removed the lock, pressed the button for floor twenty-seven, and watched the doors close, as the lift began its descent to Lauren and Yvonne.

The floor beyond the lift was one large hallway with a bend to the left forty feet away. The hallway had polished mirrors on either side and a blood-red tiled floor, which Miles was sure was meant to be symbolic of something or other.

Miles walked along the hallway, stopping before he reached the turn. There was something waiting . . . no, not someone . . . two someones. Vampires. He stepped around the corner.

There were two Inquisitors. The first was the woman who sported an eyepatch after their encounter in the cells, and the second caused a low growl to build up in Miles's chest.

"You remember me," the man said. He wasn't wearing his tactical helmet anymore, so Miles could see his pale skin, his short hair, the tattoos on his forehead.

"You hurt my dog," Miles said, letting his vampire form out. His fangs elongated, his fingers becoming talons.

The woman screamed in incandescent rage, having given in to her vampire form, and threw herself at Miles, who ducked under a swipe and clawed at the male Inquisitor's legs, forcing him back. Miles spun on his heel and planted a kick in the chest of the female Inquisitor, sending her flying back down the hallway with a crash.

The male Inquisitor barrelled into Miles, who managed to move a fraction too slow and was thrown against the wall, his head bouncing off the back of the glass with a crack.

Miles dropped to the floor, blocking a knee from the male Inquisitor, and drove his talons into the man's thigh. He twisted his hand and dragged it down, opening the thigh from crotch to knee.

Blood poured out of the male Inquisitor's wound, and he staggered back, but Miles wasn't done. He leapt up, driving his talons into the throat of the Inquisitor, over and over again, blood pouring out of the wound as he fell to the floor.

Miles looked up at the female Inquisitor. She removed a pair of UV knuckles from her pocket and slipped them on. She charged forward, throwing punch after punch, which pushed Miles back as he blocked and avoided as much as he could. Every blow that got through stung, and slowed Miles down, pain lacing through his arms and chest.

She dodged a swipe from Miles and drove her knuckled fist into his kidney, kicking out his knee and slashing him across the face as he dropped. Miles rolled from the blow, his head dizzy, his vision blurry. His whole face hurt.

The male Inquisitor grabbed Miles's leg as he moved by, trying to pull him down to the ground. The Inquisitor's hands were slick with his own blood, and Miles twisted in his grip, slashing his talons across the wrist of the Inquisitor, almost taking his hand in the process.

Miles managed to get out of the way of another knuckled punch from the female Inquisitor, but stepped back in as a second shot came toward him. He drove his hand into the woman's side, between the gap where her tactical gear and trousers met, and unleashed his bloodline gift.

She collapsed to the floor, convulsing, and Miles lifted her up, throwing her along the hallway, where she smashed into the mirror at the end and fell to the floor with a thud.

Miles leaned back against the wall beside him, grateful for a moment's respite. He caught a look of himself in the mirror opposite. He had a nasty cut across his forehead, and his entire face was a mask of crimson, but he'd seen worse.

He pushed himself off the wall and kicked the male Inquisitor in the face when he moved. The Inquisitor's head bounced off the wall, and Miles used his telekinesis to hold it there as he put his foot through the man's face, which made a crunch as his nose was all but destroyed.

A lash of blood-red power swept out of the male Inquisitor's hand, slashing across Miles's arm and drawing more blood as a second blast hit Miles in the side of the head. Miles grabbed the Inquisitor's arm before he could do it again and snapped the elbow. He picked the Inquisitor up and tore out his throat with one taloned hand, drinking deeply from the blood that spilled out of it.

Miles tossed the male Inquisitor down the hallway and turned back to the woman, who was now on her feet, albeit shakily. He took a step toward her as pain laced his body; his hands felt as if they were growing longer, and his head screamed out in pain. He took another step and crashed to his knees, his body seemingly fighting him. He tore at his shirt in an effort to stop it from feeling so constricted, so tight against his torso.

The female Inquisitor threw herself toward Miles, who in an instant was back on his feet and caught her by the throat. He crushed her throat with ease, grabbed her head, and decapitated her, letting her body drop to the floor. He turned back to the male Inquisitor and threw the head of the female at him before rushing forward and using his talons to decapitate him, too.

Miles looked at his blood-covered hands. "What the fuck?" he said. They were longer than they should be, each finger twice the length as usual, his talons now longer and black.

He kicked open the door, which came off its hinges, and stepped into the large office. There was a desk in front of a large circular window, and in the chair was Kyle. He saw Miles and shot twice, both bullets stopping in mid-air as Miles raised one hand. With a push, he shoved them back toward Kyle, who had to throw himself to the side to avoid them, but Miles crossed the twenty-foot gap in an instant.

He grabbed Kyle by the neck and smashed the back of his head into a large, ornate mirror, smashing it. Kyle tried to fight, but Miles threw him back across the office with ease before more pain tore through him. A scream left Miles's throat, and he dropped to his knees as his ribs cracked, popping like bubble wrap as they broke and reset themselves. His arms, his legs, every part of him broke and healed almost instantly. His arms grew longer, his hands and fingers elongating even further than in his vampire form. Fur grew over his body as blood poured from a hundred wounds all over him, which were all instantly healed.

He staggered to his feet and agony refused to let go of him as two wings ripped out of his back. They were each longer than he was tall and were made of a thin black membrane that didn't look strong enough to hold his weight.

A glimpse in a broken mirror showed Miles the horror he'd become. A true vampire beast. His face was still vampiric in appearance, but his jaw jutted out, his ears long and pointed, his eyes bright pools of blazing red with black centres. Hardened ridges of bone sat over each eye, and his cheeks were sunken. He opened his mouth, the fangs on the top row now accompanied by every other tooth razor sharp and sharklike, except for two more fangs on the bottom.

Miles screamed at the mirror, beat his wings, and exploded up through the circular window beside him. He flew up, farther and farther, faster, and faster, as the pain that had wracked his body only moments before dissipated, to be replaced with a euphoric joy of flight. The whole transformation had taken only seconds, but to Miles's tortured mind, it had been minutes of agony.

He soared through the night sky, skimming the buildings of Seattle, going faster and faster, never wanting to stop, until he remembered Kyle, back in the Magistrate Headquarters. He stopped flying, beat his wings, and turned back to the skyscraper. He'd flown miles in no time at all. He'd known how to fly, known exactly what this new form was capable of, and that his bloodline gift and telekinesis wouldn't work while he was in his beast form. It was as if the information had always been there and just needed to be unlocked.

"Kyle," Miles said, his voice rough and low. He growled, feeling the low rumble in his chest, and flew back toward his prey.

Miles spotted Kyle back at the workstation, using a computer. He didn't see Miles until it was far too late.

Miles grabbed the man by the throat and lifted him off the ground with one hand, holding him out of the window. He was close to nine feet tall in his new form, and Kyle's legs dangled helplessly hundreds of feet in the air. He flew out of the destroyed window and landed on the rooftop, dropping Kyle beside him, who scrambled away.

"I was told that you were a highly trained assassin," Miles said. "I expected better."

"I didn't expect this," Kyle said. "More used to killing human-looking vampires."

"I give you two options," Miles said, looking around the rooftop, which contained pipes, air conditioning units, and probably some other bits that Miles had no interest in. "Option one is you tell me what I want to know, and I hand you over to the ATO."

"No," Kyle said.

"Option two is I take you a thousand feet up, let you fall," Miles said. "I know you're Vedran's familiar, so you'd probably survive a fall, but I don't think you'd survive that."

"Option one it is," Kyle said. "Vedran wants the West Coast."

Miles turned back into his human form. He was naked, but he felt no pain from doing so. He would need to invest in a bag to carry clothes around if he was going to be turning into a beast on a regular basis. "Explain better," Miles said.

"Vedran is going to kill the First Lord of House Umbra," Kyle explained. "But he can't just go ahead and do it; there are far too many people in House Umbra who wouldn't allow it. Who would fight back. He has to get them all to follow him, to show the current Lord to be incompetent.

"Umbra has a stake in Oregon, and Vedran made a deal with the Magistrate to instigate a . . . mini Maine problem here. Vedran comes here, fixes everything, saves a load of humans, goes back to House Umbra, and says the guy in charge is not worthy because he's let this happen on his own watch."

"And then what?" Miles asked.

"Blake and Vedran have a deal," Kyle said. "Vedran helps Blake to commit his Maine, and Vedran fixes it. In return, Blake gets what he wants. Vampire monitoring in the States."

"The whole country?" Miles asked.

"No, just Oregon, a few others along the Canadian border, a few more along the southern border," Kyle said. "Vedran will push for it, will say it'll benefit vampires in the long run. That we need humans to trust us and this will help with that. So you either say join the list, or you move."

"And Vedran has access to this list," Miles said. "He gets to find out who works for whom, and who could be a problem."

"Part of it," Kyle said. "He gets California. For the first time in history, one House would control an entire state alone. And it has one of the biggest economies in the country. New York and the like are too entwined with the Assembly, but California was always meant to be neutral. It'll be passed into law by the lawmakers in D.C."

"Vedran gets it put into law that House Umbra is the sole controller of California," Miles said. "And all it takes is him having his own people killed, betrayed, and working with Blake, who wants us all to wear collars. The Magistrate will know where every vampire lives, they'll know their families, friends, everything. People are going to die."

"Large numbers of vampires will leave the states that the Magistrate have forced monitoring in," Kyle said. "Those who stay, it's kind of on them."

"You're all insane," Miles said. "You're selling out your own people."

"For money, power, prestige," Kyle said. "Unfortunately, in the aftermath of what happened in Tottenham, we found out that Oliver works for that bitch Danica. Had to off him, but he ran before we could. We searched London for him, had the Inquisitors out, and nothing. Turned out, he ran here, where he found Lauren, who had found out everything we'd planned.

"Now you have two people who know parts of your plan," Miles said.

"Not ideal, I'll admit," Kyle said. "Anyway, it meant we had to deal with her, but she vanished with Oliver before those Magistrate idiots could finish the job, so Vedran came here to help hunt them. He's at Garibaldi. There's an estate out there on the lake. Blake was going to meet them so they could decide what to do next. Lauren kind of screwed up our timescale. The creation of the desolate old guy in London screwed up Vedran's plans of having people in the London political system who could help introduce him to people in America."

"Those same people who help fund the Magistrate," Miles said.

"You've already heard," Kyle said.

"Vedran wants to move the whole House Umbra here?" Miles asked. "To California. Where it is hot."

"California is a big place," Kyle said. "Lots of wonderful vampire real estate up for grabs. Now, you said you'd let me go, that still true?"

"You're going to be handed over to the Assembly," Miles said. "You're going to be going to jail for a *really* long time. And you're Vedran's familiar and personal assassin, so I'm assuming you won't make it to any trial just in case you tell people something House Umbra doesn't want you to know."

Kyle laughed. "Working for Vedran paid better than working for the House."

"How'd that work out?" Miles asked.

"I'll be fine," Kyle said. "What were you?"

Miles motioned for Kyle to get walking. "None of your concern."

"You weren't a fucking Librarian," Kyle said with a chuckle. "Never met a Librarian who can take down two Inquisitors at the same time. And they weren't pushovers."

Miles had a thought. "The Inquisitors," he said. "How long has Vedran had them in his pocket?"

"A long time," Kyle replied. "Couldn't get this far without their help. The Inquisition members are just like everyone else; they all want a piece of the pie, so to speak. Vedran offered them something, and they agreed. And then you killed them all. He's not going to be happy about that; they cost him a lot of money."

"Oh no, I am truly heartbroken," Miles said sarcastically.

Kyle and Miles walked by a bunch of HVAC units and by some pipes, and Kyle stopped walking. He looked over the bay. "You know what, it's nice here. How high up do you think we are? Four, five hundred feet? Would you really have taken me a thousand feet up and dropped me?"

"Yes," Miles said.

Kyle turned back to Miles. "What's it like, turning into a beast?"

Before Miles could answer, Kyle shot forward. Miles saw the glint of the blade and dodged back, avoiding the lunge. Miles immediately snapped forward, kicking Kyle in the chest, and sending him tumbling over the edge of the rooftop.

Miles ran to the edge and looked over, his night vision letting him see Kyle turn and look up at him, right before he impacted back first with a van, all but destroying the car in the process.

"Was that Kyle?" Lauren asked from behind Miles.

Miles nodded.

"He dead?" Lauren asked.

Miles looked over the edge of the building. "He's a familiar, so odds are he survived. Probably hurts like hell, though."

"Yvonne went back to Oliver; she's taking his body to the ATOs, who are out at the front of the building, by the way," Lauren said. "And a dog. A *really* big dog."

Miles smiled. "Church," he said, his grin widening. "She probably followed my scent here. She can run a long way in a few hours."

"I'm glad she's okay," Lauren said, passing Miles his phone. "It was in the office."

Miles nodded a thank you and switched the phone on, happy to see it still had battery. "Blake?" Miles asked, knowing he needed to focus on work for a while longer.

"He got out before we could get him," Lauren said, more than a hint of anger in her voice. "I found Reese. He was cowering."

"Is he . . ." Miles let the question hang in the air.

"Yes," Lauren said. "Very. I'm not done with these people, Miles. I need to know where to next."

"Garibaldi," Miles said. "That's where Blake will go. He knows you're coming. Vedran will be there, too."

"What's Garibaldi?" Lauren asked.

"It's an estate," Miles said. "That's pretty much all I know, though. I've never been there."

"I'm going to need more desolate," Lauren said. "I stopped the computer drive from wiping itself. Also, you're naked. You do know that, yes?"

"Aye," Miles said, looking back over the edge of the building as several ATO agents dragged Kyle off the top of the van roof. "Wish I wasn't. I'm going to go find some clothes, take the data from that computer, and stop Vedran and Blake from ever being able to get away with this. I assume I can meet you in Garibaldi in twenty-four hours. You've got a few hours until dawn. How'd you get here, anyway?"

"Stole a truck; the desolate hide in the back," Lauren said. "How do we get out of here?"

"There's a tunnel back where you first found us; the access code is *111876*," Miles said. "Get out of here, stay safe. Thank you for your help."

Lauren left without another word.

Miles looked over the edge again, but it was empty. Blake wasn't dead, Vedran had betrayed his own kind for power and money, and Lauren wasn't done getting revenge on everyone who had hurt her.

"Time to get to work," Miles said to himself.

CHAPTER THIRTY-ONE

Miles returned to the large office where he'd fought Kyle and set to work, using the computer there to search for everything he needed. Kyle had been attempting to find and delete anything that pertained to Vedran's involvement in what the Magistrate was doing.

Judging from the USB flash drive in the computer, Kyle was also trying to make a copy of everything for himself. A little bit of covering his own arse, which Miles had to admit was smart. The drive had several gigabytes of data, including photos, recordings between the various parties, and enough information to make everyone involved have a very squeaky bum.

Miles went online, opened a secure cloud storage, and copied everything over to there, too. He had plans of his own.

As the data transferred, he looked around the office and found a small closet next to a much larger bathroom with black and gold marbled everything, in a display of money over style.

He found some clothes in the closet, and while they were just a pair of blue faded jeans and a black T-shirt that barely fit, at least he wasn't going to be doing the next part of his plan naked. He searched for a pair of shoes that might fit, too, but apparently Blake had the smallest feet known to man and Miles would rather go barefoot than be in pain.

After washing himself of the blood that covered his upper body and getting dressed, he went back to the computer. There were sirens outside now, human police more than likely. The building would be searched by the ATOs and human police, working side by side, so that the Magistrate couldn't say that the vampires were responsible.

Miles didn't have long, and he watched as the last files downloaded onto his cloud drive. He pocketed the USB drive, and using the computer, called Charlotte.

Her face came up on the screen. "How bad is everything?" she asked, a smile on her face but a slight concern to her tone. She sat in the main house, close to Drest's office, which would certainly save time.

"Can you get Gideon?" Miles asked her; he didn't have time for their usual playful relationship.

"Sure, he's with Drest," Charlotte said, getting up and walking away.

Miles stared at the empty screen for a minute, as the sound of Gideon's irritation came through the computer's tiny speakers.

"I do not work for Miles Watson," Gideon said as Charlotte came into view again. Gideon stood behind her, his arms folded over his chest. "Oh good, it's the lord and saviour."

"Shut the fuck up for two minutes," Miles snapped. "This is more important than your preening and posturing, and it's certainly more important than our mutual dislike."

He walked through everything he'd done and found in the Magistrate office, including everything Vedran was involved in, and how he'd saved the data on a cloud drive. The expressions of Charlotte and Gideon turned sourer with every passing sentence.

"Charlotte," Miles said as he opened the encrypted drive on his phone and sent Charlotte read and write access. "This is everything I've found on Vedran. This will end him and anyone working with him. Gideon, this is enough for you to request an open investigation into House Umbra, but more importantly, it's enough to open an investigation into the Inquisitors and the Assembly."

"Holy shit, Miles," Charlotte said, scrolling through the data on her end. "There's so much."

"Have you lost your mind?" Gideon asked, his eyes widening as Charlotte continued to look through everything Miles had sent her. "Oh fucking hell, Miles. This is going to end a lot of people."

"Good," Miles said. "Vedran couldn't do all of this without help, and he already has several Inquisitors in his pocket. Or had; they're dead now."

"You killed Inquisitors?" Gideon asked.

"Five at last count," Miles said.

Charlotte leaned back in her chair. "You killed five Inquisitors?"

"Well, three were desolate at the time," Miles said. "It's complicated.

Anyway, both of you together can get these investigations started. I trust Anya and the ATOs here, but I have no idea who else to trust. If you need any help with what happened in Fortress Falls, there's a cop there called Amber Lambert. She should be your first contact. Also a Doc Hammond. They're good people, they want to help."

"Where are you going?" Charlotte asked.

"I need to get Vedran," Miles said, seeing no point in lying.

"You're going after the Umbra First Captain?" Charlotte said, genuine fear in her words. "He'll kill you."

"You killed five Inquisitors," Gideon said. "How? You're an investigator. You were a Librarian, for God's sake. I don't care how much training you get as an Arbiter, how did you kill five Inquisitors?"

"Got lucky," Miles said. "Look, can you two do this?"

"Yes," Charlotte said.

"Yes," Gideon told him. "This will change the vampire world forever, Miles."

"And you'll both be the head of that change," Miles told them. "The ATOs have Kyle, Vedran's pet assassin. He's probably not in a position to talk right now; he went diving and banged his head. Contact Henry Shaw and he'll sort out access."

"You beat a highly trained assassin. Who the fuck are you?" Gideon asked. "Seriously."

"Long story, Gideon," Miles said.

"Is that Miles?" Drest asked, his voice booming in the enclosed space of the House Venator foyer.

"Yes, my Lord," Gideon said with a bow of his head.

"I need a word alone," Drest told them both.

Gideon walked away without another word, but Charlotte lingered. "Be safe, Miles. Come back to us. Please." She left before Miles could reply.

Drest took a seat, replacing Charlotte on Miles's screen. "You've been busy."

"Did you know?" Miles asked. "About Vedran trying to create his own little empire in America? About him trying to get people in positions of power in the UK to become vampires? He was never going to be satisfied with America; he wanted London, too, is my guess."

"I knew he was ambitious," Drest said. "Didn't know he was capable of all this. I thought him a peacock of a man, flamboyant and loud. He was always dangerous, though. I knew he wasn't loyal to his Lord. I don't think First Captain was ever going to be his endgame."

"I've got to go after him," Miles said. "He's at Garibaldi; you ever been?"

"It's an estate," Drest said. "There was a little too much party throwing for my tastes. Vedran will have a lot of people there who will die for him."

"I'll be happy to accommodate them," Miles said.

Drest stared at the screen for several seconds. "Can you beat him?"

"In a fair one-on-one fight? Probably not," Miles said. "He's one of the best fighters I've ever seen."

"That's not what I asked," Drest said.

"You know, when I took the job as First Librarian, I hoped I'd never have to do this shit again," Miles said sadly. "I left to become an Arbiter because there was so much bullshit that Houses were just getting away with. I hoped to change that, even a little bit."

"You're not answering my question," Drest said.

"Yes, I can kill him," Miles snapped.

For over a century Miles had been content with not reverting back to the man who had first met Drest. He'd hoped that he would never have to revert to his old ways. He saw now that he had been at best somewhat optimistically, and at worse genuinely naive, to believe he was done forever with his old talents.

"Goodbye, Drest," Miles said. "I don't know what's going to happen next, but this is going to end for Vedran."

Drest nodded slowly. "Return if you can. And if you can't . . . it was an honour . . . my friend."

The screen went blank, and Miles sat and stared at it, feeling a hollowness inside of him. If going after Vedran was how it was all going to end, then so be it. He left the computer where it was; he had his own copy of the files now, so it didn't much matter if anyone tried to delete it all.

Miles considered undressing, dropping out of the window, changing into his beast form, and flying down, but he decided he'd rather have the time to himself. He made his way back through the building until he reached the foyer, where several armed police all pointed guns at him and started shouting, only stopping when Anya ran in with Henry beside her. Both wore tactical gear, and neither looked happy to be there.

"How bad is it?" Anya asked.

"Do you ever just say hello?" Miles replied.

"Hi, Miles," Anya said, sounding bubbly and excitable. "How fucking bad is it? Also, why are you barefoot?"

Miles laughed. "I'm recreating *Die Hard*. Also, I need some clothes that fit me."

"Why are you wearing clothes that don't fit?" she asked as Henry spoke to the police in charge.

"Long story," Miles said.

The pair walked out of the crowded foyer and left the building. It was still going to be dark for a few hours, but the number of headlights and flashing lights made everything look brighter than it was. Miles was taken over to a large blue truck used as a field HQ. Anya stepped inside first and told everyone to get out, which they did immediately.

"You, in," Anya said.

Miles used the steps to get inside the truck, which had computers and monitors down one side and a locked gun rack on the other. At the far end, just before the driving cabin, were several seats. Miles sat as Henry stepped into the truck and passed Miles a set of the same tactical gear they all wore. Miles was soon dressed in black combats and a black top, with a stab vest over the top. Vampires were much more likely to get stabbed than shot. Even with an enemy who more than likely had incendiary rounds in their inventory. At least, that was how Henry phrased it. Miles just figured that they didn't have enough bulletproof vests, and besides, the stab vest didn't limit his mobility as much as the bulletproof one, so he was fine with it.

"Explain, please," Anya said.

Miles explained everything that had happened, leaving nothing out. There was no point in doing anything else; he actually trusted Henry and Anya.

"Where's your Arbiter bracelet?" Anya asked when all was said and done.

"That's what you took out of it?" Miles replied.

"Sorry, it's been bugging me," Anya said.

Miles looked down at his bare wrist. "Probably in the building after I turned into my beast form. I guess it snapped from the strain."

"We'll get you a new one," Anya said.

"No," Miles told her. "I need to go to finish this. Vedran, Blake, and company are too dangerous to leave out there, and with Inquisition involvement, I'm genuinely unsure who I can and can't trust. Present company excepted."

"You're quitting as an Arbiter?" Anya asked.

"What needs to be done can't be linked to you, the Assembly, or the Great Houses," Miles told her, passing over the USB drive. "I have actual evidence of everything they've done. It's backed up, too. It details Vedran's involvement. Vedran doesn't know that Blake kept records of everything."

"So we can arrest Vedran," Henry said.

"We both know that's not going to be allowed to happen," Miles told him. "Vedran will stick in, he'll fight tooth and nail. Assembly personnel will die trying to get him. He's in his estate at Garibaldi. I used the walk down through the building to check out the maps of the area on my phone. It's Fort Knox, but without the gold. This has to be done quietly, and quickly."

"What about the Desolate Queen?" Anya asked.

"She's got her own agenda," Miles said. "She can be trusted. I think. She's definitely been able to kill me a dozen times over and hasn't. Don't see why she'd try now. I don't think I'd test that theory with the desolate and ATO squads in the same proximity. She's basically our nuclear option. If I can't do it, if I get caught or killed, it can't come back on you."

Anya drummed the fingers of one hand on her knee. "I mean, if you go there and you watch in horror as a Desolate Queen has her desolates kill everyone, you got there too late to save them. And by then we have Vedran's name flooding through the Assembly to find and arrest him. You were too late to save the humans, but you can make it up by arresting the vampire who helped set them up to a desolate attack. Or something like that, I'll figure it out. I can delay telling people that there's a Desolate Queen running around Canada, but not indefinitely. And not if it all goes to shit and she invades Quebec or something. Keep her close; keep her where you have access."

"Have I ever told you that you're quite marvellously devious?" Miles asked, a smirk on his lips.

"No, but I still like to be told it," Anya said. "Do what you need to do, Miles. Just stay in one piece. What do we do with the Desolate Queen after this is done?"

"I don't know," Miles admitted.

Anya clicked her tongue against the roof of her mouth. "I'll trust your judgment, but if she lives, she's going to be hunted forever, and there's nothing you or I can do to stop that. And honestly, at some point, she'll die, and her desolate will be free. No one wants that. Also, because I'm just full of brilliant questions, how do we explain the death of a Vampire Greater House First Captain, if it's necessary?"

"I've sent the info you have to First Counsel of House Venator," Miles said. "She'll figure out a legal route to get the investigation put together. She's going to include the Assembly and Inquisitors in it."

"Good," Henry said. "We don't have room for people like those who would work with Vedran against their own kind. Getting vampires registered, getting them tracked, their friends and families, too. It'll get people killed. And he must know it."

"He does," Miles said. "He's never been an idiot. He just doesn't care."

There was a knock at the door, which Henry opened, and Church bounded in, saw Miles, and immediately started licking his face as he crouched down to greet her.

"Glad you're okay," Amber said from the doorway.

Miles looked up from Church as she tried to sit on his lap. "Thank you for bringing her."

"She ran right into the hospital and started going mad," Amber said. "Doc Hammond called me. I called Henry, and he said you were here causing trouble. Seems to follow you around."

"I'm lucky like that," Miles said. "You seen Yvonne?"

Amber nodded sadly. "I'll take her back home; she can stay with us."

"Oliver saved Lauren's life," Miles said and turned to Anya. "I think he tried to do the right thing. The illegal vampire ring will go down with Vedran being at the head of it. If Oliver hadn't run here, hadn't sought out his sister, he never would have found Lauren, and I never would have needed to come here and get embroiled in all this. He saved lives by coming here, Anya."

"I'll make sure his record shows that," Anya told him.

Amber shook Henry's hand and went to shake Miles's, but Church got in the way and needed to be given attention. Eventually, Amber shook Miles's hand. "Thank you," she said. "Maybe sometime come back to our little town and you can see it in a better light. We arrested Shilton, by the way. He's not best pleased, and the Red Demon won't be a problem, considering the CCTV inside showed Lauren murdering everyone, or turning them into desolate."

"I thought I recognised a few of them," Miles said. "I'll be sure to say hi before I go back to Scotland."

Amber left, and Miles hoped that everyone in Fortress Falls would be able to move forward after all the deaths and hate that flowed through there.

"You need weapons?" Henry asked Miles.

"A car," he said. "I just need a car. Maybe a knife or two. Possibly a tank. Do you have a tank?"

"Not on me," Henry said. "But I think I can do the rest."

Henry went outside, and Miles turned to Anya. "It's been a pleasure making your life more difficult," he told her.

"Fuck off," Anya said with a laugh and gave Miles a hug. "Make them all pay for this. If Vedran won't surrender, his life is forfeit."

Miles was never going to ask Vedran to surrender, but he nodded that he understood. "Daylight is in a few hours," he said. "I could use somewhere to sleep. It's four hours to Vedran's estate, according to the internet."

Anya assured Miles they would sort something out, which ended up being Miles and Church in a Transit van driving through the darkness while the local radio played hits from the 1970s. Miles felt the daylight break over the horizon, and he used the satnav to find the nearest parking area in the dense forest that surrounded the whole area.

Once parked, Miles and Church climbed into the rear of the truck, where someone—presumably on Henry or Anya's orders—had put a rucksack with snacks and drinks, a small cooler with several blood packs, and a second holdall. The latter contained two daggers and a Winchester rifle with a box of incendiary rounds. Miles leaned up against the side of the van with Church beside him, and both fell sleep.

CHAPTER THIRTY-TWO

It was early afternoon when Miles woke up. He let Church out for a quick run, while he drank a blood pack. He hadn't realised how thirsty he was, considering he'd practically drained Cody and drunk from one of the Inquisitors. Apparently, turning into his beast form took a lot out of him.

With Church exercised, and with a few hours of driving to go and nightfall to descend before they reached their destination, Miles took the van back out onto the main road and set off.

He was an hour into the drive when his phone went off; *Yvonne.*

Miles answered it, but it wasn't Yvonne who spoke, "How far out are you?" Lauren asked.

"How'd you get Yvonne's phone?" he replied.

"Yvonne gave it to me," Lauren said. "The desolate and I are in the back of a sixteen-wheeler. I just woke up. Couldn't risk getting farther before daylight broke. It's forty-nine minutes before nightfall. I'm at a truck stop on the other side of Vancouver, near Whyte Lake Parking."

"I'm going through Vancouver right now," Miles said. "It's half an hour, depending on traffic."

"You are not putting your Assembly and own kind ahead of me," Lauren said softly, as though she didn't want to wake someone. "You allowed me to leave to do what must be done. I'm not sure many vampires would do that."

Miles considered the best way to respond to this. He'd wondered why he was allowing a Desolate Queen to be a part of anything he did. It was true that he couldn't afford to kill the queen while several dozen desolate remained with access to the outside world. They were in the rear of a truck, near a massive city like Vancouver. And that truck wasn't going to stop them from tearing through it like paper if enough of them started to attack it at once. The more accurate answer, however, was much simpler. "You don't deserve to die for what others did to you."

Lauren said nothing for several seconds, and Miles had started to believe that the conversation was over with a satisfactory response. Eventually, she said, "Thank you."

"Do not thank me," Miles said softly, stopping the truck at a set of traffic lights as people went about their lives all around him, with no idea what was only a short distance from them. "I'm not sure I'm doing you a kindness by letting you come along. You say that you are not changed from the woman you were, but you slaughtered those who turned you. You slaughtered those Inquisitors, drinking their blood, and turning them into a weapon to slow us down. You are changed, Lauren. You are not the woman you were, and you will never be her again. You are . . . something else. The woman you were might be there, and I'm not saying you're a monster, but you are capable of exceptional levels of violence without batting an eye. It would be naive of you to think that nothing has changed."

"When I killed for the first time," Lauren said, "when I killed Liam, I expected to feel something like remorse. I expected to feel shame and hurt for the action, but all I felt was relief. A deep overriding sense of having done the right thing. Tell me you wouldn't have done the same."

"I would have killed him," Miles said, as the lights turned, and he set off again. "I told Anya that you were involved. The Assembly will have to be told of your existence, but we have a little time."

"Can I ask you something before I let you go?" Lauren asked.

"Sure," Miles said, making the most British of hand gestures to a moron who cut him up.

"If it comes to it," Lauren repeated, "kill me. If I become a true monster, unable to distinguish friend from foe, unable to see beyond my own hunger, end me. Please."

"I will," Miles said softly, feeling a sense of relief that she had asked. "I'll be there soon."

The call ended, and half an hour later, Miles arrived at the parking lot just as the sun set. He thought that in hindsight they should have just gone together, but Miles wasn't so sure how he felt about having to sleep in the same truck as a whole lot of desolate. He parked the van beside the sixteen-wheeler and got out, knocking on the closed doors of the truck and stepping back.

He looked down at Church, who sat beside him and whined.

"Aye," Miles said softly, as he stroked her head. "I'm not a fan of it either."

The doors to the truck opened and revealed the two dozen desolate, all sitting as if frozen in place, while Lauren dropped down.

"It will still be dark when we arrive at this Garibaldi," Lauren said.

Miles had done a little research during his time resting in the van and had discovered that Garibaldi was little more than a ghost town, having been created back in the early twentieth century and abandoned within a few decades. There had been attempts to put a ski resort there, but the plans were blocked by . . . no one knew. One minute there had been investment, the next nothing. It all pointed to money getting involved and telling everyone to clear out, or vampires killing everyone, but Miles assumed if it were the latter, he would have heard about it by now. After a few years, a large estate was built there, on the shores of the lake.

"I think it would be wise to get into position and not attack immediately," Miles said. "We have time on our side for now."

"They will have all had time to prepare for our arrival," Lauren said. "Blake will make sure they know we're coming. It won't save them. Do whatever you must, but Blake is mine."

"Be my guest," Miles told her. "I have little interest in hunting humans when Vedran is there for the taking."

"Do you need him alive?" Lauren asked.

"No," Miles said. "This isn't an extraction."

Lauren nodded. "My desolate are restless."

Miles checked the satnav. "It's an hour from here. Do you have a plan for getting into this fortress?"

"I thought I'd plough right through the front gate," she said.

Miles looked back at Church, who had decided to lie under the truck in what was probably a wise decision on her part.

"And your desolate?" Miles asked.

"They will be released right in their front garden," Lauren said. "I will instruct them to deal with any guards. You will have to find Vedran and deal with any resistance you meet, but we will keep more from following you. I assure you, they'll be a lot more interested in us than in you."

"Can you handle that many vampires and humans at once?" Miles asked, assuming there were going to be plenty of guards and mercenaries there.

"The desolate are like a flood of power," Lauren said.

Miles had once seen a dozen desolate hit a patrol of a hundred human soldiers, killing them all in a little under five minutes, accompanied by a lot of screaming. With every human they killed without feasting, they gained another ally. There was a reason even the most powerful of vampires rightly feared the desolate.

Miles grabbed everything from the van as Lauren closed the doors of the truck and climbed into the driver's seat, joined shortly after by Church and Miles in the passenger seat beside her. They set off immediately, with no conversation between the occupants of the cab, and even Church keeping noise to herself. They were going to war and didn't need the distractions.

Lauren turned the truck off the main road and down a path that led into a densely wooded area. "Not long now," she said softly, rolling her shoulders.

"Stop the truck; let me and Church off," Miles said.

After switching off the headlights, Lauren stopped the truck as they rounded a corner. The lights of the compound were easily visible five hundred meters in front.

"What's your plan?" Lauren said, the truck's engine idling in the darkness.

"You're the distraction," Miles said. "So I'm going to scale the side of the wall and find a way into the compound. I think if we're both in the truck and they see us leave, any semblance of my being able to get away from the resulting firefight is going to leave us with unnecessary problems to deal with. Besides, I'm a vampire, not the Incredible Hulk, I get hurt, I'm going to need to heal. That's hard to do when you're being shot at."

"I heal quickly," Lauren said, looking down at imaginary wounds. "I will see you soon."

Miles looked over at Lauren, and he wasn't entirely sure she planned on surviving the coming battle. There was a finite tone to her voice and a sadness in her demeanour that she hadn't had when setting out on their quest for vengeance.

Miles opened the door, letting the freezing air into the cab, and dropped down to the soft snow, letting Church jump out a moment later. The dog ran in circles for a moment, trying to catch the snow in her mouth before looking over at Miles and snorting.

"When this is done, we'll try to find somewhere for you to go," Miles said to Lauren. "I don't know how, but we will."

Lauren stared at Miles before finally smiling. "You are a good man," Miles Watson. "I wish I'd met you in better times. I think I would have enjoyed your friendship."

"Me too, Lauren," Miles said. "Good hunting."

"Good hunting," Lauren repeated and Miles closed the door, running off to the side of the road with Church at his side. The pair were quickly shrouded in the darkness of the trees, both of them keeping an eye out for traps as they ran through the woods toward the compound at the end.

They'd covered a few hundred meters when they stopped and looked down at the compound from their vantage point of a rocky outcrop. It wasn't the best view of the compound, but Miles made out the helipad on the roof, complete with a helicopter and five large black SUVs in the drive at the front.

The compound itself was indeed large, with thirty-foot concrete walls surrounding three sides of it, while Miles could just about make out the rear of the compound as it sat against the river. The front entrance was manned by a guard station, and there were people atop the walls themselves with rifles and submachine guns.

Within the compound was a large drive that snaked from the front entrance, around a large grassy mound, and back the way it had come, creating in Miles's mind a small roundabout, with concrete barriers around it. Beyond the driveway was a large piece of wooden decking that stretched the length of the hundred-foot-long building, moving around the corners of the compound and continuing on toward the lake. There stood a dozen armed soldiers on the decking, all of whom looked as though they meant business.

Behind them was the compound building itself, a large, two-storey wooden and glass structure with multiple ways to get in, although Miles wasn't certain how many of those ways would let him do so with any degree of stealth, considering the slightly purple glow around them. UV lights. This was definitely a Vampires Aren't Welcome kind of place. Cameras sat on every corner of the rectangular building, and there were more guards stationed on the slightly concave roof.

Miles dropped the ten feet to the snowy ground, with Church right behind him. They moved farther along toward the compound, making sure to keep the dense trees between them and . . . Miles paused and sniffed the air. Oil.

He reached out with his senses, turning his eyes to track heat signatures, and found the soldier in the trees, twenty feet in front of him, forty feet up a tree, on top of a manmade platform. The soldier was watching the entrance of the building and hadn't yet noticed Miles or Church.

Miles looked around and found three more soldiers, farther along on his side of the forest. They would need to be dealt with.

After tapping Church on the head and raising his finger to his lips, Miles moved quickly and silently through the snow, leaping the last few feet, and turning his hands to claws as his vampire side was let out. There was no need to turn into his beast form; he had to save that for when it was completely necessary.

Miles scaled the thick tree in moments, pulling himself up onto the platform, and driving the claws into the side of the soldier's skull, killing him instantly. He used the rifle to check through the night vision scope at the other two soldiers as the sounds of the truck's engine roared through the night.

The two soldiers raised their rifles in the direction of the compound entrance, and Miles watched the guards at the compound as they began the procedure to stop a truck they couldn't yet see. At that time, no one appeared to be outwardly concerned, but Miles heard the heartbeats of the men and women as adrenaline started to flood their systems.

The truck barrelled into view, and Miles watched the two soldiers raise their rifles. When it became apparent that the sixteen-wheeler wasn't about to even slow down, they opened fire, hitting the front tires of the truck at the same moment the guards outside the front entrance opened fire with powerful weaponry, tearing the cab of the truck apart.

Miles used the noise as a distraction and put a bullet through the back of the heads of both soldiers in the trees. He turned the rifle, not bothering to watch where the soldiers fell, just as the truck smashed into the front gates, flipped up, and crashed through it with staggering force. The trailer, now sheared off from the cab, continued on, through the wall above the gate, landing in the courtyard beyond with a shriek of metal on concrete.

There was a moment of stillness as Miles searched the treetops around him for any further soldiers. He spotted two on the opposite side of the trees and watched as something moved up the tree trunk, the soldiers unaware of the danger they were in, until Lauren was on them.

Lauren didn't feed like vampires. There was no attempt at making it anything less than a rage-filled statement of violence. She tore the head off the first soldier, threw it at the second, and leapt the twenty feet across the gap between the two soldiers, knocking the second one off the platform with a kick while holding onto his arm. The man fell screaming to the ground, with Lauren still holding onto his detached limb. Miles turned away as she started to eat it.

Gunfire appeared to do little to actually slow down the desolates' advance around the courtyard. The fifty desolate pounced on anything that moved, tearing it apart, or biting it to create a new desolate. The dozen guards outside the main building barked orders at one another as metal shutters closed around anything glass. Apparently, Blake had prepared for such an eventuality.

Miles dropped from the tree, leaving the rifle where it had been, and ran through the woods to the side of the compound, ignoring the screams and pleas for help from those humans unlucky enough to be in the way of a hoard of desolate.

The desolate made Miles's skin itch. He hated being so close to so many, and knowing that in an instant if Lauren lost control, they would see him as much of a meal as any human. He was pretty sure he could get away, Church too, but he was a hundred percent certain it would not be pleasant.

Miles scaled the outer wall in seconds, looking back to Church. "Go around to the lake," he said. "Be careful."

Church barked and set off at a run down the side of the compound wall, disappearing from view when she leapt over a large boulder. Miles hoped she would be okay. Technically, he *knew* she would be okay, but he still worried. The last few days had been long for her, too, and sometimes it was easy to forget that she needed rest.

Miles pushed concerns out of his head and sprinted along the top of the wall, leaping across the thirty-foot gap to the building with ease and scrambling up the side of the wooden wall, using his claws. He pulled himself up and onto the roof, immediately throwing himself to the side as a bullet smashed into the ledge where his head had been.

He threw a blast of telekinesis at his assailant, forcing him to step back and allowing Miles to close the distance between them, using his claws to tear out the man's throat.

Miles stepped aside from the dead soldier and glanced over the edge of the roof to see Lauren and her desolate doing their necessary work. She stood atop the ruined truck, a soldier in one hand, his feet dangling over the edge of the truck's remains, his head at an angle that heads were not meant to go.

Safe in the knowledge that one of his allies was okay, Miles ran across the cambered roof, looking over at the rear of the compound. There was a slight drop from the roof onto a secondary roof a floor below, which stretched out to the lake.

Miles dropped over the edge of the roof and sprinted across the second lower roof, to the sounds of growling below. He continued on across the flat roof, springing off the edge with one hand, and dropping down on top of a soldier who aimed a gun at Church as the dog arrived, having taken a different direction to get there. Miles tore the man's throat out with one clawed hand and punched the other through the man's chest, cutting through the bulletproof vest as if it weren't there. It had been unnecessary, but he'd threatened Church, and Miles would simply not allow that to happen again.

Church had taken out two human soldiers, with one dead and a second crawling toward the lake. Miles retrieved the rifle from the dead soldier and shot the dying one through the head, tossing the rifle back to the ground once he was done.

"You can't come with me to fight Vedran," Miles said, crouching down in front of Church and taking her face in his now human hands.

Church whined.

"I know," Miles said, feeling guilty for sidelining his companion, but knowing that Vedran wouldn't think twice about killing her to get to him. "But I need someone to cover my back. I have to kill a bad vampire, and I need to know I don't have to worry about anyone shooting me in the back."

Church's tail wagged enthusiastically.

"You ready?" Miles asked.

Church barked once. She was ready.

CHAPTER THIRTY-THREE

The metal shutters all around the compound building were designed of thick steel, and while Miles could tear through one to get to whoever was inside, it would be loud work, giving someone time to attack him the second he got through.

Miles was about to go and ask for some desolate intervention, when half a dozen sprinted around the corner. They saw Miles, promptly ignored him, and with their clawed hands began to tear at the steel shutters.

They made no sound as they attacked the compound's protection, the only noise being the scraping of claw on steel. The desolate weren't generally as strong as vampires, but they had no pain receptors, and thus they just kept on going, ignoring the damage they were doing to their own bodies.

It didn't take long for the six desolate to make a hole in the steel and begin to peel it back like an orange. A desolate's head vanished in a plume of blood and gore when it got too close to the ever-increasing hole. There was a smell of burned flesh mixed in with the usual scents Miles got when someone's head exploded close by, which was an occurrence he had to admit probably had happened a lot more than he should be comfortable with.

A second shot hit a desolate in the shoulder, spinning it around, smoke pouring out of the wound. Incendiary shells. The desolate lay still for a moment, got back to its feet, and got hit again, this time in the chest as the barrel of the shotgun protruded from the twelve-inch hole in the steel shutter.

Miles took hold of the shotgun barrel with his telekinesis, jarring it forward at high enough speed to yank it out of the hands of whoever was holding it. He emptied the gun, tossing the shotgun behind him as the shutter slowly raised.

A low growl emanated from Church, as the fur on the back of her neck rose. She started barking as the desolate scrambled under the several inches of room beneath the still-raising shutter. The sounds of bodies being turned to wet meat beyond the shutter were all that Miles needed to hear to know that whatever was coming was bad and he shouldn't be standing in its way.

"To the side," Miles said to Church, who ran to the edge of the compound, lying down in the shadows of the wall there.

Miles leapt up onto the roof, crouched low, and waited.

There was a sound of crunching below, and Miles knew that something had crushed one of the bodies of the desolate.

Blake appeared from beneath the roof wearing an almost full-body suit of armour that glowed a faint purple colour from where the joints met. He turned to look up at Miles. "Coward," Blake shouted.

Miles walked the edge of the roof and dropped down. "You look *ridiculous*," he said.

Blake's outfit looked like someone had taken a suit of armour, dented the ever-loving shit out of it, sprayed it black, and added some hydraulics to the shoulders. Blake's face was obscured by a black metal mask, but Miles was pretty sure he was seething.

"You look like if someone purchased an Iron Man suit from a disreputable online retailer," Miles told Blake. "You look like you made a suit of armour for a kid's Halloween costume but got so caught up in it, you decided to make it for yourself."

"I am going to crush you, just like those desolate there," Blake said, raising one gauntlet fist.

"You look like someone ordered the Doomguy from *Doom*, but got his cousin Mild Irritation Guy," Miles continued, trying not to smirk.

"You think this is funny?" Blake shouted.

"Have you not seen you?" Miles asked. "Do you not own a mirror or a reflective surface? Did you lose a bet?"

Blake charged forward, moving much quicker than Miles had anticipated. He managed to throw himself to the side, landing awkwardly on a set of steps, and hit a railing, but he was soon back on his feet.

Blake turned back to Miles. "Fight me, you monster," he screamed.

"I can't," Miles explained, watching Church run by Blake and into the compound.

"Because you're a coward," Blake roared.

"Because I think she wants to," Miles said, pointing behind Blake to the newly arrived Lauren.

Lauren was covered in blood, presumably very little of it belonging to her. She looked wild and barely human, her features more in keeping with a vampire than humanity, and her bright red eyes burned with rage. Miles was pretty sure that if he had tried to kill Blake, Lauren would have taken it badly. "Blake, we have much to discuss," Lauren said, her voice sounding almost snakelike.

"Have fun, you crazy kids," Miles said and ran into the compound, leaving Blake and Lauren to get reacquainted.

The interior of the compound was a mass of expensive looking furniture, open-planned rooms, and artwork adorning the walls. There were anti-vampire paraphernalia strewn across one large table, but Miles didn't have time to notice anything. He spotted a red button on the wall with the word *SHUTTERS* written above it, and he ran over to hit it. The shutters encircling the building began to rise with an unpleasant squeal, but Miles continued on through the building, tearing open doors in search for Vedran until he found a door with a set of stairs leading down.

He looked out into the courtyard, noticing headlights moving quickly toward them. "Damn it," Miles said, leaving the door for a moment and running through the front door to find several more desolate feasting on their defeated foes.

"Lauren needs to know about the incoming," Miles shouted.

Two of the desolate, both wearing tattered jeans and blood covered flannel shirts, screamed a high-pitched noise that made Miles's ears hurt. The cars stopped only for gunfire to fill the courtyard, tearing into two of the desolate as Miles moved back into the building. He caught a glimpse of the desolate charging as one out toward the reinforcements.

Miles turned back to Church. "Stay here; don't let anyone who isn't friendly down there," Miles said, trying to ignore the sounds of battle being raised outside.

He ran into the stairwell and leapt down into the darkness below, using his senses to move through the hallway.

The first vampire that attacked him burst out of a nearby room, almost catching Miles by surprise. He dodged the rake of talons from the vampire and punched his own through his enemy's chest, puncturing the heart. The vampire coughed blood, and Miles drove his other clawed hand up under the vampire's chin, puncturing the brain and killing it.

Miles pushed the body of the vampire aside and continued on down the dark hallway, letting his night vision and sense of smell guide the way.

After walking down what felt like a maze of corridors and doors with nothing behind them, Miles opened a door into a large room that reminded him of the House Umbra room he'd been in not so long ago, when he'd gone to talk to the criminal who had handed himself in. It felt as though so much time had passed since that day, that so much had changed.

There were blades and other weapons adorning several black wooden racks around the room, with artwork depicting battles and warriors on every wall.

In the middle of the room sat Vedran, with three Blood Guard in front of him. The guard were all in suits of highly polished armour, a combination of metal and some kind of strengthened, extra-light polymer. The actual makeup of a Blood Guard's armour was secret, but all Miles needed to know was that it was exceptionally durable.

Miles wished he'd taken the shotgun that he'd emptied earlier. He wasn't sure it would puncture the Blood Guard's armour, but it couldn't have hurt.

The three Blood Guard each held a bladed weapon, two a sword and one a large scythe. None of them held their weapons in a threatening way, but all three guards only had eyes for Miles. Two of the three weren't wearing their helmets; their helms were sitting on the ground beside them. When they wore their helmets, there were no parts of their body that weren't covered by their white and charcoal grey armour. They looked a lot like grown-up versions of the armour that Blake had been wearing.

But without the helmet, their heads and necks were a place of weakness. And weakness could be exploited.

"You sold out your own kind, Vedran. You sold us out so you could get a little more power and money?" Miles asked, unable to keep the incredulity from his voice.

"I sold vampires out to get a get *a lot* more power and money," Vedran corrected, not standing, and making it sound as if Miles was interrupting something important. "Once I heard that you'd escaped Seattle, I knew you'd come here. I'd hoped Blake would have been able to keep you imprisoned until everything was ready for me to come talk to you. I'd hoped I'd have been able to convince you that this is the only way forward for all of us. If I had an ally in in the Assembly like you, this would all be much easier."

"That was never going to happen," Miles said. "Glad to hear you knew of my arrival so you could prepare. I'd have hated to catch you unaware."

"Humans always talk," Vedran said. "Didn't expect you to have the Desolate Queen with you. I'd hoped you might have killed each other."

"I guess your plans to control California and get friends in high places have all gone to shit," Miles said.

"There will be people to blame it on," Vedran said dismissively. "Once you're dead, I'll find another way to get what I want. The Assembly can huff and puff, but my House will protect me."

"Not this time," Miles said. "Blake kept everything. You're done."

"Blake won't speak against me," Vedran said, sounding just a little less confident than he had before. "He *needs* me."

"He's about to become food for the desolate," Miles said. "We have all the files you told Kyle to destroy. Kyle didn't get that far, by the way. He went diving off the building instead. Just so you know, we have *all* of the files. A lot about you. Photos, videos, secret conversations; it's almost like you're really shit at this spy stuff. Did you not think Blake would record you?"

Vedran's face flushed with anger.

"You didn't," Miles said with a chuckle. "You believed you were his better, and he would never go against his better. You arrogant prick."

"I will be glad when all the humans are gone," Vedran said. "Filthy, disgusting little degenerates. You killing them all just makes my life easier. Kill him."

One of the Blood Guard without a helmet, the one wielding the scythe, charged Miles, hissing, showing his long fangs as his face turned into its vampire form. Miles jumped back from a swipe of the weapon as Vedran commanded him to stop.

Miles landed on the tips of his toes and sprung back at the Blood Guard, using his telekinesis to stop another swipe of the scythe, and slamming his open palm into the neck of the guard, unleashing his bloodline gift.

The Blood Guard dropped to his knees and convulsed, releasing his grip on the scythe. Miles caught it in one hand and swung it around with all his might, catching the guard full in the face with the edge of the weapon and decapitating him.

Miles hadn't expended the Blood Guard to charge first, but the outcome had been the same.

The other two Blood Guard charged as one.

Miles used the scythe to block a sword swipe from one of the Blood Guard and parried the other guard, forcing his weapon to obscure his ally. They moved further apart to ensure it didn't happen again, and Miles smiled. A blast of telekinesis to the legs of one Blood Guard forced him to trip forward, and Miles swung the scythe down toward his helmet-covered head, but it was a feint, and as the second Blood Guard stepped in to stab Miles, he spun the scythe in his hand and drove the tip of it into the Blood Guard's throat.

A twist of the scythe and a pull with Miles's telekinesis, and the Blood Guard was impaled on the scythe that had belonged to his companion. Miles pushed the scythe and dead vampire away, picking up his broad sword as the final third and final Blood Guard got to his feet.

"You really want to do this?" Miles asked.

If all three of them had fought as one, Miles would have been killed. He was certain of it. He'd have had to grab a weapon from the rack and three on one, there was little he could have done but hold his own until one of them got a good cut. Two on one, and with them both off balance after seeing the death of their companion, that was a completely different matter.

And now it was one on one. Blood Guard blades were designed to cut through Blood Guard armour. No point in having a weapon that can only defend against some people. The other problem with Blood Guard armour was that while it stopped someone from using their bloodline gift on them, it also meant they couldn't be fully covered and use their own gift. A lot of Blood Guard removed their helms and gauntlets to be able to use their gifts. These three hadn't considered it. Or Vedran had forbidden it. Probably both.

The remaining Blood Guard charged Miles, who parried the blade strike and used his telekinesis to push the guard aside, toward Vedran, who was apoplectic with rage. The Blood Guard darted forward, but Miles easily parried the blade, and drove his claws into the exposed throat of the vampire, before bringing the sword up across the remains of his neck. The Blood Guard's head rolled away as his body collapsed.

Miles darted forward to attack the First Captain of House Umbra, but Vedran threw the body of a Blood Guard at him, forcing Miles to use his telekinesis to throw the guard aside, where he bounced off the wall headfirst and fell unmoving to the ground. If he hadn't already been dead, he would have been after that.

"These weren't Blood Guard," Miles said. "Or if they were, you really need to get a refund." He looked down at one of the decapitated vampires. They were normal vampires put in Blood Guard armour. A desecration of the role.

Vedran roared, bringing Miles's attention back to him.

Horns tore from either side of Vedran's skull. Large and black, with tips that looked razor sharp, made for goring. His body increased in size, making him nearly ten feet tall, and weighing probably half a ton. His clothes were torn free, fur covering his entire body as it changed into something resembling half man, half boar. His face remained that of Vedran, although it was twisted with rage, and where his hands had once been were now huge talons, each one as long as an average-sized adult human femur. His feet were now large cloven hooves, with dark fur covering his legs up to his thighs. He looked like something approximating an old image of the devil, or the minotaur, except a boar instead of a bull. The whole transformation happened in an instant.

"Do you see what you've made me do?" Vedran roared, his face the last thing to change, now resembling that of a massive humanoid boar, with long tusks jutting out from his jaw. "I will crush you where you stand."

He took a step toward Miles, who removed his stab vest and unbuttoned his jacket, throwing both to the floor as Vedran stopped walking and stared. "What are you doing?" he demanded to know.

"You might be a great fighter, Vedran," Miles said. "But you're thick as pig shite."

Miles's transformation to his beast form was easier than it had been before, with only a flash of agony that was quickly gone. He stood there and beat his wings as Vedran's face took on something approximating fear.

"Come on then," Miles shouted, feeling an overwhelming urge to inflict terrible violence on Vedran. "Let's see what you can do, ya fuckin' bawbag."

CHAPTER THIRTY-FOUR

Vedran charged Miles with a roar born of rage and need to be triumphant against, in his mind, a weaker foe. He slammed into Miles with terrible strength, throwing him back against the wall, which cracked from the force, showering the pair with grey concrete dust.

Miles kicked out at Vedran, the talons on his feet slicing through his opponent's belly with ease, and pushing him back with his own roar.

It was only when the pair separated that Miles noticed the blood trickling down his arm. Vedran had punctured his shoulder with one of his tusks, but Vedran's stomach was badly torn, and bled heavily for several seconds before it, like Miles's shoulder, healed.

Vedran ran a large finger across the tusk before licking it clean with a dark tongue. "You taste good," he said, his voice no longer that of the man he had once been. He charged again. Miles threw himself to the side, but Vedran grabbed his leg in one hand, swinging him around, forcing him to collide with the racks of weapons before releasing his grip.

Miles sailed across the room, smashing headfirst into the far wall, moving through items into a small room beyond. Miles had wrapped himself in his wings the moment before he hit the wall and was grateful for how much protection they offered.

He wanted to fight as he always had, but that was clearly not how vampire beasts fought. Vedran had always been strong and fast, but he was all about pinpoint repeated strikes; now in his beast form, Vedran was only power and speed. He hit like a truck with every blow.

He clambered back through the hole, noticing the blood on his right wing. He could not afford to continue on in this manner. He would be killed by Vedran before too long if he kept wanting to fight the way he had done for centuries. He was no longer even human shaped.

Vedran's laugh boomed around the mostly destroyed room. "Those little wings aren't going to do you any good in here," he shouted.

"You are right," Miles said. "Let us finish this."

Vedran charged again, moving so quickly from a standing position, and with so much power, that he left cracks in the floor. His horns were aimed low, looking to gore, to cause maximum damage by disembowelling his opponent.

Miles forced himself to remain still until the last moment, when he batted his wings and moved too quickly for Vedran to correct himself, and he smashed into the wall in front of him, finishing the earlier demolition in a cacophony of noise and dust.

Wasting no time, Miles grabbed Vedran around the neck and threw him up with all his might, smashing him into the ceiling above. Vedran hit the floor hard, dazed enough to let Miles do it a second time. When Miles threw him up to the ceiling a third time, he beat his wings and exploded up off the ground, grabbing Vedran as he moved up, crashing through the remains of the ceiling. He held Vedran aloft to ensure the impact hit him first, throwing him across the kitchen when they both exited the floor.

Vedran crashed into the fridge and bounced onto the floor, but he sprang back, picking up the six-and-a-half-foot-tall fridge and throwing it at Miles as though it were a tennis ball. Miles easily avoided it, but the fridge crashed through the window behind him, tearing out part of the wall as it went. He rushed Miles, and the two traded blows, with Vedran using nothing but clubbing forearms while trying to grapple with the lither vampire.

Miles used his wings to block and deflect several of the blows, and was happy to realise that they were as good a shield as anything he could have worn when in his human form. With wings wrapped around him, he was essentially an immobile tank, which did little to stop Vedran's onslaught but made sure that he wasn't being battered around the building. He ducked one punch that connected with the wall, obliterating part of it, and with his talons out drove them into Vedran's stomach, twisting his arms up, creating huge holes in the House Umbra vampire's lower torso.

Vedran roared in pain and anger, kicking Miles back with enough strength to send him sailing through the remains of the window and wall.

Miles landed on the soft snow outside, rolled over, and batted his wings once, lifting him off the ground. There were still armed soldiers outside fighting the desolate, although the battle appeared to be mostly confined to the woodland outside the compound.

He turned to hear Vedran's rage as the boar-vampire tore through the wall. Miles batted his wings once more with what he hoped was enough force to lift him high off the ground, but instead the wings clapped together, causing a boom of power which threw Vedran back into the building, and shattered every window that wasn't already broken.

Any desolate nearby were either thrown back or forced to sink to their knees as blood poured out of their burst ears.

Miles wondered what else he might be capable of, but there was no time for practice as Vedran stepped out of the building, picked up a desolate nearby, and crushed its head in one hand, before lifting the remains of its skull to his open mouth and letting the blood flow in.

Miles tried to create the sonic boom again, but Vedran threw the remains of the desolate at him, causing him to float to the side to avoid it, putting him directly in the path of a charging Vedran.

The House Umbra vampire hit Miles so hard that it tore every bit of breath out of his body. Vedran's arms moved around Miles's lower rib cage and squeezed, popping the ribs as he drove his right horn into Miles's stomach, tearing through muscle and organs with ease.

Miles cried out in pain, trying to move back, using his wings to put distance between them, but Vedran held on, removing the horn from Miles's stomach and standing upright, lifting him further off the ground.

A grotesque grin spread across Vedran's blood-xsplattered face. "No one beats Vedran," he screamed. "No one."

With every part of him hurting, Miles headbutted Vedran, whose tusk tore through Miles's cheek. Vedran released his grip and staggered back, but Miles wasn't done. He leapt on Vedran, sinking his teeth into the vampire's neck and biting deep.

Miles tore out the side of Vedran's throat and held on, allowing the blood to flow down his throat, feeling himself regenerate. He felt the blood pour over his open mouth, down his neck and chest, a fountain of nourishment. The more he took, the more he needed, the more he . . . *craved*.

"No," Vedran shouted, trying to throw Miles off, trying to tear himself free, but Miles's talons were punched through Vedran's shoulder and back, holding on with everything he could as the House Umbra vampire rained down blows on his shoulders, back, and neck.

Miles blocked as much as he could, but Vedran grabbed onto one of Miles's wings, and Miles instinctively let go, kicking back off Vedran's chest, leaving more gouges in his enemy's body. He tried to use his wings to create a boom again, but as one moved, pain screeched through him. He looked over and saw the tear in the membrane of the wing. Flying was one thing, but he wasn't sure how much longer the wing would be able to protect him, and he definitely wasn't creating any more booms of power.

Vedran snorted and threw himself at Miles, who dropped to the ground and sprang up as Vedran sailed over him. Miles grabbed Vedran around the waist and threw him, headfirst, into the concrete driveway. Vedran tried to push him away with one huge hand, but Miles grabbed his arm and wrenched it up and back, breaking the elbow and dislocating the shoulder.

Miles kept a hold of Vedran's arm and stomped down on his head, but Vedran twisted onto his back, pulling Miles off balance and using his tusks to gore across his still sore ribs. Miles rolled with the attack, his wings cushioning the fall. He knew he couldn't keep this up forever. Eventually, Vedran's power would trump his own. Feeding on Vedran's blood had healed his ribs, had bought him time, but it was going to be just that, time. Miles came back to his feet a little distance between himself and Vedran, who popped his arm back in place as he stood.

Vedran roared to the heavens, and Miles took the opportunity to fly at Vedran, low and fast, scooping him up before he could react, and smashing his head into the remaining roof of the compound, before throwing him up and onto the top of the concave roof.

Miles took off, hovering two dozen feet above the roof as a dazed Vedran got back to his feet. He saw his moment and took it, swooping down with lightning fast speed, turning in mid-air, and barrelling into Vedran feet first.

The First Captain of House Umbra took the blow on his chest but grabbed Miles's ankles, and the pair tumbled end over end along the rooftop, smashing over the side of it, and skidding across the lower roof that Miles had leapt off not long ago. They both fell onto the decking and tumbled toward the water, throwing blow after blow at each other, trying to separate, but trying to get in close.

Each vampire was littered with a dozen wounds around their torso, neck, and head, each one trying to get the leverage to throw the one hit that would do the most damage.

Vedran gored through Miles's shoulder, biting down on his neck as Miles bit down on Vedran's neck, and with the momentum, and neither of the pair pulling away, they plunged into the icy river.

Ice cold water felt like a million knives being driven into Miles's flesh. He kicked away from Vedran, trying to swing away, but his wings made it difficult. His need for blood rose, and by the time he reached the bank fifty feet away, he wanted nothing more than to tear into something, to feed without stopping.

He looked across the river to Vedran as he pulled himself out of the water, looked back over at Miles, turned, and sprinted off into the forest.

"Church," Miles shouted, as he beat his wings and took off across the icy water, landing on the opposite side, his arms feeling as though they were on fire.

Church barked as she arrived on the scene, her fur matted with blood that wasn't hers.

"We hunt," Miles said.

He took off to the skies as Church bounded into the forest. Miles turned his eyesight to track her heat signature, hoping to spot Vedran, but his plunge in the water made him difficult to spot below the canopies of the trees.

In his beast form, Vedran was fast. Much faster than any vampire could hope to be while looking like a human. Miles wasn't going to let him flee. He had to face justice of a permanent kind. There was no other way this ended.

Church barked far below, the noise carrying to Miles as though they were close to each other. Miles spotted Church as she changed direction, toward a large rocky section of the forest that rose up high. He dove down fast, moving between the trees at speed, only narrowly avoiding branches and trunks.

The run had increased Vedran's heat, and now he was easily visible as he scaled the side of the rocky cliff face, but he was also exposed.

Miles hit Vedran on the side at high speed, dragging him off the cliff and throwing him back down to the ground, where he impacted with a tree, causing it to splinter.

Church was on Vedran in an instant, grabbing his ankles and tearing at the Achilles, hobbling him, and darting away when Vedran swiped at her. Miles walked through the forest and watched as Church sprang back, biting the other ankle and moving away. Vedran screamed and cursed in an incoherent mass of rage. Church was too quick, and Vedran was already wounded.

Miles stood before Vedran, who knelt on the hard, frozen ground, spattered with his blood. "Please," he said. "I can give you anything you want. Money, power, anything."

"You're a bully, Vedran," Miles said. "And there's not a damn thing I want from you. Church, back to the lake."

Miles grabbed his prey by the throat, and with a beat of his wings, with everything he had, he took Vedran up into the sky, moving fast. They went higher and higher into the sky, the cold air tearing against his skin as he moved to straddle Vedran's back, wrapped his arms around him, and bit down into his throat, tearing it open and feasting on the warmth inside.

Miles's mind had returned to him; the warmth of the feed had done wonders to ensure he regained his composure, but the cold remained, and the chill would eventually rob him of his reason once again. He held Vedran by the throat in one massive, clawed hand, and Miles turned him around to face him.

"Please," Vedran said again.

Miles plunged his claws into Vedran's throat, ripping it to the bone. Vedran thrashed in his grip, his own claws tearing across Miles's chest and stomach in an effort to save himself. It was too little, too late, and with every bit of strength Miles possessed, he tore Vedran's head free, letting the two body parts fall back toward the forest. Miles continued to flutter in the moonlight, raised his head to the now clear night sky, and let out a roar.

He flew back toward the lake, moving more slowly; he was hurt and needed rest. He was only a hundred feet above the lake when he convulsed. His entire body burned, and he realised just how many wounds he had over his body. His beast form vanished, and he fell the hundred feet to the centre of the lake, slamming into the water like a cinder block, breaking bones as he connected with the unforgiving surface.

Miles spluttered and coughed as he made his way up from the bottom of the lake. His arm was broken, his knee dislocated, and he'd re-broken several ribs. His head screamed in pain, a dull roar going down his neck.

He hadn't realised how injured he'd been, and how high up he'd been. His mind had been so full of pleasure from the taking of Vedran's blood that he hadn't realised how close his body was to removing the beast form. Apparently there were limits to what it would allow him to, or at least how long he could do it.

Miles floated on the surface of the water and felt a tug on his shoulder. He tried to turn his neck but discovered he couldn't; it hurt far too much to breathe, and he coughed when water went up his nose, causing him more pain. Something was dragging him out of the lake, and for that he was grateful.

He lay on the bank of the lake as Church sat beside him.

"Good girl," Miles said softly. His body was already healing, but it would be some time before he was capable of saying more than a few words, let alone moving.

Someone else grabbed his shoulders, and he managed to look up at two desolate who pulled him further up the shore. Miles managed a painful sigh, but the lack of aggression from either the desolate or Church meant they were probably helping, not just bringing him out of the water to eat. Hopefully.

They released their grip once inside the house, propping Miles up against a partially destroyed sofa. He watched the two desolate walk away back outside at the front of the building where the dead littered the ground and the remains of the truck burned. He hadn't been sure if it had been on fire when he'd fought Vedran.

"Miles," Lauren said stepping into the room. She was freshly dressed in thick trousers, boots, and a black puffy jacket. Her face and hair were wet, but they were no longer bloody.

"You had time to shower?" Miles asked in disbelief, adding his jaw to the list of things that hurt.

"Lake," Lauren said. "I saw you fly after Vedran. I saw you fall. Thought you might like some help. Church was first on the scene."

He couldn't say what he wanted to say, that if Vedran hadn't given in to his arrogance and pride, or if he'd fought in his human form, Miles probably wouldn't have won. Miles won because Vedran allowed himself to be drawn into a fight where his emotions took over his reason. Instead of saying any of that, Miles managed to lift his arm to give a thumbs-up, but regretted it when he realised his arm hurt and lowered it again.

"Your beast form crapped out," Lauren said. "My guess is you're not used to using it."

Miles managed to wiggle his hand from side to side.

"Blake and Reese are both dead," she said and sat beside him.

"I'm going to leave you here with my desolate. The sunrise will kill them, but I can't be among their number. I don't want to die, Miles. Hell, I barely lived until I became a Desolate Queen. I need to see the world. I need to do good. I can't do those things while I'm ash."

Miles nodded.

"They'll come after me," Lauren said. "When they realise I'm not dead, they'll try to kill me. When you contact them to let them know where you are for extraction, will you tell them I escaped?"

"I'll tell them I don't know," Miles told her. "I hope that helps."

Lauren smiled sadly.

"I can't do it yet," Miles said, taking as deep a breath as he could before continuing. "Need to heal first. Need rest. Need sleep. Gives you time."

"An hour to find somewhere to sleep," Lauren said. "An hour to get away."

"Twenty-four hours," Miles corrected.

Lauren leaned down and kissed Miles on the forehead. "You are a good man, Miles Watson."

"Please don't tell everyone," Miles said with a smile.

Lauren got to her feet and scratched Church behind her ear. "I will miss you," she said, and Church barked in response, licking Lauren's hand. "I will miss you both."

"If you ever need me," Miles said.

"I have your number," Lauren told him, looking genuinely sad. "Take care Miles and Church."

Miles watched Lauren leave the house and felt a profound sadness at how everything had ended for her. She was a Desolate Queen, but even if Miles hadn't been seriously hurt, he couldn't have killed her. She deserved better than that. She'd proven she wasn't a monster; she'd proven that Desolate Royalty were not all monsters.

The desolate remained standing or sitting all around the front of the house, and by the time the first rays of sunlight appeared in the clear sky, they burst into flames. They turned to ash in seconds without a sound.

Miles's body was mostly healed by the time the sunrise happened, and he had no idea where his phone was to actually contact anyone to get him. He got to his feet and found a mobile phone on the ground that still had someone's hand attached to it. He removed the hand and dialled Anya's number from memory.

"If you're trying to sell me something, you can fuck off," she said.

"And a good morning to you, too," Miles said, rolling his shoulders to get some of the soreness out.

"How bad is it?" Anya asked.

"Everyone but me and Church are dead," Miles said. He'd wondered what he was going to say about Lauren, and he figured he'd just omit her as an issue unless asked. "The desolate all burst into flames when the sun came up."

"Including Lauren?" Anya asked.

"I presume so," Miles lied. "Bit hard to pinpoint which pile of smoking ruin is her because I was busy killing Vedran."

Anya whistled. "Vedran is dead?"

"Unless his head can regenerate itself, yes," Miles said, fully aware that his head could do no such thing, but glancing over to the forest just to make sure Vedran's headless corpse didn't come back for one last attack.

"You want an extraction?" Anya asked.

"I do," Miles said and told her his location. "You'll find me in one of the bedrooms upstairs, asleep. Church will be with me. Try not to make any sudden movements when you get here."

"You know that killing the First Captain of House Umbra will cause problems," Anya said.

"And those problems will remain after I've had some sleep," Miles pointed out.

"We'll be there in a few hours," Anya told him. "Are you okay?"

"Sore," Miles said. "Tired. Hungry. Mostly sore. See you soon, going to sleep now before I fall down." He ended the call, considered calling Drest, but decided that would wait. He tentatively walked out of the house, using his hand to test the sun's power and feeling nothing but a slight tingling in his fingers. He decided to stay in the shadows of the house and wait.

Church sat beside Miles as he looked around at the remains of the courtyard and the death that had been brought there. Deserved death, no doubt, but death nonetheless.

Miles stroked Church's head, and the large dog licked his hand in return. "So," Miles said softly. "That was a hell of a week."

Church barked once.

"You too, my friend," Miles said with a smile. "You too."

ACKNOWLEDGEMENTS

I've wanted to write a vampire book for a long time, but as is so often the case when I decide I want to write something set in a new world, I also wanted to do something a little different to what I'd done before. I hope you enjoyed reading it as much as I enjoyed writing it.

There are always numerous people who have helped me get this book written, edited, and published.

My wife, Vanessa, and my daughters, Keira, Faith, and Harley. Their support can't really be measured. They're part of the reason I write; they're part of the reason I ever decided to try and get published in the first place. Thank you for everything you do.

To my parents, who have always been supportive of my writing and read every book I publish, thank you for being there all these years, and I am sorry (not really) for the amount of space the wall of my covers now takes up.

To my family, my friends, all of those people who have supported me, who have contacted me to tell me they've loved my work, who listen to me going on about ideas and complaining about how my brain won't shut up for five minutes to let me work on one thing, you're all awesome.

My friend and agent, Paul Lucas, thank you for all you do.

To everyone at Podium. I've been working with Nicole, Victoria, Leah, Cole, and Kyle for a few books now. It's been a genuine pleasure to work with them all and I look forward to what the future brings.

My editor, Julie Crisp. An incredible editor who helps make my work better and who manages to translate the sometimes word salad that is an early draft of my book. Thank you for being awesome to work with.

To Istvan Straban, the artist who did the incredible covers to all three Riftborn books. Thank you for your amazing work.

Last, but by no means least, to everyone else who picks up my books, whether this is the first one or those who have followed my work for years, thank you.

ABOUT THE AUTHOR

Steve McHugh is the bestselling author of the Hellequin Chronicles. His novel *Scorched Shadows* was nominated for a David Gemmell Award for Fantasy in 2018. Born in Mexborough, South Yorkshire, McHugh currently lives with his wife and three daughters in Southampton.